Stories
from
our
Center

Carolyn Duncan
John J. Mistur
Katie Yusuf

Al Tietjen
Lucinda Hauser
Laura Nicol

Stories from our Center

Lives Challenged by MS

Edited by Evelyn Arvey

SWEDISH MS CENTER, SEATTLE WA

The stories and views expressed here are those of each individual author as part of the "Finding Your Voice in Writing" group. Authors are encouraged to choose their own topics for each short work. All opinions, language, or reflections are those of the author and do not represent Swedish Medical Group.

All proceeds from book sales go to support the Swedish MS Center Endowment for Supportive Care Services. Through the MS Center's comprehensive care model, patients' physical, emotional and social wellness are addressed along with clinical treatment of the disease. MS touches every part of a person's life. That's why we offer wellness programs and classes for patients and families to help maintain physical wellness, provide emotional support and build community. *Finding Your Voice in Writing* is a unique creative outlet to help students connect with themselves, each other, and you, the reader. Donations support wellness programs and vital research for those living with MS. Learn more about the MS Center at Swedish and how you can help at *www.swedishfoundation.org/neuro*

Preface

In the winter of 2020, a friend at the MS Center at Swedish Neuroscience Institute in Seattle came to me with an idea: *Why don't you teach a creative writing class, Evelyn? You'd be amazing!* She paused a beat, then added, with the sort of charming grin meant to convince me: *I'd take your class. I'd definitely take your class! Sign me up.*

I didn't quite know what to say. As a published author of three novels and numerous short stories, as well as having been a full-time working artist with a degree in Fine Arts from the University of Washington, I certainly had the creative experience and a flair for written language…but, teaching? How could I possibly do that? And then I thought of my husband, Richard.

Richard is the sort of person who can teach anything. He's so educated (and so humble) that he brushes aside questions about exactly how many degrees he has. Better yet, Richard has been a teacher for most of his life, to students at all levels from pre-school to graduate university students, including creative and expository writing. Maybe he would help me teach this writing class?

Turns out, he would. I wrote a proposal for the class and

submitted it to Erin Carper, the program manager at the MS Center. From the first she heard of it, Erin loved the idea of a long-term writing class as part of the MS Center's wellness programs. With support from the Swedish Medical Center Foundation, the group began to take shape. *Finding Your Voice in Writing* would start, in person, the fourth Monday in March of 2020.

March of 2020. Right.

When the pandemic hit and closed everything down, Erin, Richard, and I scrambled to move our class online. None of us had ever used this new thing called Zoom. We didn't know how to hold a meeting, share screens, or to mute ourselves—but we learned. Quickly. To our surprise, creative writing classes over Zoom worked very well and the class flourished. It is not an exaggeration to say that for everyone involved, including myself, this endeavor has been a lifesaver and has blossomed into something much greater than a simple writing class. We've shared parts of ourselves with heartfelt writing, feedback, and editing. We've become friends.

And, yes, my friend took the class.

Evelyn Arvey, Seattle, WA
October 2021

Foreword

Many facets of one's life and identity can feel threatened upon receiving an MS diagnosis. Family, friends, work, hobbies, interests, goals, and future plans all come into question with the unknowns of this complicated and frustrating disease. As the program manager at the Swedish MS Center, I oversee and support numerous classes and groups to help address the emotional, psychological, and social needs that arise beyond just the physical symptoms. Our goal is always to ensure that living with MS still means living life well.

With the vision of our Medical Director and fearless leader, Dr. James Bowen, and philanthropic support through donations to the Swedish Medical Center Foundation, our slate of programs includes everything from music therapy, exercise classes, book club, support groups, educational talks, art shows, and even a full-fledged MS adventure program with everything from adaptive skiing to skydiving! All free to anyone living with MS in our community, and not dependent on insurance.

We are always searching for other activities or classes that may catch someone's eye, get them out of their comfort zone, or appeal to another side of their personality that our other offerings haven't quite captured. So, when Evelyn and Richard approached me in late 2019 about starting this class, it immediately piqued my interest. While we have support groups and a book club, we didn't have anything quite like this program. It would appeal to those with a writing background as well as those who would be willing to try something new. Beyond working toward an individual goal of improving their writing, and a mutual goal of publishing a book of short works, I knew anyone involved in this group would also likely be sharing some of their own experiences with the group, and you, the reader. This, to me, was pivotal.

Little did we know that in March 2020 the first epicenter of Covid-19 in the United States was about to come knocking on our door only twenty miles away. Swift shutdowns in Seattle, specifically in medical centers like Swedish, followed. Thankfully, Evelyn and Richard were quick to convert what was meant to be an in-person program to a completely virtual class using unfamiliar software for brand-new students. During a global pandemic. Well, the students were game, and the rest is history.

During an extremely fraught and isolating time, this group became a unique opportunity for participants to connect from afar in a way that virtual support groups and exercise classes can't quite capture. As participant (and now published author) Lucinda Hauser observed, "'Finding your Voice in Writing' is my new community. A shared sense of trust, respect, and genuine support for each other has deepened over time. It is a gift that allows me a break mentally from a progressive disease that continues to take so much from me physically."

Thank you to our wonderful authors for sharing a few of their stories from the past year and a half in this book, and to Richard and Evelyn for helping them find these stories in themselves.

Erin Carper, Program Manager
Swedish MS Center
Seattle, WA
October 2021

Contents

Carolyn Duncan

About the Author

Carolyn is a true Northwesterner who favors cloudy, cool summer weather and still ventures out before dawn at the prospect of catching a salmon or a limit of razor clams. She was born in Portland, Oregon, and raised in Marysville and Everett, Washington. She was fifteen before her family expanded their vacations—and her world experiences—beyond camping, clamming, fishing, and visiting relatives in Montana. That year they went to Disneyland.

She wrote for the student newspapers in high school and community college, though the biggest influence on her career choice was Mary Tyler Moore's 1970s TV show about a television producer. Carolyn graduated from the University of Washington with a BA in Broadcast Journalism and spent thirteen years in broadcasting and twenty-five years in public relations.

She currently lives in West Seattle with her elderly cat, Amelia, and feels fortunate when asked to babysit her preschool-age grandsons. An obsessed gardener, she finds few things more disappointing than a rose without fragrance, so she has banished tea roses from her garden. She collects vintage vases, which she uses to fill her home with flowers. Carolyn paints with watercolors and also enjoys birding, boating, beach walks, and buying bargains in consignment stores.

A Life on Stage

"All the world's a stage,
And all the men and women merely players;
They have their exits and their entrances,
And one man in his time plays many parts…Last scene of all,
…mere oblivion, sans teeth, sans eyes, sans taste,
sans everything"

—*As You Like It*
by William Shakespeare

We West Seattleites have one way off the peninsula now that the high-rise bridge over the Duwamish River is perilously cracked. The detour to downtown sends us south through White Center, across the First South Bridge and then north or east through the industrial area. This detour unexpectedly gave me a Shakespearean experience where "all the world's a stage," as it lifted the curtain on one woman's life. I was one in an audience of thousands who saw only glimpses of the stage and the life played. It was a drama in scenes of two or three seconds, as we swooshed by at 45 miles an hour; people with purpose driving SUVs, semi-trucks, cement mixers and freight trains. We, along with the sterile streets and buildings, are the economic engine of Seattle and the entire state. She is a clunk in that humming engine that creates tens of billions of dollars each year. A clunk in the engine that no one seems able to repair no matter how much we try.

The first act in this tragedy began last spring when a wooden, slant-roof shack, much like a strawberry field-boss's shed, appeared one day on the sidewalk at East Marginal Way and Orcas Street. A wooden thumb of a building, alone on the cement sidewalk across from the Banner Bank billboard, and a big, anonymous factory venting clouds of steam.

White curtains fluttering out a hole cut for a window catch my eye and touch my heart as I drive by on a warm spring evening. How charming. How out of place. It must be a woman setting up house. I wonder where she got the curtains. They look like eyelet lace. Then I think this is not charming. A homeless person is so desperate she is living on a busy street corner. The curtains are nice, but will she be safe?

The house is nurtured and loved. At least that's what it looks like to me. Each time I pass, I notice new amenities—a flower box, a rickety bookcase. The house gets an addition. I never see the proprietress. But the eyelet curtains are a flag of hope and affection that I can't give to some homeless people I've encountered.

Forty years working downtown gave me a near-daily mix of experiences, and a complex set of feelings toward the homeless. Some days it was wild at my bus stop. Walking to my office I steeled myself not to be afraid of jittery men panhandling or dealing drugs and mentally ill people defecating, shouting, cursing and sometimes lashing out. I genuinely ached for people I saw sleeping in doorways as I walked. I became sorrowful for people I didn't see but learned were out there: parents with children, the working poor, the elderly. But now, I recoil at the dirty, loud men hanging out along the row of decrepit RVs on a side street near one of my exits. I actually resent the relatively new phenomena of tent cities along the freeway and in parks. How did it get like this?

I give this unseen person on the corner baseless, positive attributes. Do I empathize with her because I can relate to white lace curtains? I feel guilty for it. My internal debate rages: all homeless are human beings deserving my compassion whether living in a dome tent, beat-up RV, or shed with curtains. I have always donated to food banks and nonprofits, and faithfully bought Real Change, though I rarely have the opportunity now that I've retired. Now I'm driving in neighborhoods, not walking downtown, and don't engage with the homeless like I used to.

Weeks pass. Finally, I see a person standing near the house. I'm surprised that he is tall and thin and menacing. He's waving his arms, a crumpled fedora atop his long hair. I tell my husband Jim that this can't be the person who put up white curtains, it has to be a woman who created this little oasis. I am suspicious this scary man harmed the real resident of the little house.

The weather warms. Activity at the corner spikes. A broken office chair sits by the door, a junk heap grows alongside. And then, there she is. She's obviously the proprietress of the quaint little house! But if all the world's a stage, this is a scene I wish was never written. She's blonde and would look like one of my middle-age colleagues who worked downtown, but for the dirty, yellow wetsuit she's wearing. It is oversized, has short legs. The sleeves have been cut off, so the arm holes hang past her waist exposing her naked breasts and butt. She is furiously pulling boards off the junk pile.

I'm stunned. How could I have been so naïve and superficial? This isn't a summer cabin. This isn't an oasis. Her home is cold cement filled with castoffs and gas fumes. There is no dignity for her. Men ogle while en route to Ladybug Bikini Espresso and the nightclub just beyond it. She's in danger, sexually vulnerable, and living a tragedy on life's stage.

The woman is 'home' more often now. Sometimes she wears regular clothes, one time she's in her underwear bathing with a bucket of water. The junk pile grows and one sad scene after another unfolds. I guess we can metaphorically call it the second act when I decide in September to give her direct help. I no longer can just hope she'll somehow benefit from a few hundred dollars I give yearly to a nonprofit agency. I struggle over what to give her. Would someone steal the money if I give her cash? I decide to give her my down ski jacket and a blanket. Once I talk to her I'll know better what else she needs. Jim and my friends think I'm on the right path. But what if she won't talk to me? What if she screams or lunges at me, as happened once years ago near my office?

The weather becomes stormy and cool, yet I haven't yet gathered the coat and blanket. Jim and I drive to town one Sunday night. The white curtains are gone. A dirty, purple satin quilt is tacked over the window.

Monday, while on errands, I'm thinking of her. I abruptly change directions and drive toward the little house. I feel disoriented as I approach Orcas Street. Something is wrong. Maybe I'm at the wrong place. Then I slowly connect the "Got Junk" dump truck and two men with wide shovels to the missing house. I gasp. A mix of emotions wash through my body. The shack is gone and they are shoveling her stuff. I blink hard and try refocusing my eyes as if that will help me make sense of what I see. An unraveling straw beach bag hangs on the cyclone fence, water bottles and whole onions roll among clothes, boards, and filth. Not dirt. Black, smelly, ugly filth.

I didn't help her. Chills race across my skin. Where is she? I'm sick at the thought of what could be. Did her relatives find her and take her for help? Or was she evicted, angry, and lost? Is she safe?

The workers look at me curiously. I roll down my window and ask them if the city hired them. No, they say, it was the owners of the commercial bakery one block over. "She's been gone for five days, you know," one of the young men gently says.

"No, I didn't know," I say. We speak with a sort of reverence for her. "I drove by last night and there was a quilt on the window, but I didn't see her. I've been watching her and worrying about her for months."

"We have too," the young man softly smiles. "We wondered what would happen to her, and wondered if we'd eventually be called to do just this," he said, gesturing to his truck. "With her gone for so long—it's been five days—the bakery decided to clean up." He hesitated. "It had gotten so... bad." I quietly nod.

Still struggling, I thank them and slowly drive off, grateful to know what happened to the house rather than drive by one day to find an empty corner. I'm glad to confirm that others saw her and worried too. Yes, like Shakespeare observed, all the world's a stage. We West Seattle drivers were the audience to scenes from one woman's life ironically played surrounded by great wealth. It could have been an interactive play for any of us who drove by. Yet despite all of us, she slipped into oblivion, *"sans everything."*

She's First

I had been a reporter in Seattle for a year, but my real value to the country radio station KMPS-AM & FM where I worked was as the traffic girl who joked with the hugely popular morning DJ/host Phil Harper and news anchor Don Riggs. The station had a decent news operation, but the money-makers were the music and on-air personalities. It was cool to be on the show in the morning when people were driving to work, during the radio station's largest audience of the day. Our Morning Drive Time threesome usually had the largest audience of the Metropolitan Seattle area, which translated into higher advertising rates.

The KMPS news director knew I had left a TV anchor-reporter job in Yakima for the chance to work in big-market Seattle, even though it meant working in radio rather than the more glamorous television. He also knew morning drive traffic reporting, even on a highly rated program, was not the journalism career I aimed for, so he gave me substantive story assignments after the morning fluff.

I was getting good reporting experience, covering the

county and city councils and big breaking news stories, like the gasoline tanker truck that blew up and burned for hours on I-5 at the 405 Interchange. I was pleasantly surprised when he assigned me to a news conference with the President of the United States, Jimmy Carter. It was December 1979 and militant Iranian students had been holding fifty-two American diplomats hostage for more than a month inside the US Embassy in Tehran. That put President Carter at the center of the biggest story in the nation, if not the world. Their hellish ordeal would ultimately last 444 days and doom Carter to a one-term presidency.

It is often the case that tragedy gives news people the opportunity to shine professionally, and this was one of them. I could demonstrate my reporting skills to my boss, but it was also nearly as important that I make a good impression with reporters from the big news operations where I hoped to work someday.

I decided I would distinguish myself by asking the first question. Realistically, the odds were against me. Women worked in the local and national media, but print and broadcast journalism was still mostly a man's world. I would be out of my league with the more experienced national press corps assigned to the president. Asking questions would be tough at such a high-profile event. Several especially aggressive local TV reporters—who happened to be men—would be there, people who were known to be rude to other reporters and newsmakers.

I started my career during a time when the women's movement was high profile, and it definitely impacted my job prospects. My early career demonstrated why so many women were fed up with the status quo and wanted opportunities, jobs, and pay equal to men. In the late 1970s, women like me were getting jobs in professions where few, if any, women worked. Sure, women had worked in radio since it was first invented in the 1920s, but men eventually dominated the industry and convinced the world that women weren't credible delivering important news. Besides, they said, women's voices were shrill.

My own news director spoke frankly about his beliefs concerning women on the radio. He said I was great doing traffic reports, but I would never get a drive-time news anchor job because a woman's voice on a car's AM radio, coupled with the sound of traffic, would make the sound quality so poor that no one would want to listen. In other words, I would be bad for ratings just because I was a woman.

While the nation debated the need for the Equal Rights Amendment, several things happened in my small part of the world that made the equality issue crystal clear to me: I was definitely hired as the token female at my former job in television news. I knew this because the news director told me. I had been surprised when he called me for an interview because the station already had a female news anchor. I learned that she was about to be fired, but first they needed to find her female replacement. That is when I happened along with my audition tape.

Sex, not equal rights, was likely the determiner for getting my radio traffic-girl job—I wasn't a token, but I was a young woman who had good chemistry joking around with the two men with the *important* jobs. The news reporter part of my job may have been to get a female voice on air, but, as I said, the news director made clear there was no room for advancement. In addition, the fact that I was often the only woman at events or news conferences showed equality did not reign in the world of journalism or broadcast journalism that I aspired to.

The first real eye-opener about equality for me was covering the 1976 State-of-the-State speech by Governor Dan Evans. I was an intern at KZOK-FM and set to graduate from the University of Washington. At about the time the governor took the stage in the luxurious Olympic Hotel dining room, I realized I hadn't seen any women sitting at tables for this important speech hosted by one of Seattle's prestigious civic groups. I searched the five hundred movers and shakers assembled there, and as far as I could tell I was the only woman who wasn't wearing a waitress uniform and slogging dirty plates into the kitchen. I had a hard time concentrating on the speech as I ruminated on this observation; how could I be right about the lack of women in the room? I continued to search the sea of suits. After the speech, I watched people leaving, but my tally of five hundred men didn't change. *That* should have been the story I reported that day. But I was too green. I wasn't gutsy enough to suggest it to my news director.

Now, three years later, I was again headed to the Olympic Hotel. This time I would be covering the biggest story of my short career. However, my professional handicap had doubled since my internship: I was not just a female reporter, but this time I was a *pregnant* female reporter. I expected to be treated differently than male reporters at this presidential news conference, because that was happening to me at less important events.

For pregnant women who chose to work outside the home, good luck finding business work clothes. Women didn't have boutiques full of stylish clothes to show off what are now called "baby bumps." At the time, aside from the TV reporters, it was obvious that most reporters in the Seattle Press Corp didn't put much thought into their clothes. But given my condition, I had to think about my maternity wardrobe prior to President Carter's important news conference. My pregnancy wardrobe was minuscule, and I literally didn't have anything appropriate to wear for the President's visit. It irritated me that I was having a wardrobe crisis. It seemed like such a *girl thing*.

Most of my pregnancy clothes were from the Bon Marche's single rack of maternity clothes in the back of the women's department, an afterthought filled with tent-shaped tops and frumpy pants meant to cover what were then called large fat bellies. I decided my only option was my one good dress that I had bought for the station's upcoming Christmas party. It was peachy-pink crushed velveteen with long sleeves; it made me feel overdressed for a presidential news conference, but it beat the maternity wear in my closet.

The day of President Carter's visit was getting closer. Security checks and other preparations in advance of his arrival were nearly complete when the White House announced that President Carter had to stay in Washington DC to deal with the crisis. Vice President Mondale would come instead. I was disappointed, but I would still be covering the visit of the Vice President of the United States—and I was still determined to ask the first question.

I knew I was aiming high. There is prestige in being *first*, and many men didn't know how to treat a pregnant reporter. I might not be called on at all. Once my pregnancy became obvious, I was treated differently at news conferences, compared to when my pregnancy did not show. My brain was the same, but my body had changed. The same business leader who used to chat with me before and after events, and who called on me early for questions at news conferences wouldn't look me in the eye now that I was pregnant. He called on other reporters when it should have been me. I was perplexed the first time it happened. And really mad the second and third times.

I had many sexist career surprises, including on the first day I worked at KMPS radio. I had to elbow a handsy news guy who managed to touch my breasts as he rushed up behind me and reached around me to "fix my microphone" as I sat down to anchor the news. Mr. Handsy caught me off guard the first time. I was too embarrassed to say anything to him, but as the day progressed, I developed elbow maneuvers to push his hands away so he couldn't touch me most of the times that he tried "to fix my microphone." The second day, I was ready for him and shoved my strategically placed elbow in his ribs as I told him I didn't need his help. He left me alone after that.

Being molested just seconds before delivering a five-minute newscast each hour was embarrassing and made it hard to concentrate. I was the only woman on the air at the station and my work was thoroughly scrutinized by managers and colleagues. But I didn't want to rock the boat, so I never told my boss. Or my husband. I eventually did tell my husband, spurred by my anger over the mistreatment of Anita Hill when she testified before the US Senate judiciary, reviewing the Clarence Thomas Supreme Court nomination.

After all my preparation—getting a security clearance, staying current on the hostage situation, figuring out my clothes, practicing my question—the big day arrived. I had to get up at 4:30 a.m. to get to the station and to prepare for the 6 a.m. start of morning drive. I went home at 9 a.m. for a few hours and tried to nap. My mind was on high alert, a closed loop running through my head of the details of what could happen at the 5 p.m. news conference and the logistics of driving from my Kirkland home to downtown Seattle and not being late.

The scene at the hotel was just as I imagined. A couple of dozen print, wire service and broadcast reporters and photographers were there because Mondale was the closest reporters could get to President Carter during an international crisis where the lives of fifty-two Americans were at stake.

It was stuffy and crowded. Hot television lights brightened a wide spot in a hallway, big tripods held approximately eight or so TV cameras, over a dozen microphones were precariously mounted—some with duct tape—on the lectern. A handful of print photographers kneeled on the thick carpet between the TV cameras and the lectern, so they would stay out of the picture. Stone-faced plain clothes security agents surveyed the mob of reporters and photographers who jostled and joked as we waited. For me, it was already a heady experience and the VEEP wasn't even there yet.

My cheeks were pink and my stomach queasy from the realization of where I was and what I was doing. I had to force myself to stay focused as we got word that Air Force One had landed at Boeing Field, and later that Mondale's motorcade had arrived at the Olympic Hotel.

I battled the urge to forget about asking the first question and just sit back and let myself be in awe of the whole setup. The area jammed with the media and hot television lights grew warmer; my stomach started to flutter, and I began feeling like

I was just a shy girl from Everett unworthy of standing with all the prominent local and national news folk, secret service agents, and Mondale's staff. I didn't know anyone, so I hadn't participated in the banter among the press corps members who frequently encountered each other on the job. I hated my party dress and silently noted the irony when I realized I was standing next to the local TV reporter who I dreaded most in my planning. In my opinion, he was cocky, rude, and overly aggressive in asking questions at news events.

Suddenly, the area was filled with the distinct sound of rapid clicks and whorls of multiple 35-millimeter cameras as Vice President Mondale stepped into the bright lights and up to the mountain of microphones. He gave a few remarks, skillfully avoiding anything substantive about the Iran hostage crisis.

I wasn't the only one who wanted the honor of asking the first question. The moment Mondale opened the news conference for questions he was bombarded by a cacophony of reporters trying to out shout each other for his attention. In my mind it was happening in slow motion, but actually, it was just a flash of a few seconds when most reporters dropped out of the shouting match. A few other reporters dropped out one at a time over the next fractions of seconds until only two reporters were left vying for Mondale's attention: me, and the TV reporter next to me.

I was startled but glad to hear only our two voices as the other reporters became quiet and dropped out. Then I dropped out too. I let Mr. Full-of-Himself finish his question.

The Vice President of the United States looked at Mr. Full-of-Himself TV reporter.

But he pointed at *me*. "I believe she was first," Mondale said.

What! Am I hearing him correctly? Wow, I thought, *I'm going to be first!* I was so impressed that I could win favor over the man next to me.

Mondale looked at me. "Go ahead," he said. He waited for my question.

My jitters instantly disappeared. Calm, collected and professional, I asked the first question: "To what degree is Carter personally involved in negotiations to free the hostages; what is the current tone of negotiations and the likelihood of their quick release?" And then the follow-up: "Do you believe the Americans will be released in time for Christmas at home?"

I remember knowing from the reactions of the other reporters and from Mondale that I had asked the perfect questions for the events of the day; that they were important questions. I felt pride in knowing they were questions all the reporters wanted to ask, questions that the world wanted answers to. I was proud that the questions were not asked by a woman, or a pregnant woman—they were asked by a young radio reporter who hustled to ask them *first.*

You Don't Need No Doctor

I don't think my mother's family was much different than many that lived in rural areas during the 1930s Depression and World War II. Money was scarce, so going to the doctor was not only a luxury, it usually meant a long drive and a lost day's work. My grandparents, mom, and her brothers were blessed by robust good health, home remedies worked fine, and they were proud that they didn't need no doctor. Heck, Grandpa was in his eighties when he went to a doctor for the first time.

Even though I was raised during the 1950s and '60s in urban Western Washington's Marysville and Everett and my dad worked at Boeing, my mother hammered the you-don't-need-no-doctor mantra into my psyche from my earliest memory. She said something like "you're fine" when I told her I twisted my ankle while playing when I was four or five years old. I couldn't walk without piercing pain, but Mom would have none of it. I remember putting my arms around two friends' shoulders who helped me hobble to the family car.

Don't get me wrong, my mother wasn't intentionally cruel,

but she wasn't about to pamper us kids either. My family speaks with good grammar except when they slip into Montana colloquialisms such as "crick" for "creek" and "ain't" for "isn't." And they *did* go to the doctor, especially as they aged, when their bodies weren't capable of spending the day baling hay, branding yearlings, or cooking for a crew. Back then, they had nothing against doctors. You just...*don't need no doctor*. In most cases. You've gotta be bleeding bad or snake-bit before doing something so rash as driving into town.

In a bit of ironic logic that some will find hard to understand, doctors were actually revered by my family—but they also believed that most of the time, doctors can't do much or don't know much, so why go? My real-life consequence of this doctor aversion was my mother's belief that we kids were usually not sick—or not sick enough—to need a doctor.

The family signature phrase was "you're not sick!" coupled with a look on Mom's face of disgust that we were even having the conversation. Most parents have had to say "you're not sick" when one of their kids pulls a stunt like pretending illness so they can skip school. Mom always erred on the side of "you're not sick," once sending me to school with a 103-degree fever. The school nurse sent me right back home shortly after I arrived.

Even having health insurance and living in an area offering high quality medical care, it was hard for my Mom to shake the no-doctor mentality she had been raised with on ranches in Montana. She had difficulty believing I ever had any real medical issues even when I was in my forties and taking medication prescribed for a dysfunctional thyroid gland. That's why I knew my Multiple Sclerosis diagnosis would be hard for her to believe.

A diagnosis of MS, an incurable brain and spinal cord affliction, is hard to process, but one of my immediate concerns after hearing the bad news was that my mother would never believe it. I could hear her in my child's mind repeating "you're not sick!"

My mother's complicated philosophy takes a little more explanation. Even though she'd trash-talked doctors, she really was impressed by their education, knowledge, and wealth. She didn't think I, or the doctor, was lying. Her whole family used my grandfather's health as an example of why doctors weren't necessary. Mom believed her mother, my grandmother, was a bit of a hypochondriac in her old age, unnecessarily wanting to go to the doctor, a one-hour drive to Butte, for the slightest ache or pain.

As my MS symptoms began manifesting in a more pronounced way, Mom didn't say much when I'd tell her about them. She knew about debilitating bouts of vertigo and my belief that I had a pinched nerve causing pain and numbness in my right leg, but I didn't tell her about the electrical pulses in my face and circling my skull. Occasionally, when I'd tell her about a new symptom, she'd revert to the only thing that made sense to her as a young girl on a lonesome ranch. "Doctor's don't do much good," she'd say.

When I could no longer shrug off the suggestion that MS was a possibility, I decided to help my mother understand our new reality by inviting her to my appointment for a spinal tap and to look at MRI results. I figured the drama of a giant needle inserted into my spine, seeing images from inside my skull, and hearing the diagnosis from my doctor's lips was my only chance of her believing I had MS. If she didn't believe the diagnosis, I would have to endure her implied and explicit skepticism that I had MS the rest of my life.

She seemed honored to be asked to my doctor's appointment and glad to go with me. She seemed eager to participate and was doing her best to take in all the information that was coming our way. Her eyes were bright and both of us were surprised when the doctor asked Mom if she would hold me while a needle was inserted between two vertebrae.

I could feel Mom's love, warmth, and confusion as we took a contorted Madonna-and-fifty-five-year-old-child pose and the doctor talked me through the pain. She gripped me even tighter as I told them I was about to faint while the needle was still drawing fluid from my spine. She spoke encouragements and joined the celebrating after I stayed conscious just long enough for the doctor to finish and withdraw the needle. But the drama of the rainy day in a brightly lit doctor's office didn't change our complicated relationship or her world view.

Our relationship slipped back to what I called normal for us. I couldn't tell what Mom really thought over the next year as I shared the tribulations of giving myself injections of medication and continuing to work while feeling like I had the flu every day. It was usually dead silence on the phone after I told her about my latest MS-related experience. She seemed to care, but her way was to not verbalize that sort of thing to me directly.

One day the phone rang and I could hear excitement in her voice when I picked up the phone. She had great news to share. She had talked to a close friend in Portland who had a friend whose daughter was diagnosed with MS about ten years ago. The daughter took the medicine prescribed by her doctor and even ate a special diet for ten years. TEN YEARS!

Imagine that. But the real news is they—I don't know exactly who "they" were—discovered that she doesn't have MS and *never* had MS. The doctors were wrong! "All that money and effort for nothin'." She didn't need no doctor.

Of course, she was telling me that I probably didn't have MS. My doctor could be wrong. I wish! Maybe that's what she was doing—wishing I didn't have MS and seeking any information she could to make her wish come true. Maybe she couldn't believe I had MS because I still looked normal. Maybe she couldn't bear to believe that bad things like MS happen to good people like me. Denial was her way to cope with a disease she couldn't control.

It put me in an odd position. Do I argue with her and remind her of the all the symptoms I've suffered? That seemed ridiculous. So I stopped sharing any information about my health and relied on my friends, mainly, for support. Many years later, I learned from my aunt and cousins that Mom shared with them her concerns about my MS and her love for me. As the years passed, I could tell Mom had accepted that I had MS and that she worried about my health. She understood that I needed doctors to keep me from becoming disabled. But during the fifteen years she lived after my diagnosis, she never told me.

Floating

Thank God the panic isn't as intense as when I first fell in. The boat floated away so fast! I'll never catch it. Michael Phelps could. Not seventy-year-old me. This evening chop is better than big waves. But I do wish I was floating on it, not in it. It'll probably calm down soon. I didn't feel like I sank very deep. What a surprise. A surprise polar plunge. I definitely gasped when I hit the cold water and gulped some in, just like they talk about in boating safety classes. Water is still pouring out of my nose. It's so salty and bitter.

How stupid that I thrashed like someone who doesn't know what to do. Ha. Barbara would sock me in the jaw like we pretended to do in high school lifeguard lessons. A panicked drowning person can sink you both; sock 'em in the jaw and pull them to the dock from behind. Hand on chin.

Wow. This water is *icy*. It definitely wakes a person up! Glad I didn't open the wine before going to get the crab pot. Oh, yeah! Those crabs are happily dining on raw chicken necks in my crab pot at the bottom of Puget Sound.

I just have to get a grip on my emotions and do what I

know. I literally could back-float for days if needed. If I relax and let my legs float in front of me, I'll be horizontal on the water. It seems like my prosthetic left leg helps my buoyancy instead of weighing me down. I won't unhook it. I'd hate to lose it, and it'd be too hard to take off. Gad, I didn't even zip or snap the clasps of my life jacket. Too hard to zip now, but these clasps are snapping and will keep the life jacket on me.

How the heck did this happen?! Especially to me, of all people. I fell out of the dang boat. I know better. I'm a safety nut.

Oh, great, it looks like thunderheads forming south of here. But the sky is blue. It seems like a nice day, but the choppy water could have gotten worse if I had waited for Alexi and the twins before getting the crab pot. Maybe the thunderheads are all show, no rain or wind. Funny to float in a Christ-on-a-cross position. My Biblical boating accident.

My eyelashes feel stuck together in salty clumps. They, the tip of my nose, and cheeks form a frame as I look up into the blue sky and float. I'm glad I'm so paranoid about losing my glasses in the water. The safety strap performed perfectly. They're still on my face. Hard to see through the water drops. Salty water drops. Right. It's not enough that I didn't lose my glasses. I'd like them dry and spot-free, please. Okay, I'm scared, but not panicked like I was at first. I'm kinda sick-to-my-stomach scared, but not frantic or in-a-panic scared like I was when I first flipped out of the boat. I know better than to lean over the side to pull up a crab pot.

Damn it. Damn it. I can't believe this happened. What's the fastest way out of this bleeping, freezin' water? All my training and experience are for naught.

Dad, I see you standing on shore waving us in when we

were young. Something is wrong, you're waving and motioning us to come in, but we can't hear you. We finally turn around in our pram to see a black, windy storm rolling fast off the glacier that feeds the lake. I've never seen the front line of a storm before. Nasty white caps, all in a line, are racing toward us. The pram is rocking and waves are splashing. We've never been in rough water alone. We try to steady ourselves as we struggle to get the oars back in the oar locks. Barb and I were dinking around, each of us with an oar, pretending to paddle a canoe. We focus and the oars clunk as they finally slip into the slot. We don't even discuss who will row. Barb, younger than I, but a strong athlete, rows hard. Luckily, the wind is headed to the same shore we are. Dad, anxiously waiting, tells my little brother to stay back. He wades into the lake, grabs the bow and pulls us the last couple feet to shore. We laugh with relief that we're safe. The storm blows through fairly fast. The campfire flames light our faces that night as we tell and retell the story of our boat ride.

Dad taught us well. But what about a big tide like I'm in now? It's sucking me into the Straights. I'm heading into the shipping lanes. This is the big time. Why didn't you teach me about this? Lake Wenatchee didn't have shipping lanes. Nor Lake Goodwin. My beach house looks so far away. Dang it. I'll be in Victoria by the time Alexi and the girls get here. Or there. This is ridiculous. This can't be me. I'm so careful. Usually.

Darn it. I'm shaking. It's just shock. Yeah, *just*. I haven't been in the water long enough for my body temp to drop. I'll back-float for a few minutes and calm down. It makes me think of all those swimming lessons at Lake Stevens. All the childhood stuff. Best friends Janet and Julie. Larry and Barb venturing out too far. Swimming and swimming. Water-logged skinny little kids. Mom was smart to insist we know how to swim. She didn't know how herself, but she made sure her kids and grandkids did. It was a main theme in her life. A swim-lesson crusader. "Too many kids drown in irrigation ditches." Irrigation ditches were part of her Montana upbringing.

Hmm. It's like I'm a floating cross. Ironic that floating in this position is how I used to reduce stress from work. I wish I was floating offshore at Auntie Donna's. Lahaina's water temperature must be twice that of Puget Sound. But then I'd have to worry about sharks. Okay, then I wish I was floating in Auntie Donna's pool.

Take a deep breath. Reach deep, fill my lungs. SSSHHHHH, exhale with my diaphragm. Inhale...exhale... Ha, my new invention, back-floating yoga. It's actually helping. Inhale...SSSSHHH. Inhale...SSSSSHHHHH. Again, suck it in deep inside. SSSSSHHHHH. Be calm. Be calm. That's better.

I wish I could remember what percentage of the human body is water. Ha. Here I am, water in the form of flesh, bone, and blood with innards that are filled with water. Am I more than 100 per cent water? Yuk. My stomach feels so full and queasy. RRUP! Water and bile. Crap. No, not crap. Just barf. Retching hurts and ruins my back float. Ugh, here comes more. RRUP! At least it's easy to rinse my life jacket off. How revolting. Interesting concept, though, water giveth and water taketh away. Same with fire, I guess.

Well, that was a setback. I should have called for help before I barfed. Note to self. Always call 911 before wasting time barfing. I can't even see the boat anymore and there's no way I can swim to shore. Even if I was young again. Well, maybe I could if Barb swam with me. She was so strong. Even so, Uncle Dean rowed beside us when we swam across D Lake in Oregon when she was fourteen and I was fifteen. I can still feel the amazement I felt when she stayed in the water and swam back, while cousin Steve and I rode in the boat. The lake water was warm and cousin John was still alive. We all hated—he, most of all—that his heart was too weak for him to swim with us. Our moms tried to cheer us up and grilled shish kebabs for dinner. We thought that was cool.

Damn it. Pay attention, Claire. Unclip the phone dry-pouch from your life jacket. Lucky, I bought this dry pouch. I can even dial while the phone's still inside the plastic, nice and dry. Well, theoretically. My fingers are shaky. How many times do I have to hit "9" before it takes? Nine. Nope. Nine. Nope. NINE. Click! One. One. It's ringing! Alexi is going to kill me. Instead of surprising her with dinner already cooked, I'm out here drowning. I shouldn't say that. It's not funny. This is serious. I'm in trouble.

This life jacket is a kick. I thought the whistle was overkill when I bought it. The twins love blowing it. Too bad it's a weekday in March and the neighbor's houses still locked up for the winter. Hey, I have a whistle for emergencies. WHIRRRL. WHHIIRRRRL. It's a lonesome whistle. Like our resident loon that hangs out offshore. I think he's a widower. There used to be two. Now it's a singular loon, lonesome and calling. No one answers.

Hey, what's for dinner? Lemons, parsley, butter and… saltwater. Oh, yeah, and a nice Pinot Grigio. Chilled. Lemon butter. Melted. Oh, and there's dessert, too…a pocketful of kelp. And a whistle for ambiance instead of Ted playing acoustic guitar.

Thank God I had my life vest on. It and my phone would still be in my dinghy floating out to the Pacific if I hadn't slipped my arms through it before picking up the oars. I'm so glad it wasn't one of the times I just threw it in the boat. I know that life jackets don't work unless you're wearing them. That will be my *absolute* rule from now on, I promise. I will always put it on and zip it up, even for quick trips to the crab pot.

The cell service is so shitty out here. Maybe I'll hit it lucky. Yeah, of course, can't you see, it's my lucky day? I do hear it ringing and ringing. Maybe it's the emergency service that is shitty out here. Maybe nobody's there to hear it ring. Maybe I'm not ringing the dispatcher. I don't dare hang up and try again.

Alexi and the girls are probably crossing Deception Pass about now. I'll be another forty-five minutes before they get to the house. She is going to be so mad at me. I broke my own safety rule and my promise to her that I will always tell someone and wear my life jacket when I take the boat out alone. She's always been a worrier. I raised her right. But she's reached new heights of worry since my amputation. Getting rid of the bum leg actually feels better. No pain in my plastic leg. That's an advantage when you're drifting into the Straits of Juan de Fuca in forty-six-degree water and about to be run over by a container ship from Japan the size of three football fields. Your plastic leg isn't cold, and it helps one to stay afloat.

I don't know if she believes me when I explain that I'm more stable when I walk because I'm pain-free. My right thigh and calf muscles are much stronger too from all the physical therapy. It was a good decision. A relief to get rid of it. The bum left leg.

I wish the tide wasn't racing like this. It's a total waste to try to swim against it. I'll just poop out. And the exertion won't warm me. In fact, the brochure with my new life vest said to curl into a ball and conserve body heat. Don't swim. How the heck is anyone going to see me? No one is around, and, of course, I got the fashionable aqua-and-blue life vest, and I'm curled into a ball. I'll just blend in. The orange life vests weren't attractive. Yeah, that's one of the important things to consider when buying a life jacket. Is it fashionably on trend?

"This is 911, what is your emergency?"

"Oh, my goodness. My phone works! I'm so embarrassed. I fell out of my little boat while pulling in the crab pot."

"Ma'am, what is your location? Do not hang up. What is your location?"

"Well, the tide is pulling me into the straits. My summer house is on West Beach Road."

"Ma'am, what is your exact address and name?"

"Fourteen West Beach Road. I'm Claire Johnson. If you know where Senator Murray and her husband live, my place is about a mile south of them."

"Whidbey Island?"

"Yes."

"Claire, you're in the water, right?"

"Yes."

"Do you have a life vest on?"

"Yes, but it's the blue one. I hate the orange one. How will anyone slee me?"

"Claire, we will find you. How far are you from shore?"

"A long way. Too far to sllwim, and the tide is pulling me out to those strong currents."

"Tell me what land can you see?"

"Just the beach and all the empty houses. No one's home this time of shlear."

"Can you see Fort Casey or Ebby's Prairie? Can you see a town?"

"Yes, I can see Fort Casey, but it's far away. I can see Port Townslend when I turn. I'm sorry my teeth are chattering so loud. I mean sloudly."

"Claire, you're doing great. Help is on the way. Just relax and hang onto your phone. Is it hooked to your vest?"

"My hands don't work. It was like little knives in my fingertips. They quit hurting and are just numb. But my dang teeth won't quit chattering. Good that my sleg is amputated, so it's not cold."

"Ma'am, are you injured?"

"Yes, my pride. I shouldn't be here. I have sea slegs. I mean one sea leg. One got mangled in a car wreck. Do you know container shlips come through here at twenty-three knots? How will they slee me in my blue vest floating out here?"

"Ma'am, help is on the way. Can you see any boats or a helicopter? The Naval Air Station and the Coast Guard are sending help. Even the State Ferry that's leaving from Port Townsend can help."

"AUUUUUHHH! A boat is roaring straight at me. It's targeting me. It'll hit me...my vlue best..."

"Ma'am, ma'am...?"

"Whoa! Thank God, it stopped. It's a big boat with people"

"HELLO!" A voice calls from the boat. "Are you Claire? Looks like you need a lift."

"Ha, ha, ha. Yeah, I need help. I thought you were going to plow over me. I'm out too far to swim."

What a handsome man. Long, thick, gray hair. His voice

is so nice. He must be Native American. He has such a gentle voice, even when he's calling out to me over the sound of the boat's engine. No edges or boom to his voice. It's round and smooth. Low and gentle.

"No more swimming for you, Claire. We just caught some fish and now we are going to catch you."

SPLAAASHSHS.

"Whoa! You jumped into the water with your clothes on!"

"Yes. You're not exactly dressed for a swim either. You're doing great, ma'am; just relax. We'll get you out of this ice bath."

"Thank you. Don't sock me in the jaw. I won't slhrash. Or slrash. Sorry, I can't talk. My teeth won't quiiiiittt cha-t-t-t-er-ing."

"Just relax. Zach will lift you on the boat's back platform. We'll wrap you in a down sleeping bag and get you a cup of tea. You can sit by our heater. We have twin 350 hp engines that will get you home fast."

"My daughter is going to kill me. Am I slurring? I didn't open the wine before I left. I didn't lose my sleg or my glasses. We don't have anything for dinner or I'd invite you."

Wooooh, I'm so drowsy. How impolite if I fall asleep before I have a cup of tea. But I can't keep my eyes open any longer.

A Gardener's High

I work quickly as dusk quietly melts the light, and robins begin repeating their short melodic riff signaling time for bed. The dirt is rich and the air sweet as a gentle, tender darkness slowly engulfs me. The centers of the shrubs grow dark and soon all the plants are simple silhouettes in the warm night. I think of my grandfather Vic's ranching life and thank him for my love of this good earth.

I don't want to go in for the night. Every molecule of my being is an exquisite balance of energy and peace. Joyous and thankful for the plants, the birds, and the pleasures of gardening, I dreamily imagine ancestors, their rustic tools digging the soil like I do tonight.

I am a creature of the early night's garden, traveling on a higher plane than my conscious being. This moment in time is in harmonic layers. I'm floating above the neighborhood voices, traffic, and friendly barking dog.

My body is a smile. Not a broad charismatic smile with bright white teeth. It's a personal, Mona Lisa smile; a suggestion of an upward turn on the corners of the lips and a knowing look in the eyes that make you want to know what she knows.

Reluctantly, I tidy the walkway and put away my spade and mismatched garden gloves. I move ethereally, one fiber in the fabric of this young night. I stop on the cobble-stone path between the garage and the house and view two sharp rectangles of bright light shining from the windows of my empty kitchen. I am an alien, a voyeur, an outsider of my daytime self, happy to be outside looking in.

This magical June night in my garden was a dozen years ago, an apex of my lifelong avocation. I have never completely duplicated that dreamy evening again, though gardening is still like a runner's high for me, not the work many people equate with gardening. At about that time in my life I became weary of my late mother's bitter complaints about the arthritic aches and pains caused by gardening in her eighties. She had introduced me to gardening when I was a bored grade-schooler. She assigned me to deadhead the common, prolific pansies in the flowerbeds of my youth. I spent hours over-thinking where to cut the stem of each withered blossom. Gardening became such a part of my early persona that Mom snapped a black and white photo of me that she had me pose for with my favorite doll. My haired is pulled tight into a blond ponytail. I'm wearing a pastel cotton dress that she had sewn. The skirt is spread out into a circle like a ballerina's tutu onto the bed of pansies, the precise spot at my childhood home where I began gardening.

I was in my early fifties when I bought a home where I could create garden beds from my dreams. Ironically, a painful divorce caused me to sell a house that sat in the shade of tall trees and buy a brick Tudor by Puget Sound that gave me unimaginable joy. It had perfect southern and western expo-sure to the sun, exactly what was needed to grow my favorite lilacs, roses, tulips, and hydrangeas. It not only had great sun-light but it was also free of the dreaded garden monster: glacial till, commonly known as clay.

The 4,500-square foot lot was nearly a blank slate with sad remnants of iris beds tended long ago when its original owner was in her prime. The backyard was a patchwork of concrete, connecting the driveway, clothes-line pad, and sidewalk, so two cars could pull up to the back porch and park. My pri-ority was plants, not parking, so for the first time in my life I spent money on a landscape design and a crew with a back-hoe to create a sentimental garden inspired by photos clipped from magazines and the work of my parents and grandparents. Brick, cobble-stone pavers, paths and rock walls that echoed parts of my neighbor's meticulously groomed, French-inspired yard. But mine had a more carefree flounce of flowers and a wave of branches from dogwood, lilac, magnolia and, red vine maple trees.

I created lush, secluded garden vignettes with arbors, varie-gated leaves, fragrant heirloom flowers, and vintage chairs and benches, so I could sit quietly and be in Zen with my universe. I planted flowers in colors of sunrise and sunset, all selected for fragrance and their future role in beautiful bouquets. I nurtured dahlia bulbs from a plant my mother got from a co-worker twenty years earlier. I added a patch of luscious raspberries that tasted like roses smell, a nod to my grandfa-ther's garden. Then, like a fairy tale, buzzing bees and delicate butterflies found my gardens. Black-capped chickadees, Anna's hummingbirds and robins began nesting and fledging babies in my yard and next door.

Although my neighbor David had a difficult time under-standing why I refused to clip my shrubs into ridged topiaries like his, harmony was rarely broken even when my two new kittens, Chloe and Amelia, stalked butterflies and tumbled in the grass. One day a woman appeared in my yard from the West Seattle Garden Club. She said someone had nominated both my garden and David's garden to be included in the annual tour. We were so flattered that for the next nine months we threw ourselves whole-heartedly into to weeding, mulching and prepping our yards in anticipation of the tour. We couldn't believe our bad luck when recording-breaking buckets of rain fell from a dark sky the July day of the tour. But that didn't stop nearly one thousand people from tromping through our yards, many stopping at the neighbor children's lavender cookie and lemonade stand.

As I aged and was diagnosed with MS, I began to empa-thize with my Mother's 'oh-my-aching-back' complaints and I hired a gardener to help, and then to do it all. When the real estate market grew hot, I sold my house and my beloved garden and moved to a condo. I had thought hard and long about the pros and cons before letting go. The four-bedroom house was too big and I was only using part of it. My daughter had finished college, had a good job, was engaged, and no longer needed a room. The yard was beautiful, but in addition to a small view of Puget Sound, on the other side of the front hedge were cars lined up on the street waiting for ferries to Vashon Island and the Kitsap Peninsula.

Traffic bogged down when a ferry unloaded one hundred and thirty cars into our neighborhood. Every year on New Year's Day, we enjoyed watching five hundred or more motorcyclists in formation, with flags and banners flying, roar by as they head for the Vashon ferry dock. Unfortunately, Vashon was a favorite motorcycle-group ride on weekends and many commuters switched to motorcycles in the spring for the cheaper ferry fare. The ferry system groups all motorcycles at the front of the ferry and they drive off first—together—when the ferry docks. We neighbors of the ferry dock didn't need alarm clocks to wake up in time for work when seventy-five Marlon Brando clones roared off the 5:05 a.m. boat—and again every half-hour or so—on weekdays. I don't understand how someone can enjoy the cracking BLAT of an engine minus its muffler. Fun for them, but it broke my garden reverie.

One evening when the sunset colored the sky fuchsia, pink, and gold, I went looking for a secluded waterfront condominium property I had looked at twelve years earlier. I remembered the condominium location was quiet and sat on the shore with an unobstructed view. I couldn't quite remember the street it was on, so wandered a little on streets that dead-ended. I eventually found it just a mile from my house in an area of greenbelts on a narrow dead-end road and a steep driveway to the beach. I was right, the sunset was even better at the condominium property.

Oddly, or maybe presciently, the ground-floor unit with a garden that I had looked at all those years ago was for sale. Even with ferry boats and cargo ships offshore, the area was remarkably serene. The silence was a sharp contrast to the sounds of the city I had lived with just a mile away.

I bought the condo a week later, dug up starts of some of my favorite plants, got rid of lots of furniture, packed the rest, and left without regrets. Now, with a bum knee, arthritic hands, tremors, and heat intolerance, I sit on my patio like an old-timer on the front porch of the store in a small town.

I smile subtly and remember white French lilacs, old antique roses, baby birds, and cobble stones. I reminisce about the perfume of artful bouquets arranged in prized vases and standing at the berry patch with my friends eating warm raspberries.

I still marvel at the stunning colors of sunrise and sunset, but not just the color scheme of flowers in my garden. I see the colors in astonishing sunrises that reflect from behind my home onto the Olympic Mountains in front of me. Night after night I am graced with a sky filled with a mélange of gold, pink, and fuchsia as the sun sinks behind Mount Constance, The Brothers, and Mount Washington. On clear nights, the moon's reflection shimmers across the shipping lanes in front of my home. I'm retired and if I want, I can sit for hours entranced by the twinkling galaxy above, the gentle lap of waves on shore, and the sparkle of lights on the Vashon ferry dock four miles across the shipping lanes.

Summers, my neighbors and I paddle in our kayaks and cool off in the swimming pool near my patio door. I don't see my favorite little chick-a-dees, but my flower beds are home to warbling wrens, melodic white-crown sparrows, and zippy barn swallows that nest in the eaves of the garage. Among the babies that fledge each year are one or two gangly Great Blue herons who provide a little comedy as they awkwardly learn to fish and fly and grow into elegant adults. Osprey, eagles, and terns dive for fish. Seals, otters, and sea lions hang out. Orca pods or a lone humpback occasionally swim by. Cargo ships a thousand feet long head out to the Pacific, colorful spinnakers dot the water during weekend sailing regattas and every year dozens of Native Americans paddle ornate, hand-hewed canoes to their annual gathering.

Yes, I once lived in a brick house with a blissful garden.

It was a jewel in my life—my own little Camelot. While I still savor the Fauntleroy garden memories, I find new joys walking the beach, collecting agates, shells, and driftwood; and painting and sketching the mountains, flowers, birds, and creatures from the sea. I'm fortunate that plants can be moved and that I am still able to admire the beauty and history of my Mom's large, velvety purple dahlia bloom resting in my Grandmother's favorite vase. It's a ninety-year-old vase that once held tulips, peonies, and roses from my Grandmother's yard high in the Rocky Mountains; it now sits on my sea-level dining room table. The flowers in the vase are a sentimental connection from my past to my new, quiet life on the beach.

She Loves You, Yeah, Yeah, Yeah!

It's as vivid as yesterday. My younger sister and I were happily headed to downtown Everett when KJR radio announced The Beatles concert had sold out, so they were adding a Saturday matinee. My sister turned to me with a light in her eyes that instantly told me she was thinking what I was: my purse held twenty dollars. Mom had given it to me, so I could pay the Bon Marche bill. Mom thoughtfully created such errands, so I could drive her new Bonneville.

My sister, my natural-born adversary, was now my instant ally. We both knew calling to ask for permission to attend the concert would take too long, and what if Mom said no?

Seattle was the big city to us small-town Everett girls, yet our parents had unwittingly equipped us with the skills and confidence to pull off our plan to see The Fab Four. Multiple trips to the 1962 World's Fair, site of the Coliseum, where the Beatles concert was being held, meant we knew the way and where to park.

Cars were not complicated by computers in the 1960s. In our community, it was a rite of passage for friends to teach the newly licensed sixteen-year-old drivers (even girls) how to manage the mileage on the family car by disconnecting the odometer. So, my sister and I filled the Bonneville up with gas, disconnected the odometer, and hit the highway for Seattle.

The Coliseum was already dark as we found our seats low on the sloping left side of the main floor. Below, a sea of restless girls were deliriously screaming and dancing. A bit overwhelmed, we hesitated, then I followed my fearless little sister to empty seats closer to the bright circle on stage and sang along with John, Paul, George and Ringo.

"Love, love me do…" and "She loves you, yeah, yeah, yeah…"

Life couldn't get better.

We played it cool at home, implying we had visited friends. I delayed giving Mom her receipt, saying my purse was in the bedroom. The mistake that almost got us caught wasn't the money. I covered it on Monday with a month's pay from my after-school job, and put the receipt on her dresser. We slipped back into our summer routine, confident that danger from our adventure was gone.

Our undoing was using Mom's regular gas station. Next time she filled up, the attendant ran out with a wad of S&H Green Stamps. "Mrs. Duncan! Mrs. Duncan! Your daughters didn't wait for their stamps on Saturday."

We admitted to disconnecting the odometer and driving to Seattle, but we kept The Beatles and the twenty misspent dollars secret for decades. At dozens of family gatherings my sister would whisper: "Shall we tell Mom about the Beatles?"

"No!" I'd counsel. "Shhh."

Years later, when we were in our late thirties, we decided the timing was right for confession. By then, we were reasonably successful adults with children of our own, but Mom reacted as if we were untrustworthy, impulsive teenagers: she got *mad*. We were stunned that she didn't appreciate that her daughters were the envy of millions for having sung along with The Beatles at one of their last concerts.

We were, rightly, contrite.

In hindsight, she was right to believe she deserved better, but couldn't she have been a little bit glad that we saw them? You can guess the answer. We will carry the guilt of the Beatles Concert to our graves, wishing we'd done it differently, but *so glad we did it!*

Sorry, Moscow is Closed

My colleagues Bill and Vic knew something was up—cops with side arms were staked outside our Red Square hotel. Soviet flags with black ribbons were stacked against storefronts. When we asked why, we got the brush off: "It's nothing. This isn't anything unusual."

It was Thursday, November 11, 1982, and we were in our second week in the U.S.S.R. The weather was glum as we headed out to collect information for stories to broadcast on KIRO Newsradio beginning at 5 p.m. Moscow time and 6 a.m. Seattle time. We were a bit paranoid and totally exhausted by eighteen-hour days working reverse clocks in Seattle and Moscow.

The Cold War, a nuclear-tinged chess game between the world's two largest adversaries, was going strong. Access to the sinister nation behind the Iron Curtain was next to none for Westerners, especially reporters. We were there thanks to our station's management team brain-storming inventive ways to highlight KIRO's programming. The station was considered among the top ten, nationally.

The idea was so outlandish that it wasn't just my grandmother who thought we shouldn't go. News Director Vic Bremer was warned—and visited—by one of our nation's most prominent war hawks, Senator Henry (Scoop) Jackson, informing him how untrustworthy the Soviets could be. Even our network affiliate, CBS, was against us broadcasting our morning program from the communist nation via one of the satellites that had been launched that year. KIRO managers were actually a little surprised when the Soviets said "yes" to four of us attending the sixty-fifth anniversary of the 1917 Russian Revolution.

I want to take a moment to explain that a reporter's blood is different than that of other people. Or maybe it's the way our brains are wired. We drive *toward*, instead of *away from* something bad that has happened. We are the free press, privileged to act as the eyes and ears of the people of our nation. We don't presume to be invincible, but using common sense and taking precautions, we believe that we can go most places and survive while others might not even try.

It's 3 p.m., the second-to-last day of our broadcasts. We're standing in front of the Intourist Hotel, the only place Westerners can stay in central Moscow, when our assigned host, Alexander, drives up in the usual black Mercedes. We head to Radio Moscow, the center of a sophisticated communist propaganda machine that broadcast in seventy languages, from Swahili, to German to Japanese.

The Soviets graciously gave us a huge studio that looked like it was designed for 1930s live radio shows with orchestra. Given the Soviet's notoriety for censorship, we said "thanks, but no thanks" to using their broadcast equipment complete with two engineers behind a large glass window at one end of the studio. They were a bit insulted and fully staffed each evening as we put together our broadcast-station-in-a-suitcase that Norm, our amiable, clever engineer back home, had created. We could see the Soviet engineers talking about us as we plugged cord "A" into socket "A," "B" into "B" and so on. Norm trained us, so we were self-sufficient, although the Soviets made the final link to the satellite.

But I digress. Once in the Mercedes, Alexander, our tall, thirty-something host who spoke perfect English, soberly pointed out the window. "See the flags?" he said as our driver maneuvered through Thursday afternoon Moscow traffic. "Brezhnev is dead. You might not get a satellite connection tonight."

Our minds raced. Our first thought was we had a leg up on the biggest story in the world since we were the only Western broadcasters in Moscow. But will the Soviets silence us? We absolutely needed the satellite connection. KIRO had spent so much money and effort to get us here, and the Seattle staff would be scrambling to fill two hours of the highest listenership and the most important airtime of the day. And oh, yeah, what about us? What might the Soviets do with us—members of the fearless, free press?

Vic cautiously probed for more information. As we pulled up to Radio Moscow, Alexander laid out the government's position. If the satellite connection happens, our stories about Brezhnev are to be respectful. Alexander said the government did not want us to ridicule or criticize the man. The man, we all knew, had ruled the vast empire for thirty years with an oppressive, seemingly heartless fist. Our pitch to the Soviets when proposing the trip was that we were *not* going there to cover politics, but to explore the city and life there. Vic told Alexander that we had journalistic standards for covering the facts of the story and would not ridicule Brezhnev or editorialize.

Alexander had set up and escorted us on great excursions and interviews like the Olympic Village children's gymnastics class; tea and chocolates with the Assistant Artistic Director of the Bolshoi Ballet; and watching couples on their wedding day visit the tomb of the unknown soldier, a Soviet tradition.

We also took trips without Alexander to do things like interview the *New York Times* Bureau Chief, and the Siberian Seven, persecuted Pentecostalists seeking asylum who had lived in the basement of the US Embassy for four years.

The day of the celebration, Alexander steered us through thousands of parade goers, passed countless buildings covered in red and gold fabric with giant images of the hammer and sickle, Lenin, Brezhnev and idealized young revolutionaries. He eased us through the tightest security I had ever experienced to a roped off reporters' area close to Brezhnev and the politburo lined up in front of the Kremlin. We were the only Western reporters there.

Brezhnev was known to have health problems. This was the time of year when the annual rumors circulated that he was near death and was only propped up during the parade to show the world that he was still in power. Earlier that week, we shared with Seattle listeners the sight of him standing, or possibly propped up, above Lenin's mausoleum watching the long parade of rockets, tanks, and thousands of soldiers and citizens pass through Red Square.

Alexander usually dropped us off at Radio Moscow, but today he went inside. We tried to stay focused producing the broadcast during our usual two-hour prep. Despite "what if" thoughts, all we could do was prepare as though we would connect with the satellite.

I was thirty-four years old and had been a reporter at KIRO for one year when I was among those named to the station's new Action Team that would expand our station's horizons beyond the Seattle Metro area and even beyond the United States. This was my first trip.

That night in Moscow, the fourth member of our team, Jim, who was proficient in Slavic languages, monitored Radio Moscow and confirmed Brezhnev had died, Wednesday, November 10, the day before we and Soviet citizens were told. Now, we needed a way to tell Seattle listeners.

Our clock was synced with CBS. Our routine was to assemble our radio-station-in-a-suitcase, the Soviets would connect to the satellite, and we'd listen to KIRO in Seattle for an hour while we prepared. At precisely 6 a.m. Seattle time, 5 p.m. Moscow time, the station picked up the five-minute CBS newscast from New York. KIRO's popular morning host, Bill Yeend, would open his microphone on the anchor's cue "this is CBS News."

Today was different. We triple checked that the "A" cord was in the "A" sprocket, but couldn't hear KIRO's air. We continued collecting info and writing about Brezhnev's death and edited interviews done earlier in the day on other topics. We were silent but calm as we watched the clock tick toward 5 p.m. in Moscow. Still no sound. No satellite. No KIRO radio. We looked into each other's eyes; all of us knew the stakes. The Soviet engineers watched us, and we watched them for possible clues. Alexander, whom we had grown to call Sasha, watched us and the clock with us, his blue eyes seemed to say he was powerless to change what was happening or not happening.

The clock finally reached 5 p.m. The CBS newscast had started, but we couldn't hear it. All eyes were on the clock as the minutes quietly passed. Five-oh-one. Five-oh-two. Five-oh-three. We had no control over our broadcast or our fate. The Seattle crew was ready to take it.

The minute hand moved to five-oh-four, and suddenly, we heard the CBS anchor begin the last minute of the newscast. We whooped and shouted, the Soviet engineers and Alexander joined in.

"We have the satellite! We have the satellite!" Bill put on his headset, waited the few short seconds until he heard "This is CBS news."

"Good Morning from Moscow, the Soviet Union," Bill said. "It's been an historic, eventful day," and immediately tossed it to Vic, whose baritone voice dramatically, simply, announced the stunning news. "Leonoid Brezhnev is dead."

It was the first that the Western world had heard the news that could impact the nuclear arms race, world peace, and the future of the Communist nation itself. In Moscow on a fluke, we were scooping the big boys. I did the non-Brezhnev stories, while Vic and Jim delivered the Brezhnev news. Bill said he knew before going on-air that he'd have to do some "tap dancing" as host while the story was unfolding. But we were energized and did everything right. We aced it, and we knew it after the broadcast that would eventually win many prestigious journalism awards.

"I didn't feel any pressure, I had such a great time!" Vic smiled was we recapped the excitement of the story unveiling itself, the drama of the satellite, and our collective instincts on how to deliver this exclusive information to our Seattle listeners.

Proud, but exhausted and ravenously hungry, we headed back to the hotel where we usually ate dinner in a sad, deserted cabaret, the only place available to us to eat after 10 p.m. Bill was diabetic, and it was a challenge not knowing when or where we would have access to food except at the hotel.

The Intourist was brightly lit as we approached. "Wow, look at all the people. Maybe we'll party and have a little fun tonight," Bill said.

As we got closer, we could tell people were lugging suit-cases and upset. Some climbed into big tourist buses outside. One of the porters told us they were evacuating the hotel for dignitaries who would attend Brezhnev's funeral. Vic joined the noisy crowd at the front desk to argue in vain that they couldn't make us leave. "But we have reservations! We have reservations!"

"I'm sorry, Moscow is closed," the hotel clerk informed Vic.

Vic pushed his way back to us. "We have thirty minutes to pack and board bus Number Two. They're clearing the city of foreigners!"

Astonished and protesting, we did as we were told. We learned it was a well-planned scheme created in anticipation of Brezhnev's death. At 9 p.m., staff started clearing two floors at a time, knocking on doors and giving people a half hour to pack and go to their assigned bus. The buses took everyone across town to a hotel built in collaboration with the French for the 1980 Moscow Summer Olympics. But the hotel was barely used because the Olympics were boycotted after the Soviets invaded Afghanistan.

Where was Alexander when we needed him? He had

rescued us once when police surrounded us and demanded Bill's camera after he snapped a souvenir photo of Radio Moscow. A tough, unwavering policeman argued with Alexander on the steps, up the steps, and into the lobby's security office. We hated the thought of losing our all our photos. After a nerve-wracking hour, we were allowed to keep the camera and go with Alexander.

On our own now, I felt like we were characters in a movie as we moved in this mass expulsion of foreigners. We had so many questions as we rode in the cushy, quiet bus. What was going to happen to us? To our last broadcast? And we're hungry!

Arriving at the hotel, the chaotic scene matched the one we just left except the lobby was modern. Vic took a deep breath and dived into the crowd determined to get us rooms before the night was over. Surprisingly, he returned fairly soon, and we headed upstairs.

The men had rooms on one side of the hallway. Mine was on the opposite side, the side that I would learn in the morning was the one with no hot water. But tonight, we were impressed with the attractive quarters and the classic French furniture. Once settled, we rendezvoused in my room when Vic sat down on a chair that instantly collapsed with a bang, dropping him to the floor. Stunned, we burst into uproarious laughter and couldn't stop. We laughed so hard we cried, and we laughed some more when someone snorted and set us off again.

Phew, that felt good. Happy, we went in search of food.

The foreign currency bar was open and it too was jammed. Unlike the lobby, people were happy, though no one seemed to speak English. The menu promised food. But as was often the case, only a couple of items were available. That's okay, we'll eat whatever you've got.

It was the wee hours of the morning when I made it back to my room, not feeling well. Eventually, I was violently ill. I had heeded warnings to not drink Moscow's tap water. But I used it for brushing my teeth. Or was it the weird bar food? No matter, it was nasty. Vic said my skin looked green. Sasha was concerned and said the hospital care would be free if needed.

"Oh, by the way," Alexander informed Vic, "no more satellite broadcasts. You need to leave the country. Foreigners have to leave. Hundreds of thousands of people descended on Red Square when Lenin died and some were crushed by the crowds. We need the hotel for diplomats."

So, that was the end. After such a spectacular broadcast the day before, we were okay with losing our last day. We rested and marveled at an astounding two weeks and looked forward to the next morning when we'd emerge from behind the Iron Curtain and head for home, land of the free.

Acknowledgements

Thank you to my eighth grade, home-room teacher, Mr. Hay. His enlightened approach to punishing my friend and me for talking too much in class was more homework. We wrote several punishment-for-talking-in-class-essays that year, two thousand words per talking episode. My writing was purposely wordy in order to meet the hefty word count. But the exercise showed me I enjoyed writing and had a knack for it.

Thank you to my mother, Mary Duncan, who had ever higher expectations of me during my childhood and optimism that I could do most anything if I tried. To my dad, Carl Duncan, for his humor, good character, and DNA that seems to contain a creative gene. To my Aunt Shirley Redfield Magnus, and Uncle Vic Magnus, A.K.A. Dutze, for helping fill in details of the Montana part of my childhood. And to my Grandfather Vic Magnus and my Uncle John who, like Dad and Dutze, were master story-tellers.

Thanks to Tim Lewis for his support and advice. Thanks, also, to friends Rebecca Hale, Pam Bissonnette, Maureen Welch, and Sally Mangold, and to former colleagues Frank Abe, Vic Bremer and Bill Yeend. Special thanks to my MS Writing Class teachers Richard Arvey and Evelyn Arvey, whose nurturing and critiques took my writing to new places. And also to my cohorts Lucinda, John, Al, Laura, and Katie for their encouragement, insights and new friendship. Thanks, especially, to the Swedish Medical Center Foundation for making the class and my personal growth possible.

John J. Mistur

About the Author

John J. Mistur lives in downtown Seattle with his pussycat, Bootsy. He enjoys writing memoirs and stories about living with Multiple Sclerosis.

Originally from Ohio, he graduated from Ohio University with a BA in marketing. (Go Bobby's!) As early as high school he was very creative. He wrote songs for his band, The KnuckleBeasts. He also wrote a speech while running for student council that helped him win the position of treasurer—by a landslide.

Since March of 2020, John has been actively writing with the Swedish MS group and improving his skills. Even though the progression of his disease has taken away his mobility, John has optimistically adapted by dictating his work into his smartphone. As a result, some of his work has a "travelogue" feel. John's raw writing style brings out the emotions and intensity of his stories.

John is currently working on his own memoir, some of which is excerpted here.

What's Happening to Me?

My story begins in Athens, Ohio, a small Southern rural college town one hour north of the West Virginia state line. I live with my little brother Mike in a small two-bedroom green house in the corner lot at the end of Court Street. I'm in the middle of finals week of my senior year at the college. Instead of studying for my exam during the end of spring quarter, I partied all night. Drinking whiskey and taking Vicodin at The Union with my friend Carrie, like a dumb ass.

What did I get myself into last night? Screw it. My final today is for a pass-fail elective and all I have to do is show up and take an easy true-false test. Piece of cake. It's only 12:30 p.m. and the final isn't until 2 o'clock. As I sit myself up on my red produce-print sofa, my head is pounding from the alcohol, but there's something else severely wrong with me.

I'm having trouble lifting up my left leg.

Come to think of it, my left arm feels the same way.

I can barely sit myself up on the couch. I continuously stretch out my left arm trying to figure out what the hell is going on. This is so messed up. Feels like my extremities are rubber bands that I have to stretch out with extra effort in order for them to function. I really need to concentrate and moving is no longer a natural phenomenon. Maybe this is just the effects of the Vicodin I took last night. I'm fine. I just need to get up and get ready for this final.

I stand up from my couch and then I trip over my Chukka Boots going into my bedroom! I put my other leg down to save me from falling, but walking around with my crippled leg like this is difficult so far. I hobble into my bedroom to get out of these pungent clothes. I bend down and grab a cleaner t-shirt on the floor, using my good hand because my left hand feels useless. Just hanging by my side. I can move my paralyzed arm a little bit, up and down, but I'm also having trouble grabbing shit with that hand.

I take my shirt off and throw it down in frustration. I start putting on the *new* one, strategically getting my left arm through the sleeve by using my other hand and then pull the shirt over my head. There's no way I'll be able to change into any fresher jeans. I'm already freaking exhausted, so I sit down on my bed to rest and catch my breath. I start rubbing my sweaty hands on my knees while I breathe heavier to the point of hyperventilation.

I look up at my python, Rex, and begin to have a mental breakdown. I'm realizing how serious the situation is becoming. I start to worry about every worst possibility, like if this is permanent, or when I'll get better. What is happening to me? Why do I deserve this? Especially now when I have to take my final exam in the next hour! Jesus Christ!

I take a couple deep breaths to compose myself. I'll see if my brother can drive me. I put my orange Adidas next to me on the bed and limp over to his room. I open the door, but he's not even there. Looks like I'm on my own. I proceed into the bathroom to wash my face, put deodorant on, and then go into the kitchen for a quick breakfast. Walking around the house is difficult, but at least I am getting around. Full concentration is the key and thinking of my next step is something I will need to focus on if I'm going to make this final. Morton Hall is only a twenty-minute walk so I should be okay. I've got to leave now if I'm going to get there in time.

Especially in my current condition.

Opening the front porch screen door, I look around and see that my brother took the van! Crap! I've got no choice. Right off the bat, I run into my first obstacle, the cement stairs. I grab the handrail, carefully going down them one stair at a time. When I get done with the stairs, I look up at a small hill I'm going to have to climb. Damn it.

I start staggering up the hill. Dragging my left foot a little bit atop the sidewalk, making a rustling noise. I keep telling myself to "lift the leg" when I see any cracks, so I won't fall flat on my face. Almost at the top. Using all the energy I have, both physically and mentally, to get up this hill. The sun and the humidity aren't helping and I'm sweating profusely. Panting.

Finally, I make it to the top and find some much-needed shade under a blooming buckeye tree in front of the Alpha Phi Omega frat house. I sit down on a three-foot brick wall surrounding the house. Heavily breathing and sweating profusely, soaking my red t-shirt. I take a short break and my good leg is spent from doing all the extra work and already feels sore. Looking down the street, I figure out the best path, so that I can avoid people seeing me. I am a total freak show right now. I look at my watch and see I still have a half an hour with six more blocks to go. I've got to hurry.

Each block feels like I'm walking a mile as I start getting close to my destination. I try to walk faster, but the faster I go the more I'm putting myself into danger. Every step I make I look down to make sure my paralyzed leg is lifting up high enough. Especially when I cross the roads and go up curb cuts, grabbing the poles of street signs to lift myself up. I'm almost there and can see Morton Hall now. Just one more block to go. I keep dragging my foot along until I find a cement bench to sit on in front of the building. I need to take a quick rest and focus before I go inside to take the test.

I look up and everybody is staring at me. I just don't give a crap though, because I made it here on time. I'm drenched with sweat and still breathing heavy, but I'm smiling because I'm here on time. I wait and watch everyone go inside. There's a sign on the entrance that says:

Starts at 2:00 Sharp!

Seat Yourself.

Test on Desk.

Okay great. I just need to sneak in there as inconspic-uously as possible. I open the door to the auditorium-style classroom and see a desk at other side of the top row. I try to play it cool and walk to the desk as smooth as possible, trying not to limp. I sit down, pulling a number two pencil out of my pocket, and start answering the questions. I'm trying to answer the questions the best I can, but I can't stop thinking about what's wrong with me. I'm so exhausted, and I just want to get home and get back in bed. I just hope I can make the trip home.

Finishing the test in record time, I drop it off in a basket by the door and get the hell out of there. Hobbling back over to the cement bench in front of the building. Just trying to compose myself again and get ready for my trek home. One of the other students comes up to me and says: "Dude, are you all right? Do you need any help getting home?"

"Yeah, yeah. I'm fine. I just sprained my ankle. Thanks anyways," I say to him. The nerve of that guy! I don't need anyone's help. I can get there myself.

When everybody clears out, I start staggering back the same way I came. Taking my time and a break every half block now. More humid than earlier. I am so tired and it's getting harder to lift my disabled leg. When I get to the frat house on the hill, my leg doesn't lift up enough. I trip over a crack in the sidewalk, falling down on the concrete landing on my knees! Nobody sees me lying helplessly, so I crawl over to the red brick wall and climb up to the top, using all the energy I have left. Rubbing my knees to ease the pain, I look down and see a big walking stick, so I bend down to pick it up for the rest of the trip.

Down the hill with my stick in hand I see the house. So close yet so far. I still don't see the van. Where the hell is Mike?! I am going crazy thinking about what's wrong with me. I need to go to the hospital now. After that fall I feel soreness all over, but I have just a little bit further to go. I use the cane and push myself up in standing position ready to get to my bed. The cane makes things *so* much easier. I can boost my leg up, plus it helps me with balance. I start going a little faster and get a little rhythm with my dragging foot. I finally get to the house. Drop the cane and use my good arm to help me get up the steps to the front door. I don't have any more energy left, so I go straight to my bedroom, take off my soaking red shirt, and instantly fall asleep.

Rex the python wakes me up trying to get out of his cage. Holy crap, it's 8:34 a.m. and I slept through the whole night. Nothing is different. I stretch out my arm and leg again, hoping, but they still feel like rubber bands. I notice the blue Ford Econoline in the street, so I get up and bust into Mike's room waking him up abruptly.

"Mike! I have to go to the hospital! There's something seriously wrong with me. My arm and leg aren't working right. I'm walking around like a freaking moron!" I lurch around his room in circles and try to lift something up to show him what's going on.

"Um. Good morning and thanks for waking me up, dude. Are you sure you have to go to the hospital right now? You don't look that bad."

"Are you crazy? I'm severely fucked up. We've got to go ASAP. Now get out of bed and get ready! I've got to see what's wrong with me, for God's sake. Let's go."

I go back into my room and find my favorite dark blue gas station shirt and put it on, and then go back to the living room couch to put on my Chukka Boots. While my brother gets ready, I call my parents long distance in Cleveland on my Cadillac phone. They agree with my decision and recommend that that I go to Athens Hospital, *not* the University Hospital. They want me to go see *real* doctors, not up-and-comers. Mike grabs the keys. We leave the house and get in the van.

After watching me struggle getting to, and getting into the van, my brother looks at me and says, "What the *hell* is wrong with you? You do kind of look weird."

"Screw you, Mike. I told you this is serious. Let's go! Step on it!"

We get to the hospital emergency room, and he drops me off at the front door to check in. After an hour, I am finally able to see a doctor. He does a full examination, including stretching my arm and leg out. He says he wants to consult with other docs and leaves the room. When he gets back into the exam room, he stands there looking at me, tapping his pencil on his clipboard.

"Please tell me what's happening to me doc," I beg. "I need help!"

He looks at me. "After examining you and speaking with my colleagues, I cannot diagnose you or explain why you're having paralysis. We have to give you a MRI, but our hospital does not have one."

He keeps going on and on about how there's nothing he can do to help my symptoms, and I'll have to cope. I'll have to see a neurologist first before a diagnosis or any treatments. This is the second time in my life a *real* doctor has told me they don't know what's wrong with me. What is happening to me?

Please somebody tell me!

I'm totally furious. I get off the exam table and hobble out of the office as quickly as possible to the waiting room, where Mike is reading a *People* magazine.

"Let's go. Let's get the hell out of here!"

"Where are you going, John? Don't you have to stay to get more help?"

"No! They can't do shit. Useless hospital! I have to go back home to Cleveland to see a neurologist. Where is the van?"

"Right out front. Quit spazzing out, John. So you have to go back to Cleveland. You'll get some help. Don't worry."

We start walking through the parking lot toward the van. He is standing by my side, so I grab a hold of his arm.

"Don't *worry*? Look at me! You have to help me to the van, for Christ's sake. Plus, I have my last final on Monday!"

Mike helps me into the luxury van and gets in the driver side. He looks at me and says, "Relax, John. Let's go home and figure out what to do next. Call Mom and Dad. How about we stop at Skyline Chili and I get us some chili dogs with extra cheese?"

"Okay. That sounds nice. Let's get the hell outta here. Thanks for your help, jerk."

We drive down to Skyline, got the dogs to go, and then go back to the house. After sitting down on my couch, I start eating while I call my parents. Letting them know my current situation. My Dad tells me not to stress out too much and he's going to find me the best neurologist in town to get the help I need. They want me home right away.

Then I call Dr. Gupta to reschedule my Quantitative Statistics final on Monday and tell him my medical situation. He doesn't care. He tells me I'll have to retake the *whole class*. There is no rescheduling the final and these are his class rules.

I slam down the phone. "Arrogant prick!"

"What's up, John?" Mike says.

"I got to retake the whole damn class. Plus, I got to figure out a way to get home ASAP. Can you take me on Sunday?"

"I still have a final next week. But Shep Dog is in town this weekend. I'm sure he can drive you back in the van."

Shep Dog is a friend of the family, Richard Shepherd, who does anything to help us out. He lives in the suburb over on the east side of Cleveland. This plan will work out perfectly. I will be leaving on Sunday to find out my fate, and to find out what's happening to me. I hope this neurologist will have all the answers and get me some treatment.

To get me back to normal.

Damn Phone Bill

I have Secondary Progressive Multiple Sclerosis and for me every day can be a challenge. The disease has progressed so badly that I can no longer walk or use my hands, so I need help every day with daily activities, so I can survive and live life. Everything from eating, dressing, and even using a Hoyer lift to hoist me up out of my bed and into my power chair, so I have mobility. And some independence.

Living like this and getting all this help can be frustrating and demoralizing. I've had to learn to be very patient and accept all the help. Sometimes it drives me crazy that I cannot do all the daily activities that I used to be able to. I don't let these frustrations control me or stop me from living my life. I find myself getting up every day with help from home nurses, so I can live every day the best way I can.

However, things don't always go as planned.

Sometimes I have to improvise to make things work. Even the simplest of tasks like paying a phone bill can be a challenge. Let me tell you a story of a day that one of my only tasks was to pay the phone bill.

My story begins after getting Hoyer-lifted into my power chair, with help from Susan. Since I cannot use my hands to drive my power chair, I have to use the complicated headset (with my head) to drive myself around by using various sensors. We finally got everything perfectly straightened out on the headset and I can get out and pay my phone bill.

I left my apartment on 12th Avenue in Seattle's Capitol Hill neighborhood and headed towards Pine Street by the police station at the corner. It was a beautiful sunny day with clear skies, and I was glad I got outside. When I got to Pine, I crossed over 12th, but the pavement was bumpy and when I went up on the yellow curb, my headset suddenly dropped down. Now I couldn't hit the back of the headset, which made it impossible for me to move forward.

I was completely stuck now, sitting next to a tree on the sidewalk.

There was nothing I could do. Normally, in this situation I would call someone to rescue me, but my phone was shut off. Oh *shit*. I was going to have to ask somebody to help me fix my headset.

I looked around and couldn't see anybody nearby except for a police officer in an undercover dark blue Crown Royal Cruiser parked in front of me. He got out of his car. He was wearing a Seattle Police Department navy blue polo shirt, and had the perfect policeman bushy brown mustache. He opened the trunk and pulled out five dry-cleaned police uniforms.

I tried to get his attention. "Excuse me, officer," I called to him, but my words were faint and he didn't hear me. I watched him run across the street to drop the uniforms off at the Precinct. Opportunity lost.

I sat there next to the tree on the sidewalk as people

walked by. I tried to get their attention by saying I needed help, but everyone just nodded their head to greet me or completely ignored me. There were people listening to their headphones or looking at their phones and I couldn't get anyone's attention. I was screwed. Stuck eight blocks away from the phone company.

After about thirty minutes, I saw the police officer that dropped off the uniforms crossing back over Pine Street to his car.

"Excuse me, officer! Can you help me?" *This* time I was a little more vocal.

"What's going on?" he asked.

"I'm in a little bit of the pickle. My headset fell down and I was wondering if you could help me fix it?"

He agreed. I gave him instructions on what to do. He lifted the back of the headset and made sure everything was back into place, so I could drive.

"I think that's good, officer. Thanks for all the help."

He got back into his cruiser and drove off. I was saved by the mustachio officer! I could finally head to the phone company to pay the phone bill.

I headed back down Pine Street toward Broadway, the street the phone company was on. For a few blocks my headset was holding up until I reached Broadway. Suddenly I hit a big giant crack in the sidewalk and again my headset fell down.

Dammit!

I was stuck right in front of Blick Art Supply, in front of the rusted bronze Jimmy Hendricks statue. I was going to have to ask for more help.

There wasn't anybody coming out of the store. Yet again,

I just patiently waited for someone to come by, so I could ask for help. And then, I heard a woman's voice behind me.

"Beautiful day outside," she said. "This is a nice place to sit in the sun."

I turned my head and I saw a stunning redhead with her hair in a ponytail. She was wearing multi-colored yoga pants and a black sports bra. Her camera was out and she was taking pictures of the Jimi Hendrix statue.

"Yes!" I said. "It's a beautiful day and I love this statue. It reminds me of the old rock days."

She smiled. "He's a Seattle icon!"

At this point, I couldn't believe that this gorgeous woman was even *talking* to me. This was my window of opportunity to get some help. I looked at her with puppy dog eyes and asked her politely, "I was wondering if you could help me out. My headset fell down, and I'm having trouble driving. Could you help me fix it?"

She raised her arms and said in a concerned voice, "Oh my goodness! I didn't know this was why you were sitting here. No problem. What can I do?"

She jumped on the opportunity and was eager to help. I gave her instructions on what to do and trained her how to reposition my headset, so I could drive again. She double-checked to make sure everything was all right, until I drove off again.

Ready to pay the stupid phone bill.

I drove down Broadway until I got to the phone company. Thankfully, nothing else went wrong and I finally made it. Success! Nothing was going to stop me from paying my phone bill. This was truly a small victory.

So, why the hell did I want to tell you a story about paying a phone bill? Because I wanted you to go through some challenges I may go through every day. I have to accept all the extra help I need throughout the day. Accepting is tough, but that is what I need to do to continue enjoying life. I may struggle dealing with my MS at times, but that doesn't mean I'm going to give up on life. Even if it's just a simple task like paying my damn phone bill.

Hey, I even got to meet and get help from a beautiful woman.

Who knows what tomorrow will bring?

Earning My Homecoming

As I sit here eating another soggy hamburger and curly fries from the hospital cafeteria, I can't help but wonder when I'm going to be able to go home again. I've been here for three months because of a major MS attack, which weakened my arms and legs so much that I couldn't get out of bed one morning and had to be taken to the ICU.

Now I'm doing rehab six days a week here at the rehab center and I'm feeling confident enough to live on my own again. Although I'm a bit nervous because it's been so long since I've lived on my own. Who am I kidding? I'm *so* ready to get the hell out of here. I miss my apartment in the Interbay neighborhood of Seattle, home cooking, and my cat Bootsy so much.

I am going to show the physical therapists (PTs) and the occupational therapists (OTs) that I am ready to get out of rehab. During today's four hours of therapy, I will do all my activities with confidence. Right off the bat, the transfer to my manual wheelchair from the bed is easy. I quickly propel myself down the hallways to the small gym where we usually get started. I pull myself up to the arm bike and start pedaling as fast as I can, even working overtime. I want to show my OT that my strength is coming back.

"Keep going, John!" she encourages me. "Five more minutes."

So I give her ten more minutes.

After strengthening my arms, we decide to cool down and work on hand-eye coordination. She sets up the Nintendo Wii, so I can do light exercises while I bowl with the Wii controllers in my hands. It's my favorite activity because it doesn't even feel like I'm exercising, just having fun.

I move into the big gym after finishing the OT activities and start more intense exercises with the PT. First, we go to the standing frame where I lock my brakes and get ready to stand. I pull myself up until I'm able to straighten my legs and hold myself up for as long as I can. I beat my record of three minutes and the PT is thrilled by my progress. He wants to work on my core, so I transfer onto the giant mat in the middle of the gym and sit myself up at the edge of the mat with my feet on the floor to keep myself balanced. He hands me a beach ball and sits in front of me, so we can play catch, challenging me by throwing the ball in different directions.

I keep catching everything and throwing the ball back to him as I keep my balance.

"Just a couple more, John. You're doing great!"

We finish up and I transfer back into my manual chair to head back to my room for the evening. I can tell everybody is so proud of me and of the progress I've made. I transfer one last time into bed without a hitch.

As I sit in bed waiting for dinner, I get a visit from the lead doctor of the rehab center. I *knew* I'd impressed the therapists!

I hope there's good news because this doctor doesn't visit me every day. He stands in front of me with his white doctor coat, miniature golf pencil, and clipboard, looking very serious. "Your progress the past week has been remarkable according to everyone, John," he says. "I'm ready to start the discharge process and get you back home."

Hell *yeah*! I knew I killed it today!

But he has more to say. "However, I won't be able to discharge you until I know that your home is safe, and you've got some extra help. At home."

"What do you mean, help at home?" I respond nervously.

"I want to make sure you have a caregiver helping you out at least every other day in the beginning. Once you have somebody in place, then I will be able to release you."

He goes on to tell me that this kind of thing is normal for people in my situation and says that the extra assistance will help me conserve energy with everyday living tasks. Almost on the verge of tears, I plead with him that I'll be fine on my own, but there isn't anything I can say to change his mind. I *have* to get someone in place right away or I can't go home. The doctor briefly goes over the discharge process and congratulates me on the way out.

All my hard work has paid off. I can finally leave.

But I can't believe it's come to this. I come to the hard realization that my MS is getting worse and I'm going to have to start adjusting my lifestyle to stay independent again. Not to mention that I have to stay in this shithole for another week while I prepare.

The following week we do everything for the discharge process. We work with the OTs to set my apartment up to be safe. We get a stand-up pole to help me dress, a commode chair that fits over the toilet, so it's safe to go to the bathroom, and a transfer board so I can get into the brand-new, hospital-style bed.

I meet with the intake woman from Chesterfield Caregiving Agency for Home Care. After an hour of discussing my needs and doing paperwork, she says she already has somebody in mind for me, someone who will be a perfect fit to help me out. We make a plan: the day I get home, I will put a key under my front door mat, so the caregiver can get inside my apartment.

Seems a little shady. But I'll do whatever it takes to get me back home.

On my last day in rehab, my sister Holly comes by. We take a yellow cab back to my apartment. I get out of the cab and roll myself up my ramp to the front door as fast as I can. When I open the door, Bootsy jumps in my lap to greet me. She's so happy to see me and purrs loudly when I pet her.

Home sweet home!

My lazy boy. My big screen TV. My stereo. I am free at last. This is a glorious day!

Holly and I get some delicious Thai delivery to celebrate.

"So, she's just going to come here in the morning? And she'll let herself in?" Holly asks, "Do you want me to be here?"

"That's how it's going down. I already put the key under the mat. I'll be fine. I'll call if something goes wrong."

After finishing up dinner and enjoying being in my cozy apartment again, it's time for bed. I use my brand-new transfer board to get into my brand-new hospital bed. I lay there with my cat, wondering what life is going to be like with a caregiver. It feels is so awkward and frustrating that some strange woman will be here in a matter of hours.

In the morning, I hear a loud knock on my front door. Bootsy jumps out of bed and the front door opens.

"Hello? I'm back here!" I call from my bedroom.

She comes into my room and bobs her head to greet me. She's a tall African woman with dreadlocks wrapped in an orange headdress. She's wearing sandals, glitter jeans, and a thick bright purple blouse. She gives me a big warm smile and starts talking with a heavy accent. "I am Florence from Chesterfield. Don't worry, John. I know what you're going through. I'm here to help you settle in your home again."

Florence tells me stories about Ghana and about being a caregiver for years, including her parents in hospice and having autistic children. She is so bubbly and friendly, speaking to me with that thick accent, laughing all the time. I can tell Florence is a natural-born caregiver.

"Relax, John. Everything's going to be fine. We'll get along just great!" she says in a warm tender voice. Then she lets out another jovial laugh.

I am starting to feel more comfortable around her already.

The next few hours she makes me a hearty breakfast that she gives me in bed. After breakfast, she helps me transfer into my wheelchair even though I didn't really need her. Then she helps me get dressed by pulling my pants up after I lift myself up using the standing pole in the middle of my living room. After I am ready for the day, she starts making me dinner for later. While she works on my chicken stir fry with bell peppers, we talk some more and quickly become friends. Maybe having a caregiver isn't going to be so bad.

I can't believe that the progression has gotten this far, and that this is my new adaption reality. I'm just glad I'm living independently again and that I'm out of the damn hospital. I have nothing to be nervous about anymore.

Everything's going to be fine.

Happiness in MS

Multiple Sclerosis is a horrible disease. There's an endless list of debilitating symptoms to deal with all the time. Especially depression. Always leaves you wondering if and when progression will get worse. So what do you do when the nightmare comes true and things get worse? Well, the dream has come true for me, and I want to share some examples of how I've been able to cope and continue enjoying life.

During my working years in the 2000s, my progression started rapidly getting worse. Seemed like every other year I was getting a new piece of DME (Durable Medical Equipment). I call these my "DME years" and I needed the tools for safety and to continue working.

When I started walking like a drunken fisherman, I bought a walking Redwood cane with a shiny brass cobra on top. Then, when it got even more difficult to walk, I decided to buy a souped-up walker, so I could get back and forth to the office. The walker was dark red and became a bench when I put the brakes on. At this point, things got awkward at work, but that didn't stop me from becoming a successful salesman of EMR (Electronic Medical Records) software. I took pride in my job and formed bonds with my coworkers as well as clients. I did well, balancing work and living with a debilitating disease getting worse.

Eventually, I got fitted for a manual chair because I started fatiguing quickly and was losing my balance. The chair was a shiny black Ti Lite that only weighed four pounds. At the time, that chair made my life so much easier, saving me energy and not having to worry about falling unless I went too far back while popping a wheelie. MS kept punching me in the face, trying to knock me down, but I kept fighting back. I still lived life the best way I could.

Progression just got worse. Plus, I lost my job, and my truck, and eventually I had to get set up in a power chair. Three more devastating blows that slowed me down, but I just wouldn't stay down. My TDX SP wheelchair actually sped things up and opened new doors. I signed up for Access Rideline, a shuttle service in Seattle, and learned the bus routes. I started volunteering at the Seattle Aquarium, learned about all the wildlife of the ocean, and then educated visitors. I also started volunteering at the Southeast senior center teaching them how to use "the electronics" and joined their chess club. I still play there to this day and formed several friendships.

My arms and hands started to get weaker, but that didn't stop me from my favorite hobby, taking photos. For Christmas, my parents got me a Samsung Galaxy smart camera with a bendable tripod that I could hold onto with my weak left hand to line up the shots. The camera also had voice recognition so when I had the picture perfectly lined up, I'd say *capture that* and it would take a picture! The camera was amazing and made taking pictures a lot easier. I spent a lot of time taking pictures of the giant Pacific octopus at the aquarium or traveling up and down the Canal Trail in Interbay, taking pictures of sailboats and cormorants during their mating season. I even submitted some of my pieces to the Swedish MS Art Show where they displayed them in the middle of the Armory at Seattle Center for everyone to view while they got food. I volunteered for that event as well talking to visitors about the artwork or answering questions about my mysterious disease. Swedish threw a viewing party at the end of the show, so all the artists could get together to meet each other while we ate cookies and tried to win raffle prizes.

Suddenly, the progression of my MS got so bad I lost most of the functionality of my arms and hands altogether. Presented with yet another challenge, I figured out a solution. I worked with my OT plus another DME vendor and got fitted for a headset, so I could drive my power chair with my head. Problem was the headset wouldn't be ready for two months! So I was stuck in bed during that time, but I didn't let that bring me down. I stayed positive and thought of starting a GoFundMe page to raise money for a wheelchair van. This helped me pass the time while I was waiting for the headset. The response was overwhelming. After only two weeks, I raised all the funds that I needed get a used Town & Country minivan. I call her Black Lightning. This brought me great joy and helped me deal with another MS progression setback. When I finally got the headset back, I learned how to use it and I was back in business. Then I took Black Lightning out to different accessible trails in the beautiful Northwest. I used my new headset to drive as fast as I could down a paved path surrounded by evergreens.

I can't write this story without mentioning importance of

accepting help and finding an excellent support system. Since my progression has gotten so bad, I need help with everything—tasks from eating and dressing, to even going to the bathroom. MS kept beating me up, but I found a solution for that too. I started working with a team of caregivers, including my sister, that help me with everything. I'm devastated that my life has come to this, but I have no choice but to get the help I need. Now I can stay in my own apartment with my cat Bootsy, continuing to live my life the best way I can, even though I'm severely beat up by MS.

I can't stress enough the importance of being a part of some kind of an MS support group. Being around others challenged with the disease like me has helped out tremendously. I've been lucky to get my care from the Swedish MS Center in Seattle, which has groups like The Adventure Club, where I got to go camping on Blake Island just outside of Seattle. My favorite group has been the MS Writing Group where I've learned how to become a better writer and shared my personal stories with everyone in the group. The experience has been very therapeutic and I've bonded with everybody. I've meet so many wonderful people coping just like me by joining these groups. They're like my "MS family." Just another way MS has opened up doors for the better.

These are only just a few examples in my life that I've been able to deal with this horrible disease. You may not be able to control the Orange Beast, but you can tame the evil monster. There may be an endless amount of challenges, but look at them as opportunities. You just need positivity and patience. Then I guarantee you'll learn to adapt and live with MS. Find internal peace. If I can do it, then I know you can too. Just don't give up. Try to turn lemons into a wheelchair van. Even though you've been dealt a bad hand you can still win in this precious life.

You never know what each day will bring you. I mean, just yesterday I drove around Seattle and someone gave me a Neon green polo shirt and some chocolate frosted donuts with sprinkles. Now that's a pretty good day and I couldn't have made it happened if I gave up. You can still do whatever you want to do even though you have MS. Might take you a little longer to complete your goals, but anything's still possible. Believe me when I tell you my life has not always been a bed of roses, but when life gets bad I always look for that beautiful bouquet.

You should try it too.

Hotdog Chop Life

There is so much going on in the world today that the world feels like total chaos and things are out of control. I'm trying to live through this awful pandemic, and to top things off there are protests in my neighborhood for the BLM (Black Lives Matter) movement the past two weeks. Between the social distancing, isolation, and living in the middle of CHOP (Capitol Hill Occupy Protest) in Seattle, I'm trying to keep my stress level low and keep myself from going insane.

I'm going to get out today even though there's rain. I want to see what's going on because last night I heard protesters breaking glass at the police station and chanting all night. Total anarchy. After getting up and into my power chair with help from Azeb, my caregiver, I leave my apartment on 12th Avenue and head north to Pine Street. I see dozens of people walking in the middle of the streets; they're curious to see what is going on. Feels like a Block Party.

The police station is boarded up already and protesters dressed in Black Bloc are sitting all around the entrance like they own the place. There's a huge black cloth mural draped over the entrance that says in white spray paint: "Property of the People of Seattle." The police are nowhere to be found and everyone is doing whatever they want.

Driving my chair further west down Pine on the sidewalk, I find an awning to sit under to get out of the rain. Since I am not wearing a mask, I sit by myself away from people observing all activity. Looking down Pine, I feel like I'm a giant outside the Urban Art Museum because of the way all the buildings are tagged with colorful graffiti and murals. It's like being in a dream. Dozens of versions of BLM tags are everywhere. Some are orange, blue, purple, made with different fonts. Every artist has a different unique rendition. Some tags decorating the walls include "Fuck SPD," "ACAB," "Cop-Free Zone," and "Remember Brianna Taylor." On the boarded-up Stout restaurant there is a huge realistic mural of George Floyd's face and underneath it says, "RIP."

More and more people are showing up, including families with kids. Hard to believe that a couple weeks ago everyone was told by Governor Inslee to stay inside and socially distance, but nobody cares anymore. Now it's a free-for-all shitshow and everybody is getting along while they check out the festivities at Chop.

There's a DJ playing music while he preaches social injustice. On the corner of Pine and 11th in front of the Rhino Room, someone has set up a pop-up market and giving away hot meals and fresh produce to anyone hungry. The Dirty Dog hot dog vendor at the other corner by me is making a killing right now with all these people hanging around. He's probably selling more Seattle dogs today than he has all of last month.

After the rain subsides, I drive around checking things out. I go down Pine to 11th, passing Dirty Dogs. The smell of the grilling dogs makes me feel like I am at a summer cookout.

Turning down 11th, there are people smoking weed on couches and La-Z-Boys set up in the middle of the road. I love that pungent skunky smell.

I keep going and see that the Hugo House is all boarded up. The plywood on the windows says "Black Lives Matter" in black and white paint with different color stick figures underneath, the thick brush strokes signifying unity. Stopping in front of the Hugo House under a green metal awning, I see a big group of protesters marching across the field of Cal Anderson Park. The sea of different colored umbrellas looks surreal, like a floating Chinese dragon at a New Year's Festival.

As I sit there, my talkative middle-aged black home-less friend Chris slowly walks towards me. He is wearing a light green fisherman's cap, dirty blue jeans, and a brown Carhartt jacket.

He greets me. "You know this Black Lives Matter move-ment ain't so bad," he says. "I am benefiting from it right now."

"What do you mean? Like people are giving you money?"

"Yeees! Big time." Nodding with a smile and his eyes wide open. "I think everyone giving me money makes them feel good about themselves. Like they're making a contribution to the movement. Whatever the reason. I can't complain!" Letting out a bellowing sneaky laugh like he just won the lotto.

After I enthusiastically congratulate him, he goes to Uma Bop restaurant at the corner and gets some pork pot stickers with his newfound fortune for us to share. I'm a little bit nervous sharing with him, but he uses hand sanitizer before helping me eat, so I think I'm safe from Covid. He dips a couple of pot stickers in sweet spicy sauce and feeds them to me. He tries to finish the rest, but they gave him so many extra he is unable. He puts the rest in a small backpack for later.

"Best damn pot stickers I've ever had!" he says, busting out his sneaky laugh again. He pulls out a joint. "You wanna smoke? Someone gave me a whole bunch of weed."

"Sure! I'll puff with you. But let me start it up just to be safe."

He puts the joint in my mouth and lights me up. Screw it. I've been dealing with enough lately so maybe this will chill me out and help me deal. When in Rome...plus the cops aren't around anyways, so fuck it. I take a few drags, coughing, and then he takes it from my mouth and finishes the tiny rolly joint.

He starts babbling. "I just heard that people are making flour out of crickets for consumption. Crickets! Can you believe that? Disgusting."

"I heard that too," I said. "I think it's because of the protein content. Like a protein powder."

"Would you try it?"

"Hell yeah! I'd try a cricket protein powder buttered waffle with maple syrup. That sounds delicious right now."

We both laugh really hard.

Someone approaches us slowly, hunched over, wearing a skull face mask and a blue bandana holding back her long purple hair.

"What up, dudes? It's me, Darcy." She pulls down her mask and points to herself.

I've met her a couple of times. She's one of my bartender friends.

"Hey, Darcy!" I say. "We're just chilling in Chop. You want to hang? We were just about to have a drink. I have some vodka but no mixers"

"Oh, I got you," she says, taking charge. "I know the owner of Dirty Dogs. I'll get us something."

She runs down to the hot dog stand and hooks us up with some orange soda and red plastic party cups. She grabs the Four Freedoms out of my bag and makes us all drinks. She holds up the drinks for a toast. "To Chop Life."

"To Chop Life," we both respond, taking a sip of the delicious mixed drink she created.

"I should get that tattooed across my knuckles," I said, joking around with her.

"I could put it on with a Sharpie! I have one in my bag," she says wittily.

"No, no, no. I'm not going to do it. I'll never be able to get that shit off," I reply with a big smirk on my face.

"So, are you going to give me a tour of your hood or what?" Darcy demands.

"Hell yeah, we can show you around the park and see what's going on. I want to see what they're doing on Pine Street. Then we can head over to the park benches by the basketball courts and see what's going on over there."

After finishing our cocktails, we turn around and head back towards Pine, passing the smoking lounge area and Dirty Dogs. By now, it's not raining, so I don't have to worry about getting my wheelchair wet. Strolling down the road on Pine, I can finally see what's happening. In the middle two lanes, people are painting a huge Black Lives Matter mural that stretches a whole block from 10th to 11th. Each letter is being painted by different artists, so every letter has its own unique personality. The coolest art I've seen all day.

We stop at all the snack vendors set up along the sidewalk to pick up some free munchies and drinks. We get some

Cheez-Its, Tim's potato chips, Clif bars, and Gatorade. Score! Everyone's being so kind and generous. Like a small little loving community. Everyone's got each other's backs and are willing to help anyone out.

After entering the park, I go ahead, leading the way to the basketball court benches, passing the skatepark and the tennis courts. Once I get to the empty basketball courts, I speed up my chair as fast as it can go. I do a long drift on the damp cement as I turn around and face them, showing off my donut driving skills.

"I knew you were going to do that! Did I not tell you he was going to do that?" Chris says to Darcy, laughing hysterically.

We decide to have another drink, so Darcy works her magic and sets us up for round two. We hang around looking at all the changes in the park, including a freshly erected thirty-foot tall wood statue of a Black Power fist placed on home plate of the baseball field and more food vendor canopy tents set up along the first and third base lines.

Darcy suddenly lifts her glass and screams to random strangers. "Chop Life!"

As we sit there enjoying each other's company, I look at Chris. "So, you think all this is going to make a difference?" I ask. "You think there will be change?

"Are you kidding? I've been living through this kind of thing for decades and ain't nothing ever changes. They're still going to kill us."

Spending the day with Chris and Darcy helped me cope with all the stresses and turmoil going on in the world right now. I felt like I was living in a once-in-a-lifetime political movement. Only time will tell if there will be any changes because of what happened at CHOP.

Human Interaction

I was up all night.

    I was thinking about bullshit and I was depressed about everything going on in my life right now. Like dealing with the fear of the pandemic and total social isolation. Even after a Zoom call with all my best high school buds yesterday, you would think that I would be in a better mood, but I wasn't. Seeing every single one of them showing off their children except for me made me feel even more alone and sad. All I could do is tell them about my beautiful pussycat Bootsy. I felt like wet stinky trash down in the dumps.

    I had to do something to get out of this depressing lonely funk. I read an article that said making at least eight social contacts a day helps with mental health and curbs loneliness. I decided to make a goal to get out and test that theory. Maybe that would lift my spirits, like freshly blossomed roses in the garden.

    If I was going to do this, right I'd have to take advantage of every person, starting with my motherly Ugandan Certified

Nursing Assistant, Suzanne. When she came over, I acted like I'd never seen her before.

"Good morning, Suzanne! How are you today?" I cheerfully greeted her.

She just gave me a weird look and started laughing at me. Told me she's fine, and then went to the kitchen to make me breakfast. The sizzling bacon smelled amazing and made my stomach grumble. Little did she know she was my first contact of the day.

Only seven more to go.

I left the apartment slowly, so I could adjust to the bitter cold wind blowing down the street. I headed towards Cal Anderson Park a block away from my apartment. I rode down Olive Street and ran into some of my punk rock blue-haired neighbors from my building walking their old Shih Tzus.

"Hey, neighbors!" I greeted them.

They waited for me to drive by on the sidewalk.

"Looks like the sun's coming out!" I said enthusiastically when I passed them. "Have a good day!"

I'd knocked off a couple more contacts from my list. I was almost halfway there already.

I drove through the park and parked myself by the entrance near the basketball courts and started checking my emails on my phone. My hands and bald head were starting to freeze up like a popsicle. Out of nowhere, from around the corner, Emilio greeted me. He was a young man that I'd seen around the park, my senior friend Gary's nephew. The shitty English joint he was smoking emitted the nasty smell of burning car tires. We sat there and talked a little bit, and then he called his Uncle Gary, so I could talk to him too.

"What's up, Uncle Gary? Is it cool if got your number? Maybe you can text it to me."

The grouchy old man shouted back to me. "Yes, John, you can have my number. But you know I can't text!"

We both laughed at his reaction.

Emilio said, "I got you", and texted me his Uncle Gary's phone number.

I could now officially count him as a contact. I was half-way there already!

I decided to head to the Denny Way light-rail train station to warm up. I cut through the park and took the gravel trail. I could hear the tires on my power chair crunch over the rocks like I was driving on sandpaper. When I got to the station, I sat under the space heaters that were hanging above me on the ceiling. Those little heaters felt like a warm blanket as they melted my frozen bald head and hands.

I took a phone call from my sister Holly, and she told me about the exotic spicy spices she bought for me at Uwajimaya Asian market. As I was talking to her, a couple of Metro Transit officers wearing blue gray uniforms with flak jackets and stun guns approached. "You okay, buddy?"

I looked up at them. "I'm okay. Just talking on the phone. Thanks for checking in on me, guys."

After I got toasted from the heat lamps and made another contact with the officers, I left the station and headed towards Broadway Street on Denny Way. Right before I crossed Broadway, I saw someone else I know crossing towards me. Shorty Mac was wearing a University of Washington sweat-shirt and ball cap. He had his headphones on. He lifted one of the speakers from his ear and spoke with me.

He told me a story about how there are no Key Banks

on Broadway and he desperately needed money for alcohol. His stimulus check hasn't come yet either. I told him I was broke and he walked away in frustration. I can now count Shorty Mac as another contact even though he was bitching the whole time.

I crossed Broadway to Starbucks and the smell of mocha lattes filled the air. I knew I only had a few more contacts to go, so I decided to go into the Metro PCS to get my voicemail switched over from Spanish back to English. I don't know how I did that, but I had to get that fixed.

When I got inside, a heavy-set African American woman wore a purple PCS shirt with lavender perfume asked me how she could help out. I told her my situation and she went to the computer to reset my voicemail. When we were finished, she walked me out through the lavender fields and opened the door for me.

My contacts were building up, but I still had a few to go. I decided to go visit Harry at the tobacco shop. I'd known him for years from when I used to smoke, so I went to pay him a visit. I drove past Dicks Drive-In, and the wonderful smell of Dicks Deluxe cheeseburgers and fresh-cut fries surrounded me. I was hungry again.

I got to the mini-mall and drove to the back where Broadway Tobacco is located. I passed his cigar room where he keeps the thousands of freshly rolled cigars from around the world that gave the hallway a rich vanilla aroma. I pushed open the metal gated door and he had the heat blasting, which was just what I needed. He was burning patchouli incense.

"Hello, John! How are you?" He happily greeted me in his Indian accent.

I told him I was cold and asked him if I could stick around and warm up for a little bit.

He was delighted and didn't mind at all. We talked for about fifteen minutes about religion and politics until I got warm enough to go back out to the frigid ice cave. When I left, I felt great about going to visit Harry again. I had not seen him in months. Plus, he was another contact for the day!

I was on a roll and practically had all my contacts, but I wasn't satisfied. I wanted to see if I could find some more victims. I left the mini-mall and headed back home. I passed Dick's Drive-In again, went through the hamburger clouds, and found a place to sit in the sun on Denny Street by Starbucks. Across the street, Albacha Mediterranean restaurant was cooking up their famous Gyro special with garlic fries for lunch. The combo of smells hovered around me, and I was no longer thinking about a Dick's deluxe burger.

After I called Uncle Gary confirming that Emilio gave me his correct number, I saw my weird neighbor, Antonio, leaving Starbucks with a large coffee in his hand. He saw me sitting there and headed right towards me. My chance for another contact!

"What's up, Antonio? What kind of coffee you drinking?" I asked him.

"Pistachio soy latte. Why do you ask?" he sounded nervous.

"I was just curious. I enjoy mocha lattes myself."

Little did he know that he had just become another one of my contact victims.

I told him that I'd been at Broadway Tobacco in the mini-mall visiting Harry, and that opened a flood gate for him to tell me a yarn of a story. He said that Kurt Cobain shot up heroin in the wood-furnished bathrooms on the top floor of the very same mini-mall. I could never tell if Antonio told me the truth or not when I talked to him, but this story seemed believable enough. Who knows?

I spoke with Antonio for a little longer, and then he left to go to Raucous Weed dispensary to re-up on some flowers to smoke. I had frozen up again even though I was in the sun, so I decided to go to the other train station on Broadway to sit under the little heaters.

Suddenly, I saw Eric, a tall, slender, dirty young homeless man whom I'd seen wandering the streets. Me and Uncle Gary sometimes call him "The Neanderthal." He was wearing a pink plaid hoodie wool pullover, dirty-ass jeans, and purple flip-flops. He came over to greet me and smelled like the old cigarette butt that he was holding in his black hand. I backed up a little, so he wouldn't get too close. Mainly because of paranoia from shitty Covid.

"Hey, Eric. How are you? I see you got a smoke," I calmly said to him.

"Good, good. Just walking around," he scratched his head with one hand and lifted the garbage can lid with his other.

"I'm pretty warm in here. Do you ever stay here at night?"

"No, no," he said. "They kick you out!"

"That's bullshit! Well, maybe they'll let you stay for a little while. Good seeing you, Eric. I got to meet somebody."

"Okay, John. Love you, buddy"

I zoomed out of the train station to get away from the germ-infested gentleman. Don't get me wrong about Eric. He's a very nice homeless guy and wouldn't hurt a bug except the ones he scratches off his body.

I'd made yet another contact. It was time for me to head home.

I drove back through Cal Anderson Park, but nobody was

there except for dog walkers and soccer players. I thought I still needed one more contact though; I was starting to lose track. When I got to the front of my building, my neighbor Topher was sitting on the bench smoking an American Spirit. This was my chance, so I drove right towards him.

"Hello, Topher!" I shouted.

We hung out until he got done smoking. While we were surrounded by smoke, he told me a story about being on vacation with his friends in a cabin near Olympia. He needed to get out of his room and get away from all the pandemic bullshit. Then he was kind enough to offer me help to get back up to my apartment. Since we live on the same floor, this was the perfect plan.

I succeeded in getting eight human contacts for the day. Maybe more! I completed the study and felt proud of myself for accomplishing my goal. I had connected with the whole community in some way and lifted up my spirits. I didn't feel so lonely after all. I just needed to get out and make some kind of human interaction to help me feel better about myself again.

These short interactions really put everything into perspective for me. Everyone seems to be dealing with the pandemic, depression, and loneliness their own way, just like me. This is how I dealt with those issues on this day to make myself feel better. Maybe if *you* reach out like I did, and spread the love, then you might feel better about yourself too.

Not Again

After waking up this morning and transferring into my manual wheelchair, I feel like I have just ran a marathon. If I *could* run a marathon. The weather has been boiling hot all week and today is no exception. The heat is aggravating my MS symptoms, fatiguing me and wearing me out quickly. Everything I do is at a turtle pace and I'm feeling like an out-of-shape, two-toed sloth.

After taking a break and petting my cat, Bootsy, in my lap, I roll into the kitchen to grab some ice water because I feel like I ran a 4k. Just standing up to reach for some ice in the freezer feels like I'm climbing Mount Baker and chiseling some ice from a glacier. I haven't felt this worn out from doing everyday tasks in a long time.

I snatch some Cheez-Its and crunchy granola bars from the lowered kitchen shelves and slowly push myself into the living room in front of my big-screen TV. I finish my "breakfast," cool off from the mountain ice water, and fall asleep.

I wake up to Judge Judy screaming "Shut up!" while she pretends to zip her lips with her fingers. I can't help but snicker and can't believe how long I slept. This heat is getting unbearable and making my life more difficult. I really hope I have enough stamina to finish this day.

I have to figure out a plan of action for tonight, so I can conserve the most energy while I'm dealing with this crap. King 5 weather says sunny and almost 95°. I'm baking in my house right now and need to get some air circulating in here.

My arms feel like floppy wet noodles and I'm struggling to roll my wheelchair over to the side porch door to open it all the way. Bootsy zips past me to go outside and get out of the sauna. The warm breeze flows into my apartment, making the heat more bearable. I smell the fishy water from the canal and hear the seagulls fighting with the crows.

I go to the fridge and reach in for a chilled bottle of Lipton green tea to quench my thirst. Even doing these small tasks is pooping me out; I'm starting to worry my MS symptoms are acting up more than usual. I *hate* dealing with this disease and how it affects my body. So frustrating. I know from experience that I just need to relax and stay calm until dusk when the blistering sun sets over the Olympics. Otherwise, my symptoms will get even worse.

Until then, I'm going to eat dinner and just try to take it easy. There's no way I'm cooking dinner tonight and wasting my valuable energy. So I reach into the fridge for beef jerky and a banana, then go over to the kitchen table by the open side porch door.

As I watch the boats head back to Lake Union, I worry about how I'm going to get myself into bed tonight. I'll have to be extra careful and make sure I have my phone on me in case something goes wrong, like if I fall on the floor during the transfer.

As soon as the sun goes down, I know this is the best time to get ready for bed. I'm feeling a little better since I ate and because the weather cooled down. Slowly, I head to the bathroom. I drank way too much green tea, so now I really need to take a piss.

After parking myself in front of the toilet, I lock the brakes, so my wheelchair will stay put. Then, using the arms of the chair, I lift myself to a standing position. Using every ounce of energy and every muscle in my body, I finally stand up. I can barely stand. I keep rocking back and forth like I am a drunk sailor on a ship.

I need to hurry, so I quickly start letting everything out. Still rocking back and forth, I barely hit the center of the toilet and start peeing all over the floor. When I can't stand anymore, I fall back into my chair, peeing all over myself. I go over to the sink to wash off my hands and just splash water all over my face, cleaning myself off for the night. Screw brushing my teeth.

Going back into the kitchen, I see Bootsy run in the side door straight to her food. I lock all my doors and now I'm ready to get into bed for the evening, something I've dreaded doing all day. In my room, I place myself next to my hospital bed. I'm not going to bother taking off my pee-soaked clothes or my shoes because I need every ounce of remaining energy.

Locking the wheels once again, I lift the side arm of the chair, so I can transfer to my bed. Then I unlock the legs of the chair and put my feet down on the hardwood floor to sturdy myself. I got my wire loop leg-lifter ready just in case, and double check that my phone is in my pocket.

Now I'm ready to go.

The thin, slick wooden transfer board is still sitting on the bed from this morning, so I shove it under my butt to make a little wood slide to my bed. I put my fist down on the bed and brace myself for the transfer. Taking a deep breath, I tell myself, *I can do this*. I use my free arm to push myself off the other wheelchair armrest.

"1-2-3," I say out loud. Every time I slide an inch toward the bed, I have to take a long break. Finally, after an hour of meticulous and careful sliding, I safely land on the bed.

Now I sit at the edge of my bed, breathing heavy and sweating. The hardest part is over, but I still need to get my legs up onto the bed. I put the head of the hospital bed up and unlock the brakes of my chair to get it out of the way. I grab my leg-lifter, putting the loop around my foot, so I can use my arms to help lift my legs. There's no way I can lift my legs on their own because I'm so tired. I lay back on the bed, and with all the energy I have left; I get both legs on the bed and finish up with the transfer.

Hell yes!

As I lay in bed breathing a sigh of relief, Bootsy jumps into my bed and sits down on my stomach to congratulate me. As I pet her, I worry again about how my symptoms are getting worse. How hard it was to get through the day today. Then I drift off to sleep.

When I wake up in the morning, there is something seriously wrong with me. I can't move my legs at all, and I can barely move my arms. No matter how hard I try or think about it, my legs aren't budging. My brain isn't communicating to my legs to move anymore. I am freaking out, wondering if I'm having another MS attack. If I am, then this one is worse than my first one when I had temporary paralysis of the whole left side of my body. I don't know what I can to do with the little movement I have, so I reach in my pocket and grab my phone to call my sister Holly.

"Hello?"

"Holly! There's something wrong with me! I can't move my legs and I can barely reach in my pocket to get my phone. I've been struggling all week and yesterday was bad."

"Whoa, whoa, slow down. I'm sure you're fine. Just relax."

"Relax? I can't move! There's no way I'll be able to get out bed today. I think I'm having another attack. I need your help."

"Okay, okay. Calm down. I'll come over right away."

When she comes from work, we decide to try to get me up into the manual chair. She lifts my lifeless legs off the mattress, putting my feet on the hardwood floor and sitting me on the edge of the bed.

"Why are you still wearing your shoes?" she asks.

As I sit there, I can't keep myself up with my arms and I slowly fall sideways back into bed. There is no use in trying anymore and we both know it. She lays me back into bed and lifts my legs up while we think about the next move.

"I think you need to call your doctor and see what they tell you to do," she says.

At that moment of hard realization, I start to cry. Holly gives me a big comforting hug, which makes me cry even harder.

"Why is this happening to me, Holls? Why me? It's not fair!" Tears pour down my face.

Tearing up and sniffling herself, Holly consoles me. "It's going to be okay, John. Don't worry. They will give you the help you need right now."

Bootsy jumps up on the bed and sits down on the other side of me, so I can pet her. Making both Holly and me smile because I think Bootsy senses something is wrong as well. She seems to have an unknown fifth-dimensional power, a sixth sense.

Finally settling down from the harsh realization, I call my neurologist. But I can't get through to the doctor. Begging and pleading doesn't work either. Doesn't he understand this is an emergency? I really need some guidance right now, but it's like he doesn't care. What's the point of having a neurologist? He's not even willing to help me out during my time of need.

Eventually, after an hour, his nurse practitioner gets on the phone and I urgently tell her what's happening to me.

"I think it's best if you go to the hospital and get checked out," she says, "We need to run some tests and see what's going on with you. Just call 911 and tell them you need to go to the ER."

Hanging up the phone in frustration, I am just so angry, but I have no choice. I am bound to go to the hospital. So I call 911 like she told me to, and then wait for the ambulance to arrive.

I hear the sirens getting louder and louder as they get closer to the house. Suddenly, at the door there is a loud knock, accompanied with "Fire Department!" Bootsy runs off the bed into the bathroom. The whole Fire Department, including 3 EMTs, enter my room with a large gurney. They take my vitals, and then four of the bigger firemen lift me off the bed onto the gurney. They strap me in tight.

With tears in my eyes, I say goodbye to Holly as they push me out to the ambulance. "I'll come and visit you later, John," Holly shouts when we leave the front door. "Don't worry, you're going to be fine."

My nosey neighbor on the front porch is watching as they

lift and squeeze me inside the small AMS truck. One of the EMTs urgently puts a one-inch IV needle in my hand because she says I need fluids right away. Above her, hanging from the ceiling, is a bag of saline water that the IV tube is attached to. The situation is getting really serious now, and I feel frightened. This is the first time I've been in an ambulance, and everything sucks right now. I'm going to the hospital for God knows how long. Who knows when I'll see Bootsy again.

After finishing up with me she hits the front window to signal the driver. He turns the sirens on and we head to the ER. Putting his foot on the gas, going faster, the driver swerves in and out of traffic. The EMT touches my hand. "Your heart rate is high," she says. "Calm down. Take a couple of deep breaths and just breathe."

I don't want to believe this is happening to me. Not again.

The ambulance gets me to the ER in no time and they start unloading me out of the back. The saline bag shakes over me as they put me on the sidewalk in front of the hospital's entrance. As they rush me through the halls, the bright overhead lights burn my eyeballs and make me realize I'm in the hospital again. This sucks. We get to the first open room and the EMTs transfer me on to another uncomfortable hospital bed.

"Good luck, John. Our job is done. Somebody should see you shortly," she tells me. They leave. Now I'm alone in a cramped office at the end of the hallway.

I try to move my legs and arms, but there's little communication from my brain still and it's almost impossible to move most of my extremities. My arms move a little, but my legs aren't budging. This is really freaking me out and I have never been so scared in my life. My progression is getting worse.

All I think about is getting steroids, hoping the infusion will relieve my symptoms.

One of the nurses comes into my room and takes my vitals. My blood pressure and heart rate are still high. She gets me a Sprite and some peanut butter Ritz Bits, then tells me "We're swamped," and it may be a while. Not what you want to hear when you need help.

After an hour, the lead ER doctor finally shows up and starts her examination. Stretches out my arms and tests my sensation with a mini hammer that's in the pocket of her lab coat. "Why did you come and see us today, John?" the ER doctor asks.

"I'm pretty sure I'm having an MS attack. I can't move my legs and my arms are weak. My neurologist told me to come here to get some help. I just want some steroids, so I can feel better."

"Okay. Well, try to relax because we're waiting for an ICU unit to open up. You'll be getting other doctors, including a new neurologist once you're on that floor. I did put an order for an MRI, so Radiology will come by and get you soon, so we can get started with your evaluation. Unfortunately, I can't get your steroid treatment started because I don't have authorization. You're going to have to wait until you get to the ICU."

"Jesus Christ, that sucks. Can't you see I need help now? And wait a minute. Did you say I'll be getting a *new* neurologist? What about the one I already have?"

"You'll be assigned to one of our wonderful neurologists here at this hospital campus. Don't worry, you'll be in good hands. In the meantime, please make yourself comfortable because I can't give you an ETA yet. Press the call button if you need anything."

This seriously sucks!

I'm not going to get help for a while. To top it off, my damn neurologist is not even going to help me out. I feel betrayed in my time of need. What a numbskull.

I grab my Motorola flip phone on the table next to my bed and call Holly to let her know what's going on.

"What the hell, John. What are you going to do?"

"There's nothing I can do! I just have to sit here like a useless box of rocks and wait in this lousy hard bed."

"Calm down, John. I'm sure a room will open up soon. I'll come visit you after work."

Two young lab technicians knock on my door, ready to escort me.

"Okay. Thanks, Holls. I got to run. Radiology just came by. I'm getting an MRI. See you later." I close my phone.

One of the technicians unlocks my bed and they start pushing me through the halls. When we get to the radiology lab, I tell them I won't be able to transfer, so we wait an extra half hour for a power Hoyer lift to get me on the MRI bed. I feel so helpless not being able to transfer and it's so painstakingly frustrating. After an hour of listening to loud clicks and being claustrophobic, they finish the test and Hoyer me back to my shitty bed. Taking me back to my little dungeon room in the ER.

They gave me mushy mac and cheese with tater tots for dinner, and then around eight o'clock, Holly comes by to see me and to drop off my manual chair and medications. She's also got magazines, Lipton Blue Label, and some Reese's Peanut Butter Cups for me. Bootsy is staying with Holly and her cat, Tony. She shows me some pictures of the two cats on her fancy new iPhone. We call Mom and Dad in Cleveland and give them the lowdown. Pops wants to talk to the hospital administrator, but I tell him not to embarrass me and there's nothing he'll be able to do. At ten o'clock, visiting hours end.

"I'll come by as soon as I can, John. Hang in there, Slugger," she tells me as she leaves.

I'm stuck in the ER for the night all alone again, reading *Time* magazine and counting holes in the white ceiling tiles. Wondering when I'm going to get treatment for my worst "MS Attack" ever.

I can't sleep. The light above the sink is on and my ass is hurting me. Plus, I have to pee. I've got no clue how I'm going to do that since I can't get up. I press the red call button.

"How can I help you, John?" the night nurse asks me, entering the room.

"My bum hurts from this bed and I have to take a piss really bad. Not sure how I'll do that. Any suggestions?"

"Let me grab you a urinal, so you can pee in that. I'll bring a couple extra pillows too. I'll be right back."

She returns and gives me a clear plastic portable urinal to pee in, and then rearranges the pillows by my butt to relieve the pressure. "So you think that urinal will work for you?" she asks.

"I have no other option. I'll try to make it happen."

"I'll be right across the hall. Just give me a holler if you need help."

I unbutton my pants and grab the urinal sitting next to me. This is *so* annoying that I can't just get up to pee! At least I still have some dexterity with my hands. I hold down my pants with one hand and hold the urinal with the other while

I relieve myself until it's filled with warm yellow fluid. I carefully lift the urinal upward when I finish, so I don't spill piss all over me again.

"I'm done!" I yell, holding the urinal by the handle.

The nurse rushes in, grabs the handle, dumps the piss in the toilet, and then washes the urinal out. Then she put it on the table. "Just in case you need it later."

Christ.

"So, are there any updates on my ICU room?" I ask. "What's going on?"

"I just got off the phone with them. They said maybe tomorrow at 9 a.m."

"Nine a.m.! That's ridiculous. I've been here almost twenty-four hours. Can't you see I'm struggling? I'm pissing in plastic bottles, for Christ's sake. Let me talk to my ER doctor."

"She isn't here anymore. And the other on-call doctor is busy right now. There is nothing that can be done anyway until your room is open. Please calm down."

"How can I calm down when I'm like this? Damn it!"

The nurse leaves with her head down, and I lay back to try to get some rest. I shrug my shoulders and settle down. I don't want to make my symptoms even worse by stressing out.

At 7 a.m. sharp, another nurse comes in and checks my blood pressure. It's finally back to normal. He also gives me a banana, an apple, and cheese spread with Club crackers. My room is finally ready at 9:30 a.m. One of the ICU nurses comes by to transport me.

"Hello. My name is Ken. I'll be taking you upstairs."

"Thank God! Let's get out of here."

When I get up to the ICU, I feel like I am in a whole other world. Everything is more organized with many nurses and doctors walking up and down the halls. Taking care of business. We get to my room, and it's humongous compared to my ER room. I even have a window with a view of Mount Rainier. Ken pushes my tiny ER bed next to a much bigger hospital bed. "I need help for a transfer!" he yells.

Two nurses stand behind me. Ken is at the base of my bed. They lift the bedsheet under me, sliding me safely over.

"Thanks, guys. I'll take it from here," Ken tells them. He comes over to me and says, "I got good news for you, John. We got you an air mattress."

He presses a button on the side of the bed and a small fan starts filling up the mattress with air. My body floats like I'm on a cloud at the base of the mountain. That's more like it! Ken takes my blood pressure and adds a fresh bag of fluids to my IV tubing. He rolls the wheeled hospital side table close to me. "The ICU doctor will see you shortly," he says. "The TV remote is on the table, along with the lunch and dinner menu. I'll come back later and get your order."

"Thanks, Ken."

For a second there I felt like I was living large, but the reality is I'm still in the hospital. There's no glamour being here. I just need to talk to a doctor, for Christ's sake. I need someone that can heal me and get me back to normal. Also, I don't understand why this is happening to me. I've been taking my Tysabri, a disease-modifying drug, and living a healthy lifestyle.

I need answers.

The ICU doctor comes into my room and does a complete exam while he introduces himself and tells me what's going on with my care. He's in charge of me while I'm in ICU, and also of the steroids. He wants to keep me in observation for a few more days. Something I don't want to hear.

"Our head neurologist will see you soon to answer your questions and discuss your MRI. Just relax and get some lunch. You're in good hands now," the ICU doctor tells me before he leaves.

Ken storms in, pushing an IV pump stand with a thousand CC bags dangling from the top. "What's up, John? I got you prednisone," he says. "Know what you want for lunch?"

He puts the IV pump next to my bed and sets everything up for my infusion. I browse the menu and order a turkey sandwich, BBQ Baked Lays, and a fruit salad.

"Thanks, Ken," I tell him. But my head is down.

As I'm eating lunch and getting the IV treatment, another doctor walks into my room, pushing his workstation with a laptop.

"Hello, John. I'm the hospital neurologist. I'll be going over the MRI with you. I can answer any of your questions."

"Okay. Doc, can you tell me why this happened to me? I've been taking my Tysabri, eating right, and doing physical therapy. I just don't understand." I beg for answers.

"Unfortunately, I cannot tell you exactly *why*. Multiple sclerosis is unpredictable and sometimes unexplainable. However, I did notice something on your MRI that may help explain why your legs are feeling weak."

He turns the computer around and my brain image is plastered on the screen. Then he circles a light-colored area around my spinal cord caused by the dye. He also circles an area on the left side of my brain.

"I compared your images to others that were in the system.

I notice the lesions around your spinal cord have gotten larger. This may explain why your symptoms are acting up."

"Is there anything you can do to heal those lesions in my brain and spinal cord? Maybe you can make them smaller?" I already know the answer to the questions, but I thought I'd ask him anyway. He's fresh blood. Maybe he's got a different perspective on the disease.

"Unfortunately, there isn't a cure for MS right now. We have no way to fix the lesions that are already there. We can just hope your body responds well to the steroids. Then with some rehabilitation we can get you back home."

Just what I thought. It was worth a shot to ask him, though. Just for once I want to hear something else. Something optimistic, so I know I won't become permanently disabled. Or at least get me a wonder drug that'll fix the lesions, so I'll be able to continue enjoying my life. Driving my Nissan Frontier and hiking in Mount Rainier. But the disease progression is getting worse and my nightmare is coming true. There's nothing any MS neurologist can do about it. Which makes me wonder: why would anyone *want* to become an MS neurologist?

This is the biggest annoyance of living with MS. All the "not knowing" and "what if's" add up and always leave you wondering. With MS, you constantly have to learn how to live and adapt. It's a non-stop battle juggling all the irritations and frustrations *all* the time. But I'm sick of juggling all these emotions every day. I'm not sure how much more of this I can take.

Now I'm being faced with MS progression head-on because I have no choice. I have to recover from this horrible attack and deal with another setback. What I *do* know is I want to get back home ASAP. Pet my little Bootsy.

"Rehab, huh."

"Yes. That will be after your observation time here at ICU. We will eventually transfer you to the rehab hospital. I'll check back with you in a couple days after the steroids fully settle in, then we'll work on a plan to get you home."

The doctor leaves.

I continue eating my lunch. I'm too angry and upset to talk about this any longer. The doctor just dropped an atomic bombshell on me and I need to take it all in. I have such a long road ahead of me. MS is disrupting my life, putting me in check, but I'm not going to let the disease slow me down. After treatment I'm going to do everything I can to take that road and get the *hell* out of here.

Acknowledgements

I would like to thank Richard and Evelyn Arvey for helping me build confidence in my writing, and for running the Swedish MS writing group. Their help was invaluable (and not that strict!). I am also thankful for the thoughtful comments and guidance from everyone else in the group; sharing my stories was very therapeutic and I feel like we've all formed a bond.

Thank you to Erin Carper at the Swedish MS Center for her support of the group, and to the Swedish Medical Center Foundation for providing us with resources to make this book a reality.

I am incredibly grateful for the love and support from my family, especially my sister Holly. She's lived through all my stages and has been my biggest, most patient support.

Finally, I couldn't survive without the help from all my wonderful caregivers, especially Susan and Azeb. They are my unsung heroes.

Katie Yusuf

About the Author

Katie Yusuf grew up in rural Kansas and developed a love for books and reading at an early age. She learned a good book would carry her out of the isolated prairie and transport her to a new world, AKA *Wizard of Oz* syndrome. Hopes of penning an adventure of her own were placed on hold and writing was pushed to a pastime, however, when she decided to pursue a Doctor of Pharmacy degree at the University of Kentucky.

When MS ended her career as a pharmacist in 2009, books and writing helped get her through this loss and then escorted her into a new phase of her life. What was once a dream to chase 'one day' quickly became a new axis for her world to spin on. Writing has since flourished into a beloved activity of hers and an outlet for her personal experiences. Katie draws on her carefree, childhood memories on the farm in addition to the distressing, adult memories of her diagnosis and disease to inject life and feeling into her stories.

Katie has published one children's book, *Grandma's Precious Memories*—meant to help parents explain a grandparent's dementia to a small child—and is currently working on her first science fiction novel. She lives in the Pacific Northwest with her husband, Arman.

Face Behind the Numbers

Often times, real-life scenarios in pharmacy school were verbosely explained and coated with sugar like Saturday morning cereals. When I ran out of options for my uncontrolled multiple sclerosis (MS) and had to become a lab rat in a clinical trial, I quickly learned I had been taught nothing useful about trials in my classes or perchance I had slept through the lecture "How to be a Science Experiment." However, my knowledge grew exponentially after my MS forced me to step through the looking glass and learn firsthand the realities of a drug study.

I was so excited for my second year of pharmacy school in September 2003, until a shadowy curtain was dropped on my world in the late summer and my eyesight went dark. At my optometrist, he had me hit a button each time I saw a red dot flash on the screen. This ended up being pointless and a complete waste of time. My lack of vision formed a big black period with the flickers I missed. He took one look at my printout, shook his head regretfully, and referred me to a neuro-ophthalmologist. After steroids, an MRI, and a lumbar puncture, my life was permanently turned upside down with a sentence of MS. Prescribed an interferon, I was referred to the neurology clinic and hustled out the door.

In the beginning, I averaged one or two relapses a year, but was always able to bounce back after an infusion of steroids. When I completed my Doctor of Pharmacy degree (PharmD), I believed I had complete control of my MS. My blinders were ripped off after the adrenaline that had been propelling me through school wore off, and I suffered two severe relapses shortly into my residency. A new MRI revealed the lesions on my brain and spinal cord had dramatically increased in quantity over the past four years. I was still on my original interferon beta-1b, and it had obviously overstayed its usefulness.

In 2008, there weren't many therapies on the market yet, so I had few options. Having recently changed neurologists, he proposed I consider a clinical trial, but my husband, Jason, and I were skittish of this suggestion. We had considered this road with the natalizumab (Tysabri) trial. However, the week before I was to join, it was removed from the market because of its association with progressive multifocal leukoencephalopathy (think MS on steroids.) Jason was leery about me trying something without a proven history. I was a little more trusting, but only because I genuinely thought I knew more about trials. After explaining a Phase 3 trial should be safer since the previous two phases were supposed to identify the majority of side effects, Jason reluctantly agreed.

We decided that I would join the trial for alemtuzumab, which was already on the market to treat chronic lymphocytic leukemia (CLL) under the name Campath. My neurologist informed us this was the second enrollment of the trial, and the first had shown good results with very few adverse events.

I would have the infusion once a year for two years and then be followed four more with physicals and labs. This medicine sounded unbelievable; only two years of treatment and then nothing else needed? I allowed myself to be cautiously hopeful.

I began the process of signing consent forms, having initial blood samples drawn, and preliminary neurological exams. This was all part of the in-depth entrance exam to be in the study. Knowing to expect this didn't change the fact that I felt like I was trying to get accepted into a private club where I would be served the good "candy."

My initial blood work showed a low CD4+ T-lymphocyte count, which would exclude me from the study—that is, my test scores weren't high enough to gain acceptance. However, I was informed that there had been some reports of a low CD4+ being associated with long-term interferon beta-1b treatment. The study investigators decided to include patients with initial low counts if they normalized after the washout period. I was saved on a technicality with the condition that my test scores had to improve. I had been waitlisted. Yay!

The next step before I could even begin the physical entrance evaluations was to undergo a thirty-day washout period, during which I could take no MS disease-modifying medications. One month? Shoot! This was going to be a piece of cake. What could possibly happen in one piddily month?

The first two weeks passed with no problems, and I started wondering why I needed any medication at all. Then reality started to creep in like a pungent smell; mild at first but it grew stronger as more time passed. It started as little things: heat affected me quicker, my fatigue increased, and I could do almost naught—less than one thing a day equals worthless. Things that used to be trivial, like scooting on my butt from bed to couch, became virtually impossible to accomplish. I wanted to stab an empty syringe in my arm and hope for the placebo effect to kick in. My feebleness physically had shattered me mentally.

After the washout period, my bloodwork showed everything to be in the normal range, so I was deemed suitable. I made an appointment to have my pretreatment neurological tests and MRI and anticipated beginning my treatment four days later. However, the researchers had made a few adjustments to the consent form, so I had to sacrifice precious time to raze more trees and sign an amended version. Over time, I found out I would be required to autograph a new copy every time the authors changed a single word, thus resulting in a collection of over twenty manuscripts.

By the day of the tests, I could barely walk with assistance and my new cane, and if I stood too long, my legs would fold like an accordion despite the stick. Between the washout period, tests, and lag time, it had been almost two months since I had received any treatment, and I could really feel it. They buried the lead about the thirty-day washout period. To clarify, it was thirty days before I could even begin the trial's physical exams, not thirty days until I could begin a symptom-treating medication.

Although the study was blinded, when I found out my regimen would be a six-hour infusion, for five days, I knew straightaway I had been randomized into the alemtuzumab group seeing as it was IV. The control, interferon beta-1a, was a subcutaneous injection that was self-administered three times a week. Elated at my good fortune, I could only cross my fingers that it worked, because I couldn't feel my toes by then.

I was also told housing would be provided at a nearby hotel for Jason and me, which was great news. When I had started to lose feeling in my legs and feet four weeks back, Jason had decided it wasn't safe for me to drive and began taking time away from work to transport me to and from my countless appointments. Being able to subtract the daily six-ty-mile round-trip drive from the five, already lengthy, days of treatment, would greatly help.

After enduring almost eight weeks without medication, or what felt like three years in MS time, my first day of treatment finally arrived. My five-day itinerary was: a one-hour infusion of methylprednisolone on days one through three and then the study drug over six hours on all five days. Then I had to stay at least an hour to be sure boredom was the only adverse effect. It baffled me why no steroids were given on day four and five. Were they trying to evoke side effects on the last two days to enhance their study? As troublesome as this thought was, I chose to focus on my nervous anticipation of receiving a potentially life-changing medication and my naïve optimism that it would wipe out my MS symptoms.

Day one seemed to start fairly well. Following the methylprednisolone, I was given metoclopramide and diphen-hydramine; the latter knocked me out, and I snored through most of the study drug infusion. When Jason came to pick me up, I was able to make it to the car with assistance, but when we arrived at the hotel, I wasn't strong enough to stand. Jason pulled me from our Honda CR-V and helped me to the com-fortable green wire bench by the sliding entrance door where I had to take my first pit-stop. I made it to the firm, blue lobby chair next, before finally making it into the elevator. As the doors closed, I leaned against the metal wall and slowly slid to the floor as my gas tank hit zero and the confusion and anguish crept in. I thought the infusion today was supposed to make my legs stronger, not turn them to jelly.

Every part of me hurt. My muscles weren't responding to my brain, and my brain was too garbled to realize it. When the doors opened on our floor, I wriggled out the door and squirmed like an inchworm down the hall. As I hauled my drained body across the carpet, I laughed and jested about how absurd I would look to anyone who rounded the corner, which exasperated my already tired, frantic husband. Months later, I confessed that I would have dissolved into a drippy puddle of emotion if I hadn't laughed at that moment. I knew he wouldn't have been able to handle that after I saw the anguish and helplessness in his eyes.

When I finally made it to our room, he helped me wiggle my way onto the double bed's flower-print bedspread, and I curled into a ball, praying for sleep or death, whichever took me first. Jason called the study coordinator who was surprised to hear about my reaction and agreed to deliver a wheelchair to the hotel the next morning. For the rest of the week, I was transported everywhere in my borrowed chariot.

On day two, the study's lead physician came to see me during my infusion. Answering him honestly when he asked how I was feeling, I told him how weak I was and about cleaning the hotel hall with my bum the previous night. His response, "You're going to feel like crap. Nothing we can do to prevent that." The investigator's candor misled me into thinking this reaction was normal. I later found out, it wasn't. His words reminded me to strengthen my resolve for the forthcoming trials. So far, things were off to a disconcerting start, and I was worried days four and five might be worse when I received no methylprednisolone. I wanted to prepare myself now for this possibility.

The rest of the week progressed as expected. I developed hives, but not as bad as I had feared. The weakness, fatigue, and muscle pain had already debilitated me on the first day, so noticing anything different was difficult. To help me ignore all the physical and mental agony I was experiencing, I tried to stay comatose by sleeping both in and out of the clinic. The nurses kept telling me the medication should start taking effect soon, but I dejectedly knew I had flunked out and was overcome with hopelessness.

A small number of earlier patients had developed immune thrombocytopenia purpura (ITP), so I was to be monitored for this with a monthly blood draw and online survey. Answering "yes" to a question suggesting a symptom indicative of ITP would prompt additional bloodwork. I also had to see two study neurologists (one blinded, one not) every three months, complete mental/physical health surveys, and have yearly MRIs. When I was wheeled out of the clinic on the last day, I was handed a calendar for important dates, depictions of what to look for with ITP, and a twenty-four-hour telephone number to call if I had any problems. Leaving the office, I was in worse shape than I had arrived in after five days of misery. This was the first time I felt completely defeated and demoralized by my MS.

The first few weeks were excruciating. During the initial days, I was covered with red, bumpy hives and wanted to scratch my skin off. I developed ulcers in my mouth and couldn't eat or drink without agonizing pain. The weakness and fatigue increased to the point that I could barely stand or stumble to the restroom. Between struggling to survive another day and cursing the one that I had signed my first consent form on, I hardly noticed three weeks had gone by until the ITP survey reminder arrived in my inbox.

Before I opened my laptop, I was already set up for failure on the questionnaire. A few things I needed to look for that could indicate ITP were increased bruising, red dots or petechiae, and fatigue. Naturally pale as Casper the ghost, I bruised if I hit a wall too hard. Also, I was always fatigued and still covered in polka dots because my hives hadn't cleared up. These all skewed my answers and when they were added to the weakness and immobility I was still experiencing, I won a trip for more bloodwork. Thankfully, the results were normal, and I was sent out unto the world for another month.

After suffering through six weeks of washing the poison from my body, the aftereffects of the infusion were fading, my MS was flaring, and my sanity was waning. My neurologist gave me a steroid bolus in hopes of granting me some relief and to prepare me to begin my medication search again. It was infuriating that my body had suffered significantly from this medication, but my MS had come through unscathed. Alemtuzumab had been as effective as a six-hour bolus of normal saline for me. Due to my adverse reactions, I only received one year of the two-year regimen. Although I was no longer on the medication, they nonetheless wanted to follow me for four years. Ultimately, this turned into twelve when the study was extended to look for long-term side effects.

Throughout the trial, I was compensated. Nevertheless, a hotel room and $35 a visit did not adequately cover the pain, suffering, and emotional/physical toll we endured. Jason was brutally traumatized from watching his wife weaken right in front of him and go from walking to crawling, literally, in a matter of minutes. I felt responsible for inflicting this anguish on him and was also haunted by the hellish nightmare of my own personal struggle. In a mere five days, this experience left us both with permanent scars.

Despite my wicked reaction, alemtuzumab was FDA-approved under the name Lemtrada in 2014. My sacrifices could not be quantified when my entire personal journey was transformed into a faceless number and converted into a final percentage. All my misfortunes, agony, and anguish were simply rolled into ratios and displayed on the package insert. Even though I knew this was how studies were reported, it was disconcerting to see everything I went through boiled down to pharma talk.

I had become nothing more than a "Rare but Serious Side Effect."

Before and After

On the way home, I had stopped at the clinic, picked up my MRI films, and was now sitting at the dining room table staring at them. It would be a few weeks before I received an actual diagnosis from the neurologist, but I had learned enough from numerous anatomy and physiology classes to recognize that the white spots on my brain were not supposed to be there. I was afraid my optometrist had been right, and I might have multiple sclerosis (MS.) He had suggested this before referring me to the neuro-ophthalmologist for the MRI, and these images seemed to prove him correct. This would change things forever, but at that moment I couldn't have known how much.

I slid the films back into the purple-plastic sleeve. Falling apart wasn't an option. I had to stay composed until Jason got home. If I broke down now, I knew I wouldn't be able to put myself back together before he walked in. With a few hours to kill, I started cleaning the kitchen in preparation to make dinner. If I could keep my hands busy, I hoped my mind would follow. No such luck.

First, my mind was flooded with all the 'why' questions. Why me? I had finally put my wild ways behind me, settled down, and was focused on a solid path. The second year of my pharmacy education was starting in a few weeks, and I was looking forward to the challenge. Why us? We had recently celebrated our first anniversary; our story had barely started. We should get time to enjoy writing it. Why now? We were in the beginning stages of having our first house built.

The second wave of thoughts was about money. Jason was a contract worker at Lexmark, so he had little to no health insurance. I was a student with no full-time job, so I had none. In 2003, we were only twenty-four and had minimal savings. Our new house was only possible through a FHA loan, which made closing costs negligible. After seeing the charge for the MRI, I had no idea where we would find the money for that new bill, much less all that might follow.

The final one came crashing down, pulling me under, and making my heart seize—would Jason still want me? This wasn't what he signed up for. I knew he said "in sickness and in health," but sickness usually didn't come this soon. This would impact all our future plans in some way. What if I couldn't have kids? What if I couldn't walk? What if I couldn't work? Could he handle the possibility of these changes and challenges? We were already in the boat together. Was he willing to stay and row to help me navigate the rough waters ahead? Or would he jump and swim for solid land? I didn't want him to bail in the future if the waters became choppy. It would hurt to lose him now, but devastating to lose him later. Of all my thoughts, this one scared me the most.

As my mind continued to spin, Jason walked through the door and tossed his bag down on the futon. Spotting the transparent-purple MRI sleeve on the table, his eyes immediately began scanning the room for me. By the time they locked on my face, I had already started quietly crying. Jason's mere presence in the room had relaxed me enough to let my emotional barriers down. Instantly encased in his arms, I began creating a snot patch on his white polo. He let me cry until I began to sniffle and then gently wiped tears from my wet cheeks and told me— "Together, we can deal with whatever happens. We can do this."

Picking up the purple folder, he asked me to explain the scans to him. We sat on the floor in the living room and spread the MRI images out in front of us on the beige carpet. I began showing him the spots that concerned me and explaining what the white areas might mean. It was now his turn to fall apart. We held each other and cried knowing these images held answers that could change our lives. When the tears finally ran dry, we spent the rest of the evening trying to avoid the five-ton elephant.

The next morning, my only task was to schedule a follow-up visit at the neuro-ophthalmology clinic to find out conclusively what the MRI showed. This not-knowing-nightmare had begun over a month ago, and I needed to wake up. Alas, I had the misfortune of speaking to a heartless scheduling lady who did not seem to comprehend the urgency of my situation. She couldn't understand, or didn't want to, how *my life* had been halted and was currently hanging in limbo. My voice grew louder and more forceful every time I refused to wait two or three months for an appointment. Every day of not knowing that passed felt like a month of my life had slipped by wasted, and I couldn't take it anymore. Eventually,

Miss Cold-Blooded dug up a date in three weeks, and I took it without hesitation and hung up.

By pushing for the earliest appointment, I locked myself into whatever opening was offered, but there was no alternative. Regrettably, this meant Jason wouldn't be able to go with me, and I would be receiving my results alone. We had discussed this possibility earlier, and as agonizing and terrifying as this decision had been, we both knew I had to go regardless. Neither of us had slept well since my symptoms first occurred, and our sleepless nights needed to end. Good or bad, we had to know and couldn't afford to wait.

So now, here I was three weeks later, sitting by myself in this sterile exam room's uncomfortable tan chair, waiting to hear the official results of my MRI. The doctor was over an hour late, so I had used this time to foolishly convince myself everything was going to be okay. I rationalized he could afford to be late because my scans were obviously a false alarm, and I had been psyching myself out over a shadow on the film. Nothing was seriously wrong with me, therefore, I was the lowest priority in his book. Deep down I knew this theory was ludicrous. There was no correlation between the two, but logic had left the building. Anything like this imaginary pipe dream was fair game, so long as it kept my mind away from the "what if" scenarios.

When a doctor finally walked through the door, he looked like he was scarcely out of med school. I knew this was a teaching hospital, but didn't that mean he needed a teacher? The tall, lanky kid barely glanced at me as he sat down at the metal consultation desk and started studying a thick, manila file that I suspected was my chart. Quickly scanning the notes, he flipped through a few sections, before turning and acknowledging my existence for the first time. Without any pleasantries, formalities, or a simple introduction, he bluntly asserted, "Well, I looked at your MRI films and I agree with the radiologist's report—you have multiple sclerosis." He closed my chart, gathered his things, and walked out of the room without another word.

My mouth was suddenly bone dry and swallowing had become complicated around the lump in my throat. MS was what I had feared when I looked at the images and had seen my brain speckled with white spots, but it felt different now that it was spoken aloud and confirmed. I could no longer hope and pretend that there was another, simpler explanation for my symptoms. This made it real. Final. My breathing became labored as I felt my eyes starting to fill. It took every morsel of my willpower to keep them from flowing over.

To distract myself and prevent a total disintegration, I shifted my focus to the insolent, unprofessional physician and started to get angry. Not only was he over an hour late but when he did grace me with his presence I also received no explanation or apology for his tardiness. He simply strolled in, dumped this life-changing diagnosis on me, and then moseyed out the door again. Taking no notice, or merely not caring, that I was alone, he left me to absorb the full impact of this bomb by myself. What kind of bedside manner was he taught? Wasn't it his job, at the very minimum, to explain my new disorder and allow me to ask questions? I knew this was a neuro-*ophthalmology* clinic, so the doctor was undoubtedly used to dealing with mostly eye patients. However, that didn't excuse him or allow him to treat me any differently.

At that moment, the doctor decided he had a few spare minutes to allocate to me and returned to my room. He again sat at the consultation desk and started flipping through my chart as if he had forgotten why I was there. Honestly, at that moment, I had no idea why I was still sitting there, either. When the physician did look in my direction, he seemed extremely surprised that I was upset.

"MS is not that bad anymore. I know many people with it that are getting along fine. We have treatment medications now, so you do have options. Do you know anything about those medicines?"

I stared at him in disbelief of his crassness. Biting my tongue, so I could just get this over with and leave, I shook my head. He made his recommendation, wrote a prescription, and referred me to the neurology clinic upstairs. Grabbing the script, I willed my static legs to stand up from the exam room chair and quickly left the office. My head was spinning, and I needed to be in the presence of someone who actually cared.

As I drove home, I tried to remember everything I had been taught and read in the past few weeks about MS. It summed up to…to…nothing: They didn't know what caused MS or why it happened; they didn't know how it would affect an individual, because no two cases were alike; and they had no idea how to fix it. So much for modern medicine. Turning into my apartment's lot, however, I did recall one random piece of late-night research that might be helpful—wasn't there something about an MRI not being enough to diagnose MS? Didn't a different test need to be done to confirm it? Did that mean they may have misdiagnosed me? What was the name of that test?

Taking the stairs two at a time, I fumbled with my keys before eventually getting into our apartment and running down the hall to the computer. I found the evasive answer straightaway—a lumbar puncture. As awful as that sounded, I picked up the phone and requested the procedure. Surprisingly, I received a call within a few hours. The clinic had sent the order, and the hospital could fit me in the day after tomorrow. They had also slated my follow-up appointment with a primary care doctor for next week. It appeared I was being sent through the system as quickly as possible now; almost as if my name was marked with an asterisk signally an "aggravated/aggravating patient." If that's what it took, I wasn't going to apologize.

Two days later, I was lying in the fetal position on a table, half-naked, and draped in a paper gown. The doctor told me the first shot—lidocaine—would feel like a bee sting and would numb my back. Later, when I played this back for Jason, all I could remember was it was an awfully large bee. As I lay on that table for the next forty-five minutes, I tried not to think about the four-inch needle in my back and instead just prayed that this was going to prove I had been misdiagnosed. The following week I would learn these prayers weren't answered; I was undoubtedly living with multiple sclerosis.

Jason and I started scrutinizing and questioning all the plans we had made. Was it safe for us to have a family? Would I be able to finish pharmacy school? Work? What about traveling? We planned to go visit his family and my sister overseas—was that still okay? The single answer we received to all these questions was "It depends…" No one could tell us if I would get worse, and if I did, what to expect or when it might happen. Every answer we wanted hinged on these uncertainties. All they knew for certain was: 1) There was no cure, so I was trapped in this pitch-black tunnel for the rest of my life, and 2) I needed to start my Disease-Modifying Therapy (DMT) as soon as possible.

While I was waiting at the pharmacy for my Betaseron to be filled, I recalled a conversation I had had with my boss earlier this year. Filling an insulin prescription at the pharmacy where I worked, I remember telling the pharmacist: "I would hate it if I had to give myself an injection every day. I don't think I could." This wonderful jaunt down my memory highway continued as I called forth my next comments: "I would also hate it if my body quit working, but my mind was still fully functional. It would be like I was trapped inside myself." These comments must have been too great a temptation for fate, and they broke his resistance.

This was years before the convenience of pre-filled syringes, thus that evening I had to mix my own medication prior to drawing up the injection. Jason wiped my hip with an alcohol pad before gritting his teeth and bravely administering my first shot. I had pre-medicated with naproxen and went straight to bed after the jab as instructed, hoping to sleep through any negative reactions. That didn't happen. The pharmacy and doctor's office had briefly skimmed over the possible side effects—fever, chills, muscle pain—but they had not fully prepared me for the agony and wretchedness of the next twenty-four hours.

First came the cramping and burning in my muscles. Lying on the bed, I curled into a tight ball and tried to will myself to sleep. It wasn't long before I was overtaken with intense shivering, sweating, and nausea. I wanted to strip my clothes off, but also huddle under a blanket. Most crucial at that moment, however, was a mad dash to the bathroom across the hall to rid myself of dinner. When I returned, I resumed the fetal position in my sweat-soaked clothes and pulled a comforter over me. Until then, I never thought it was possible to freeze and sweat that much simultaneously.

By this point, Jason was panicking and convinced I was dying; I was hoping I would, so I would be put out of my misery. He sat vigil by the bed for the remainder of the night, occasionally checking to make sure I was still breathing. Meanwhile, I moved as little as possible, thinking this would make the pain stop. Somehow, I survived the night, and as light was beginning to sneak through the blinds, I fell into a fitful sleep. I never experienced another side effect from Betaseron after that night. Perhaps, since I had already survived them all once, there was no fun in torturing me further.

A few nights later, my dad finally called me, and I had a chance to tell him of my diagnosis. His matter-of-fact response: "Well, not surprised." At that moment, I felt like I had been hit in the gut and my knees kicked from behind at the same time. There was just enough time to grab a dining room chair before my legs crumpled completely, and I met the kitchen linoleum. He calmly continued: "Your cousin has that, so I was expecting one of you kids to have it too. Just didn't know which one yet." He made it sound like I had won some prize in the genetics lottery. I was hurt by his insensitivity and callousness, but in the back of my mind I was asking myself, *What did you want him to say? What do you want anyone to say for that matter?*

A clear example of what *not* to say came a few nights later when a good friend from high school, and now my brother's roommate, phoned. His opening question was "So, how long do you have?" I was once again doubled over, but this time from trying to hold in my laughter. MS wasn't one of the most commonly talked about diseases, but surely people knew enough to know it wasn't fatal…Right? I soon learned that people knew the title "multiple sclerosis" and they knew the letters "M" and "S," but that was about where their knowledge and the association ended. Little did I know, I would come to rely on the explanation of MS I gave my friend that night and would have to use it frequently in the future.

One of the biggest questions hanging over our heads was: how was I going to handle pharmacy school? I had been able to go to classes for the past few weeks between my appointments because my school was conveniently located next to the hospital. However, entering the classroom now seemed like walking into a new world. The room hadn't changed: still a hundred and forty chairs divided with two sloping aisles and a wall of white erase boards down front. My classes hadn't changed: still three hours in the morning, three in the afternoon sitting in the middle section, second row. But I had changed: I felt I now needed to work twice as hard to prove I deserved to be here and could do this despite my MS diagnosis.

My professors were supportive and willing to assist me in whatever accommodations I may need now or in the future. They were all familiar with MS either from a healthcare, pharmacology, or physiology standpoint, so I knew I was surrounded by a group of very informed and understanding professionals. There was one, though, that strongly encouraged me to leave school. He felt it would be too much, and I should focus on and prioritize my health. I was stunned and slightly miffed that he would suggest such a thing. Nevertheless, it emboldened me to dig down deep and demonstrate to him, myself, and everyone else it wasn't too much.

That night when I got home, there was a noticeably

different spin on our dinner conversation. Instead of dwelling on what *might* change in the future, Jason and I made plans for how we would enjoy and take advantage of life right now. We would prepare for when things might get harder, but we wouldn't squander any day before then. The "after" chapter of our eighteen-month marriage had just begun.

A Hike in the Hoh Rainforest

(This story is split into two parts—the first is from the perspective of the person with MS, and the second is the same walk through the eyes of her caregiver.)

Conquering Hoh

Jason and I moved to Washington State two years ago from Kentucky, but this was our first excursion out of Seattle. I was the one with MS, but Jason was the one that had fallen down the stairs in our townhouse and fractured his foot. It had kept us home the first summer we were residents in the Evergreen State.

As we parked in front of the red-brick Visitor Center in Hoh Rain Forest, I sent a little prayer out into the infinite unknown: *Please let me be able to do this. I don't want us to miss out on something else because of me.* Over the past ten years, we had been forced to greatly alter our vacation itineraries due to my increased physical limitations, but I was hoping I wouldn't have to add this stop to that list.

The first thing Jason did was go see if there was a trail that I could manage. This allowed me time to take stock of my surroundings. We had arrived early, so the parking lot was less than a fourth full. I watched as small groups of vacationers in shorts and hiking boots disappeared down the dirt paths into groves of remarkably striking, gigantic trees. When he had told me where we were headed, I truly hadn't known what to expect, but this certainly wasn't it. This looked magnificent.

When he returned, Jason said we had two options. The first, simpler track was a short, paved trail that we could use the wheelchair on with no problems. A more challenging possibility offered a lot more to see, but was a non-paved route. He had been told it was fairly smooth with only a few bumps, but wheelchairs weren't allowed. It was a little over half-a-mile and called the *Hall of Mosses*. Jason was worried I couldn't walk that much but left the decision solely up to me.

It was obvious how much he wanted to see this. I didn't want him to miss out yet again because I had to stay on the kiddie trail. Just a few months ago, I had walked, pushing my wheelchair, half-a-mile over a variable terrain in the MS walk. Surely, I would be able to accomplish this scenic stroll with the help of my one-of-a-kind personal walking device alongside me. Besides, I genuinely wanted to behold the Pacific Northwest foliage and prove to myself that I could keep up with the big kids.

I cinched my ankle brace up, covered myself in bug spray/SPF 30, and filled a backpack with water bottles and dark chocolate-cherry-nut granola bars. Leaving my wheelchair in the car, we headed for the trailheads. Left was for four wheels, but right was for two feet. We veered to the right, and I set my feet on the packed dirt track to begin my trial through the kingdom of trees.

The first five minutes gave me the false impression that this was going to be a long, but not too difficult, meander through nature's wonderland. It didn't appear to be difficult terrain, and Jason could help me if I got tired. Then the shaky wooden bridge appeared followed by ten steep steps situated along a jagged rock face that led up to the real pathway. For someone with unsure footing and difficulty picking up their feet, this was akin to a big piece of green kryptonite. *Okay, I can do this. One step at a time. No hurry.*

Crossing the short bridge and tackling the first few steps was no problem. However. the stupid things had to go and get taller, forcing me to lift my weak legs even more. I had to step up with the stronger right leg, and then, while pulling on the handrail and Jason, use it to muscle the wimpy left up beside it. Carefully navigating each one meant I slowed down considerably and caused a traffic jam on the narrow walkway. Multiple times, we had to press against the sharp uneven wall and let the other travelers pass. This gave me a chance to rest my legs, but it also introduced me to the phrase of the day: "Are you okay?" (sometimes they thought I was mute as well as lame: "Is she okay?") By the time we had completed our jaunt that day, this would become a joke of ours, and a despised phrase of mine.

Reaching the top of the grueling wood steps, I saw a park bench in front of us. Thinking a short rest now would save my strength for later, I set my trajectory for it. However, I hadn't anticipated the bench would simply be a mirage on the horizon. It seemed the forest nymphs decided to keep moving it backwards just out of reach. When I finally caught up to it and was able to rest for a minute or five, Jason and I got our first chance to fully appreciate our environment.

We were encircled by various shades of green-leaved ferns sprouting from the soil. A light avocado spray of plants lorded over a ground-hugging lime grouping. The leaves were feather-shaped fans that were composed of smaller and smaller versions of the feather form. They filled in the space between the mammoth reddish-brown barked trees. Just the wonder of these colossal creations of nature and the years it took to cultivate them was awe-inspiring on its own, but the sheer beauty and strength they harnessed was spirit-stirring.

A choir of voices made up the fragrance of the forest. The light, soft soprano of the small, almost hidden flowers under the ferns was accompanied by the fresh rain smell that carried a calming alto. Musty scents from fallen leaves joined with the tenor, and the bold tree bark added the bass. Together they formed a signature botanical arrangement.

When we started out again, things went exceptionally well for the next stretch of our venture. I was tremendously proud of myself and had no earthly idea why I had ever questioned my ability to conquer this. With rest stops and remembering to drink, I would have no problems. I should not doubt myself, and people needed to stop mistrusting my faculties as well. They just worried too much.

Pride goeth before the fall…literally. We started encountering bumpy, uneven bulges of roots sprouting up along the trail. They had just enough ground clearance to fit the toe of a New Balance sneaker nicely. I found this out when the first one I tried to step over, grabbed my shoe and sent me plunging forward. If Jason hadn't caught me, I would have had dirt for lunch and possibly a trip to the dentist when we got home.

When I had climbed the stairs earlier, I had been able to use my strong leg to force the other up. Conversely, stepping over the knobby tubers not only required both legs to be raised independently, but also advancing over the hump at the same time. It looked like a track and field hurdle bar to me; I had to get close enough to make the first vault shorter, but not too close and allow the tree to eat my shoe. It was a pass/fail test that I couldn't have passed without Jason's help lifting my left leg over.

Traveling deeper into the rainforest, I found my head was swiveling continuously like a barn owl at dusk. On one side were hemlock trees covered with fuzzy emerald-green lichen, while on the other side there were numerous fallen, wooden soldiers of the forest lying in a pond. Ground between the lofty shooting timbers was covered with a mix of old leaves and lush new foliage. Topping it off was a high-ceilinged crown of intertwined branches sprinkled with hints of aqua-blue sky.

Focusing my eyes on the road ahead, I saw shorter maples standing in the shadows of their cousins. The stooped-over smaller trees had bent, crooked limbs reminiscent of arms and branches of distorted, broken fingers. There was green and brown moss resembling long, tangled hair hanging from the trunk of the tree and its pointy, twisted appendages. It reminded me of something small children might see in their nightmares or in a Disney movie with apples and a princess.

Jason and I stopped for a photo-op with one of the stately Sitka Spruce whose width was wider than my arm span. If I tilted my head all the way back to see the point where the towering king scratched the sky, I started to get woozy. I have never felt so diminutive as I did when I pressed up against that rough dun-colored, centuries-old bark. Maybe if I stood there long enough, I could absorb just a fraction of its longevity or power? Then I would be able to reset my broken clock and place the gears back in order.

Besides the huge granddaddy trees, there were also those standing on groups of twisted, woven stilts. Almost as if the dirt around the roots had fully eroded leaving them exposed. The supports formed meandering patterns, making crevices and caves between them. These trees were smaller in width and looked like they had not been in line when the height gene was passed out. I would guess their lumber just hadn't seen many summers yet.

I rested every chance I got, and the forest nymphs were kind enough to leave permanent benches for me along the way. By this point, I had sweated enough that my bug repellent had melted away like a citronella candle. Every time I sat or paused for a moment of recuperation, the lookout notified the others, and I soon became a chew toy for mosquitos and gnats. That was a great incentive to keep moving.

Another reason to keep going was brought forth before we reached the "Halfway Point" sign. Jason asked how I was doing and then very seriously and earnestly offered to turn around if I needed to return to the car. I gave him a confused, unblinking stare wondering if he was joking. Geometry 101: if you're halfway around a circle, it's the same distance in either direction back to the starting point. His rationale: we knew what's behind us, not in front. My rationale: It couldn't get any worse.

Beginning the back half of the green, I was weary but

determined. We weren't in a hurry, and those stuck behind us could slow down to enjoy the scenery or could power walk on past and miss the diverse surroundings. As surprising as this may seem to some people, the rainforest was a huge, ever-changing portrait gallery with no two sections the same. The artist of these paintings was a virtuoso with his paintbrush and never tired of updating his work.

Farther down the path, there were large stumps with fallen decaying logs still partially attached lying beside them. It was obvious the timbers were not purposefully cut down, and this was part of the forest's natural regeneration. The tops of the pedestals were shaped like stalagmites and the tumbled tree bases were jagged like fallen, horizontal stalactites. Paying homage at the base of the tree, small seedlings had begun their two-hundred-year battle against the elements to live up to their ancestor's legacies. Even then, they would still only be teenagers.

When we turned a corner, we came across the most original collapsed giant of our outing. This behemoth had decided to lie down for its final nap right across the footpath. Nevertheless, one limb had kept the path clear by keeping the giant propped up. This formed an arc and established a new area for the tree to keep growing. Branches were shooting up off the back of their bent brother's arm, and it resulted in a wooden, spiny arch.

Jason took numerous shots of this picturesque wonder and then used it as a backdrop for selfies. Nevertheless, he still wanted his photo taken underneath the botanical rainbow. Knowing I was only able to stand unaided for an extremely brief time, he made a mad dash to pose after leaving me wobbling in the middle of the road. A quick sprint back to check on the shot and support me for a few minutes before he decided to make another frenzied run for one more snap. He was ultimately satisfied with the result, so we pushed on.

There were quite a few areas that were roped off on this half of the trail; some contained pools of stagnant green water, while others were simply places of denser woods. I was tiring out quicker, and this was only intensified by the increased thermal temperature and humidity. The canopy of the trees should have been providing some shade, but instead it was simply locking us in this sweltering hot box. In one spot, I bent the posted rules and left the assigned dirt pathway to venture into a small alcove. Jason knew I needed to stop and spied a bulky, grey stone off the beaten path. It curved into a seat made just for me and looked so inviting and comfortable. Off the trail, but it was still inside the velvet rope. In my book, bending a rule a little was not officially breaking it.

We pulled over, so I could rest and quench my thirst while Jason scouted ahead for upcoming obstacles. As I sat there, for the umpteenth time since the halfway point, the thought *What if I can't make it?* crossed my mind. Did they send a golf cart to pick people up when they got hurt or gave up, or was there a hidden helipad in the roped off area? My bravado from when we set out had slowly seeped out of me, along with my strength, energy, and a bucket of sweat. It seemed as if we had been hiking for hours, so the finish line should be close. Giving up now would negate all my struggle up to this point. I had to finish.

As soon as we started out again, Jason wrapped his arm around my waist to support some of my weight and started reminding me to "pick your foot up." When my weak left limb grew tired, it had a tendency to not fully detach my foot from the ground, causing me to stumble over the smallest of pebbles. My legs were becoming fluid while my feet were solidifying into cement blocks. I was glad I had seen the landscape earlier since my full concentration had to be focused on moving each foot forward. My eyes were fixed on the densely packed dirt path in front of me, and all I saw now were brown dried leaves and twigs.

My arduous trudge was a slow, tedious process, but I told myself it would be okay as long as I kept advancing. It might take me a few hours and might only be a hundred feet at a time, but I would finish. This time, I would not let MS defeat me. I scheduled my stops more frequently and rested longer, but I kept trekking. Jason kept my spirits up, and his encouragement gave me the strength to push forward.

By now my deodorant had died from exhaustion, and my delightful aroma was inviting guests from all parts. It was hard to slap a blood sucker or swat at buzzing swarms when I was doing my best to balance and keep my arm around Jason's shoulder. He was kind enough not to comment on the smell or the friends I had invited. Because of me, we unwillingly added to the health and nutrition of the pest community that day.

At one stop, when I was splayed out on a bench trying to recoup, a hiker stopped and inquired if I needed help. The sarcastic me thought: *Yeah, do you know the secret recipe for myelin or how to make nerves work again?* The polite me thanked her and said I only needed to catch my breath.

A short time later, I didn't make it to a bench and had to sit on a compacted earth pile underneath a hemlock. I took out the half-melted granola bar I had forgotten, hoping it would infuse me with enough stamina to complete the course.

Everyone that walked by assumed there had to be something seriously wrong with me. No one would be silly enough to come out here that couldn't handle it, so something must have happened if I was on the ground.

As considerate as it was for people to stop and ask *Jason* if I was all right, I only wanted them to avert their eyes and move along. I was already frustrated and embarrassed enough, and each conscientious stranger simply added to my heap of failure feelings. It was childish, I knew, but I had always been extremely independent and self-reliant. Even after sixteen years, I didn't want to show weakness or ask for help because of my MS.

When we finally completed the loop and arrived back at the dreaded staircase, I had to psych myself up to undertake the horrible task of going down; this was so much worse for me. If I fell going up, I hit the next step, but if I fell going down, I became a human slinky. *One step at a time, right to stabilize left, Jason to stabilize me.* It was an extremely slow process. An overly impatient gentleman even offered to carry me down. This sparked a t-shirt idea for our next adventure— yellow shirt with the back reading "CAUTION: MS (Moves Slow)." Maybe then I wouldn't have to incessantly regurgitate the same explanation.

By gripping Jason's shoulder and methodically lowering one foot at a time, I made it to the bottom. As we started the final part back to the Visitor Center, Jason made the mistake of trying to embolden me for the last bit. He stopped, pointed out our car, and told me we were almost there. As the last word floated off his lips, it triggered my body's shutdown function and caused the remaining milliliter of adrenaline coursing through my veins to evaporate. This infuriating reflex had happened previously when I was told I was about to complete something, and I had no control of it. I felt my strength dissipate instantly, and my legs crumpled underneath me. The only things that kept me from becoming a dirt hole cover were Jason's arms wrapped tightly around me.

Every inch forward after that was a hard-fought battle to stay upright. I had my left arm around Jason's neck with a vice grip on his shoulder and my right hand braced on his chest for balance. His arms were still around my waist, and he began slightly lifting me on each step to assist my weakened thigh muscles in raising my sapped limbs. Those seeing us emerge from the darkened woods would think that I had partaken of a little too much forest nymph wine.

Jason deposited me on a bench to rest while he took his own respite. Out of curiosity, I looked up *Hall of Mosses* while I was resting and found out the trail I had barely survived was closer to a mile long, not "just over half a mile" as Jason had been told. Part of me was glad I hadn't known, or I might have been too scared to try. As it was, I persevered and got to behold a splendor of nature. I knew I wouldn't be able to accomplish something this strenuous again, but for today MS didn't win.

Hoh Redux

Pulling into the parking lot of Hoh Rainforest, I am filled with a swirl of so many emotions. Our surroundings are lush, serene, and breathtaking, and I can't wait to get on the trail to bring life to the pictures I saw on the Internet. At the same time, I'm worried and nervous about the accessibility factor. Will there be a route that can handle a wheelchair or possibly a shorter trail that Nicky can manage on foot? Or will we need to scratch this off our vacation sightseeing list?

At the ranger station, they tell me about all the available trails—the lengths, terrain, and what is available to see on each one. By the vivid description, I know right away the *Hall of Mosses* is where all the awe-inspiring pictures were taken that had prompted me to add this to the "must-see" agenda. However, this path is a little over a half a mile long and not wheelchair-accessible; that one is much shorter and not as scenic. My heart drops a bit knowing the latter will be the sensible choice, and the online pictures will have to suffice. At least I will get to see some of the rainforest.

Back at the car, Nicky is adamant that she will be able to handle the longer trail. Seeing as she usually tries to do things she knows she can't and shouldn't do anymore, I am skeptical and concerned that she will tire out halfway through and be stuck. She assures me this is not the case and grumbles that I don't give her enough credit. Perhaps it is because I know we will both enjoy the scenic trail more, or maybe I have a moment of pure selfish weakness, whatever the reason, I give in. We pack up our things and head across the road to the *Hall of Mosses*.

As we step into the towering western hemlocks and red cedars, I am surrounded by a peacefulness that only nature can provide. I hurry Nicky across a dilapidated wood bridge traversing a crystal-clear, gurgling stream. Then our relaxing nature walk takes a steep turn north. While describing the even terrain and "only a few bumps" on this trail, the rangers forgot to mention the staircase built into the side of a cliff. I am infuriated by this lazy oversight, but that feeling is overshadowed by my terror of Nicky climbing the precipitous staircase. Stairs are an unnerving challenge for her, and my only consolation is she is still fresh.

The stairs are just wide enough for me to climb beside her and help her up each step. With her arm around my neck, she grips the rusted, metal handrail and steps up with her stronger right leg. Using it to push herself up while she pulls on the rail, Nicky is able to lift herself up to the next stair. We take each step in-sync, so I can help stabilize her as we move up the uneven staircase. The determination and effort are written on her face, and I encourage her until we reach the top.

Knowing she will need to rest before we can proceed, I steer us towards a green-iron bench beside the trail. We take a seat so Nicky can recuperate, and I can continue to fret in the back of my mind. Concerned over a challenge this taxing so early in our walk, I offer to turn back. She scoffs at the suggestion and sees no reason not to push forward. Trying to settle my nerves, I look around and try to focus on my calm surroundings. This is the first real glimpse I get of the forest.

Ferns of all shapes and varieties fan out in front of us. With assorted sizes, patterns, and colors, they weave multi-layered skirts around each of the trees. There are more shades of green than a Sherwin-Williams store and all complement each other beautifully. I am surrounded by ancient Sitka Spruce that stretch their trunks until their limbs can tickle the clouds. Taking a deep breath, it smells a bit musty and earthy, like wet-garden soil. That makes sense since I'm sitting in a rainforest.

When Nicky is ready, we set out on the twig-strewn path through the forest. She has her left arm draped over my shoulder, and my right is wrapped loosely around her waist. The extra balance and stability I provide is helping her enjoy the stunning landscape until we literally hit a bump in the road. A tree has decided that a monopoly on one side of the path is not enough. It has tried to lay claim to our trail by bisecting it with a large, bulging root. This makes another big step for Nicky and more palpitations for me. At this rate, I'll qualify for my family's history of high blood pressure by the time we make it back to the car.

Once I step over the offending root, I turn and face Nicky. She reaches across the wooden obstacle and grabs ahold of my shoulders for support. I wince when I feel her fingernails take hold, but stand firm so she doesn't lose her balance. Slowly, she lifts her right foot over the hump and sets it next to me, straddling the obstruction. The weak left is next, and I must lift her knee to help her clear the top of the bump. This routine works, and I'm sure it will be needed again farther down the road.

After successfully hurdling the hump, we slowly press on, deeper into this vast greenhouse. Our pace gives me a chance to fully absorb my surrounding. I'm fenced in by trees that are anywhere from saplings to centuries old, inches to feet in diameter, and are heights that end only when my chin is completely vertical. The pale-grey hue of broken, decaying stumps and fallen timbers that have succumbed to Mother Nature and Father Time accentuates the beauty of the russet-brown, lichen-covered hemlocks towering over them.

I see shorter maples hiding in the shadows of their loftier cousins that could be used as stage props for the Broadway version of Tim Burton's *The Nightmare Before Christmas.* Bent and deformed branches protruding from the warped and twisted limbs will leave a frightful shadow on a child's wall. The green, flowing moss hanging from each bough makes lovely tinsel to transform these deformed trees into Christmas trees worthy of any ghoul's holiday.

I look around and find the biggest tree—in the surrounding few hundred feet—and assist Nicky to pose against it for a photo-op. Even when she spreads her arms wide, as if to fly away, the tree is still larger than her wingspan. As she is leaning against the rough bark, I can see weariness begin to subtly emerge on her face, causing me to wrinkle my brow in concern. Such a small tell will be overlooked by most, but I can read her better. I have become more perceptive of the smallest of changes since the MS diagnosis. She carries a dormant bomb, and I must be able to spot and preemptively neutralize anything that may set it off.

Despite my growing concerns about her fatigue and my willingness to turn around, Nicky is steadfast in her decision to continue. Agonizingly respecting her wishes, we again embark down the dusty path. I know I probably sound like the chirping bird in the morning that repeats the same tune over and over again until she wants to shoot it. Nevertheless, I'm concerned because I don't know how much trail is left for us, or how much gas is left for her. A thought briefly crosses my mind to make an executive decision to turn around and not chance her health, but I know the fallout from this will be brutal. For now, we will stay the course.

A short distance down the trail, the debate is definitively settled when we approach a sign that reads "Halfway Point." As Nicky so sweetly reminds me, "It is the same distance on both sides of the loop back to the bridge, so there's no point in turning back now." We go around the corner and begin the slow-and-steady/shaky walk back to the car. All my senses are in overdrive as I try to soak in the natural beauty around me, as well as be hyper-vigilant to Nicky's demeanor. I know things can go downhill very quickly when she is tired, and she has already begun leaning on me more.

This half of the path offers its own scenic beauty. The ferns are lighter shades of green and seem to be standing a little straighter. With fewer of the shorter moss-covered, disfigured maples lurking in the shadows, the Sitka somehow even appear taller. There is more sun peeking through the canopy of leaves, so maybe that is contributing to the change in foliage.

As we round a corner, I can barely contain my excitement when I see we are approaching the forest's wooden rainbow. This sizable tree branch bends over the pedestrian walkway and forms a seamless arch. It truly is a masterpiece of engineering created by nature. This marvel is something I saw in multiple photographs whilst researching Hoh Rainforest and is at the top of my mental "Hoh Pictures" list. After multiple selfies with Hoh's arc, Nicky volunteers to take some photos of me standing underneath it. I'm not entirely sure how, but she carefully balances in the middle of the road long enough to take a few shots before I run back to steady her. Her feats and actions never cease to amaze me.

I start to feel the difference a little sun makes in this steamy sweatbox and worry about this element being added to Nicky's already overloaded table. Heat turns her muscles into jelly and renders her a rag doll. Recognizing we will need to take more rest and water breaks, I plan for a stop at the large, grey rock I spot up ahead. It's slightly off the path, but taking care of her is more important than following the "Stay on the Trail" rule. An indentation on the side of the oversized stone curves perfectly into a makeshift chair for Nicky. She can now sit down, rest, and rehydrate before we tackle the final stretch.

After a much too short of a rest in my opinion, she is antsy to start again. We both are acutely aware that her hourglass of energy is quickly slipping away, and we're playing with borrowed time. I only wish she would rest for a few minutes longer, so she might gain a few extra minutes down the road. However, I've learned when she has her mind set on something, standing in her way is futile.

As we commence walking, I notice her left foot is barely clearing the ground. Her concentration and focus tell me she is laboring to elevate it. The bottom of her dirt-coated, blue New Balance is audibly scraping the ground, so I start to remind her with every step to lift her foot. Hoping to assist the left leg in raising this foot, I try to support more of its weight. I'm concerned because there are so many small, loose stones on the path for her to skid and trip on so easily. I don't want that to be our undoing.

With each step, as I feel her struggle and slow a bit more, my insides knot and my heart begins to skip every few beats with growing anxiety and worry. Our rest breaks become more and more frequent until finally we are stopping about every hundred feet. She keeps apologizing for ruining my vacation, but I should be the one groveling for forgiveness after dragging her into this. I was aware of her limitations, and I should have *made* her turn back. If she gets hurt or has a relapse, it will be all my fault, and I won't be able to do anything. I am supposed to be preventing her from overdoing it; not instigating it.

At one point along the route, Nicky's legs are about to fold underneath her, and there are no benches in sight. She ends up plopping down on a hemlock's dirt-packed, root mound. We drink our lukewarm water and chew our melted chocolate-cherry granola bars while she recovers. Unfortunately, the forest's smallest predators take this opportunity to begin drinking from us and chewing on our exposed skin.

Numerous hikers stop to ask *me* if *she* is injured, as if comprehension and speech are only possible for standing, walking individuals. I can barely contain my irritation and struggle to reply civilly. Judging by the strained look on her face, their blatant disrespect and ignorance are wearing on Nicky as well. Although a longer break would be nice, neither of us has the patience or tolerance to deal with the witlessness right now and cut our break short.

Moving forward, I continue to offer support and reassurance vocally, but am silently stewing and panicking. The stairs are near and descending them will present a new challenge for her already spent legs. I make sure we are stopping frequently, so she conserves all her lingering energy for that challenge. This also gives our new entourage of tiny pillagers a chance to replenish themselves. I'm positive the swarm has grown since it began patiently following us. A stationary target *is* much easier to catch than a moving one, so I guess I can't fault them for wanting a sit-down meal over drive-thru for a change.

The top of the dreaded steps appears, and I see glimpses of fear, dismay, and anxiety cross Nicky's face before her steely fortitude sets in. Going down stairs is much more difficult for her than going up, and each step presents a new challenge. Moving to the second step, I turn to steady her as she grips the handrail and begins to gingerly descend. Stepping down first with her strong right, she uses it, the railing, and my shoulder to support herself as she brings the weaker left foot down. Basically, we are reversing the process of going up.

We are slowly and methodically repeating this process step by grueling step, when I notice we have created a traffic jam and are delaying some extremely impatient people. One unhappy man even offers to carry Nicky down, so the line can move faster! As nice, albeit highly inappropriate, as his offer is, we choose to press our backs firmly against the stairway's rock wall and let people scurry past to return to their all-consuming, hectic lives. Without asking, I knew there is no chance of her giving up now when she is so close to the finish line—even if it takes her another two hours to cross it.

Relief and gratitude wash over me when I help her off the last step. When we then cross the bridge, I take a deep breath and finally allow myself to relax a little. Even though I was worried and stressed throughout the walk, this whole experience was amazing. We got to see astoundingly, stunning wonders of nature and were able to make it back safely—what more could I ask for?

Anticipating the end of the hike and wanting to give Nicky one last boost of inspiration, I get too comfortable and make a grievous mistake. In the past, when I have said how close we were to the end or pointed out our destination, regardless of the distance remaining, her body has instantly drained all remaining energy and collapsed. I know this, but am unfocused and make the thoughtless, stupid slip-up; I point to our car and tell her we are almost there. Before the last syllable floats off my tongue, I realize my error, and what I have done. Nicky will now face unnecessary torment and struggle for the rest of our walk because of my carelessness. How can I be so foolish? We are so close!

I feel her slump against me as her legs fold and crumple beneath her. She clings to my neck, and I quickly tighten my grip on her waist to hold her up. Every step from here to the car is like a three-legged race. Her right leg still has a bit of strength, but I am fully in charge of lifting her left. With every step of my right foot, I lift her leg off the ground and help move the left foot forward. This improvised system carries us out of the *Hall of Mosses*.

Emerging from the forest, I'm sure we look like the downtrodden pair, but we are quite the opposite. I am thankful we made it safely, happy we're finished, ecstatic about the things we have seen and pictures we have taken, but more than anything, I'm proud of Nicky for what she has accomplished today. She was determined to walk the whole trail, and she didn't let anything stand in her way. Not me. Not her fatigue. And most certainly—not her MS. She conquered it today. Together *we* conquered it today.

Memories Are Made of This

When I was young, I had walked through these head-stones to visit Grandpa's grave on Memorial Day many times with my grandma. We would wear our hand-made, red-tissue paper poppies from the local VFW (Veterans of Foreign Wars), and she would buy a red and white, plastic flower wreath to leave. This was our yearly tradition to honor my grandfather's WWII service. Today's visit, however, was my own private memorial to honor my grandma.

Having missed her funeral for health reasons, this was the first and only time I would be able to come home and visit the cemetery. Walking through the rows of smooth granite stones, I tried to find my kinfolk's plot. I recognized so many of the family names I passed, but I guess that was to be expected in a small community. When I reached my grandparent's stone and read her newly chiseled name next to Grandpa's, the shock of Grandma being gone finally hit me.

As I laid my fresh flowers down, I focused my grief on anger at the weeds sprouting up around her headstone. Didn't we pay for it to be maintained? Wrapping my hand around the noxious intruders, I started to pull them when I was hit with nostalgia of Grandma's yard in summertime. I always loved running through the grass on a sunny, summer afternoon, collecting a spray of these pretty flowers before the mower came and chopped them up. It was even more fun if their white puffballs had appeared. If I picked one of those, I would blow on it and send all the petal's seeds floating away on a gust of air before making a wish. The little yellow blooms in my hand had unexpectedly unearthed a bushel of buried memories with Grandma.

What instantly came to mind was planting a garden with her. I grew up in the same rural, country house she had, so the sizable yard was her old stomping ground. From the patch of bamboo Grandma had planted as a young girl for fishing poles, to the designated gardening plot that she had made with her mother, my grandma had left her mark on every inch.

The vegetable-planting parcel was nestled between the back shed and the poisonous, scarlet-berry bushes and was guarded by a row of evergreens, which hid a yellow water hydrant specifically for the garden. When she got married, Grandma moved down the road, but her garden stayed here with her mother. Every year, Dad would spend an afternoon breaking up this overgrown patch for us, using the old, red push tiller, and he knew exactly how many brown-trenches to carve. He had been in charge of digging these channels with a hoe when he was a boy, and Grandma's layout had never changed. That consistency may be why I could still remember her preferred order perfectly to this day.

The various tomatoes always started the arrangement on the left. My palate was beginning to water as I reminisced on popping a plump, sweet cherry tomato into my mouth straight from the vine. That was a taste synonymous with summer. As the tomato plants had grown taller, I would help Grandma wrap them in chicken wire, so they would grow straight and so their delicate tomatoes would be protected.

Broccoli seedlings would be planted in the next row, followed by lettuce. This would eventually have expansive green leaves that would tickle my bare legs as I walked past. The cool soft dirt squished between my fingers as I helped plant each area. Back then, I didn't care if I got dirt underneath my fingernails or a sticker in my hand, so garden gloves were never considered. Especially since a wriggly, slick earthworm or a small, delicate roly-poly could only be fully appreciated with bare fingers.

Grandma always put a line of onions straight down the middle of her garden, so the pungent odor could work as a natural insecticide. Young green bean plants, which would be droopy and full of pods in a few weeks, were next. The root vegetables, carrots and potatoes, rounded out the final two vertical rows. Every year, I would grow impatient not being able to see their growth progression and pull these too early.

One of my most hated jobs every summer was checking the leaves of the potato plants for the decimating potato beetles and crushing them. The sickening smell emitted when I smashed their hard black and yellow striped shells was nauseating. Nevertheless, this disgusting job had to be done, seeing as this disastrous pest could devour the leaves and kill a potato plant in a matter of days. I merely wished I wasn't assigned the chore.

Grandma liked to save room behind these orderly lines for the lofty, pink stalks of rhubarb that she would later mix with strawberries to make my favorite pie. There was also space for tangled vines of round, beige cantaloupes and plump, green watermelons to spread out and thrive. After we had everything planted, she would slice open a bale of golden straw and have me mulch around all our baby plants. I preferred protecting my garden in this manner, but straw bales were hard to find after I left the farm to become a city dweller.

I had been away for over two decades, but I had no problem recalling the hours spent down the road at Grandma's house. She lived a quarter mile from us, down a white gravel road that passed a field, a pasture, and the one-room schoolhouse that Dad had attended as a boy. On my '69 Schwinn that I inherited from Mom, I had no problem biking there, provided I remembered to gain enough speed to get up the last, steep hill. More times than not, though, I would get distracted and forget, which resulted in me walking in her driveway pushing my bike.

For some reason, Grandma would want to feed me whenever I came over, so many of my memories revolved around her fluorescently lighted kitchen. Like her cooking staples, I don't think her kitchen had ever changed. Her favorite cutlery tool to chop, peel, or skin anything with, and the only one I ever saw her use, had been a honed, black-handled paring knife that she wielded like a five-star chef with a Wüsthof blade. She could strip a potato bare, forming a single, curling cable of skin, in mere seconds. If I ever attempted that, I would have fewer fingers than a high school shop teacher.

All meals were cooked in a heavy, cast-iron skillet, which had been seasoning since my dad was a boy, and only lard had ever been allowed to touch it. An old soup can on the stove kept any leftover fat drippings, so every artery clogging bit could be saved and used. Try as I might, I wasn't able to recall a hot meal that didn't include at least one fried item. Yet, there was always a bowl of green beans or black-eyed peas to put on your plate next to your golden, fried potatoes and chicken-fried steak to make it look healthier.

One of my favorite meals was when Grandma made her famous, homemade beef noodles for dinner. After she flattened out the soft dough on a white dusted counter, she would roll it into a tight cylinder, and cut it into half inch pieces. If I had been good that day, Grandma would let me flour my hands and unwind the sticky spirals. The plump noodles would be cooked in the beef gravy made from the flavorful brown bits stuck to the bottom of the skillet after cooking the meal. No relative had ever been able to duplicate this family favorite recipe. I think the years seasoning the cast iron and her magical paring knife added something that could not be replicated.

Since she never knew when she would get to town again, Grandma stockpiled enough food for the apocalypse in three, full-sized freezers. Once, while helping to defrost one, my brother regretfully found out Grandma used her ice boxes to preserve more than fixins for dinner. As a bulky package he thought was a sirloin thawed, pink gums and white molars started to appear. Grandma had been so thrilled that my brother had found her spare set of teeth; he had been so thrilled he hadn't found *Grandpa*. Though, he did later find a twenty-year-old 3Musketeers bar from the early '80s.

With my bare thighs stuck to one of Grandma's vinyl kitchen chairs, I listened to the sweet crooning of Kenny Rogers and REO Speedwagon on the radio that played faintly in the background. This was where I got hooked on the obscure tales and tidbits provided by Paul Harvey's "The Rest of the Story." It was considered required listening after we finished watching

The Young and the Restless. Today, if I was lucky enough to catch a rerun of Paul Harvey on NPR, I would have a flashback to drinking Tang with dinner at Grandma's Formica table.

Besides the radio, the other persistent sound in Grandma's kitchen was the random squawk of activities announced over the police scanner. A simple black box on the counter with scrolling yellow numbers kept her apprised of anything in surrounding counties that involved law enforcement. It was her polite way of keeping tabs on her neighbors without being labeled a nosy gossip. I never paid attention to the police scanner while I was younger, but when I turned fourteen and started driving, that mechanical announcer of infractions became my arch nemesis.

I would be the first to admit that I loved to play hard and drive fast during my teenage years. Blue and red flashing lights were in my rearview mirror more than once. This should not have been a problem seeing as I never drove off with more than a verbal chastisement, so no one needed to or should have known my transgressions. Nonetheless, when I got home, regardless of the time, I would be met at the door and promptly asked to surrender my keys for a week due to my indiscretion. Grandma's box had squealed on me, so she had felt the need to call and promptly inform my father. A hunk of plastic and a busybody octogenarian had sold me out.

When I last had a chance to visit Grandma five years ago, it warmed my heart to see the time capsule of my youth, and my dad's before me, had not been opened or disturbed. The home she had built over sixty-five years would be the American Picker's dream discovery, but the generations of buried finds were solely proprietary. Old farm machinery and pickup trucks parked in the fields; a silver-antique, hand-crank cistern by

Grandma's front door; rare glass power line insulators displayed on the top of wooden fence poles. Each was a portion of my grandma's history that belonged with her and not with a swap-meet collector.

Dropping by in mid-June, Grandma's yard was in bloom with the bouquet of colors I held captured on countless Polaroids in my mind. The lavender and yellow irises played against a backdrop of orange and fuchsia gladiolus in the front, while the white and pink peony bushes supplied supporting roles along the sides. Unfortunately, the intoxicating, floral fragrances that were suspended in the air could not be transferred to pictures, so I had to let them soak into every pore while I was visiting. When I had bought my first house, I planted all these gorgeous perennials in my garden, so I could recreate this snapshot and aroma.

There had been many furry additions in her yard, however, that appeared in none of my memories. Dozens upon dozens of cats were strolling around the premises. Grandma had always had a stray barn cat or two, which resulted in the occasional litter of kittens, but this population put the most feverish cat ladies to shame. From big tabbies and pure black kittens to mangled tomcats and sherbet mousers, there was no discrimination in their variety. When I inquired about her new pets, I had to harness all my self-control to keep a straight face as Grandma relayed her tale of woe.

A few months prior, one or two cats wandered in and were followed shortly by a few more stragglers. She didn't want the damn things, but couldn't get them to leave. They kept multiplying by both new arrivals and procreation. Now, there were so many, she was going through almost fifty pounds of cat food a week. Turns out, Grandma had been feeding the nomadic kitties from day one, and they had decided to stay for the free food and had invited their friends to the "no reservations required" table.

As if this could not have gotten more unbelievable, she had also informed me of trying to stealthily thin the herd. My eighty-five-year-old Grandma had been making midnight runs five miles down the road to leave bags of felines on her neighbor's doorstep. I had inadvertently found the explanation for the mysterious parcel of cats our longtime family friends had received and spoken of when I visited them earlier. Grandma had become a reverse cat burglar!

Eliciting these treasured memories of my feisty, salt-of-the-earth Grandma brought me a reassuring peace, and I locked them tightly away in my heart. Lovingly tracing the fresh carvings on her headstone, I thought the rough-edged letters with their cool-smooth interior perfectly symbolized my grandma. Whispering a final goodbye and placing a kiss gently by her name with my salty fingertips, I stood up to leave this hallowed ground, knowing I would not be back.

Walking to my car, I realized the morning of sentimental memories had filled me with a desire to visit our family farm and see my childhood home. As I drove out of the cemetery onto the white chalk road, a wheat truck lumbered by signaling everyone would be preoccupied with the harvest. Kids out here were driving their family's gold-filled trucks to the grain elevators as soon as they could tap their toes on the pedals, which was usually by the age of ten. When I thought of my nephews doing this in a few years, I laughed. My sister would never allow it, and I would strongly discourage the boys from asking. Nonetheless, I would love a fly's seat if they tried.

Reminiscing on harvests when I was young, I remembered

the first time Dad had let me ride on his lap in the cabin of the combine. I had been riveted watching the waving, golden stalks of wheat get sucked up, then sheared down by the spinning head out front. If I had turned and peered out the back window, I could see a stream of reddish-brown kernels continuously gushing into a grain bin. Behind the combine, we were leaving a trail of stripped chaff and discarded wheat stalks that would later be turned into straw bales. The whole process had fascinated me.

As fun as this was to see from the cockpit, I would barely last an hour underneath the scorching Kansas sun. It was blistering hot, and I melted faster than a marshmallow at a campfire. We didn't have one of the fancy machines with all the perks, like a radio and an air conditioner. No, I was pretty sure this was a first edition model that Dad had been fixing since his granddad retired the scythe. It still got the job done, and that was all that mattered.

My dad was born with MacGyver skills in his blood and could repair anything using a screwdriver and a welding gun. If those didn't work, there was always duct tape. He would keep his equipment running for as long as possible before ultimately discarding it in a machinery graveyard somewhere in the back pasture. Our poor, ancient combine should have been granted this benefit years ago, but it had been denied the honor.

For a few summers, a custom cutting crew had helped with our harvest. Like a cloud of locusts, they traveled across the country, leaving a trail of stubbled fields behind them. One day, I saw campers and RVs pulling into our drive filled with wives and kids. They were followed by flatbed trailers that were carrying the best combines on the market. A small city moved into our backyard, and I had had new gypsy friends to play with for a week.

When tornadoes started dropping around us one year, everyone had moved from their motorhomes into our house for shelter. As they ran indoors, a cutter's hat blew off, and I, being a fearless six-year-old, had run into the screaming, swirling wind to retrieve it. Right as my pudgy little fingers were about to grab the visor, someone had felt the need to seize me and drag me back into the house for a public dressing down. If that story was told at a family gathering today, I would still stand by my decision to save the hat.

After a few years, Dad chose not to invite the crew back. He knew he would still need extra help, and his options had been his seventy-year-old mom, five-year-old son, or his wife. As I thought about his choices now, I believed wholeheartedly Grandma would have enjoyed being in a hot, dusty combine more than being left at home babysitting sweaty, stinky kids. However, Dad had decided to put my terrified mom on a combine. This was something she had never wanted to add to "skills" on her resume, but it has since provided a great conversation starter at parties.

Without a doubt, my favorite part of harvest had always been when Grandma brought us home at twilight, and Dad was there with a truck full of fresh-cut wheat. He had let us climb up the wood slat side and play in the berries that were still warm from the sun. I would pick up a handful and watch the cascading waterfall of kernels slide through my fingers before chewing on a few until they were the consistency of gum. It never bothered me that I was getting coated in dust or that wheat was stuck in my hair, seeing as I would be forced to take a shower that night regardless.

Turning off my memory's super-highway, I realized I was about to drive past my old, white Quaker church. I could be found here every Sunday morning when I was young, freezing in the drafty basement for Sunday School and then fidgeting on a hard, wooden pew during the sermon. This was the time of year for camp meeting at the dilapidated tabernacle down the road. I had watched mice run across the stage behind the preacher over there and had the joy of using a timeworn, wood outhouse. Mom had taught the Vacation Bible School, where I learned how to tie-dye, wheat weave, and play red-rover-red-rover. I was fairly certain she still had her wheat art from that time.

Turning down the long road that led to our farm's drive-way, I rolled down the window and let the warm summertime air engulf me. The pure, unadulterated smells of the country slowly drifted into the car. Ahhh...the scent of pure, warm cow pasture with a hint of wildflowers couldn't be replicated. I rested my arm on the car window to work on my farmer's tan, took a deep breath in, and knew I was officially home.

Both sides of the road were lined with rusted, barbed wire fences to corral the roaming cattle. Red Herefords and their spring calves on the left, while herds of Black Angus mixed with a spattering of White Charolais cows chewing their cuds on the right. Mixed in between the weathered, wood fence posts were the occasional wild, black-current bush or wind-blown tumbleweed. Glancing in the rearview mirror, I saw the white cloud of dust I was kicking up and knew I would need to find a carwash before returning the rental.

As I was turning down our gravel drive, I tried to remember the last time I was here. Grandma was alive, I lived in a dryer state, and I didn't have these strands of grey hair, so a lifetime ago. I knew I wouldn't be bothered since this place had sat empty for years. Reaching the three-way split in the road, I elected to take the left roundabout. This passed my great-grandma's little yellow two-bedroom house that my family of five had shared for eight years. The towering pine tree that I drove past had been no taller than two-year-old me when Mom had planted it as a willowy sapling. She had nurtured us both and helped us plant solid roots, but the pine had inherited Grandpa's height genes.

I parked between the irises and mature apricot tree. Stepping out of the car, I stepped back into my childhood. The dark, blue irises had already started to bloom and unroll their petals to show their furry, white caterpillar stripe. The air was filled with their earthy and spicy scent. Although the apricot tree no longer produced fruit, I drooled a little, thinking of how juicy and delicious the delicate, fuzz covered bounty had been every summer while I was young. A farmer's market or roadside stand could not compare to what's picked straight from the tree.

I was walking toward the three cement steps in front of the house, when I had a change of heart. There was nothing I wanted to see within the cramped four walls that stood behind that aluminum screen door. Instead, I veered to the right, towards the ancient storm cellar facing the side of the house. The air was filled with the sweet nectar emanating from the line of peonies along its periphery. They were full of round buds ready to burst into pink and white flowers.

Making my way to the backyard, I had visions of my siblings and me chasing the blinking, yellow firefly bottoms in our underwear on a sweltering summer evening, trying to see who could catch one first. Gathered around the victor's cupped hands, we would watch the bulb flip on and off before letting our prize fly free again. We found this more entertaining at that age than most Saturday morning cartoons.

By retracing my steps, I passed my car and crossed the main driveway to our broke down, red and yellow striped play-set. The little slide, that I had loved sending our unsuspecting barn cats down, was lopsided and barely hanging onto the side frame. One swing had succumbed to gravity and was dangling by a single chain, while the other's plastic seat was cracked and almost split in two. I used to think if I pumped my pint-sized legs really hard, I could get high enough to flip the swing over the top bar. Sadly, I hadn't been committed enough to succeed.

Standing a few feet away, our mulberry tree had shrunk considerably since I last visited. The tree was stocky enough that, as a kid, I had liked to climb out on the sturdy limbs to reach every delectable, dark purple berry. The nursery rhythm said the monkey went *around the* mulberry bush; well, this monkey had gone *up* one. By the time I had finally returned to the house, I would have tree scrapes on my bare arms and legs and magenta berry juice stains on my clothes, mouth, hands, face…pretty much everywhere. As I recalled, Mom had not been amused.

Glancing across the road at the weather-worn, red barn, I thought of the day Dad brought my cherished pony, Brown Sugar, home. When he had led her out of the cow trailer, I squealed and ran right up to stroke her downy-soft nose and bristly whiskers. Hot breath snorted on my hand as she sniffed me and huffed my scent. All these years later, I could still recall the musky fragrance of horse, hay, and droppings that I had committed to memory that day.

Brown Sugar stood about four feet tall, or twelve hands in

horse, and had a soft, reddish-brown coat with a coarse black mane. Brushing her coat after a long, dusty trail ride or combing her mane to get the sandburs and tangles out had been as enjoyable for me as calming for her. We had many good rides and marshmallow fluff sandwiches together before I graduated to my mother's light-brown quarter horse, Mitze, and Brown Sugar got to begin grazing her way through the green grass of retirement.

Mitze was a foot taller, fifteen hands, and became my 4-H show horse. I had learned to ride on Brown Sugar, but Mitze and I mastered barrel and pole racing and competition riding. When I slackened my grip on her leather reins and metal bit and kicked my spinning spurs into her soft belly, she knew it was time to kick up dust and start galloping towards the first barrel. I kept the bit in her mouth loose, held onto the saddle horn, and leaned against her swaying, bouncing neck as we tore across the dirt arena. Wind whipping my face, Mitze snorting as her iron-shod hooves hit the ground, our bodies rocking to their own rhythm—we were one unstoppable machine. I had loved that feeling of unbridled freedom.

Looking at my watch, I realized I had to leave straightaway if I was going to make my last stop by sunset. Walking back to my car, I took one last look around before getting in, returning to the driveway, and subsequently the main road. Mom, a talented artist, had painted this road from our mailboxes as well as paintings of Mitze and Brown Sugar for me, so two of my fondest memories, returning home and my horses, were hanging on my living room wall. Regardless of where I landed, two watercolors of my childhood on a farm in Kansas hitchhiked.

Driving past the little green, one-room schoolhouse, I saw the old equipment in one of Grandpa's machinery graveyards decorating the playground. I was still amazed that Dad and Uncle Bill had started school here with three other local farm boys. My Dad would have had an easy commute seeing as the schoolhouse was right across the road from Grandma's. It was closed when he was in grade school, and Dad had had to transfer to the same itty-bitty school in Natoma that I would later attend.

With the intention of coming back another day, I drove past Grandma's house to Dad's big, cream-colored machine shed. He would be in the field till he wasn't burnin' daylight, so it was deserted. Parking alongside the gigantic sliding doors, I went in the side entrance to unlock the bolts and glide them open. As my eyes adjusted, they instantly latched on to the antique black Chevy in the corner.

I had loved pretending to drive that truck, with its snazzy red interior, like a race truck at Daytona. What I never knew back then was how it had gotten the hole through its floor-board. Recently, Dad shared that Grandma created it when she had moved Grandpa's gun without making sure the safety had been locked. I also discovered that what I had always thought was onyx paint with a white crystal effect was simply black with white paint flecks. My grandparents had been standing in the truck bed trying to spray paint something white, when a gust of wind blew paint back on the pristine, black truck exterior. All this abuse my black beauty had suffered in silence, and I had never known.

Finding Dad's blue four-wheeler, I was able to get it started with enough time to make the overlook by sunset if I hurried. Pulling out onto the shifty, loose rocks, I had to remind myself how to use the throttle and clutch, so I wouldn't spin out. Soon, I was zipping up the road to the far north pasture and the hilltop lookout. This was the best vantage point to observe and absorb all the beauty emitted from our land, and it was especially gorgeous during a summer twilight.

After turning into the bare milo field, I followed the fence line down its far side. If I had continued straight, I would have crossed the creek bed and circled back to Grandma's house. She would bring us down here to scrounge around in the dirt for the flint arrowhead fragments that were buried throughout our land. My family's homestead was in the Kill Creek township and was named for an Indian massacre that occurred there in the 1860s. I couldn't take a step in these hills without absorbing generations of history's blood and carnage through my soles.

Pulling up to the first gate, I quickly unhooked the barbed wire loop, opened the fence, and drove into the pasture. I was extra vigilant to return and refasten each gate behind me, so the cows couldn't take a holiday trip into the neighbor's field. Driving across the open grasslands, I repeated the process two more times, gaining elevation as I crossed the pastures. Cows were grazing in the distance, and their calves were nearby frolicking carefree before they had to come find their mom's teat for dinner.

Reaching the last meadow, I parked and walked the final hundred feet to the rocky ledge, so I could pick some wildflowers along the way. A handful of mustard-yellow thin goldenrods started my bundle followed by a grouping of violet petaled asters with sunshine-yellow middles. Rounding out my pack were pinkish coneflowers and the easily recognizable black-eyed Susan. With its dark-brown eye surrounded by bright-yellow petals, a black-eyed Susan could be picked out of any crowd. The variety in my bouquet formed a fragrant wildflower melody. Blooms in hand, I took a seat on the edge of the sheer limestone drop-off and waited for the setting sun's radiance.

From here, I had a panoramic, aerial view: Grandma's house and barn, Dad's shed and schoolhouse, and, if I squinted hard enough, my childhood home. Wheat fields that were still golden, but would be reduced to stubs by the end of the week. There was the creek I had just passed, twisting, turning, and slicing a line through the land. Below me, where the limestone met the water, was one of the best ways to keep a child entertained...a shale hill

This slope was composed of loose, black shale rock that stopped right at the edge of the freezing, cold water. My siblings and I would scoot out on a slippery ledge that years of erosion had cut into the limestone wall at the top of the shale. It had been wide enough for me to sit and push off, so I could skid all the way to the bottom on the unattached, ebony slivers. I had to stop myself before I slid into a frigid bath, which happened more than once, resulting in a black, sludgy mess.

The real challenge came when I had tried to climb back up this steep, shifty mountain. When I had almost reached the top, the unattached pieces would move under my feet sending me sliding. By the time I was finally able to reach the ledge, I would be covered head-to-toe in black, sooty dust and ready for my next turn. I never tired of this endless merry-go-round.

Before I could locate any other familiar landmarks, crickets began chirping, a low moo called a little one home to bed, and night started rolling in. The yellow of day began transforming into oranges and reds on the western horizon and flung a glow of dusk across the land. Watching as the light faded to mauve and cast a light, pink blush over the landscape, I could see the faint outline of the moon and North Star becoming visible in the night sky.

Standing, I said a prayer, threw my flowers over the side in honor of my Grandma, and walked back to the four-wheeler. What started as a sad day had ended in a peaceful reflection and tribute.

One More Chapter

With the addition of my new nemesis, multiple sclerosis (MS), I had seen the gradual subtraction of various interests and pastimes. I was forever labeled with a "Caution: Experiences Bouts of Drowsiness/Weakness/Cognitive loss" sticker that had hindered my ability to work, operate a moving vehicle, and carry objects while walking. The purposely arranged, tightly organized sectors of my life were dissolving around me, leaving me alone and empty. I turned to my oldest most beloved hobby, reading, to help me fill this void. Throughout the years, it had seen me through the good times and bad, and I knew it would not fail me now.

I read my first book, *All the Pretty Horses*, one bright, sunny afternoon sitting in the screened in back porch of our canary-yellow country house. An energetic five-year-old, I sat quietly and flipped the love-worn pages of my brown paperback. Sounding out words as I went, I looked at pictures of spirited Dapples and Greys and dreamt of one day owning my own pretty horse. Some might say I had the prose memorized after demanding it be read gazillions of times, but I credited the *Rainbow* Levar Burton created, and my mom's approach to calling the sandman.

Her soothing timbre as she made countless tales float off the pages lulled me to sleep every night throughout my tender years. Evenings were spent curled up with my sister on our bunkbeds, listening to *Little House on the Prairie* while I fought to keep my eyes open for one more chapter. Running through tall prairie grass, making little seem extravagant, camaraderie of sisters because there was no one else nearby—I could relate to all these things. The books came alive in my mind, creating vivid multicolored pictures and scenes, and ignited in me a zeal to start school so I could absorb more.

Unfortunately, as my thirteen years began at USD #399, I found my square peg couldn't be pounded through their small, oblong hole; I would never fit. To say I started forming my misfit, nerd status at an impressionable age would be no exaggeration, but I didn't care. I habitually finished my assignments early and escaped their uninspiring, insidious routines to entomb myself in the library's shelves. Taking advantage of pay-to-play in its most rudimentary form, I constructed my fourth-grade teacher's bi-monthly, educational bulletin boards, so I could then be allowed to quietly sit in the hall and become wholly engrossed in written words. I did whatever was required to escape boredom and delve into the pages of my current literary voyage.

As the years rolled on, the only significant changes were: my classes traveled six miles down the road to Paradise, and my books were lengthened by a few hundred sheets. *Gone with the Wind* were the *Boxcar Children*, and *The Babysitter's Club* took a trip to Narnia. A seed of historical fiction planted by Laura Ingalls Wilder took root when I devoured the woes of Scarlett O'Hara in three nights, and I was left thirsting for more. Bedtimes were once again forgotten in lieu of just one more chapter in the tantalizing series, *Shannara*, that my siblings and I exchanged until their covers were falling off. Eventually, however, turbulent, teenager hormones threw an opaque cover over this carefree period.

The summer before ninth grade, driven by a misguided desire to fit in, I naïvely chose conformity over content and began trying to curve my squared corners. Consequently, when I was introduced to the three Bs of my high school, Books-Boys-Beer, my life was split: parents and teachers were only privy to the first two Bs, whereas social circles were centered around the latter pair. Books were downgraded to assignments in English and could now only be enjoyed in secret like a forbidden cigarette behind the gymnasium. My fervor for literary works had to lay dormant for a bit, but there was a kindling continuously smoldering.

During this hiatus from my riveting reads, I foolhardily believed my left hand knew not what my right did. However, my classmates had been with me since we were sticking glue and crayons in orifices where they didn't belong, so my bookworm inclination was already well-known. Similarly, the biological brood and wisdom oracles of my life knew the behaviors of unwise, impulsive teenagers, and to think otherwise proved their assumptions accurate.

I eagerly planned on re-igniting my oldest obsession after I gave my valedictorian speech, walked across the stage, and flipped my tassel, but that plan was exasperatingly hindered. My yearning for a thought-provoking, penned piece would have to wait as my hardbacks took on the persona of massive educational tomes. Buried under their physical weight and mental encumberment, my realm shrunk and needed to center around textbooks for the next nine years. Little did I know, when the bottom fell out of my world, they would supply a firm island for me to stand on.

In 2003, I was diagnosed with MS, and my sphere shifted and attempted to spin off its axis. I determinedly refused to let this new setback frighten me from my aspirations; I had two years left of lugging Pharmacology and Applied Therapeutics hardbacks around in my JanSport backpack followed by 1,500 hours of applied clinical practice. By propping myself up with stacks of texts and manuals, I buried myself in manuscripts of research studies and lines of 2,500-page textbooks. I wanted to concentrate on my studies and avoid dealing with my health. When I graduated and finally closed my schoolbooks after over twenty years in 2006, my new challenge became learning to ride the full-time career train with my new, unwanted, and unfamiliar baggage attached.

As a segue from student to professional, I chose to complete a year-long residency at a rural Kentucky hospital. Fortunately, housing was provided throughout my tenure at a dusty, outdated house on the property. I had started noticing a decline in my stamina level at this point and driving the fifty miles home some nights seemed like over a hundred and unmanageable. My colleague loaned me a book-on-tape to help the miles go by faster and make the drive less stressful, which *sounded* like a great idea. It was quickly returned and marked as a failed experiment, when I became so enthralled and distracted by the story that I missed my exit by twenty miles.

I was grateful for the close place to collapse after work, but I did not account for how gloomy and depressing it would be to enter the noiseless, empty two-story house every night. To fill the void and overwhelm the melancholy, as soon as I consumed supper and washed the day down the drain in a hot shower, I would retire to my room and retreat into the pages of my chosen work of fiction. Finally, able to dive back into pleasure reading, I used it to drive the spooks away and to help me relax my tired mind and body. As the words flew off the pages, they formed free picture shows in my mind that drowned out the house's deafening silence and took me away quicker than a soak in Calgon.

My MS slowly started to crawl out of hibernation and began to saw through the first, and what would become the last, three years of my tumultuous pharmacy career. I was leaning and relying more heavily on these precious hours of mental escape for stress decompression following my shifts. My one-year residency rolled into eighteen grueling months after two severe relapses. Surprisingly, after all this, the hospital still wanted to hire me upon completion and agreed to let me keep using the drafty house as my rejuvenation station. The afternoon before my shift, I would load my Honda CR-V with a suitcase and a tote of paperbacks, drive over, and use the evening hours to regroup, relax, and read.

Nevertheless, over the next year, the unsettling, accelerated pace of my neurological condition was thrust into the forefront of my mind when I started having trouble traversing the parking lot to my waiting refuge. Stumbling in one evening following a taxing shift, my eyes were too tired to clearly focus on a page, and my brain was too foggy to comprehend one word. I had pushed myself past my system's breaking point, and I painfully realized I could no longer safely perform my pharmacist responsibilities. Heartbreakingly, I made the decision to turn in my badge and house key and drove home for the last time. When I arrived home, it was determined I probably shouldn't drive anymore either, so I relinquished my car keys as well. Two very weighty volumes of my life had abruptly ended, and the sound of their covers slamming shut reverberated in my ears.

The following repetitive days at home extended into unvaried weeks, and I felt myself slipping farther and farther into a spiral of desolation. Losing my career and vehicular independence at one time was wreaking havoc on me psychologically and making me feel as if I would never get to leave my house or travel freely again. One television show had blurred into hundreds more before my clicking finger decisively froze. I ultimately concluded MS may decrease my faculties in the future, but I would not facilitate this loss by killing brain cells staring into this mindless box. Thankfully, my trusty companions had not strayed far and were patiently waiting for me on the shelves in my library with their ever-ready lifeline.

I climbed out of my self-pity pit and into an endless stream of intellectually stimulating outings and undertakings on a staircase built out of hardbacks. Whether I was learning to play Quidditch and drink butterbeer at Hogwarts, going *There and Back Again* to Mirkwood forest for *A Hobbit's Holiday*, or avoiding REDЯUM at the Overlook Hotel, by losing myself once again between the dedications and the author biographies, I found my tickets out of the isolation. I wasn't choosy and was grateful for any distraction from dwelling on the changes and losses in my circumstances. My undiscriminating range of literature carried me to numerous rousing locations, nonetheless I always circled back to my preferred genre: Historical Fiction.

Embracing a well-written narrative of the past provided me with not only a ticket to travel but also the keys to a DeLorean to reach my destinations. I emphatically stepped into a print-lined cavern that would lead me around the globe by way of bifurcations and tunnels. Plantagenets and Tudors, Henrys and Elizabeth—the tales of these English pedigrees directed my journeys through times gone by throughout Europe as royal families were married beyond borders for alliances. Other cave passageways led me to the czars of Russia, dynasties of China, and eventually, back across the saltwater. Here, I again rode in a covered wagon, strolled down unpaved streets, and experienced the chaotic growing pains of a baby country trying to form its own identity.

There was a genuine cord of truth running through all these stories, but every author added their own spin to the enthralling narratives. Since my late nights spent with Laura and Scarlett, advances in technology now allowed me to instantaneously unravel the authentic facts from the imaginative fabrications on my phone or laptop. These threads would lead me back to nonfiction collections to further educate myself on the historical details.

Technology had also changed how and where I could enjoy my favorite books. High-tech gadgets had been developed to store a small library of manuscripts on a single device, making the stacks portable and negating trips to brick-and-mortar shops. As I had previously found out, literary compositions were now available in a completely audible format as well. These had returned the joy of the written word back to those previously deprived audiences. I knew eventually I may need to utilize this, but preferred to flip my pages for as long as I could.

When my siblings and I were drawn in by the melodic beckoning of *A Song of Ice and Fire,* we had finally found a series captivating enough to once again entice our three unique tastes and diverse minds. Recommended first by my brother, the books soon had us all addicted, including my mother. Before Hollywood claimed the Iron Throne, the tales of Westeros had been perused and consumed by each of us. We no longer shared the same copy of a book, but we could still share the mythical quest within.

I learned to use a good page-turner to supplement my other new pastime, sitting in doctor's waiting rooms, as a distraction to the tedious schedule. The problem with this was that the nurse always appeared with her clipboard and called my name when I was in the middle of a riveting section. This recurring frustration occasionally made me consider reading one of their mind-numbing, year-old magazines instead, but I quickly banished that thought. My brain was damaging itself enough as is. I needed to try to strengthen it, not add to the injury.

When MS drove my other pastimes away, I barely noticed as my mind and attention were focused on my written getaways and were wandering to places my tired, uncooperative legs couldn't carry me. Books were taking me to the lands I had dreamt of one day seeing and leaving my footprints on before MS rendered my body almost incapable of travel. I would never be able to physically visit, much less climb, the three hundred and sixty-five steps of El Castillo, but I could easily reach it by climbing into the history of Chichén Itzá and the mystery surrounding the Mayans.

My love and draw to written words and the emotions and images they could invoke also inspired me to pursue a new pastime—writing. Books had taken me on so many fantastical journeys that I wanted to learn to paint the pictures and form the expeditions. One day, I would like to write something that makes younger generations want to stay up past their bedtimes, reading with a flashlight under their covers.

All those years ago in a little house on the Kansas prairie, when my mother began reading my sister and me *Little House on the Prairie*, she knew she was starting us on a trail to endless explorations, adventures, and discoveries. Our love for reading grew from that nighttime story time. Regardless of how muddled or messy my life had been since then, reading was always playing a central role in helping me grow, succeed, and overcome adversities. My MS may have restricted my movements, but I knew that by opening a front cover, I could unlock a portal into any location or time and the only restriction was the strength of my imagination.

My momma taught me that.

Acknowledgments

I would like to start by thanking the Swedish MS Center and its benefactors, the Swedish Medical Center Foundation, for helping this book come to fruition. Without their support, my stories and truths would still be rolling around inside my head. I would like to thank my emboldening writing teachers, Richard and Evelyn Arvey, who taught me to unscramble my thoughts and words and present them in meaningful, expressive stories. You have patiently handled my overanxious, slightly obsessive fussing and editing with grace and humor… always humor.

My five supportive writing classmates—Laura, Al, Carolyn, Lucinda, and John—who have graciously accepted my occasional ramblings and tendency for extensive proofreading. Your encouragement has helped me grow as a writer, and your friendships have fortified me as a person.

And to my three biggest cheerleaders and supporters: you are the force that drives me to keep going and finish the next chapter:

Bill Martin, a loving father figure, who is always eager to be a sounding board for my latest literary inspiration and who I have come to rely on for his proofreading, editing, and suggestions to facilitate my writing.

My beloved mother, Marilyn Martin, who was with me when I thought I had no one, a backer when others simply backed away, and a voice that will forever be encouraging me from the best seat in the house.

And my adoring—and adored—husband, Arman, who has been through substantially more of the "in sickness" part, yet has never once wavered as my rock. Always the calming sound of reason in my storm and the light in my darkest hour.

Al Tietjen

About the Author

Al is a (nearly) lifelong writer. He has used this affliction to amuse and impress others throughout different phases of his life. He is an inveterate punster who has relied on both his silly and serious sides to support himself. A few of his attempts at life-fulfilling strategies have been self-publishing humorist and graphic designer *extraordinaire*.

He claims he was the sillier half of the dynamic Seattle duo known as Fusion Studios in the 1980s, when he pawned his life for the chance to sell "bad jokes on postcards" throughout the Pacific Northwest. Later, he turned his serious side to designing and scripting unforgettable promotional materials for discerning small business owners.

When that streak ended, he found a new mission: teaching and helping children compose and breathe life into their own stories. He continues that passion today in his retirement years by volunteering at local child-learning centers.

He has authored and self-published three books: the pun-derful *Groan in Washington,* co-creation and illustration by Elizabeth Bryant; a reflective memoir, *Restoration*; and an 1890s era photo essay *His World Through a Pinhole* (all still available on Amazon!).

But wait... there's more. He whiles away some of his time these days composing a definitive narrative of his life, snippets of which appear in this compendium. The complete story might be available after he dies.

Remembering Dad

I piloted my new trike with the rocket theme (complete with battery-powered afterburner) on a lifetime of interstellar trips around the block in the five short months since Christmas. Then I crashed it accidentally one morning when I launched it unceremoniously off the back porch in anticipation of the latest exploratory journey. Mission aborted; broken spokes on the rear wheel with no replacement parts at the store proved fatal. Dad tried to fix it with the limited tools at his disposal, but it happened during spring baseball season, and took a weak second place to coaching my older brother's team. He never got back to it; he died that summer.

Trying to remember him now, I don't have much to go on. I don't really remember him much from our six years together, though I still feel his presence everywhere.

I know him largely through scenes from the poorly edited film replaying in my head.

He'd usually be off to work already when I awoke. I know where he went, driving off in that shiny new '59 Ford Fairlane, two-tone (white over cream), because I visited him there, once.

It was a late Saturday morning. We pulled into the gravel parking lot on the side of the building, a humble monument on the corner of a busy thoroughfare near my grade school. The building had classic Art Deco lines, complete with a false tower and a big clock. I can still summon a vivid picture of its other features: tall, two-story windows all around; yellowish-green stucco; a grand, double front door opening onto a modest brown-tile hallway floor. Dad's office was at the end, on the right.

His pretty, younger secretary was typing at her desk as we entered. She looked just like Della Street on Perry Mason. No, she was Della. All attorneys in the 1950s had attractive secretaries. I shrunk sheepishly in her presence, and looked away from her when she looked up at us—my mother, my just-older sister, and my way-younger sister, still a babe-in-arms.

"Al is expecting you. Let me show you into the lounge where you can wait for him. Would anyone like something to drink? Soda? Coffee? Water?" We sat on a green plastic-leather couch, the kind with large swooping chrome end rails, and waited for him. Della followed us in short order and chirped, "The pop machine is just around the corner. You don't need any money. It's set-up to work without. Just pull out the bottle you want. Al will be right in."

When he came in, the long sleeves of his crisp, white shirt were rolled up to mid-forearm. His tie was loosened slightly, the unbuttoned neck of the collar declaring that the cooler summer morning was over. A big smile soared above his 6'1" stature. I don't know why we visited him that day, but I was in awe before we went and after we left. That's one of the few scenes I can replay anytime from the archive tracks in my head, but other snippets with Dad are equally vivid. Like the summertime office picnic at the boss's fancy retreat at the big lake in the mountains.

It was a blue-sky sunny Saturday morning. Dad's co-worker's small family of two kids, and three of my family piled into their fake wood panel station-wagon at curbside in front of our house. Mom and Dad followed behind us in the *Fairlane* with my two older brothers. Somehow after a nearly two-hour drive, we arrived together. The "cabin" was more of a "palace," but it had the requisite log construction and knotty-pine paneling that meant its heart was in the right place.

"Hello, hello, welcome everyone!" the hostess greeted us brightly as she threw open the door. "Kids, grab your swimsuits and towels, change in the downstairs bathroom. The rest of you, meet us out back and grab a beer from the cooler. So glad you all could come."

Out back, Dad was already comfortably ensconced in the colorfully-webbed lawn chair, beer in one hand, cigarette in the other, sunglasses on his nose, sporting rarely-seen plaid Bermuda shorts when we found him on the deck. "If you don't swim, don't jump off the dock," we were admonished happily by God's female voice. "Go down to the beach below and grab an innertube." We did as told; this was a heaven-sent day and we weren't about to abuse it.

In a little while, Dad came down to the dock to check on us.

"How's it goin', Junior?" he happily inquired. I had rarely seen him so comfortable.

"I wanna' jump off the dock like the big kids," was my imploring, not-much-hope-of-that-happening request.

"Hmm...that's a problem. Let's see...I've got it. How

about the two of us go down closer to the shore where it's shallower and jump in together?"

"Really? Can we? Oh-boy!"

When we were in place, he grabbed me up in his huge, hairy arms, "Hold your nose when we jump. Ready? One-two-*three*!"

I'm pretty sure he hit bottom easily, but I clutched him tightly and never let go. We both went under for a few brief seconds, long enough to come up both sputtering:

"Let's do it again!" was my rapture-filled response. How could he refuse?

"Okay, once more, but then you grab an innertube and paddle around close to shore here," he gently commanded, still clutching me tightly.

That's a moment in time I won't forget. It meant as much to me that day as the endless hotdogs and all the root beer you could drink. I remember other scenes from our life, but few as vividly as that day he co-starred in *my* movie. In a lot of them, he was the leading actor, and I only had a supporting role, but they were important for my nascent career.

I remember him, wistfully now, when he took off to "go fishin'" with my two older brothers and old Mr. Shaw. I was usually waiting for him when he got home because he always brought back something.

"How'd you do? How'd you do?" I'd shout as I ran up to the car, anticipating a haul.

"We caught our legal limit early," was what I wanted to hear.

The green cooler was ceremoniously dumped on the front yard grass, and out flowed ice chips and water with mess of trout. The smell of fresh fish on the lawn glittering in the noon-day sun stays with me even now.

"Look! That one's still wiggling. He's alive!" I'd exclaim.

It wasn't always so good.

"Bad luck today. Only bites and not enough of those to stick around all day," was the remorseful news. I took it in stride because I knew I always caught *something*. A left-over glazed donut or potato chips, maybe a bottle of pop or a funny postcard from the 'lodge' at Banks:

"They grow 'em big out here" was the teaser inscription above the oversize trout on the flatbed trailer.

On the back,

"The one that got away."

It never occurred to me to ponder, "If it got away, what was it doing on the truck? They must have used good worms."

"Nightcrawlers" was actually the correct vernacular. They were "goin' fishin'" tomorrow because Dad was watering the lawn in the dark at 10 o'clock. Flooding the lawn would draw the nightcrawlers out of the ground, gasping for air. I was there, and sometimes dad would hand me the flashlight and let me help catch 'em.

"When they stretch out of their holes real long, grab 'em quick," he'd instruct. "But you gotta' be quick because they leave just enough in their hole, so they can get back real fast if they need to."

I approached stealthily with the big ol' flashlight. After a few zipped away, Dad would provide more critical information.

"If you see them with the flashlight, turn away real quick. They're light-sensitive. Always walk slow and careful, too. They can feel you coming. When you're real sure which end is nearest the hole, grab there. Be quick, they're fast and most times you only get about an inch to hold."

I tried again and it took me a few attempts to guess which end was which. "Darn, that was a real monster." Finally I got the hang of it with a good grip on one. I called out loud in supplication, "Don't you dare slip away. Don't make me break you in half. Let go! Let go, darn it. That's it. Nice and easy. Gotcha'!"

"Sshhh. they can hear you. You'll scare the others away," was my father's imploring advice, still clear in my memory.

Remembering back now, that had to be the perfect activity for any boy who loved his father. Who could resist mud, worm slime, the thrill of the chase, and "helping out Dad, 'cause he's "goin' fishin'." I hold onto that moment. I knew I was still a long way from going fishing with him, but I wanted to be there. Out fishin' with Dad. Letting the big one get away. Catching a soda pop at the Banks Lodge while he filled up the gas in the Ford.

I never got that chance, but I can replay other scenes from our shortened time together.

It's Saturday morning at home. The bright sun streams in through the clerestory windows above the fireplace in the living room. Dad is occupying his beloved recliner chair, laid-back and nestled in like he owned it. The smoke from his pipe curls up from his face then spreads out above him. Sunbeams pierce this lightly fogged corner of the room in multiple places, dancing with each subsequent puff before dispersing out of reach.

I'm watching him settle in from the adjoining dining room while I gallop across the landscape on my favorite hobby-steed. He looks like he's "headin' for a nap, podner" and then it crosses my mind that he's missing something. Me.

I dismount quickly and saunter across the room. The attempted leap into his lap is temporarily aborted by a "whoah, what's up, Cowboy?" but I'm in a not-to-be-denied mood.

"Can I take a nap with you?" is my honest and thin-ly-veiled request to satisfy a deeper need.

"Sure, come on up," he agrees without hesitation.

When I wrinkle my nose at the too-fragrant smoke cloud, he responds without words by putting down his pipe on the ashtray in the bookshelf beside us. His left arm is cradling me, keeping me from sliding out under the open arm of the chair. He is soft and warm, and the dad fragrance he exudes from his undershirt blends softly with today's tobacco choice. Together, we have a moment. I don't know "how" or "why" it ended, but I know all about the "when."

It never did.

Help

All kinds of questions arise when you receive a diagnosis of multiple sclerosis. Most of the answers medical professionals give you at the time just create more questions. The one question they do have an answer to, and the one that is the most certain, is "Will I need help?" But they're MDs and not mystics, so they can't say anything more definite than "Yes." As with all other aspects of the condition, "yes" is equivocal. So is "help." More than that they can't say that one person's help is another person's hindrance. Uncertainty is the name of the game. So are the pained, puzzled looks people give you when they learn of your affliction. That look is the physical manifestation of what you feel inside. They just don't know what to say, and neither do you. You can only help them ponder the uncertainty.

It's hard to ponder a future where all the expected outcomes are uncertain and unpleasant. Nobody wants to go there, least of all you. So everyone important you ask puts on their best brave face, intones something about the best possible narrative to live with, and you try to get on with your life.

As you confront the scourges MS brings, your own response (normal or otherwise) will be the only one that really matters.

Mine is still "pride goeth before the fall."

The first time I breeched the "normal response" range was also the first significant time when observers tried to "help" me avert the fall but injured my pride. I was at my then fifth grade son's end-of-year camp week. The chaperones and kids were taking a short trek through the woods to the talking circle. The afternoon sun was waning and the filtered light in the forest was beginning to fade. The path was uneven and hard for me to judge in the dimming light. I stumbled visibly more than once; my cane couldn't help. Most of the parents knew something of my MS-induced condition (it's hard to hide when you walk with a cane), but scarce acknowledged what was obvious, as I preferred. All at once, it seemed, everyone was watching and uncomfortably aware.

As I slowed down, the kids brushed by initially, until one of their mothers leapt to my assistance.

"Let me help you," was the supplication proffered.

"Thank you. I thought this would be easier," was my shaky reply as I stepped off the uneven path to let others pass by.

Arriving at the circle a bit tardy but now arm in arm with one of the mothers, all eyes burned into me with that pained and puzzled look. The game was up. I had nothing to fall back on. For the rest of the week, I was the cripple who shouldn't be doing much.

"Will you be all right with this activity?" was the qualifying query du jure put to me by all instructors, in increasingly uncomfortable ways, before all events. I had become a question; I was someone who needed "help."

Help was something other people needed. "I'm fine"

worked really well until other people began to notice and started to "help" me, asking directly or not. There goes my independent spirit—a lifetime to cultivate, a week to lose.

The wounds were largely self-inflicted, and I got over that incident, but the collateral damage was done and would continue. In the remainder of the school year, after word had spread, I was going to face a different kind of "help" from well-meaning sources. Sometimes, it wasn't as helpful as well-meant. It could easily push a hot button on my pet-peeve o'meter.

I began to particularly dread unsolicited advice.

"Have you tried taking mass quantities of Vitamin D?" was one of the parents hallway query. "I've got fibromyalgia. I hurt all the time. Sometimes I can barely crawl out of bed. It's a neurologic disorder that's similar to MS. My Naturopath recommended taking an infusion of 20-30,000 iu's once a week. I feel great now. It gave me back my life. You should try it."

"Thank you, I'll ask my neurologist," was my demurring response.

His reply was "there have been studies about mass vitamin injections to treat MS, but nothing at all indicative that anything beyond a normal dose works. I wouldn't go there without good data. Might do more harm than good, and not likely to do as much good as you imagine it does. Stay away from miracle cures is my best advice."

So now I had two new problems, maybe three: with "helpful" advice. First, she was a valuable volunteer in my weekly noontime writing club initiative at school. Second, rejecting her in a way that came off as "a personal slam" was bound to have repercussions. Third, I liked her, though we were not close friends and probably never would be. We were different people and now, it was confirmed, with known different philosophies.

In a way, she was initially helpful offering her medical "advice." It was an opportunity to confirm to myself the people I sought out for advice were there for a reason. The credentials of my sources, real and imagined, are everything to me when I have to sort out irresolute questions. I'm not a rudderless vessel. I steer the path presented, full consequences ahead. I sail the outcome seas into what will become my future—successful and otherwise.

So I took the course of least resistance.

"My doctor doesn't recommend this for me. I'm glad that it works for you." End of conversation.

Her helpful advice would go nowhere, but her unsolicited volunteer "help" was ultimately responsible for who I am today. Her assistance with my writing group would make the endeavor successful and led to a life-changing fruitful encounter at the end of the second year as "captain" of the writing club.

The "helpful" shoe dropped when another parent, mother of one of my students, grabbed my arm while I pondered the dessert table at the end-of-year class picnic. She offered a different kind of "help" in the form of a thank you, a compliment and open-ended advice rolled into one conversation that I could act upon. It turned out to be a marker for the end of one era of my life, and the beginning of the next.

"Thank you *so much* for what you did for my daughter with your writing club," the conversation string began. "She has always struggled with schoolwork, but being in your club and writing gave her an identity and has changed her attitude.

She does her homework without my begging now, is happy to go to school every day. She has learning disabilities, but I'm seeing scholastic improvement across subjects. Whatever you're doing, it's working. Have you ever given any thought to becoming a real teacher?"

"Thank you! No, I never have. I like doing this, though. Maybe I should."

After she wandered off, I called up her daughter on the "remember-me-forever-line" phone. Her daughter was a reliable "regular," choosing to voluntarily give up one noon recess once a week and spend the time writing with me. Of all the students in our club, she was the happiest, the most verbal (usually excessively so), and the most brightly enthusiastic about assigning herself things to write about. I liked her spirit.

Three months later, at age fifty-five, I followed her in that same spirit back to college.

Over the summer, I had gone through the seven stages of grief regarding my existing career choice as a graphic designer, and was high on hope for the future again. The college intake counselor threw all her best questions at me. What do you want to be? Where do you see yourself in five years? Will your MS hold you back from performing? Apparently, I hit enough of the pitches out of the ballpark to earn an appointment ticket to grad school in teaching that afternoon. Oh, the fun was just beginning.

When the smoke of my elation cleared, I found myself walking in late on a classroom full of mostly twenty-some-things at "night-school." The only seat left was at the front of the room. I could feel eyes burning not only on my advanced age, but on my cane. It was the last time they did. In the next one-and-a-half years, I don't recall any of them feeling the need to "help" me because I had MS.

The profs were equally enthusiastic about my chances for success, and they all knew I had MS. One of them volunteered to be my "mentor" during an emotionally difficult classroom observation period. I had chosen a struggling inner-city school with at-risk kids, and was disturbed by some of the teacher-student interactions I had observed. I relayed to him that watching the teacher interact was like watching a train wreck in motion. I tried to describe the intellectual and emotional carnage I was witnessing.

"We know about that school. We don't send students to observe there anymore. We want you to have a better view of good teaching," was his warning.

"I chose for myself. If I don't see things at their worst, how will I recognize the best in my own teaching?" was my rational for being there.

"Okay, but just know what you're looking at," he proffered reluctantly. Then almost immediately, "I'd like to be a close adviser to you. I can help you make sense of what you are seeing."

He stayed at my side through the "observation" and he didn't discourage me when I told him I wanted to stay overtime to conduct a special writing class for the most needy there. Unfortunately, he couldn't be with me during the "student candidate teaching" in the next quarter when the shit hit the fan.

My repeated attempts to contact him were met with silence, so I did some sleuthing. I learned the university was under certification review. Someone outside the school faculty needed to be put in charge of judging the "teaching certificate" portion of their education program "to ensure fairness." No regular faculty was allowed to have contact.

Fairness was absent when the woman in charge learned I had tripped over a pile of shoes and fell in the third week. Word traveled back to her through the site monitor and now she knew I had MS and was fully determined to use it against me. I was asked to withdraw because I was a "safety liability." When I refused to exit for medical reasons, she piled on through the site monitor. Together, they offered lip service only to the concept of "help" they professed repeatedly in the reviews. I never got any form of "help," except that their prejudice "helped" them decide I wasn't qualified on any level. They pre-judged my chances for success as near zero, and made it happen as they built a case around the MS symptoms that surfaced during the next seven weeks.

Now, instead of the "constructive observations" promised, I was routinely being checked off in the "not demonstrating competence" boxes on the report form. The classroom instructor who knew me best was outraged.

"I've never seen anything like this in twenty-five years. You're not the best teacher candidate I've watched, but you're far from the worst," was his honest assessment. He did what he could to help keep me in the game, but he knew the cards were marked. The heavy, unfamiliar workload and susceptibility to relapse due to stress were the bad cards that were dealt to me.

The knock-out blow of failing sent me reeling for a couple of years. I woke up in one of my therapy sessions with a counselor who decidedly changed my downward cycling path with a single "helpful" suggestion: "Find something that makes you happy and embrace it."

I immediately took a pleasure tour of the local antique store after my session. An early twentieth-century penny gumball machine helped me smile briefly, but I demurred at the price.

I was still so new to the critical question that I needed to ask, "What price happiness?"

On the way home that day, I took a precipitous turn trying to avoid street work ahead of me. Around the first corner, someone had decorated a large section of the detour street with multi-colored large circles. It was so *happy*. Too happy to pass over without reflective pause.

The Gumball Machine! I did a 180 back to the junk store and plunked down $75 asking price without reservation.

"You're on your way back!" my therapist exclaimed the following week. "Don't ever forget why."

In the years to come (and not long after), I found a way to return to what I know is the best possible end-of-life endeavor for me. I haven't forgotten the things that "helped" me when people and incidents didn't.

I started the current path I am walking with a purpose: to help children learn how to write. Along the way, I learned that when I'm with them, I'm in third, fourth or fifth grade all over again. Those were my best years then, and they still are in their presence. I can forget I have MS for as long as I'm in that zone.

Sometime, a new child is initially curious about why I "walk funny," but soon enough they will want to grab my cane and my hat and dance around the room (or at least they did in pre-pandemic times).

They ask me how old I am—I usually say twelve—and they know it's not true, but will entertain the proposition long enough to write and share their best stories with me. They help me smile, I help them laugh. It's symbiotic happiness at its best.

As I learn what the terms "to help" and "to be helped" mean, I look ahead now, and take stock of the current ravages of MS not helping my body. I am not looking forward to *all* the help I will need in the future that waits for me. But I don't need to dwell on it. I know the future always arrives and will be here soon enough without trying to imagine how imperfect my condition will become.

I will find something important to do most days—and I'm sure to need somebody to help me. More importantly, I'm gonna look for somebody that needs my help, too.

What's in a Name?

The way your name was chosen for you is a major folkway of your family and community group. You usually don't get any say in the matter—until you come of age. In the case of my particular inheritance, when I noticed the name I was given just wasn't right, there was still time to do something about it.

I noticed early; to take action would require three more years of discomfort.

There was something wrong with "Alfred" in the second grade roll-calls. I couldn't say exactly, but something wasn't right. Too formal? Too old? Too…something; just not me. Maybe it was the intonation the teacher used when she getting ready to "call me out" for something.

"ALFRED!"

I was on the defensive already. All I could think of to say was "I didn't do it."

I'm acknowledging this in hindsight, but I knew it in the moment that didn't make the fallout any better. It was my father's name, and his father's, too. I didn't know either of them well enough to find out how they did or didn't like their name. In the second grade, I reflected that my recently deceased father had taken on the shortened "Al" successfully in his life. I couldn't recall anyone who knew him—his boss, his relatives, my mom—calling him anything else. Hmm… maybe there's hope for me. How do I get there?

I disliked the chosen, unsolicited family-generated nick-name: "Junior." That informal branding was diminishing, and somehow, disrespectful, even if used only inside my own sibling group. It reduced me to an "also ran" in theory and in fact. It was a moniker relegating me to the non-distinct fourth-of-five position. They didn't have to call me "Junior" often, they didn't need to—I was already beneath them. I was going nowhere fast. But when distant aunts and uncles brought it out, it burned.

Thank God "Junior" never made it to the playground, where everyone seemed to have a shortened "nickname" ver-sion of their given name. Most of the versions were descended from their given names of revered Saints or holy Apostles. They already had cache´. I knew I wasn't a direct descendant of one of the chosen founding Catholic fathers, but "Alfred?" Where does that come from? Where could I go with that?

My plight of being left until the last round standing when choosing sides for teams at recess was a given. My name was already waiting there. I took up the roll my then-known athletic abilities dictated without visible complaint while I wondered in my head if the two things went together. How much of my life was being pre-determined by my given name? I didn't have any inherent qualities that could overturn the verdict. The sentencing had already been delivered.

I served my time until the beginning of the fifth grade.

It was a seminal year in more ways than one. In preparation for changing my nom-de-guerre, a lot had happened in quick succession. By that time, I was acutely aware of how much was missing from my own life. The list kept growing larger with every social call to friends, family, and neighbors. Kids notice things.

I noticed most of their homes were nicer by some visible degree. I knew our "house" wasn't our "home" because my mother's words "If you break that, we'll have to pay the landlord to fix it" rung in my ears. I could put two and two together. I too easily felt the very real difference between living in house or living in a home.

Cognitive awareness began at the ever-widening crack in the concrete running vertically up the walkway through the front steps. I didn't see this in other people's homes. That ragged, dirt-filled gap grew larger in my mind as I tracked it through the worn, mismatched furniture; the frayed carpet seam running the length of the front room; the paint peeling on kitchen cabinets.

The benign squalor continued down the rickety steps to the unfinished basement (watch your head!) with the depression-era dugout root cellar. I had already begrudgingly adopted the go-to mantra of my mother's less-than-monetarily-blessed childhood. "We can't afford that" was applied to everything we didn't have or were unlikely to acquire. I understood why implicitly.

My father had been deceased for more than a year by the time third grade was a stage of my life. I deeply wished the situation would change. As a work in progress, my life didn't seem to be making much headway. But unbeknownst to me, my life began to change in the previous summer after my third-grade year ended.

In that summer of hope, our family took a languid vacation from Boise to Oregon in our increasingly fading old blue sedan. We looked in on any number of houses for sale that were all better than our house by measures that I could see and feel—yard, size, polish, street appeal. We had family discussions about the pros and cons of each one on the way to the next one or to a favorite friends' or relative's home that was also decidedly nicer by a factor than the rental dump we inhabited in Boise.

I got my hopes up for nothing that summer, it seemed. In the months afterward, in our now *very* dilapidated feeling house, I grew resigned to the current condition. What's an eight-year-old to do? When the search resumed in the following spring in Boise, my heart wasn't in it.

Until that fateful day in April when we all knew, in unison, this was the one. To say it was perfect was a gross understatement. It had the perfect yard, a perfect ceramic-tiled kitchen with a real dishwasher. It had a perfect, blue-tiled bathroom with a shower stall. It had a real upstairs—not just an attic—with real stairs. At the top was the most perfect feature of all, my own room. When do we move in, Mom?

In the new hood, life was immediately improved in ways beyond living quarters. Things began to open socially with a new set of acquaintances now living a short distance away. My new circle included Joe who lived a block away on the same street. We knew each other from four years in school together, but that was it. Now, close proximity set up a burgeoning relationship that was about to turn my world right-side up.

Joe was a triple sport star, and as such, also a charter member of the "in" crowd. Joe had a basketball court in his backyard driveway, which was also a whiffle-ball diamond and by extension, the neighborhood community center. Anytime there were at least two kids on court, there were bound to be six in a few minutes more. I now lived in the spontaneous activity zone inhabited by most of the rest of my grade school class. This was where it all happened. Joe was my new best friend, and I was his.

With my newfound social status, my ticket was punched in a number of ways I never dreamed possible. Suddenly at school, I went from being ignored at recess to being picked well before last when sides were chosen, though my athletic skills were roughly the same as before

The Big Move. Joe was willing to take a chance on me, so his friends acceded as well. I was only marginally better at sports, but for now, being Joe's friend was enough to raise my value.

Joe and I shared a lot of other things that we both needed. Like me, his siblings were also all older by a factor and we were both lacking for an age-adjacent brother relationship. Now we both had a confidant. As well, he could be the slightly older wisdom fount, and I could be his foil. We formed a union of shared needs. He got to teach me what he knew, and I was bent on showing my worth for the work it took to mentor me.

As my self-confidence grew, there didn't seem to be any downside to my life in that summer of changing social status, until the first day of fifth grade when I was reminded I didn't have a nickname like everyone else. My heart sank during the first roll call of the new school year when the unfamiliar teacher started reading the equally unfamiliar formal first names and asked out loud: "What would you prefer to be called?" Dave, Joe, Nick, Dan—everyone was pretty chummy this morning. It didn't look good for "Alfred" again, but I knew my last name was near the end of the list alphabetically, so I had time to think.

I don't remember everything for a fact as I write this, but I could swear the room went silent when I blurted out "Al." By recess time, it was a *fait accompli*. No longer would I cringe in silence when addressed. "I choose Al" also had a nice ring to it in the potential team line-up on the playground that day—and forever after.

I didn't let the new ego stand idle for very long. When Joe cajoled me into joining the football team that fall, my only real trepidation was knowing I would be one of the smallest players. Joe was already nearly a head above me. That, I couldn't change. I accepted that trait as one of the youngest kids in my grade, but I was now full speed ahead with the new me.

In the first practice, the coach watched me repeatedly break up plays by squirting untouched through the offensive line composed primarily of the larger players. He alertly recognized the game-winning potential with me on the defensive line near the center where he was trying me out. It paid off big for both of us. I broke up more than a few plays that year in Saturday morning games, and for the next three, in every game I played. Opposing teams quickly and wisely chose to run their plays to the side I wasn't on. I was a force to be reckoned with, as was the confidence-building effect on my nascent superego this induced.

Slaps on my back from teammates weren't my only reward. I had also found a kindly father figure in my coach who not only believed in me, but routinely praised me in team pep talks as an example to follow. During one game, my exploits were met by the placement of increasingly larger players on every new set of downs. Finally, they placed the largest guy they had opposite me, who simply sat on me to thwart my role. I limped off the field in full complaint mode to my coach. His smirking response was, "That just shows you how much they respect you, Al." My new name was serving me well.

Nothing was going to hold me back now. With my new persona established, I was able to overcome the social setback of the new "geeky" look made possible by becoming an eye-glasses wearer. I'll admit to this day that I looked like I just fell off the turnip truck. The expected ribbing from classmates set me back until I picked up the benefit.

I could see the blackboard clearly, now. Question prompts flew fast and furious in the days of the forty-five-student class-room. You had to bring your A-game; delays in responses signaled poor academic progress or attention behavior issues. I had them both in spades until I could see, read, and antic-ipate the response. Eyeglasses were a game changer in more ways than one.

Within a few months, I was positioned to take on the mantle of near-perfect student that my three older siblings held. "Another Tietjen in glasses" soon morphed into "Another smart Tietjen" because that's the bar I was expected to clear. Making a name change had nothing to do with the fact, and at the same time, everything to do with it.

I rode that long-delayed confidence into all things through the fall and winter of the fifth grade. There was little "Al" couldn't do that "Alfred" wouldn't. Being seen is the precursor to being acknowledged. Creating a name for myself was surely on the horizon.

Previously, my only recognizable talents were being "last man standing" after spelling bees, and a nascent ability as "likely to create something unusual" at the art table. I had to share both of those persona-defining inherent traits with a couple of the smarter girls and the more popular boys who already had more confidence than they needed. I was already known for something, but that quantification didn't separate me as much as put me on an equal footing with a limited number of banal known qualities.

I finally found my own place unexpectedly in English class that spring. The assignment was nondescript: write a two hundred and fifty-word story about something. I agonized over the subject for a week. The night before, I took a chance on nonsense…er…fiction. Somewhere in the composition creation, the storyline took a turn toward the dark side, but I kept it light. Amid the multiple bumps and bruises suffered by the protagonist, there was mirth.

I had found something else in this confidence-building year: I had found a funny voice. Satire was probably still a vestigial concept in my limited comedic brain, but as I wrote, I also found and recognized the effect of exaggeration to drive home an image. I finished writing the piece with some self-satisfaction, but the uncertainty of the effect on a staid, Catholic nun was still an unknown.

I was quaking inside when my turn to read aloud came up. There was a limited form of silent attention as I began to read, which was mysteriously replaced by random tittering laughter. As quickly, the delivery morphed into unbroken, full-class guffawing. I had a rapt audience.

"That was very funny," was the understated response from the teacher. I heard something else, though, when the class refused to settle down easily as I settled into my seat. What I heard was life-affirming. Al had arrived.

Irony in the Aphorism

There was irony in the aphorism *all things come to he who waits*.

Roberto learned patience early. "You should be patient" were his mother's now-hollow words. He had spent his life up to this point working under that principle. He bided his time in all things. Something would happen if he waited.

Nothing came. The aphorism was wrong.

Roberto was twenty-eight years old, and two weeks into Art Class by the time something came to him. That good-looking girl who always came in late, Sheila, had a nice smile. He vowed to find out what was behind the wrinkled reticence he detected in her laugh. He decided not to wait.

Maybe he overplayed his hand a bit. He had displayed depth and skill with his impressive knowledge of art during the discussion. As a late-twenty-something, he was worldly where the classroom of early-twenty-somethings was not. But he thought he came off brash and aloof. Still, he wondered, *Did I catch a smile back there? Is it time to act?* It seemed like a great opportunity. Lunchtime, hunger, cash to spare, time to kill—and no one to share it with. Roberto asked her out to lunch. She turned him down, but not coldly.

"Sorry, have to be somewhere. Maybe next week," and nothing more.

She got up and went away. He was sure he had hesitated too long without a rejoinder. Class was over for another week. He'd have to hang a lot on that "maybe."

Next week, he resolved.

In the third week, he held back a while, then made his move to her desk during individual work time. The gambit worked; they were almost old friends now. She shared her colored pens with him. They also shared small talk and a few laughs together while they worked side by side. Then, class was over again, and he mustered his courage.

"Sorry, not today, gotta go."

Not even a maybe this time, but the sharing went well today.

The fourth week was different. Sheila had come in early. Roberto had arrived late and sat behind her on purpose. He was sure he had come off a little over-eager during "show and tell" time. He hadn't heard wrongly the teacher's instructions to "have a good concept and one poster complete" by the next class. But he had misgauged the work ethic of his classmates, who were still noodling out a concept for the first poster. He had a full four-poster concept worked out to finish, and he was halfway through his second series already. It was hard not to feel everyone was stunned. It didn't make "work in class time" comfortable, so he avoided any extended conversion with anyone, including Sheila, before he issued his now-feeble plea.

"Okay," she said. "I'd like to go out today. Where do you want to go?"

Roberto's heart did a standing long jump.

Ironically, in a way he had waited, and something *did* come to him.

His humbled ego backtracked at full speed. *What do I say now?*

Wish fulfillment was a new and strange sensation.

These Are a Few of My Favorite Things

A list of my favorite things would be long and probably tedious without parameters, so here they are: things which I partake in from the comfort of my living room.

1. My easy-chair.

Mine is the second tired butt to call this unremarkable item a primary residence after 6 p.m. I use the term "unremarkable" not as a pejorative, but primarily because there are only a few praiseworthy things to say about this chair. The best thing I can say about the '90s-era black leather, non-porous repose facilitator is that it is easy to clean up the numerous liquid spills I subject it to. Still, for all the casual abuse, it doesn't smell funny (like me most days), reclines with little difficulty (also like me most days), and has been everything, including "easy", to me.

"Easy to me" can be illusory. A less clever man would have

thrown up his hands in despair and replaced it long ago, but I am not that person. The list of relaxation-delaying repairs is ongoing, like the unspecified terms of its service. "Oh boy! Something to fix!" is my mantra, so anything short of a cat-astrophic calamity will be abided as worthy to repair. In the remembered past, it refused to recline once. I turned it upside-down and found the mysteriously-bent offending part. I deftly applied a crowbar and a vice-grip pliers simultaneously to the wonky mechanism and straightened it unceremoniously, no cursing involved.

The Gods of Self-help thanked me in short order by giving me two sproinged springs to be dutifully re-attached. Currently, this benignly evil chair begs for a new primary seat cushion. I don't know why, but my aging hiny hurts even more if I have to sit there without moving for two hours because of one of my other favorite things:

2. The Cat.

Dogs let you know you are their favorite thing; cats make you prove you are theirs. Oh, they're built to tempt you—from the contented purr in the pre-warmed lap they seek, to the extra-soft fur they present for a mutual purring session.

But there's a catch. Don't get me wrong, I'm as susceptible as the next person to a sloppy wet tongue on the cheek or to a constantly wagging tail that is the evidence of unquestioning favor in dog-persons.

With most cats, however, you'll have to keep earning it. Not so with The Cat. She is the first cat I've known who acts more like a dog. She needs constant human companionship, from the alarm-clock-worthy time in early morning hours when she loudly and purposefully claws the side of the mattress, until the last easy-chair nap of the evening that is too precipitously interrupted by *her* standards.

Like a dog, she is disappointed if someone is not in the room with her at any time. If you leave the room or, God forbid, the house, and appear to be foresaking her, she follows you. She will go to the door with you to give you that "where are you going?" look, not to be outdone by that "where have you been all day?" hard-to-hide gleeful demeanor when you return. Just like a dog, you're forgiven your transgressions. If she could wag her tail, she would.

Instead, she might bring you a fraying pipe cleaner to play with (dog is to bone as cat is to toy). If you land in the easy chair, she will glare at you unnervingly, waiting patiently for you to "make a lap." That you might want to get up sometime in the next two hours isn't considered. If she had a question, it would be:

3. "But where is the blanket?" another of my favorite things I keep handy beside my favorite chair.

Old age requires an adherence to grandpa standards. Those rules include feeling colder than normal inside and out, whenever the air surrounding me isn't exactly balmy. I bought this blanket at Costco twenty-five years ago. I don't have to admit it's the first (and only) blanket I've ever bought, but I will.

I would have preferred a scratchy or otherwise woolly blend, but life is full of compromises when you need to live larger than your paycheck. The price-point purchase has proved up against drafts, offering luxurious enough accompaniment to many an afternoon nap on a soft couch, which

MS demands of me most days. Extra colorful it is not, unless you think shades of white, grey, and black are colors. The saving grace here is the red highlighting, carefully woven in blanket-wide by delicate machinery hands.

As a bonus, if you have a purring cat on your lap on a blanket, and your easy chair will still recline in its ripe old age, you've got a triumvirate that is only missing:

4. A fire crackling in the hearth.

If you are *not* starting to see a theme so far in "a few of my favorite things," hang in there. In the meantime, grab your own comfortable chair, make a lap for the cat (or leave room at your feet for the dog), put on a blanket, and…burn 'em if you've got 'em—chopped, dried wood that is. Life in your retirement years is about to get as good as this current moment can present.

Nothing completes a cold night in a not-yet warm house like a crackling fire. I'm a bit old-fashioned, so it has to be an open hearth for me (no modern insert stoves will do). Half of the pleasure here is visual. Add a few pine-y bows to the olfactory mix, and you've really got something. Ask any caveman, or modern equivalent.

I can easily return to simpler times while I stare into my reward for enduring whatever trauma the day provided and it sends back the right message: This is going to be a peaceful, reflective interlude.

I don't get enough solitude without anxiety these days. At moments when I do, I feel like I'm in a really good commercial where nobody is going to ask me to buy anything, or in which I'm not going to wish I had something I don't really need. I've already got it all, including feeling guilty for enjoying this respite, notwithstanding knowing others are not as blessed. Life is good for *me* in this moment. *I've* arrived. The only thing missing is someone to bring me (around here, we call this particular smug-inducing fealty "cat immunity").

5. A mug of steaming cocoa.

It's not enough that my body is all warm, my brain is having warming thoughts too—something is still missing inside. The brain is telling the body (or is it the other way?) that warm, liquid chocolate is a good thing. I've been here before, that's why I always try to come prepared. Fine-grained cocoa powder (any brand but Hershey's), a beaker of micro-waved soy beverage mixed half and half with water, and one lump of sugar (unless someone already ate all the tiny marshmallows) are all I need to complete the physical and begin the metaphysical in this heightened sensual pleasure.

There's only one thing in the room left to praise:

6. The wife person.

Also known as my life partner, she has never really been missing in the last forty or so years from any scene in the multi-act play we are staging. In my rare soliloquies, she is still there, just offstage to feed me lines or offer a "bravo" when the inevitable applause comes. She may utter "what were you thinking?" equally in sincerity when I finish the scene, but I digress. This is supposed to be a "heightened-awareness of the senses" essay, so let's get back to it.

She's as lovely as the day I met her, maybe more so because I see beyond the trappings of her youthful mortal beauty. The heart sees what it needs to see, but the brain, if it gets the chance, will discover the soul of real beauty resides more than just momentarily skin deep. I know she views me the same way.

She's never smelled liked French perfume, nor has anything falsely fragrant ever been added to her laundry detergent. Both of them would have her breaking out in an abhorrent rash, physically and otherwise. So I guess it's down to "organic" as far as smell goes.

I rarely hear birds tweeting when she enters the room these days, but it wasn't always so. Her voice now brings the comfort of quality companionship daily. It is a mature and lovely tone on most occasions. She does not mince her words, not because she doesn't know how, but because I often need to hear it like it is.

If she were a caramel, that is how she would taste. But she is not—she is an apple, sweet and crisp as the day she was picked. Sometimes she is a cool, juicy peach on a warm sunny day. She can't always avoid it, but some days she is a sour pickle. I love the full range of smells and tastes her personality represents.

What does she feel like? This is a PG-rated essay, so I can only say she feels like all the best hugs small children ever gave to their parents. Sorry kitty, you can't begin to come close to what she feels like lying beside me in the dead of night. When I roll over in the morning and she grabs my hand, I instinctively return the warmth of the gesture. The purr is consensual.

That's the basic sensory overload I am subjected to while I try to shut out the sensory underload that is my day.

But wait…there's more.

Contrary to the opening statement, it's about to get

tedious. No overblown list of sensory experiences from my front room perch of choice would be complete without:

7. That big picture window to my right.

No impressionist painter worth the weight of art materials could fully capture the ever-changing masterpiece that is the scene outside, just beyond my backyard. I pull the curtain back on what might be the best scene in the city, every day. From here, I can watch all the weather patterns develop in real time. I can feel the sunny and overcast days. I am in here, and out there, simultaneously.

At the furthest visible edge, there are the Olympic Mountains, a backdrop thirty-five million years in the making, perfectly placed for my viewing pleasure. Add an occasional spectacular sunset or accept the usually ordinary grey day, and you always have something worth relishing. I won't even get into the endlessly exhilarating cloud patterns—that would be overkill, or worse.

When we moved in, we often joked about overstaying our timeshare privileges. It's not a subject of concern anymore. Three generations of my wife's family died in this house for the rights to this scenery. What we didn't inherit outright was paid for with our own life sacrifices.

Still, it goes blankly dark once every day, a bit like my mind. That's when I turn to the medium of choice:

8. The immortal TV portal.

Thoughtfully located beyond the outer edges of the common passage through the room, it waits for me to wear myself out every day, on sentinel duty a few feet from where I will collapse.

If (or when) I can stay awake, it may relinquish duty to a book or magazine, neither of which anyone sharing a home with someone in possession of a BA in English Lit will lack.

When the signal received must also be obeyed, it will take me to all the places I need to go for an hour or two, maybe three. News of the day is usually already known at this time, having been over-augmented by the ubiquitous hand-held communication device (now, where did I leave my phone?). If the hour is right, I may also replay in my dreams what happened today on the Snooze Hour go-to channel on public television.

What is left that I still go to this window on the world for is enhanced imagination, science of many forms, history, old Hollywood, the TV world of my youth (ah, youth), and whatever else offered that will keep me awake until actual bedtime (ah, old age).

Shakespeare started it when he penned "the world is my oyster." I can only humbly offer this carefully slurped down observation in paraphrase form: "the world is my Barcalounger."

* For those who live without cats, first

1. Get one—

2. Because a cat on your lap is the best excuse for asking anyone (anywhere in the house) to bring to you anything reasonable you desire. The rule is "A cat on your lap must not be disturbed." Violation of this unwritten law will induce disfavor in the eyes (literally) of the cat. And:

3. You will have to work extra hard to get The Cat back in your lap. They don't forget slights easily. If you had a cat, you'd know.

New Beginning

Chicago, early May, 1903

Joe walked to the bicycle assembly shop on South Clinton Street slower than usual. The news that he would give to the workmen today would not be pleasant. He would not deliver it gladly, the hollow in his stomach that rose before the sun that morning told him. His sleep had been restless and he had awoken more than once during the night. He couldn't resolve the paths his brain was plotting this morning. It had taken him ten years to earn the money he and his two brothers used to buy into this business. In less than nine months, that money was all but gone. He should be assembling high-end bicycles today, not wondering how to pay the rent.

Yesterday, Joe thought the business had money and a good plan. Today they had neither. The bicycle they were producing was clearly one-of-a-kind: a three-speed changeable gear bike that was supposed to change the bicycle world. Its inventor, Peter O'Leary, had touted it as an investment path to "one day soon" making an automobile, and make them all millionaires.

He had convinced his family—and many in town—to become his partners; today they had only become partners in debt. The bile in Joe's stomach was palpable.

Joe's mind wandered back in time to the day he and his family arrived in America from Switzerland—dirt poor and dream rich. They were ready for anything when they learned about homesteading. Free land "out west" came with a seeming endless supply of "money-on-the-hoof" in the form of very large trees. It was dusk-to-dawn back-bending work clearing those massive trees, but they accepted it happily and with Swiss vigor.

The trees came down too quickly. The custom sawmill they built and operated had slowed cutting as the supply waned. They were one of many small mills for whom this was all too apparent. Regretfully, they had to sell out to a larger mill operation and dismantle their own. The money they put in their pockets tickled their dreams in the way that only money could tease.

Peter O'Leary tweaked their interest the day he peddled up the rut-filled road to their farm on a strange-looking bike. He looked oddly wrong perched on that delicate machine—a burly man in a bowler hat—but he was amiable enough. He had heard through the grapevine they were looking for an investment opportunity. "This was it!" he exclaimed, holding the bicycle at arm's length away from his portly frame. "Nobody else had variable speeds yet; this is the first!" was his overly enthusiastic sales pitch.

Joe and his family listened to Peter with rapt attention, though they knew little of the economics surrounding this potential adventure. News traveled slowly in rural America, and they were unaware that investing in *any* bicycle manufacturing operation was risky. Nobody wanted bikes in 1902—they wanted automobiles. Had they known, they would have held onto their largesse a bit longer.

Peter was a fast talker. They initially mistrusted his enthusiasm, but the more they listened, the more it intrigued them. It sounded simple—raise a pile of money, set up an assembly plant in Chicago, ship in parts from both coasts, ship out bicycles, make lots of money, repeat.

In reality, it was not that easy. They were poor country folk without deep business smarts: Swiss craftsmen and farmers by heritage, not financiers or admen. Joe's gut had warned him the signs they were reading all too good to be true. Intuition should have saved them, but greed took the upper hand—and betrayed them.

When truth caught up with intuition in Chicago, fascination with bicycles had already turned to automobiles. Here, it was common knowledge that the explosive bicycle business of the '90s was oversupplied with cheap products, but they were too far into it to stop. Not only could they not sell enough bicycles yesterday but they also couldn't make them today. They were a long way from making automobiles. Curse you, O'Leary!

There was only one thing to do. Joe couldn't hold the workmen if he couldn't pay them. The uncertainty surrounding their enterprise killed the enthusiasm he once held. It was apparent now that something was wrong when O'Leary stopped sending the drive train gears from San Francisco. Joe was looking for a way to keep his end of the bargain, but could not build enough bicycles to fill the few standing orders they had. His brother John could not raise any more capital from inside their small circle of friends, relatives, and hometown residents. Today, they faced eviction. O'Leary had stopped communicating two weeks ago, but the list of things that bothered him was already long.

In order to assemble a bicycle, he needed parts from both coasts. If he ordered parts for fifty bicycles today, it would be a month or more before they all arrived at the shop. O'Leary was not prompt about paying the bills or supplying parts. If he could get his hands on the cash in Chicago, he could pay the bills, order the parts he needed, keep the wheels in motion. Complicating the assembly, when the parts from third-party suppliers arrived, often they were poorly made and unfit to use. This was supposed to be a high-end bicycle, not a department store product. He was stressed to breaking, wondering how long he could hold out.

Yesterday broke his back. At noon, he received a telegram from O'Leary saying there would be no more payments to suppliers until July. Today was May 15. Without payments, there would be no more parts arriving until August, no more bicycles completed until September. If he could not fill orders, he could not pay the workmen. He was being strangled!

At 2 p.m., he got a phone call from the landlord, the rent had not been paid for three months and he was threatening to lock the doors if the account was not brought current immediately. Damn O'Leary! He thought there was enough cash on hand to buy three months' rent, but he could not pay the workmen if he turned this over to the landlord. Without parts, both these options were gone—and what about the next three months? The chance to sell bicycles all summer was a fast-fading dream. He left early; he needed time to think.

When he arrived at the front door this morning, the space between a rock and a hard place had disappeared. The heavy chains over the front door meant the decision had already been made. He read the yellow notice posted on the door and his bile rose again. Hard as it was to see this, it was even harder to accept. It was over.

It took him a few moments to collect his thoughts; they converged in a place he was not used to going. Remorse, resentment, anger, revenge—he had had enough! There were eight bikes inside that they had finished yesterday. They were worth about $250 to a re-seller and were scheduled for delivery to a North Chicago bike shop today. *Was their business really bankrupt?* If so, the cash from that sale would buy him and his brother, Frank, three months in Chicago. *Was this still HIS company, weren't these still HIS bikes?* These were foul thoughts; stealing went against his core. But this was not stealing, just reclaiming personal property.

His stomach turned a few more times while he wrapped his head around a plan. He remembered that the latch on the loading dock door was sticky and did not always hold if it was not wiggled just right when closed. He had run out yesterday to make a plea to the landlord and left closing up to Frank. He couldn't find the landlord, and he had not returned to the shop, but spent the afternoon walking home, alone, thinking about what he might have to do tomorrow.

He walked around the back of the shop, checking for witnesses while he skulked. It was early yet, 6 a.m.; the morning light was still dim and few were up. At the door now, he looked left and right, and then left again. Assured that he was alone, he grabbed the handle of the heavy overhead door and yanked. It was not latched at all. Then another thought crossed his mind—he could get the bikes out of the shop, but how would he move eight bicycles to his flat without a wagon?

He didn't have an easy answer. While he slowly lowered the door, he heard a rustling sound come from behind the crates piled up near the shop foreman's office.

It was dark inside, what little light that came through the large windows at the front did not reach the back of the shop to reveal the source. He switched on a small light that hovered over a bearing press. Out of the corner of his eye, he caught a furtive shadow darting around the corner of the foreman's office.

"Who's there?" he shouted.

"Joe! It's me, Frank."

"Frank, what are you doing here?"

"Uh…collecting some personal things. How about you?"

"Stealing bicycles. Damn, this is a mess, Frank. What are we gonna do?"

"Not much we can do, Joe. You saw the notice. I guess O'Leary made that choice for us already. I checked the bank account yesterday after you left. Empty. Zero. There was a transfer out yesterday around 2:45 p.m. He didn't leave us a dollar. I tried to find you, but couldn't."

"Frank, stealing is all wrong," said Joe, "but what O'Leary did wasn't right either. Not a matter of two wrongs turning out right, just trying to keep it from getting worse for us while we figure out how to deal with it. These bikes were paid for when O'Leary took that money yesterday. No sense letting good go to bad. I figure we're just holding onto them for interest on the $10,000 we used to buy into this mess."

"Never see that again in this life," Frank said. "Too bad. This all looked good in December, now it's upside down. How we gonna get these out of the shop, Joe?"

"Don't know…let me think," offered Joe. "Can't roll more

than four at a time, and we don't have time to get them all out that way. Wait…milkman comes by at 6 a.m. with an empty wagon. Figure he'd like to make a buck on his way back to the dairy, Frank? If we can get these crated up, he could drop them off at your place."

They worked quickly. Crates were already prepared; the bikes were ready to go, just shove them inside, nail some tops on and push them out to the loading dock. Joe walked out onto the loading dock to listen for the milk wagon. The Chicago air was stagnant; it was unusually hot for May, but it had rained last night for the first time in a month. The foulness of the day rose up out of the cobblestones with the steam. Within a few minutes, he heard the familiar clop, clip, clop, clop of the milk wagon horse on the street. Joe hauled the heavy door up by its chain.

The sounds he made triggered a flashback. He turned around, paused, and in a brief moment the entire American Dream chapter crashed to the front of his brain—the sound of horses and chains dragging huge trees along the forest floor, whirring steel blades throwing sawdust in the mill—then hammers striking nails on a coffin lid. Inside the coffin—purloined bicycles. It was over. There was a hollow echo in his stomach. Fifteen years ago was a long time ago; yesterday was another lifetime. That dream was over.

The rising sun did not relieve the stench of manure, sawdust, and garbage in the alley as the two men pushed the crates out to the loading dock. Frank stepped off the dock to hail the deliveryman. In a few silent minutes, the bikes were loaded, and their new life was well underway. They stood silently in the alley, watching the milk wagon disappear with what remained of their fortune.

"It could have turned out a lot different, Joe," Frank remarked wistfully.

"Yeah, Frank, story of our lives so far," said Joe. "Work like a bastard, save your money, then watch some shifty idea man take it all away. We didn't go wrong, Frank, just didn't see it all in time to avoid getting taken. It was a gamble, but an honest one."

"Joe, what are we gonna tell John, and Eb, and the others back home," asked Frank.

"Tell 'em the truth, Frank," Joe snapped. "It hurts plenty, but they gotta know who stabbed 'em in the back. Maybe we can pool what money we got left and get a fancy lawyer to go after him?"

"Don't figure there's much future in that, Joe," Frank muttered scornfully. "Just throwin' perfectly good money after bad. O'Leary was dishonest, but he wasn't stupid. That money's gone, Joe. He's already burned it, probably got a pile of debt building that automobile he was always talkin' about. Think they'll make out any better than we did? You're still dreamin'. Let it go, Joe. You got any change? Let's go get some coffee and a sausage. Start a new dream."

Dawn crept up on them as they walked into their new lives. It wasn't the first time they had been broke. They were near penniless when they came to America. Eventually, they would put some money back in their pockets, but their pride was scorched today. The bicycle business had been a whirlwind affair that they had both gotten swept into. Joe knew that dreams and hard work were a good team, but he hadn't figured out the relationship between desperation and deceit until it was too late. O'Leary had taught them a new lesson. They had built their world around honesty and trust, but it turned out to be a rigged game with O'Leary dealing. Money changes everything.

As the two men walked away, Frank's arm around Joe, brothers and best friends, their next dream was just beginning.

I Can Do This

On a sweltering Thursday afternoon one August, I dipped my toes into the shark-infested waters of publishing in the early twenty-first century. The pool of choice was a Hilton Hotel conference suite. The occasion was a dubiously titled writer's symposium: "Everything you need to know about publishing your book." The big draw was the promise of two personal conferences with agents from noted publishers. Three hundred wannabe authors would soon be swimming furiously toward the chance of being eaten alive. I didn't want to miss that.

The first thing I did miss was the irony of the overly air-conditioned hallway I had to negotiate on my way to claim a seat in the modern second level of hell—a cooler place than the lust-filled room Dante imagined. I knew where I was going, but scoring a chair in the first over-booked seminar, "Building Your Platform," wasn't easy. Neither was digesting the informative construction how-to talk.

I could only hope the second session, a workshop titled, "How to Pitch Your Story," would be better. It held promise when it was moved to the ballroom because more victims than expected signed up. We were all waiting breathlessly in our chairs of ignominy to hear the secrets to be revealed. Holding back our enthusiasm a few extra minutes before the speaker entered was an eternity. Then it happened:

"Listen up, authors. You've got ten minutes to get your book concept down to five sentences or less, preferably *much* less—and make it interesting. Take out your pens and start practicing—NOW!"

During the free write, I considered just hiring an agent to deal with the agents. Of course, the moderator returned too soon for any real success. "Time's up, how'd you do? Don't applaud yourself too early—you've got a whole weekend to get this right. By the way, start *every* conversation in the next three days with *'Can I tell you about my book?'*"

Two workshops in, I still needed something to get my adrenaline started. How about some sugary pastries and coffee in the hallway after a promising slate filled with divine self-revelation and trauma-filled ignorance? Three donuts later, I looked around and noticed the agents and editors seemed to be conspicuously absent. I guess they just couldn't wait for a chance to listen to three hundred pushy type-B word slingers pitching anemic pleas about their books.

"Hello, there, can I tell you about my book?" came with a tap on my shoulder. Almost before I could turn, a mid-thirties woman standing too close in a too-crowded room launched into her soliloquy. I'm perplexed: you've got a book about… what? A sleeping, fairy princess who marries a warlock troll and their kingdom is blown up by terrorist elves before her half-brother the ugly heir to the throne can wake up from his poison-sword induced stupor?

That sounds really a…a…interesting. Stop already, you're about to wipe out a good coffee and sugar-induced buzz. Let me get a comment in edgewise. I'm guessing this is your fifth conference because you needed that many to get to the end of your pitch. You've written fifteen books? And you're still looking for an agent? Hmm. Get a clue, sister. And lose the cowgirl hat.

My next thought was, "find the exit," but I quickly settled on "find the bar, fast." Inside the cooling waterhole just this side of an early escape, I sidled up to a weary looking middle-aged woman. She had an unwritten memoir to publish about her life while married to a disgraced former diplomat in Iran in the early '90s. She was currently being forced to choose between two teenage daughters and a day job as a counselor in a chemical dependency detox clinic. We had a pleasant conversation while she was ignored by the bartender. I think she was still emitting woman-behind-the-burkha vibes, so I flagged down the barkeep for her. She needed a drink worse than I did.

After drinks and a forgettable bar-food dinner, we stumbled back upstairs to the main event. Bing. The elevator disgorged its glassy-eyed load—all about to be jazzed by colorful anecdotes from the highly-successful former-law-yer-turned-pulp-mystery-writer. A revelation hit me halfway through the entertainment.

He's successful; you're not, and you won't be anytime soon because everyone is pushing pulp fiction and science fantasy. That's where the feeding frenzy is. Never mind, go practice your pitch on another playwright wannabe. The room blurred, then…ahhhh, I'm out on the curb in front of the hotel again. The stagnant night air had cooled everything to a pleasant 85 degrees– instantly preferable to a full day of anxiety-induced 67-degree tension that I'd just experienced.

On the nearly empty light-rail home, the doors opened too often to let nobody in and all the marginally conditioned air out at every stop. Soon enough, "Third and Pike, last stop," signified an official break in today's action.

Home was a stifling, yet mentally-relief-engorged oasis. I couldn't fully explain to my wife how I had a good time today, and demurred by muttering meekly, "My ego is too deflated to talk about it now." There was still time to recover my self-respect before morning.

Morning always comes, so at 7:30 I inserted myself into the sparsely filled bus to downtown, found my way underground to the light-rail, and considered today's program options. A half-hour on the train is plenty of time to rewrite yesterday's sorry excuse for a pitch and practice giving it to myself in the window reflection without wincing noticeably. Too quickly, the train braked at the end-of-line. Day two is not yet a dream come true.

Inside the hotel now, coffee and continental breakfast is waiting in the crowded, noisy hallway. I somehow decided "I'll let a panel of editors/agents disabuse me of believing this conference will be a ticket to somewhere." Curiously, during the panel nearly everyone seemed eager to meet me, if only for the allotted ten-minute interview.

Only one problem. My randomly pre-assigned agents at the panel were all trolling for women. Next stop: the appointment desk. "Do you think I could see someone who is only 50 per cent more gender friendly?" My assigned editor had seven openings, and I didn't wonder why. Feeling super-A for a moment, I scored three appointments with people who might not be openly passive-aggressive.

Coming up: meetings about something, coffee, meetings about something else, and "Can I tell you about my book?" everywhere. One more "that's a great story idea you should write it down," and, look at the time! Get ready for your first high-wire act with an agent. Are you feeling charged yet? My conscious self speed-dated through unconscious micro-conversations.

Then I'm up. "Hello, my book is about a lot of things…" Wait, let me finish, I haven't got to the good part yet. You already love it? Are you supposed to say that? Yes, the book is finished. Yes, you can buy it on Kindle. Wait…don't buy it on Kindle, it's a lousy format. I can send you a real book next week, and, what was that…you can't wait to read it? Are you supposed to say that? You're giving me your *personal* business card? Are you supposed to do that? Here's mine, you're not supposed to pretend like you want it.

Scrape me off the ceiling, and shovel in the next round. Did I do well, or just imagine it? What's this in my pocket? William/Morris Agency, New York. "Damn, this might actually work," I delude myself.

After floating around for the next three hours, I woke up and wondered if the workshops I think I just attended would have been more useful if I could have heard anything over the elation-inflated din in my head. Time to hit the no-host bar. I'm feeling good, and I want to buy.

Inside, I met an eighty-something woman from Canada who, her name badge said, is a finalist this year in her category, Children's Literature. We have nothing in common aside from attending this conference, but we proceed to have a more-than-pleasant time *not* pitching our book ideas to each other.

In reward, she offered to show me the alternate route to the conference ballroom via the pool and garden. I've just been picked up by an old lady in a hotel bar, and now I'm going to be her date for dinner. This is different.

We shared a delightful conversation at dinner and many cute quips between pauses in the highly entertaining spy-thriller-author's speech about his life in the CIA. He does not discourage us from attempting to become authors, but cautions that the best work, even fiction, comes from personal experience.

I flashed back to the night before and the woman in the cowboy hat who was fantasizing about her life. She wasn't going to be a fairy princess in this or any life, but she might wake up one day at a writer's conference and find out she was really the troll.

Back to my date, who is enthusiastically upbeat about having little more than a snowball's chance in hell of winning in her category ("never got higher than third place in three years"), and yet still entered again. You go, granny!

When I woke up, I was outside the hotel entrance being overwhelmed by the day while I fondled the agent's card in my pocket. I felt relief in the 85+ degree climate as the endorphins of the day drifted away.

At home, Elizabeth doesn't have to guess how I think I just hit the lottery because I called her from the hotel. She will get another happy earful before I run out of ways to re-tell the day's events. Sleep? Not much chance of that happening. Gotta re-write that pitch in my head all night until it's just right.

Darn, dozed off and now I can't remember a thing, except what's next. Long bus ride, light rail, short bus ride, airporter to hotel. Then, coffee, European pastries, coffee, and more seminars in tension-filled rooms. At least I'm breathing now, and I'm feeling good about my chances today. I'm looking forward to my confab with yesterday's delightful panel guest who seemed hugely informative along with being sardonic, relaxing, and erudite. I wish I could emulate those qualities in a crowded room.

Today, he was none of that. Now, he was humorless, decidedly unemotional. He clipped me off before the second line of my pitch. "That's enough. Have you finished it yet? Good, send me the first fifty pages. If you've got a good storyline, I'll know by then. You can sell anything that has a good storyline. How do you feel about editing changes? Good, I'll read it."

Whoah, two for two! Have I really enticed two agents? The good fortune made me giddy enough to sit down at lunch next to a perplexed-looking forty-something guy, who seamlessly proceeded to pitch his book about the sexual deviances of middle-aged Americans. Sort of a Kinsey Report follow-up written in an advice column format for the truly kinky Ann Landers crowd. He's still trying to figure out what to cut because apparently no self-respecting publisher wants to know you can write an eight hundred-page book about this subject.

I presciently tell him it sounds more like two books than one, maybe he doesn't need to cut it, just serialize it. The suggestion doesn't surprise him. This is not his first conference and not the first time it has been suggested.

I broke away after lunch to hear the spy-thriller guy again, who is no less entertaining just because the crowd is only overflowing a smaller room. Then I queued up for the next round

of interviews. Waiting in line for the afternoon's personal conference, I made a disparaging comment to my line-mate about
waiting in line for everything in '70s Russia. The running joke
was if a line formed, you joined and didn't ask why. They were
very likely giving out something you didn't have, there being
not much you actually did have.

Inside, I had a brief sit-down next to my acquaintance
from Iran. She was deriding the "rule" you couldn't sell a
memoir on concept. I didn't reveal mine was written already
when I said I had an offer to send the first chapter when it
was. I was still feeling more lucky than guilty. We congratu-
lated each other on current successes and she ta-ta-ed to her
next appointment.

While I waited in the row of chairs with the next round
of shark bait, I practiced my pitch and thought how much
like Catholic grade school this was—naughty students waiting
outside the principal's office to receive their forty whacks for
talking in class. How truly hopeful and earnest we all were
today, muttering mea-culpas to ourselves one last time.

My final interview was with the nun from hell. I was only
four sentences into my pitch before she cut me off cold. Then
she turned the table upside down and beat me senseless with
the leg she ripped off in the process.

"What's your platform, who's going to buy this, and why
should I care?" were the kinder questions. "Why did I have to
drag that out of you?" was her way of saying we weren't communicating just right. I could only sit in dumb silence until I
saw my opening to plead "sorry, first-timer."

She lit into me for at least four minutes longer than my
allotted punishment time, and still wanted me to send the
first fifty pages to read. But...she wasn't going to even touch

the manuscript without a "really grade-A" query letter, and "I had better do my homework or else!" I slunk off with my tail still attached when it occurred to me that I had just batted three for three against some pretty heavy strike-out pros, good enough in any league, especially for a rookie.

The game was nearly over; the endorphins would be draining soon. I took a moment to congratulate myself silently. I had just done a reasonable job of impersonating Type-A behavior for three days, and now it was time to find that bar again. Another line-up? No problem. Suddenly everyone seems friendlier and it's not because there's a line at the open host bar. File in, find a seat, one-drink limit, back in line for dinner and closing ceremonies.

Tonight's feature is the contest winners, and I'm more than a little curious about how grandma will finish this year. Too many categories, too many need-not-be-present-to-win awards. 'Children's Literature' finalists are the last call, and the winner is...wait for it: You did it Granny—First Place! A resounding cheer went up—she was the audience favorite, and finally broke the tape. Smiles and enthusiastic clapping all around.

I'm going to try to emulate her attitude in the coming days. I believe good things *do* happen to those who persist. I've got three agents' cards in my pocket to prove it.

Fly Away Now, Little Bird

I received the notice inviting me to attend an AP college course in Archaeology two months before the end of my junior year of high school. I thought that meant I could now claim a level of certifiable intelligence among my peers. Little did I figure it didn't mean that, or even that I knew something. Rather it would come to mean that I didn't know much yet—about life.

I thought I knew a lot already. I was fearless because I just didn't know what to be afraid of. I knew there was a world out there, away from home, and I wanted to join it. My mother was already experiencing difficulty holding me back. I was ready and willing, and now I was acceptable enough to join forty-nine other fledglings at a six-week seminar/life test-flight in Pennsylvania.

Actually, I didn't care or reflect on what it would mean—I was just going.

"What it meant" hit me while I was sitting in the pre-flight boarding area with my mother when the silence was punctuated by a disembodied voice offering an ETD update: "Flight 319 to Pittsburgh will be boarding now."

I was going to be on my own in a few minutes.

When the plane was fully cruising at 25,000 feet, stress and fatigue got the best of me and I succumbed. I woke up to the controlled chaos that is seventy or so strangers trying desperately to shed their fear of flying in a mad rush to the exit. Everyone was hurriedly abandoning the controlled strangeness that cross-continental travel at 600 mph invokes.

The next six hours would be an equivalent blur of unfamiliar faces and places, punctuated by a hotel door being slammed behind an untipped, disgruntled valet in a now frigid hotel room 2,000 miles from home.

I woke up in that room the next morning, my brain churning out questions.

How far to the bus depot? How do I get there? Walk or Taxi? Breakfast…where? How will I tip people—I've only got Traveler's checks? How much do I pay them? This city is big. I'm alone.

I fumbled my way downstairs to the lobby, where I crossed paths with the valet who had slammed the door as he left my room last night. It was a valid response to being stiffed when I didn't know I should tip him. I didn't know his revenge plan was already in place when the overly-friendly concierge told me extra cheerfully that walking twelve blocks to the bus depot lugging a forty pound suitcase was his best pennywise advice. It was also intentionally vindictive. I could still hear them both laughing when I collapsed at the bus depot.

And the real fun had only just begun.

"The bus leaves at 6 o'clock tonight" was delivered without eye contact or emotion by the terse ticket agent.

"Are you sure there's not another bus?"

"Oh, there's another bus. Tomorrow night at 6 o'clock. You want that one? Take a seat. Make yourself comfortable."

I took up residence in one of the hard plastic orange chairs in the bleak lobby and nervously watched a steady stream of riders come and go before my stomach had something to say about how good my life wasn't.

So, it was back to the ticket counter with a suddenly urgent question about food:

"White Castle, one block that way," was the no-frills answer, accompanied by vague hand signal directions. It was clear he was more than a little grouchy. Just say "thank you" and beat it. You've been lucky so far, not everything you don't know has really hurt you, yet. Shortly, the pain that only tiny, tasteless hamburgers can produce was replaced by the ear-splitting terminal loudspeaker: "The bus to Clarion is delayed with mechanical problems."

Okay, it can get worse. This must be what Purgatory feels like. I know I'll get out, I just don't know when.

"Sometime after eight o'clock. Best I can guess," was all I was gonna learn in the moment from the grumpy Greyhound guy.

Then, quickly anticipating my next question, he pounced: "Joy's Café. Three blocks that way. Stay away from the Chili."

Joy's Café was a veritable oasis. Even after finding out a blue-plate special wasn't anything to write home about, I was comfortable enough to ask the unhappiest guy in the Pittsburgh about my release date.

"Eleven o'clock."

All things come to he who waits. I'll survive the next four hours, somehow. Relief was soon enough delivered from overhead: "Number 29 coach to Coreapolis, New Castle, Eau Claire, and Clarion will be boarding in fifteen minutes."

Sweet release! The bus is finally moving. Tired. Getting dark. Going into black hole. Everything feeling strange. So tired...then—

"Clarion."

I'm here. In one piece. Hey, those other kids are getting off the bus, too!

"Hi. I'm Jerry, from Akron. Where you from?"

"Boise. Idaho."

"Wow, that's a long way. Maybe we'll be roommates. How long does it take to get here from...boy...Idaho?"

"Too long...but it was fun."

I lied. I had barely passed most of the flight test with a "C-" grade. I still had a lot to learn, but at least I was standing at the entrance to an obscure college campus in Pennsylvania, in the dark, a few thousand miles from somewhere I didn't want to be anymore. The world was now *my* oyster.

The reasonably jolly man who greeted our seedy group of ten or so sleepy travelers street-side at 1 a.m. sounded like he had done this before.

"Gather round sprouts, welcome to my life this summer. I'm Jim, from the Archeology department and your best friend tonight. I can't promise this summer will be the time of your life, too (ahem). Only you can make that happen." After he hit that note, all the testy, irresolute interactions of the most recent hours in Pittsburgh vanished. As we walked and he talked, I started to reflect on the trip so far.

Deeper thought was interrupted by Jerry with the horn-rim glasses, who had sidled up beside me.

"Pleased to meet ya."

"I'm Al. Likewise."

Life does improve. Compatible friendship was finding me—randomly.

The next morning, it was pretty easy to spot the young cohort in the cafeteria, but, ever the wallflower, I demurred their company until Jerry, now my best friend, called me out while I carried my tray to the corner table.

"Hey, Boise, over here!"

"Wow. Boise. Idaho. I don't even know where that is," someone commented.

"Hey, Boisey, meet Joisey. Guess where he's from?" Joisey smirked the way you'd expect him to smirk.

As we got further into introductions, "Your roommate is Jeff? Sorry. I met him yesterday. He's a dork. Too bad." The group fault lines had already started to appear.

My heavy sigh of relief was surely audible. I had found my way to the fun table. Only a day into the event, abject strangeness was slipping into yesterday. If I didn't yet know where I was, it was comforting to know who I was going to be sharing it with, and they were comfortable sharing it with me.

Jerry had an attitude. I liked that. We were kindred spirits. During breakfast, we discovered we had a lot of things in common, but few of them could be called rigorous academic leanings or scholarly pursuits. Being here was a lark for both of us and we vowed to take best advantage of the fun wherever it could be found—together.

In the hallway after Monday's first class, we agreed the Archeology lecture we just sat through was interesting but stiff, and the professor was more than a bit pretentious. Worse yet, he was a living, breathing parody of every archeologist we had ever seen on TV.

He spoke in fluent English, but it came with a thick German accent that was going to take some getting used to. The hidden laughter we had to suppress while he droned through a lecture was going to be hard to hold.

It didn't help that he wore khaki, below-the-knee shorts, and the tops of his black socks poked out of his scruffy desert boots—the ones with the re-tied broken laces. His chin sported a reddish-brown goatee that didn't match his balding, soon-to-be-white hair. We respected him because he knew something and we didn't, but if this was what being an Archeologist looked like, well, "what were we thinking?" It was going to be a stretch to think any of us, including the prone-to-giggle-at-anything girls were heading into this profession. Naturally, my dorky roommate Jeff worshipped the ground he walked on.

At the end of the first week in class, "Fritz" (as he became known) revealed we would be partnering in groups of four for the field work next week. It was like Noah's Ark all over again when he delivered the selection protocol:

1. Each partnership would need two girls and two boys.

2. No partnership would contain any best friends. "Choose someone you don't know yet. There's plenty of time to socialize elsewhere".

3. We would need to self-select—*now*. Then he exited the classroom quickly, vowing to return in fifteen minutes, and we were left to sort it out.

Items one and three were no-brainers, but two was going to prove challenging for some, already. What did he expect?

We were all trembling on some level outside our familiar

social environs, and most had already formed tightening friendships in a week. The library, the cafeteria, and the dorm lobby proved productive bonding grounds, even if some of us were a bit prone to shyness. This order was almost draconian.

Jerry and I, of course, were built to eschew rules when presented, and we already had a "fun at any cost" pact in place, so we formed the male half of a group without question, and began scanning the room for girls whose standards were low.

"Over there, blonde, good-looking...damn. We moved too slow!"

"By the window, short, funny nose, nice smile. Look, she's already got a girlfriend. No guys yet. Let's move in."

Speed dating was not yet invented, but we did our best to improvise. Ten minutes of pleasantries were soon over, and Professor Fritz came back as promised to survey the damage. He looked momentarily disappointed when he found out everyone was seated in seemingly appropriate partnership groups, but didn't press his luck any further by asking too many questions.

He did, however, catch us on the back foot.

"Okay. Now that you all know each other a bit better, it's time to find out how much you really do know. It's Pop Quiz time."

Everyone did their best impression of one hand clapping, which was quickly followed by a fifty-person gulp.

"Don't worry about your grade," he chortled with his too-merry, English-German accent. As if a group of high grade-achievers would give a damn about achieving a high grade.

He continued: "After a week in class, I'm just trying to get a handle on what you still need to know."

The break-neck learning curve presented so far was my own pop-quiz, but none of it would expose me as the poser I was like a random written version. Jerry gave me a slow eye roll. Neither of us relished any more tests after a week of random life testing. Commiseration was surely called for.

I wasn't finding anything yet about this adventure to regret, though failing an early pop quiz qualified. Even so, I was enjoying being a student for the first time in my life. I was reading all the pull-out material in the library. I had excelled at the first week of in-class conversational summaries of lectural dronings, even though the subject matter was unfamiliar. I knew what I didn't know already, and breathlessly looked forward to inhaling the early morning dew at "the site" when we actually started "the dig" next week.

I had even started to like cafeteria food. I was in charge of my life for the first time and it felt good. Maybe this was finally a subject I was interested in. It could also have been that inclusion in a group of brilliant teenagers was finally going to my head because I wanted to shout "Bring it on, life!"

There was something new and wonderful around every corner. Even three-hour interminable archeology labs sorting potshards couldn't dent my enthusiasm. The prospect of "fieldwork" was luring me on to the extent that I didn't resent being told over and over what was unlikely to happen. Finding anything significant under a couple thousand years of riverbank deposits was remote at best.

By the end of the first "dig" week, I didn't mind that there was nothing to *believably* like about digging large square holes a half-inch at a time while the sun baked you and the biting flies lunched indiscriminately. None of us were there for the warm bologna sandwiches we all ingested with fervor. We just loved being there, all of us—the whole group of sweaty, mostly cheerful, new friends. You had to be there to know why the time together held so much promise.

When the first artifact of worth was barely uncovered, you could have sworn hearing a shout of "possible fire-pit" meant that "GOLD!" was discovered. Nobody complained about the self-imposed double-time digging that this induced for the remainder of the afternoon. Finding the pre-contact Paleo-Indigenous Native artifacts (and cultural evidence) we sought was going to be a slog, but a beautiful one.

The evenings were beginning to turn golden, too, as Jerry and I dug deeper into available diversions. Exactly what we were looking for I don't know, but I'm pretty sure we found most of what we sought in a 3 a.m. walk to skinny-dip in the river. We dared not expose it to those who were unable to ponder adventure successfully—like my roommate:

"Geez! It's 3.a.m.! Where have you been?" he groused when startled awake. "There's a class tomorrow. Go to sleep already." I forgave him; he was a dork.

Soon enough, there were more things to explore without Jerry. In the third week, I had started making eyes at Hope, the dark-haired, mousey girl who sat nearby in the back row, and she returned them. I didn't throw him over immediately, but Jerry had to know he was now a short-timer. If he minded, he didn't let on. He was proud of me and explicitly encouraged "getting some action." Raging hormones must be obeyed, after all.

Hope represented the last vestige of shackled youth to vanish that summer. It was liberating not to have to ask mom to borrow the car to see my girl. She was right there on campus, and she didn't need to ask her mother to receive me. Anytime. Oh, she still had a curfew, but there were ways around that.

My new life was everywhere I looked. Significantly, I found a lot of it in becoming a learner in my own right—for myself. For the first time in my schooling, I could converse on a subject with others in a group, and feel like I had something unique to add to the conversation. My peers started respecting me for what I knew as well as for who I thought I was.

I was the bad boy from Boise, and most of them contributed where they could. When Martha, my pit partner, offered to replace the tattered liner of the leather bomber jacket I proudly sported, I took her up on it and promptly marched down to the local Woolworth's for a fabric solution. Shortly, I would feel even badder wearing my hidden fake-leopard-skin persona-liner, and that was a good thing. I didn't need a motorcycle to make the scene, but I wore that old jacket even more proudly wherever I went. Staying out past curfew with Hope was done with a new conviction now.

I wasn't the only one finding a wrinkle in the learning time that was supposed to be *A Summer Love Affair with Archeology*. July 4 was coming up and Joisey was hatching a plan for the extended weekend.

In short order, Joisey and his goil, with Hope and I in tow, were all water skiing behind the wake of a power boat on the Sound in Seaside, New Jersey. To call it the time of our lives didn't do it full justice.

After the rapture, the final week of Fritz's lectures were somehow less...rapt. Suffering through biting flies in half-dug square holes to nowhere was never the same kind of fun. It wasn't just me, or the thrill that was New Jersey. Even my pseudo-scholarly roommate Jeff started drifting somewhere else. When I caught him red-faced studying comic books in our dorm room, the only thing I could think was, "Jeff, we hardly knew ye." That leaden *thud* you just heard was the experiment in crafting future archeologists falling on the floor.

The focus was now turned squarely to fun, and there would be no looking away from it for the duration of our conscription. Fritz must have picked up on the vibe because his hard-hitting lecture time was morphing into plot-simpler movies. The only thing missing by the end of the fifth week was the popcorn.

On site in the sixth week, we dug faster with less diligent searching. We didn't find less, there was just less to find, and everyone was less interested in not finding it.

Thursday, Fritz changed the strategy of attack to finding geological strata. Two selected half-holes would now become "find the bottomless" pits. "Dig 'em to China," was the directive.

By the time we hit the water table, the rigorous pursuit of knowledge was officially over. Fritz dutifully proclaimed the next and last day useless, except in that we would all, instead, scrub off the dirt one more time and take the bus on Friday evening to his villa in the country for a goodbye party. He was an okay guy, after all.

At the party, Hope couldn't see us ending yet. As the fireflies flickered romantically in the waning twilight, she invited her other best friend Sally and me to an extended week of fun in Richmond, Virginia. With her parents onboard, we piled into their family sedan on Monday, and the vacation of a lifetime that would not end, didn't.

By the time we landed in Richmond, the provincial southern parental mood had swung away from "it's going to be fun to have a little Catholic boy in the house" to "count the silverware before he leaves." I guess I stole too many kisses in the back seat on the drive across Pennsylvania. They had seen the lining of my leather jacket.

Sally was soon deployed as an extra-duty chaperone (as she related the conversation with "Mom") for a few days. Fortunately, her truer loyalties remained with teenage girl-hood because there were still plenty of kissin' and cuddlin' moments to come. Hope's older, wiser sister (the devil's hand-maiden) even participated in the debauchery as our chaperone one evening when she found a way to sneak us into the local eighteen-or-older bar in the neighborhood. I thought the caterpillar now grazing my upper lip sealed the deception, but knowing the bouncer was also critical. We had found a way to subvert parental discretion one more time. Then *everything* crashed mid-week, when Hope came down with mononucleosis.

Being bedridden is no way to end a romantic episode of your life, but it was there. The anticipated, tearful goodbye scene at the airport was now even sadder, in another way. The only thing left to do was exchange fond memories with Hope's father, shake hands in a manly fashion, and ride off into the sunrise of my new life.

By September, when "finishing school" resumed in Boise, there was only one thing I really needed to admit I had learned at summer school camp: growing up is easier when you've got nothing left to prove.

Acknowledgements

I owe a debt of thanks to the fifth-grade teacher/nun who first "let the laughter run its course." By choosing not to tamp down the response to my first delightful essay that interrupted the carefully-suppressed order of her classroom, she illuminated a path to public praise and personal fulfillment for me. Her selfless act allowed a budding wallflower at a critical time in his life to "be the best at something."

Thanks to my peers and close friends who recognized and continued to encourage my art throughout the formative years of my pre-adulthood, and now, but never let it go to my head.

I would also like to thank my young students for allowing me to briefly enter their heads long enough to coax out a bit of themselves. When they show their satisfaction by putting words to paper, smiling, and then by repeating the exercise, my life circle is complete.

Finally, I want to laud my wife and life partner of forty-plus years, who has supported me unequivocally (within reason), and criticized me roundly when that was necessary. Words alone will never be enough to fill the need for expressing gratitude. Thank you.

Lucinda Hauser

About the Author

Lucinda was born in Vancouver, BC, later moving to a farming community in Skagit County, WA, as a young child. Much of her youth was spent biking throughout the valley and working in the tulip fields. Her lifelong passion for outdoor adventures began in college where she chose rock-climbing, skiing, and sailing for PE credit. After graduating from the University of Washington, she worked for thirty-five years as an educator and advocate for teens before reluctantly leaving her career due to the progression of her multiple sclerosis.

Lucinda now lives in North Bend, WA, with her husband and two Labradors. Her two adult children and "other" various wildlife regularly visit her home nestled against the Cascade mountains. It is not uncommon to hoot with barred owls or chase elk from the garden!

At the onset of Covid, Lucinda joined the writing class at the Swedish MS Center for new virtual connections, and to learn the never-before attempted craft of creative writing. She enjoys reading historical fiction and memoirs, so now gravitates toward both for her own writing. The stories in this collection are inspired by true events, although creative license was liberally used when accurate memories or living ancestors were missing.

The Secret Room

(De Geheime Kamer)

The Nazis are coming! Henk DeGoede's mother received the dreaded call from a friend in town, and she immediately alerted her two elder sons, Henk and Siem, who were out working in the field. The brothers, and Kars, the farm helper, dropped their hoes and sprinted to the family bulb barn next to their home. They dashed into the secret room. *The Nazis are coming!*

Once the men were inside the hidden space, Henk's younger brothers burst into action. From inside the barn, they locked the makeshift door to the secret room and quickly shoved hay bales and equipment in front of the sham wall to hide the men from the workspace of the barn. The secret room filled with the musty stench of three young men who had rushed off the fields in the middle of a hot day, damp soil, and field mud still sticking to their sweaty skin and clothes. The hint of sweet, fresh hale bales mixed with the oily odor of the tools and bikes surrounding them. Their breath came in shallow, rapid puffs. Would they be discovered?

It was dark in the small room. A few tiny streams of sun slipped through cracks between the boards on the outside wall. The men were behind the tenth split door, at the very end of the long, single-story bulb barn. Each of the doors had a window on the upper half, which opened into a separate stall inside the barn. Rows of metal mesh shelves lined each side, filled with bulbs dug from the fields after the blooming season. The outside door was normally left open to allow air and light into the room, so that the tulip and daffodil bulbs could dry from the fresh air that found its way through the wire mesh.

But these days the ten doors on the outside of the barn were closed and locked. There were three split doors near the road, then a window for the barn's central work area, then two large doors next to allow entrance for a car or the plows, followed by seven more split doors, each with a window on the top half. The family had agreed: the story to be told was that the bulb-drying season was over and the outside doors needed to be secured against potential bulb thieves.

Pa would tell Nazi soldiers that they were welcome to inspect the contents of the rooms from the inside of the barn. *No*, he would say, *I am not sure where the key is at the moment. Would have to ask my sons who used it last. Why not follow me into the barn and I will show you the rooms from inside?* Hopefully, the soldiers would believe the illusion that the farmer needed to protect his bulbs by keeping exterior doors locked.

It was all part of the family's war plan. Inside the barn, at the end of the stalls, a false wall had been placed across the narrow end of the last stall with a small door in its corner, transforming the tenth stall into an undetected small room. The new wall was blocked with hay bales, crates, and old farm equipment, with a small doorway to be covered with a small stack of hay bales once the men were safely inside. The other nine stalls along the wall were filled with the shelves of bulbs, along with miscellaneous shovels and other stored farm tools. The inquisitive soldiers would hopefully not notice that there were *ten* doors outside, yet only *nine* corresponding rooms inside.

The three young Dutch men crouched in the room, careful to avoid knocking down one of the six bikes the family owned, or the jars of Ma's vegetable and meat preserves, or any of the other precious items stored in the tiny space. Such items, if found, would be seized by the Nazi army but were necessary for the family's survival through the winter. The three men were careful not to talk, to sneeze...or even to breathe audibly. They must not let their mud-covered wooden shoes clump on the stone floor. They must keep their presence secret in this tiny hidden room at the end of the barn. The bikes, the glass jars of food, and especially the young men themselves were valuable commodities, not only to their family of sixteen, but to the soldiers searching to feed their troops and to add to their number of combatants.

It was 1943. Although the Third Reich had already occupied the Netherlands for two years, Henk DeGoede and his family had not felt the effects until last year. Their bulb farm was on the outskirts of Anna Paulowna, a small farming village on the northern edge of the country near the Noord Sea. The war seemed so far away...strange stories coming from the cities. Nothing the hardworking family worried about much.

Then it came to their countryside.

Henk remembered his initial impression when the planes first roared by, dark metal with the black swastika on the tail. His younger brothers and sisters had waved at the pilots, marveling at the wonder of these sinister machines...until Ma and Pa sternly admonished them. Then came the ominous stories of blasted dikes, flooding in other farming areas, stolen livestock, people disappearing. Groups of bedraggled travelers suddenly came on foot from the cities, hoping for food and shelter.

Eventually, the Nazis entered the family's personal space, their idyllic piece of the Dutch countryside. Their farm. It was not enough for Pa to grow food for his large family and to run his successful bulb business. Not enough for Ma and the girls to keep the house and clothes clean, to process the food into daily meals, to can the extras into jars for the winter. The Nazis wanted things. Now every Dutch farmer was expected to "share" their livestock and preserves, even their older sons, with the Regime. Life had changed. Pa needed to protect his family, his food from the garden and the orchard, his cattle, and pigs.

The younger children thought little of the significance and danger of the war. Their lives remained one of daily chores, playing tricks on each other, the bossy older children taking care of the younger ones, and the normal boisterous family meals around the long wooden table. Henk, however, noticed the deep worry lines on his parents' faces each night after dinner as they huddled in the hall to talk on the phone with neighbors. He could hear them gasp as they learned about approaching troops and their atrocities toward Dutch citizens. Henk, one of the oldest boys, noticed and listened intently.

As the war crept insidiously toward their farm, a plan

evolved. Ma and Pa sat the older children down after dinner one evening and described urgent changes to be made immediately. Food, livestock, and fighting aged men had to be protected. Preparations for the *DeGoede family war survival plan* were to start the next day. Everyone had a job to do.

For the next two days, Henk and his older siblings followed Pa and Ma's instructions, working furiously to prepare. The younger children could not understand Ma and Pa's short tempers and curt commands, but the older siblings knew that the soldiers would be in their midst soon and they were anxious. They built a new "pigpen," a large wooden box placed near the garden and fruit trees, placed in a shallow pit in the ground. It was covered with the pile of straw previously used to keep the tree roots warm during the icy, blustery winter. The result was a large mound of sound-deafening hay that would hopefully mute the snorts and squeals of the pigs. The younger children were told to cut squares out of the rolls of landscaping cloth and cover the inside of the windows later in the evenings. Ma and Pa knew it was important to keep the light of their one lantern hidden from nighttime wanderers to avoid attention to the family home.

The main workspace of the barn was filled with clutter and the remnants of several ongoing projects meant to distract the curious inspectors. Laundry hung from beams that crossed from the bulb storage side to the opposite bare stone wall, necessary during this wet season when the clothesline was useless to dry the heavy work pants and flannel shirts from the men and boys. On one side of the large central work area worktables held piles of broken trays needing repair; bulb sorting tools, and trays lined the opposite wall. A stack of wicker baskets teetered in the corner, along with a chair, extra reams of wicker, and a box of glue, ready for someone to fix the holes that allowed bulbs to escape. Projects for the cold winter months…distractions.

Most importantly, the family prepared the secret room. The older boys made the wall with the small door. Ma supervised the older girls with the transfer of the family bikes and many of her jars of preserves to the secret room, leaving a small collection in the house to be confiscated if "needed" by the soldiers. The dozens of other precious jars stored in the secret room, along with the hanging bacon and bags of wheat and potatoes, were crucial to feed her children through the winter.

And thus, the family's routine changed. Suddenly. They kept the façade of a farming family business during the day. The boys were out in the field digging bulbs, pulling the hoe behind the work horses to prepare new planting rows, repairing equipment, and sorting the bulbs in the barn. The girls washed the laundry on scrub boards, peeled potatoes, and prepared vegetables for dinner, and made butter and buttermilk with the churn. They swept the house and prepared the meals throughout the day for their large family.

But there were many changes. The family kept the mandated curfew each night. Friends did not join at the dinner table as before. Church dances and youth activities were canceled. As the Nazi soldiers cut down the dwindling supply of wind-breaking rows of trees for their own use, they enacted a law preventing local citizens from doing the same. Firewood was then forbidden, but necessary to keep the woodstove fueled for heat and cooking. After dinner, therefore, the older boys often ventured out stealthily, in the cloak of darkness, to search for wood, further and further from the farm.

Pa and other farmers would allow temporary shelter in their barns to traveling city folks who were fleeing the food shortages and violence of Amsterdam and other nearby cities. They were allowed to stay only one night to avoid the image of hiding Jewish refugees, but the sweet hay made for soft bedding and there was food. Ma often made an extra pot of *soup met balletjes.* The delicious odor of boiled beef, meatballs, onions, and other farm vegetables reached the hungry and appreciative travelers in the barn well before they devoured the soup at dinnertime.

During the days, each older family member was to be on high alert. Once a sentinel saw or heard the slightest hint of approaching soldiers, the older boys would bolt to the secret room, followed by younger brothers assigned to block the door with crates, haybales, and farm equipment. Henk, his brother, Siem, and Kars were prime candidates to involuntarily join the Nazi regime if found by quota-driven soldiers. When they came, Pa was to be ready to distract a stern, uniformed entourage of troopers away from the family's treasures. Ma's responsibility was to keep the younger children in tow, distracting them from "friendly" soldiers searching for information from innocent youth. The plan was in place.

And it worked. Numerous times. Despite that, the anxiety never subsided for the parents and older children who knew the possible consequences if the plan failed.

Henk, Siem, and Kars were again huddled in the dark room, listening to the sounds of approaching Nazi vehicles. They heard Pa greet the soldiers and explain their predicament. "Ya, we worry about the little bit of food and having enough livestock for the winter…it has been a difficult year." Then, "we have given so much to your comrades already, you can see that our provisions are low. We are still building up supplies from last month's visit when we shared so much already."

A door slammed and the three hidden men assumed Pa had guided the soldiers into the family's home for the obligatory inspection. Suddenly, the voices were outside again. The young men heard Pa enter the barn, explaining to the soldiers that the rooms were meant to air out the stored bulbs. Each stall was searched, to verify his claims. The soldiers peered into one stall after another filled with stacked shelves of drying tulip and daffodil bulbs. They didn't notice that only nine of the ten outside doors had corresponding stalls inside.

The boys, the bikes, the food were all safe…once again.

Nineteen-year-old Henk heard his father's voice drift away as he guided the group of soldiers outside, explaining to the cadre of armed men that his younger pre-teen boys helped him on the farm. He admitted that they occasionally needed help from older boys from the village if any were even available. "No," he said, "we unfortunately do not have older boys."

The barn was silent. The three men slowed their breathing. Henk silently began to seethe with anger. He was *done*. The Nazis had no right to do this. The injustice of it infuriated him. They were forced to hide like rats. He made a decision. He vowed to continue this farming charade during the day. However, he would contact Wilhelm from church tomorrow. *De Nederlandse verzetsbeweging*, the Dutch Resistance Movement, was searching for recruits and he was finally ready to join. He might continue to hide in this room during the day.

At night, however, he would fight.

A Grand Adventure

(Een Groots Avontuur)

After a week of the hypnotic clacking of metal on rails and the soothing hum of muted conversations from other passengers, the conductor suddenly bellowed "Vancouver…next stop!" The two-week journey by ship from the Netherlands to Halifax, Nova Scotia, and then the beautiful train ride from Halifax across Canada, was ending.

Less than a month earlier, Johannes and Riet quietly and solemnly said *Ik doe* in the hushed Catholic church of their little village, Anna Paulowna, near the North Sea. The monotonous drone of the priest lulled several guests to nod their heads, with spouses poking elbows into their sides to prevent snoring. Everyone, however, sat upright as the couple said their vows, kissed, and turned to the adoring crowd of family and friends. Cheers, clapping, hoorays, and *hip hip* followed the couple as they walked down the aisle.

They both grew up in this close community, in families

who farmed the rich dirt. Riet's family of sixteen and Johannes' family of ten had several mutual friends within each clan who often went to each other's homes to share boisterous meals. The village was in the middle of a flat section of reclaimed land, a polder. Riding a bike, the main mode of transportation, meant fighting against howling, incessant wind so strong that rows of wind-break trees were bent over the landscape. The muted noise of workers, cows, and work horses were ever-present. In Anna Paulowna, you might hear one of the few cars or trucks in the area, but more likely the melodic ringing heralding an approaching bike, or the clopping of horse hooves from a wagon delivering goods to town.

Yet despite this serenity and close-knit community, Johannes and Riet decided to take the government's post-war offer to send young adults to Canada, Australia, or the United States. Few citizens at home were able to secure jobs. As middle children of large families, Johannes and Riet wanted to avoid the prospect of working for an older brother who would undoubtedly inherit the family farm and become "boss" upon his father's death.

Riet and Johannes wanted a different life. And the Dutch leaders provided that opportunity. In a blur of excitement and anticipation, they concurrently planned their wedding, secured passports, packed their suitcases, and purchased voyage tickets to Halifax, Nova Scotia. From there, they intended to travel by train to Vancouver, British Columbia to begin their life together.

That was the plan.

A month later, with no job, home nor plans of any kind, they weren't too sure of that decision. They jostled with other impatient travelers to step off the train into the Vancouver station to face the overwhelming clamor of screeching trains, foreign voices calling to each other, announcements of incoming and outgoing trains, children crying, and police whistles. Their dazed and bewildered eyes spotted a man with a hand-written sign, *WELKOM CONIJN'S!* Johannes and Riet heard the familiar greeting, *"Hallo vrienden!"* Enormously relieved, they timidly approached the man. With a strong grip familiar to Dutch farmers, he shook Johannes' hand, introduced himself as Wilhelm and explained that he was there to help them settle in town.

They had no idea who Wilhelm was, how he knew them, nor why he was helping them. Yet they also had no idea what they were going to do next in this city and he was from home. He described an apartment nearby that they could stay in, and they followed him blindly.

The walk was short, but intense. A large red firetruck startled them as it careened down the street near the sidewalk, siren screaming. Throngs of people knocked into each other, speaking words they did not understand. A jackhammer rata-tat-tatted as it bore a hole into cement, surrounded by grunting men doing repairs on the road. A streetcar drove by, ringing its bell as it prepared to stop just ahead of them.

They stopped at an apartment building and followed Wilhelm up three floors to a studio apartment. As Johannes reached for his wallet, Wilhelm assured them that no money was necessary for this company apartment. He gave them his business card and said goodbye, promising to return before lunch the next day. Riet and Johannes could think of only one thing as he closed the door. Sleep.

The Murphy bed reluctantly creaked as they pulled it down. Then, silence, as they collapsed. Johannes and Riet woke up hours later, famished. They left their belongings still stuffed in their four suitcases and descended the three floors of cracked stairs to the lobby. The dim lighting of the stairway was replaced by blinding sunlight as they opened the ornate hotel door. They were in Vancouver!

They clasped their hands and ventured out. Excited, in love, naïve, and ready to explore.

Riet had traveled to the USA months ago to see her brother in Mount Vernon, WA. Johannes had been to Berlin, Germany, during his army service. They had both traveled out of the quiet, farming community of their childhood. Yet nothing prepared them for this. A huge billboard changed from a red-haired lady, large letters below spelling "I love Lucy!"... to "Piggly Wiggly" with grocery bags...then to "Ramada Inn" with a picture of a hotel room...then back to the red-haired lady. Amazing!

People of all backgrounds and clothing bustled busily on the crowded streets. They passed a farmer's market with colorful plump vegetables and fruit. Red phone booths every few blocks. Cars of all colors...bright, yellow taxis, trucks with bright letters advertising their businesses. The buildings were *so* tall. Signs in restaurant windows enticed people in with "Pork Chops for 75 cents!" or "2 egg omelet for 50 cents!"

Every glimpse between the buildings showed beautiful snowcapped mountains and blue skies. There would be much to explore. Yet evening was setting in. They needed to eat.

Riet saw a store across the street that looked promising. The police officer held up his right gloved hand and motioned to them to cross the street with his left. With less than $50 each in their pockets, they knew they would have to be careful with their money. They bought their usual low budget food, peanut butter and bread with a few treats, and left the store to go "home."

They simultaneously realized that neither knew the address nor even the name of the apartment building! What direction did they come from? What did they pass? Where was the farmer's market? The Lucy billboard? The noisy construction crew? How could they have been so stupid?

Riet noticed John's hands shaking and sweat starting to collect on his brow. He asked her if they had *anything* that could identify Wilhelm's last name or the name of the apartment building. He searched his pockets and Riet emptied her purse on the nearby bench. There! A small card with the name, Wilhelm DeBoer. The numbers below his name must surely be a phone number. They hurried to the nearest red telephone booth across the street.

Epilogue: Wilhelm drove back to the city from his home in Burnaby to help them return to the apartment. At that point, he explained that he was an insurance salesman who got the names of Dutch immigrants from posted ship rosters. He helped travelers at arrival with the hope for a later purchase of life insurance through him. He helped Johannes and Riet—now known to me as Mom and Dad—get their first jobs as housekeeper and farm help, to find and rent their first house, and to meet other Dutch immigrants in the area. Later, once they were settled and earning money, they gladly purchased life insurance from Wilhelm.

Henry:
A Family Ghost Story

Tony and Maryann blissfully slept, recovering from the exhausting intensity of the hospital. The decision was made, but it had been hard. The life support would be turned off. The stroke had left Henry's body so useless that, had he lived, his mind and body would have been in a vegetative state. Tony believed his brother would have agreed with him, yet he had struggled to give the required signature.

For the last decade, the brothers had been embroiled in an absurd dispute involving Tony's son, Timmy, who signed his name as Tim Henry Hauser. Timmy had been only thirteen years old at the time, on a Connecticut school trip to Florida's Disney World. There had been no planning to include a visit to see Henry who lived a few miles from the park. Henry had been infuriated to discover that lapse.

The phone call.

"Are you nuts?" Tony said, aghast. "That would have been impossible on a school trip."

Henry wasn't listening. "You could have made it happen if you wanted to."

They debated, neither budging, East Coast aggression only adding to the impossibility of any form of truce.

Obscenities, followed by phones abruptly clicking on receivers. An ended relationship. The extended family would later be subjected to years of opposing accounts, but never with both brothers simultaneously present.

Outside his brother's hospital room, Tony had wondered if his decision was clouded with a desire to finally end their feud. Eventually, he signed the papers, knowing that this was what he would have wanted for himself. Tony and Maryanne left to go to their nearby vacation home, having no desire to witness the final breath of his older brother.

They later woke with a jolt. Their deep sleep abruptly disrupted. Their ears rang with the deafening clamor of doors, opening and slamming shut. *Every* cabinet door. Relentless. From the kitchen…the bathroom…the hallway. Could it be their imagination? Was this a dream after their emotional night? Was there a Florida hurricane brewing, affecting the kitchen? They knew that none of these explanations could be true, yet very cabinet door in the house seemed to join this mysterious cacophony in unison.

Their wide, frightened eyes locked as they sat up in their bed in the dim early morning light, ears pounding. Trembling hands instinctively clutched their sky-blue blanket tightly to their chins, a protective barrier to this unknown danger.

Suddenly, Tony bellowed, "Henry…STOP!"

Immediately, the house fell eerily silent. Morning birds chirped, streams of light filtered through the blinds, no sound of a windstorm outside. They barely breathed…anticipating another onslaught of deafening noise. None came.

Tony leapt from their bed and left the room, inspecting their home for intruders. None. He returned to the bedroom and looked at Maryanne. They knew that Henry had just passed. The two wordlessly acknowledged that the brothers' longstanding quarrel had obviously not ended with Henry's death.

Henry had the last say in their argument, and he had clearly won.

Short-Cut to Rosie

"*Now* what do I do?" I wondered.

An angry red hue was slowly deepening through the skin of my swelling leg, which was useless and stuck under the tangled mess of my bike. My teeth clenched as another spasm of shooting pain started up my ankle to my calf. The thin front tire of my bike was wedged firmly in the railroad track groove…the flange gap of the track perfectly sized to swallow the street tires of any ten-speed Schwinn.

It was 1977, years before the ADA mandated safety changes for track gaps to make the tracks safer for pedestrians and wheelchair users. No matter. I was in a bind. That was clear.

At fifteen-and-a-half years old, I was not quite old enough for a driver's license. My bike was my main mode of transportation to and from my afternoon job at the Riverside Deli. The eleven-mile trip only took about forty-five minutes and wasn't too bad. To ride home after work, normally I left the bright lights of the businesses surrounding the Riverside Deli, pedaled along the river for a bit, then crossed over the Skagit

River bridge to West Mount Vernon to the farming side of town. Finally, I'd arrive at our home nestled in the middle of tulip fields and vegetable patches. Actually, I loved that ride.

That Saturday night, my shift at the deli ended at 8 p.m., making it an excellent night to take my designated shortcut. If I rode fast enough through the balmy August evening, I could miss the pitch darkness that fell quickly after sunset. I cut off Riverside Drive and onto a little-used, unlit, rough side street that crossed under the I-5 freeway viaduct. I *knew* it had those damned sunken railroad tracks at that weird angle, but I had taken this route *so* many times, and I knew how to navigate the grooves.

Here's how it was supposed to work: I would veer into the road right before crossing the tracks, carefully setting myself up for a perpendicular approach. This way, I would avoid getting my tires getting caught in the shallow grooves, which crossed the road at that terribly inopportune angle. I'd bounce right over the tracks and be on my way. No problem.

Normally, there are no cars on the road. Yet, that night, there *was* one.

With unexpected headlights boring into my back and getting too close, I forgot my plan. I rode straight at those tracks. My front tire found its home in the perfectly sized groove, abruptly halting my forward progress. Bike and rider catapulted sideways to the shoulder of the road. The driver of the car impatiently honked at me as he drove by. My split-second decision was, of course, the right one, but with the predictable consequences.

I was stuck under a bike with bent spokes partially wrapped around my calf. The pain! It was excruciating. My head throbbed where it hit the ground. *Mom was right*, I thought woozily, *I should have worn a helmet. Even though it's not illegal to ride without one.*

Plenty of cars were driving above me on the freeway, but here, sixty feet below, there was nothing to flag down. No businesses, no streetlights, no phone booths. Nothing. Peering through the cement pillars supporting the freeway, I saw the brilliant colors of the sun as it settled over the river and the distant west Mount Vernon bridge silhouetted against the sky. I knew that darkness would shortly surround me.

"Help...can anyone hear me?" I cried out.

Nothing.

"Help me!"

Still nothing.

How would I get hold of Mom and Dad? Would they even know to look for me here? Memories of jumping the ditch last year flooded through my pounding head. I had been jogging on the country road and a car of sneering young men had slowed down to offer me a ride, so I'd jumped the ditch to get away from them. But who would come along *this* road on a Saturday night? If someone came, could I trust them?

That's when I heard steps.

They came near, shuffling behind me. My body tensed and my right hand instinctively grasped a large rock. A woman with grey sweats, old scuffed white tennis shoes and a sweater with a hood that partially hid her face approached. "Are you OK, honey?" she asked timidly.

Through my pain, I sensed her genuine kindness.

"Not really," I said, my words becoming an unexpected sob.

"What happened?"

My muscles relaxed a bit and somehow, I got through my

story of what happened, how my parents must be at home worrying, how my leg was throbbing and hurting. I paused and really looked at the woman for the first time. Why was I blabbering my story to this complete stranger? Who was she? Where had she come from?

"I'm Rosie," she said, sensing my sudden discomfort. She pointed up the hill under the viaduct. "I have a small place up there."

A place *up there*? What did that mean?

"Esther is a friend. She lives near me."

It dawned on me that Rosie must be one of "those" homeless people scattered throughout our town. Yet, she seemed kind and I had to trust her...I had no choice.

She turned and shouted, "Esther. It's OK. Come help."

I could barely see the other woman in the dim light, cowering behind a cement support stack. As she came forward, my companion introduced her as Esther. "Our homes are behind those stacks up the hill. It's not much, but let's get you to mine, so you can get off the road. Cars just don't come this way much at night, and who knows who would stop anyway. We'll take care of you until we can get you some help."

I could not see where she was pointing, but I knew she was right...I could not just lay on the road waiting for a car. We left my mangled bike next to the road in case Mom or Dad would come by later, and I accepted their help.

I draped my arms over Rosie and Esther's shoulders, and they helped me hop up the gravel hill to Rosie's home. It was a painful journey, but thankfully a short one. My right leg was scraped, but still holding me up. My *left* leg, however, had something seriously wrong with it. It was not twisted, but I could not put any weight on it. We slowly made our way to the base of a hill leading to the underside of noisy I-5. I groaned.

At the top of the loose gravel hill, I could barely see a cardboard structure tucked under the cement underbelly of the freeway. Rosie's house. Rosie quietly assured me that they would help. The three of us gingerly took baby steps to the top, slipping periodically on the mixture of broken cement and gravel, each misstep causing another wave of electrical pain to shoot up my leg.

Rosie's house was a cardboard hut, made of two appliance boxes taped together. She had cut out a window and door, leaving one side of each uncut to allow them to fold open and shut without hinges. Tentatively, I looked inside and was surprised to see a closet-size room, complete with a burning candle, flowering weeds in a beer bottle, a bed of pads and blankets against one wall and even a newspaper and a couple of books. A magazine photo of a river was secured with duct tape to the cardboard wall above the blanket pile. The initial coziness in the candlelit glow, however, belied the dank reality as I inhaled the stench of the musty blankets and damp cardboard.

Rosie and Esther gingerly lowered me to those same blankets. It took only a moment to realize it really didn't matter how they smelled. The weight off my bones was such a huge relief. Through the blaring truck horns and the steady drone of cars passing above us, I heard the two women talk about food and water. Esther left to get something from her place nearby, and Rosie turned to me with a dirty rag and a water bottle. "Honey. Let's clean you up a bit."

Esther came in and out with supplies, bringing a can of soup with an easy rip top. I devoured it cold. Rosie began to wipe the blood off my leg and face with her damp rag. "Is there anything else I can do?" Esther asked.

"My parents," I squealed, feeling suddenly frantic. "I need to tell them where I am. How can we get ahold of them?"

Rosie and Esther shared a look.

"We could walk to the strip..." said Rosie.

"...but the stores all close early on Saturday nights," Esther finished for her. "There won't be anyone there."

Even I knew there were no phone booths in the area. I also knew it was dark and not necessarily a safe time to walk the unlit roads for either of them. And, of course, it was 1977. No cell phones. We reluctantly agreed that it would be best to wait, leave my warped bicycle by the road, and then flag someone down in the morning.

"Thanks for the soup, Esther," I said quietly as she folded the door open to go to her tent.

Rosie took one of the dirty blankets to the other side of the shack, laid down and we began to talk...surprisingly easy in the flickering candlelight and blaring traffic above us. She wistfully listened as I told her about life on the other side of the bridge...the farming side. I told her about my loving parents, the farming community we lived and worked in near LaConner, my mom's devotion to children with the dozens of foster babies coming through our home. She asked me about my brothers and sister, what our house looked like, and the Dutch meals Mom made every night. She wistfully sighed, "That sounds so nice."

She slowly opened up when I asked about *her* story, genuinely interested. I heard about her struggles with OCD and anxiety, especially after the birth of her daughter. She proudly told me about her two young children, Isaac and Lottie, who were taken away from her by her powerful husband. He didn't have the patience (or compassion for her, I assume) to support her while she struggled and ultimately "self-medicated" to calm her nerves. He told her to "just deal with it." As a city council member, he did not want it known how much his wife was struggling with mental illness and drinking. He kept her in their home far outside of town with little contact from others before announcing one day that she was to leave... without the children.

Rosie shared her background as a para-educator and as an employee of the local school district working with troubled youth. None of that seemed to matter, she said, when her husband had gone to the judge for custody of their children and a divorce from her. Without money to hire a lawyer, it had seemed like a done deal before she stepped off the bus at the courthouse. She missed Isaac and Lottie terribly and wondered if they missed their mom...and what they heard about her.

She shared that she and Esther met over a year ago after each had found shelter in tents in the homeless camp south of town near the industrial businesses. After each experienced abuse and theft, they decided to find new shelter together on their own away from others in the homeless community. This was it...simple, near enough to Riverside Drive to beg for supplies, but far enough away from "the others," assuring them of a slightly improved modicum of safety.

I wanted to hear more, but I instead succumbed to my exhaustion and fell into a deep sleep.

Suddenly, Rosie's kind face appeared in the bright light of early morning and she was shaking me gently, quietly whispering. "Time to wake up...we think your folks are down at the road."

I peered out of the folded cardboard door and saw Dad at the bottom of the hill, inspecting my bike and looking around for me. Mom was in our ivory and wood panel station wagon, both of them calling desperately, "Theresa…where are you?"

Esther stumbled down the hill to let Dad know where I was and that I needed help. Startled, he looked up and saw me in the doorway. His suspicion of the disheveled woman left his face and he nimbly scrambled up the hill to Rosie's house. Meanwhile, Rosie helped me up, bracing me as I stood to greet my frantic father. The stoic farmer's embrace was filled with relief and love. Rosie smiled at Dad shyly.

I was proud of Dad. Years of working as field boss with crew members from various, sometimes compromised, economic backgrounds had taught him to hold back from judgments. He scanned the surroundings, noting the cardboard house, the ripped and dirty tent in the distance, the litter and outside supplies in coolers and boxes, the makeshift clothes line with dirty jeans and towels…the noise and the stench. Yet, he held out his hand to Rosie and then Esther, introducing himself and exclaiming, "I *cannot* thank you enough for taking care of Theresa. I need to get her to her mother, but is there anything I can do for you first?"

Rosie declined. "No, we are glad we could help her."

Impulsively, I hugged Rosie tightly and thanked her and Esther for helping me. Dad awkwardly gave Rosie and Esther all the money he had in his wallet to cover their hospitality and food for his daughter. Then we turned to make our way to the car, my weight heavily dependent on Dad's strong shoulder, as I limped down the hill. Rosie followed us to the car.

Mom muttered soothing words in Dutch as she hugged me close. She awkwardly greeted Rosie while inspecting my injuries. As Dad loaded me and the broken bike into the car, Mom instructed Dad to drive straight to Dr. Bryant's office. We said goodbye to Rosie, waved to Esther on the hill, and drove off to town for medical help.

Babbling with relief, I told Mom that the women would probably appreciate a thermos of her Dutch *soap met balletjes*. Maybe Mom's social worker supervisor could get mental health help for Rosie. Did the Friendship House in town offer housing for women like Rosie and Esther? Reminding Mom of her parents' help on their farm for Jews escaping Amsterdam during WWII, and Dad of his support of the farmworkers he supervised in the fields, I told them that maybe this is *our* chance to do something to help these special women…maybe others. Everyone deserved a chance to thrive and get out of an impossibly daunting situation with a helping hand.

Thinking back to the cardboard home I had spent the night in with Rosie, how the two women had cared for me, the delicious cold can of Campbell's soup from their limited stash, and the stories Rosie and I had shared, I settled back into the comfortable cushion of the back seat, knowing I would be back.

Finishing Touches

The young girl was so determined. Her indomitable spirit was obvious with each reach of a potential handhold. Skinny, scraggly, with long brown hair and freckles, she was nearly a mirror image of myself at thirteen. For me, it had been climbing the huge oak tree in the field next to my childhood home with my brothers, always against my parents' wishes. *Top priority…be safe*, they told me. This youngster was instead tackling a challenging route on the concrete climbing pillars—known to local climbers as "The Rock"—on the University of Washington waterfront.

Scanning the other climbers surrounding the pillars, I didn't spy a watchful parent.

"Grab that handhold to your right," I yelled to the girl. "Yes, you can trust it…brace the bottom of it with your thumb…got a good grip?" I waited a moment. "OK…now swing your leg to that little outcrop a couple feet over. You can do it. *Yes!*"

I knew the young girl's "sewing machine legs" meant she was experiencing stress and fatigue, but her trembling was now replaced with a strong and confident swing to the right as she accomplished the crux move. She made it! The imp nimbly scampered up the rest of the route to the top of the rock, triumphant and beaming with pride. She gave the Rocky Balboa triumphant victory stance on top of the wall with her arms reaching for the sky.

"She never would have listened to me," a voice said. "Thanks."

I turned and met "Dad."

Skinny, with curly long brown hair and a scraggly beard... he looked like a climber.

"I would have loved to be climbing at her age," I said. "Kudos to you for getting her out here. I'm Michelle, by the way." I offered my hand in greeting.

Between short climbs on the rock, after briefly sharing bios, Chris asked if I wanted to go on a trip with him and his friends to Squamish, British Columbia, that upcoming weekend. Immediately assuming this to be a come-on, I retorted that I wasn't looking for a hook-up. Chris laughed, assuring me, "My two friends are married, and I promise I'm not looking either!" He was recently divorced and *not* interested in a girlfriend...they just needed another climber for two ropes that weekend.

Why not? I was between quarters at the UW, nothing was due for my master's program for the next two weeks, and Dr. Neel, my supervising professor, told me the previous day to take a well-deserved break. I knew about the legendary walls at Squamish. I agreed.

It rained. Hard. For the entire weekend.

The four of us spent most of our time in our tents waiting for the unrelenting volume of precipitation to cease. When there was a temporary respite from the deluge, we would venture out into the drizzle and slip on the nearby wet boulders for a little exercise. There were a few top rope climbs, but it wasn't the expected epic multi-pitch climbs on the Chief. We barely had time to set up the gear and start climbing boulders before another squall hit. The misty clouds would periodically part, just long enough to show the expansive granite face of the Chief looming above Howe Sound. It was infuriating to know how close we were to some great climbing. It just wasn't going to happen that weekend.

Yet the three days solidified my friendship with Chris. I had my own tent, but finally invited him in to play cards. Rumbling snores emanated from Bob's and Bruce's tent, so it wasn't a foursome. I heard Chris rustling around, not taking advantage of the time to catch up on sleep. We often both poked our heads out of our tents at the same time when the rain seemed to subside a bit. We might as well share the hope for a salvageable weekend of climbing.

Chris made the best of the situation...which made it tolerable and fun. We talked about everything, laughed, told harrowing tales about climbing escapades gone wrong, and compared scars, boasting about the war stories that had yielded each one. And we played cards. Lots of Hearts, Spite and Malice, and Gin Rummy.

There wasn't much climbing that weekend, but we committed to other trips when we finally gave up mid-day Sunday and packed our gear into the cars. Chris and I were in one car, Bruce and Bob in the other. The four-hour drive home, along the majestic Mountain to Sound Highway, through the bustling streets of Vancouver, crossing the US/Canadian border and back to Seattle went quickly, as Chris and I enjoyed our continuous chatter.

Chris seemed like a brother, or a childhood friend. It was hard to explain, but I knew I needed a platonic relationship with a man after the intense six-year relationship with "Scrawny Ronnie," my previous boyfriend. That had ended abruptly and painfully. I needed a male friend to redeem the masculine species in my mind. At that point, it felt like all acceptable members had died off after my father's generation.

Chris and I often explored alternative venues in Seattle, met weekly at the Honey Bear Bakery above Green Lake for the legendary cinnamon rolls, and climbed locally with friends. Bill and Bob often met us at The Rock. It was great to be in such a natural and fun friendship with a man without the pressures of a relationship.

"What's up?" I asked him at brunch one Saturday morning in a steamy, aromatic bakery as we basked in the sun streaming through the window above our table. For a while now, Chris had been wearing makeup—more makeup than I would ever wear. I'd noticed cakey makeup and thick eyeliner, and today was especially ghastly. "What's with the makeup?"

Startled, confused and visibly caught off guard, he stuttered a reply.

And then, the words spilled out. And what a story it was. The words didn't stop for hours. He only took a break to go to the beverage counter for a second cup of tea after the first hour. He was, he explained, exploring makeup because he was in the process of becoming a woman. In fact, the process would be complete in a couple of months after "the surgery" in Belgium and a few following procedures.

He stumbled through the main events of his journey.

Realizing as a child that he was a girl in a boy's body. That it was not considered acceptable, especially by his father, to carefully dress, feed, and care for his dolls. To want to wear dresses himself and let his hair grow longer so that he could intertwine ribbons into the locks. That he was expected to wrestle and play ball with his male cousins when they came over…not play dress-up with the girls.

For years he tried to fit in. Soccer with the boys in middle school. His lackluster failed attempts at dating while in high school. Going to prom wearing his tuxedo. Marriage and two daughters as a young adult. It didn't work. Sex with his wife was a chore, something that was expected, not a passion.

She was smart. She figured it out. She assumed it was another woman.

And it was. Chris was not the man inside that he appeared to be on the outside.

He nervously explained that he just wanted to correct the mistake made at birth. The doctors here were giving him hormone treatments, counseling sessions, and minor preparation procedures. The final "gender affirmation" surgery was cheaper in Belgium, so he would be traveling there soon for the procedure and then would recover there with friends.

"T.M.I.!" I yelped as Chris delved into details of the actual surgery.

He quickly finished with "…and continued hormonal treatments after that."

Whew. Now what?

"So…do we need to go clothes shopping?" I asked. "I love the thrift store in Wallingford." It was a lot to process, but I seemed surprisingly okay with it all. It was a shock, for sure, but it made sense.

I had worked the flower fields in Skagit County, watching the field boss—my dad—show absolutely no racism, only respect and friendship, to the highly diverse crews. One of my favorite cousins had recently come out as gay. I live in Seattle! There were certainly same-sex couples walking arm in arm along Capitol Hill every time I explored that part of my new home city.

I had a lifetime of examples of how and why to see the value in all people. Besides, this answered so many questions that had been brewing in me for a while. For one thing, it explained how easy it was for the two of us to be in a platonic relationship, yet spend so much time with each other. Somehow, I had always sensed Chris was not who he seemed.

The next few months were a blur. We *did* go thrift store shopping, laughing at the combinations of colorful, feminine clothes added to Chris' repertoire. He and I played dress-up, Chris letting me twirl his hair into French braids. He tried to follow my advice to go easy on the makeup. We met at The Rock a few times to climb, and also continued the Saturday morning pastries. But all that came to a halt in the spring.

Finishing my master's project, the statistical analysis and write-up, and the multiple rewrites from the panel of professors consumed an enormous amount of my time. During a mid-week training hike on nearby Tiger Mountain, I met Dan. I knew this was "it" and even called Mom that night, telling her I met the guy I was going to marry. Yet I struggled to fit in time with him. Phone calls to Chris were brief and growing further apart. Then the calls just ended. I barely noticed as I juggled school and my new relationship with Dan.

Then the invitation arrived in a pink envelope. Pink confetti sprinkled to the floor as I opened it. A stork flying down with a polka dot bundle in its beak. *Please welcome Christina into the world. Help us celebrate at...*

Of course! How was this not on my radar? When had Chris—Christina—and I last talked?

Dan and I would certainly attend. Dan, always wanting to meet my friends, listened intently as I gave him a brief background of Chris' situation. The date and location of the party was set as a priority.

Two weeks later, Dan and I arrived at a brick house in the Ravenna neighborhood of Seattle, greeted by a rainbow flag in the year, loud '70s music, shouting and clinking glasses, and a huge standing-room-only crowd. Through the colorful maze of people, pink streamers and balloons, I saw Chris—now Christina—bedecked in a stunning black off-the-shoulder sheath gown. Christina had colored her hair jet black and curled it, with sparkles added to the ringlets.

With Dan's hand in mine, I approached Christina. "Welcome to womanhood, dear friend," I whispered, hugging her. "You look *mar-ve-lous!*"

Fake eyelashes and the stubbles on Christina's chin brushed against my cheek. "You have no idea how happy I am!"

She welcomed Dan with a firm handshake and the two of us left her surrounded by a colorful entourage of cross-dressers. Dan and I shimmied past a burly man dressed in sparkly gold lame cocktail dress, a tall woman in a blue dress split to her hairy thighs, and so many interesting and fun people. I waved to Bob and Bill, who were skulking in the corner drinking beers. As far as I could tell, they were possibly the only two other straight friends there.

I yelped when my butt was pinched by a large individual in a pink skirt, fishnet stocking and silvery belly dance bra.

"Cute outfit, dude!" and he/she gave me a smile, followed by a fist bump. I glanced at Dan, noticing he looked bewildered. We retreated to the beverage table and watched the party unfold.

The coming-out party was a blast. A true tribute for a wonderful man who became the woman in front of us tonight, although admittedly with a few finishing touches needed. The house was full of friends who had been loyal friends for years. I felt so honored to be a part of Christina's circle and thrilled to see her reach her goal of becoming the woman she always felt she was.

Diana Ross' "I'm coming out...I want the world to know...got to let it show!" was shouted by the crowd as everyone bounced and danced to the beat. Christina was on a small makeshift stage, belting the tune into a microphone. Everyone dancing with arms in the air, shouting the lyrics to the songs, drinking champagne, sharing endless toasts, and lots of stories. As everyone slowed down later that evening, tired and happy for the woman of the hour, Christina gave her final heartfelt words of appreciation.

Dan and I approached Christina. Giving her a hug, I promised to go climbing with her, next time in matching hot pink tights.

As Dan and I descended the front stairs to the street, I winced at his death grip suddenly on my arm. The tension of the evening seemed to explode through him. "Don't ever do that to me again," he said through clenched jaws.

Obviously, the evening was more challenging for him, as a straight man, than I had anticipated. I knew he had grown up with a brother who was gay, and I had just assumed he would see this party as a novel, exciting, and fun experience.

Yet he was clearly shaken. I cooed that everything was okay as I gingerly extracted his fingers from my arm.

Dan was a good man. He was a keeper. He would come along. I realized that, like Christina, Dan simply had a few "finishing touches" needed himself.

Our New Home

(Two Perspectives)

Lucinda

Ouch! Lucinda hit her head on the top of the car yet again. Ellie, the real estate agent, drove along the dirt road leading to the next house she was planning to show Lucinda and her husband, deftly dodging the many protruding rocks and holes. Lucinda's tall torso and the shallow back seat of the small car did not work with this steep, unpaved, bumpy road. She breathed a sigh of relief once they turned the sharp corner, driving away from the steep cliff on their right. *Where were they going?*

Lucinda and Tim both wanted space for Craig and other children they may have in the future. The large house on a quarter acre in the development they just left didn't match their vision. They'd both grown up with space, yet Lucinda shuddered when Tim told Ellie he was looking for something more "out there." What did he mean, exactly?

The drive finally ended after a winding wooded driveway opened to an area of dirt and mud. No yard, no grass, no landscaping. Mud simply covered with wood chips. They parked in front of a simple, two-story farmhouse. Literally, right in front. No garage, no carport. Just a small porch and the dining room window directly in front of the car. A dense aspen grove grew close to the house on one side, with a sparsely replanted unsightly clear cut on the other. No neighbors in sight.

Entering the house, Ellie continued her chatter. "No traffic noise here!" *Isolation from people…I won't have my morning coffee on the porch and be able to wave to my neighbors.* "The owner decided to move closer to family." *Projects every weekend…they must have gotten burned out…no wonder they are moving.* "They hand-laid this beautiful wood floor." *Soft pine, already chunked up. How do you clean THAT?* "Open living space downstairs to allow the family to all be together." *Zero privacy.* "Wood cabinets with plenty of storage." *Cheap plywood…the doors rattle.*

Ellie continued her sales pitch upstairs. Beds were on plywood floors, no carpet. No doors on the closets. "This is obviously a work in process…a labor of love." *Uhh, understatement. LOTS of labor…I'm sure I would NOT love to take on THIS work.*

The answer was clear: No. They didn't need the endless projects of an unfinished house on five acres of undeveloped land in the middle of nowhere. No.

They were starting a family. They both had full-time jobs. Weekends were already filled with friends, camping trips to the woods, spending time with extended families, including two sets of aging parents. Now she was also a new mom. No. A half-finished house with no landscaping was not her next move.

Turning to Tim and Ellie, Lucinda prepared to tactfully suggest another listing. "This is perfect!" Tim said as he looked at Lucinda, expecting mutual enthusiasm. Ready. Ready to sign. Ready to move. *He is ready to take this on...*

"Uhh...can we talk, Tim?"

Tim

Defiance, Mount Si...what is that peak...and that ridge? Tim wondered.

The views only improved as Ellie drove Tim and his wife higher up the dirt road and further away from the development they had just left. The real estate agent carefully avoided the protruding rocks and holes in the dirt road leading to the next house she was planning to show them. Apologizing for the steep and bumpy road, Tim reassured Ellie that this was an asset in providing a deterrent for people wanting to invade the privacy of this neighborhood's residents.

Are those real? There is another one. Gigantic cedar stumps appeared on either side of the driveway, randomly nestled among the recently replanted trees and a blanket of ferns and foxglove from the clear-cut a few years earlier. Ellie's chatter faded as Tim counted the remnants of those mammoth ghosts of decades past, only seen now in history books. Six in the woods along the driveway...incredible!

The drive ended at a farmhouse in the middle of a clearing. As she led them into the house, Ellie continued her chatter. "No traffic noise here!" *Only the birds, the wind, the rustling of trees.* "The owner decided to move closer to family." *Something must have happened. I would never leave this place.* "They hand laid this beautiful wood floor." Tim stopped in his tracks, noting the distressed pine floor, exactly like the old saltbox homes of New England back home. The nostalgia washed over him like an unexpected ocean swell. *I haven't seen floors like this in years. My parents would love these.* "Open living space downstairs to allow the family to all be together." *Palatial compared to our one room home we have now...plenty of space for Craig to run around.* "Wood cabinets with plenty of storage." *Probably double what we have now.*

Ellie continued her sales pitch upstairs. She chattered about the many possibilities in finishing the home...carpet or hardwood, doors. *OK, we need to finish a few things inside, but I can't wait to get outside. I wonder if Lucinda will go for a tractor...we can make this place look like a park. Every window has an incredible view of stumps...or trees...or Mount Si... or Defiance...clumps of foxglove...there isn't a bad view from ANY window!*

"This is obviously a work in process...a labor of love." *I would love to finish this project.* Lucinda was staring out of the windows, equally entranced. This was what they were looking for...space to raise their family. "This is *perfect!*" Tim said, ready to suggest they make an offer. He quickly agreed when Lucinda suggested they step outside to talk.

What Is Wrong with Me?

Clunk...well, *that* was strange.

My keys had slipped from my left hand as I tried to move them from the side of the projector table. I had to use my right hand when the third attempt to pick them up with my left fingers didn't work. Terrified, I wondered why it seemed like I was outside of my body...my head was foggy, even the messages to myself to just pick up the keys seemed fuzzy and far away.

Twenty-eight eyes looked at me, waiting to hear more about the class syllabus I had just placed on the glass of the overhead projector. *Reading Success,* it read, with bullet points of our goals, followed by more information on expectations and grading. They patiently waited for me to open my mouth and explain. As adolescents with learning disabilities, they needed clarity. Yet, I could not seem to form the words to verbalize information about our class. My first attempt was garbled. I shut my mouth.

It was second period on the first day of classes, fall term 1987. We were the purple Kangs of Lake Washington High

School. These students in front of me were my babies. I had taught some of them for the last two years in various classes since landing the job of my dreams right after graduation from Central Washington University. Some of these students had been in first period, *Current Issues*. They loved having a young teacher straight out of college. Likewise, I loved teaching teenagers. Our classes were filled with shared laughter, teasing, music, stories of our lives and references to pop culture. Guaranteed fun, despite the hard work they had come to expect.

But I couldn't teach them. Not then. Not that day. First, the keys dropped. Then my left eye blurred. My leg went numb. I struggled to stand. I tried to compensate my useless left hand with my right, but I needed both to support my sagging body to stay upright. I wanted to be normal…I could *not* freak my students out that first day of school. I needed to sit, but there was no chair nearby. I needed to talk, but I could not get my words out in a coherent sentence. I just couldn't. What was wrong with me?

I looked at Manisha in the third row nearest the door. She had been in classes with me since I started teaching two years ago. Her parents loved me and invited the new, young teacher, who had connected so well with their challenging daughter to a traditional Indian dinner last spring in their home. That's what you did in their home country. Manisha, the beautiful daughter of immigrant parents from India, had been horrified. I, however, had been incredibly honored. Her parents greeted me at the door in their traditional garments and could not have been more gracious and fun. The delectable and colorful food on the ornately designed dishes had opened my normal, bland "meat and potatoes" palette to a world of foreign spices and textures that I had never been exposed to. It was a wonderful evening and, despite instructions from administrators and past professors, I couldn't help but put Manisha on my short list of "favorites."

Now, Manisha was watching me anxiously. She knew something was wrong. My eyes pleaded with her to help. While she came up to the projector table, I quietly mumbled to the class that I wasn't feeling well and replaced the syllabus with their first assignment. Instructions to write a letter with their goals for the class, past experiences with reading, their expectations of me, and the type of books they liked. They were then to browse the books in the back of the room for one that might fit their particular interests and begin to read. We all knew they would take the opportunity to talk and horse around instead.

Manisha took my right arm and I used my left to guide myself along the wall to the door since the sensation above my left elbow gave me some stability. In the hallway, I told her that my body and head "felt weird" and that I needed help to get downstairs to the main office. I leaned heavily on the cold, smooth railing on my left and her arm on my right. The short trip taken daily without thought was a test of my endurance and concentration, as I tried to focus on each step down the cement stairs. We finally made it.

The principal's secretary, June, lifted her grey curly head, raised eyebrows above her round spectacles, showing her alarm. She was surprised to see me during class time. She saw the white pallor of my face and jumped from her desk to grab me. As the self-appointed second mother to this young teacher, June hurriedly instructed me to lie on the cot in the sick room until the nurse could come to our school from her other post in the local middle school. She brought me water, took my temperature, and tucked a comforting blanket along my sides with the assumption that I must be chilled.

Ten minutes later, I was fine. Nothing. I sat up and felt clear. I opened and closed my hands...fine. I stood up...no problem. I called June and clearly articulated the words to tell her that I was ready to head back to class. I rationalized to her...and myself...that it must have been stress and that extra coffee this morning. I had not eaten my usual high protein breakfast as I had hurried to school to get to the copy room before the rush. That must have been it...a caffeine high on an empty stomach. Despite June's protests, I went back upstairs to relieve the vice-principal who had stood in for me, promising to check in with my doctor later.

Class finished with no further interruptions. Then *Practical Writing Skills, Alternative American Government, Peer Tutoring* and my "free" period to review the thirty-two IEPs (Individual Educational Plans) I would be responsible for that year. It was a fun first day...I had almost forgotten the odd experience of second period. Until it happened again.

The out-of-body feeling slowly crept in once more as I neared the cafeteria for the faculty meeting. My eyes blurred; my left leg didn't seem to "get" what it needed to do. Oh no, oh no, oh no. The wall...get to the wall. Terrified, I staggered near the wall to steady myself as I started to wobble. I could not make it. I slumped to the floor near the double doors, waving a few of my colleagues on. "I'm just taking a quick break," I said weakly.

Finally, my teammate, Kathy, saw me. "You look awful!" She exclaimed, trying to help me up, but I was dead weight. Someone else stayed with me as Kathy left to call 911.

Vague memories between school and the hospital. The paramedics asking me to "push" several times…someone's hand against each foot, each hand. I was to try to pull my hand up toward my face, lift my leg off the floor. Raise my hands. Concerned faces as one wrote notes in a book. The ride to the hospital. The oxygen mask. The sterile white emergency room. The doctors, the nurse, the lights, the commotion. And questions.

"What year is it?"

"1987."

"Who is the president?"

"Reagan."

"Tell me about the weather today."

"Cold, but sunny."

"Stick out your tongue. Raise your hands in the air."

In the hospital, a continual stream of white-clad medical staff came in to take blood, ask more questions, test my muscle strength, shine lights in my eyes, and do more tests. Yet I was suddenly fine. It took a little longer this time, but I was back…back to normal. My thoughts were clear. My strong muscles were back. My speech was coherent. It was hard to imagine what had happened.

Until, minutes later, I warned the nurse: "It is coming back!"

As she turned to call for help, my mind seemed to drift away and everything around me blurred. Faces became fuzzy. The noises around me, the movement of equipment, the new people in the room, the chatter…it all seemed distant, like in another room down the hall. *At least it is happening in front of them,* I thought, before everything turned numb and blank. Doctors and nurses sprang into action.

In a midst of the chaos, my parents appeared; Kathy must have called them. Their furrowed brows and wringing hands broke my heart. They were not familiar with hospitals. We were from a strong farming community with few health issues. Hard outdoors work in the fields, riding bikes our whole lives, and eating well had kept all of us from utilizing our family doctor much. I wanted to reassure them…to let them know that we would figure this all out…that I would certainly be fine. But I could not get the words out. I just held out my hand to Mom.

I missed Tim, the new friend I had been hanging out with, a friend that seemed more akin to a soul mate. He was out of state for work. I so wanted to feel his reassuring hands, to have him tell me that he was there for me. Yet, it was probably a good thing that he was gone. It seemed natural to see him as a future partner and I worried that this might freak him out.

The next few hours gave me little opportunity to rest my exhausted body and mind, but I did start to feel normal again eventually. I was scanned through a Siemens MRI machine. More blood draws. A bright light to follow with my pupils. A nurse peered into my mouth, telling me to stick out my tongue. More questions. Our family history of strokes and heart attacks was clarified. My parents and I joked about our huge extended family in the Netherlands. Mom came from a family of sixteen and Dad from a family of ten, and they all had married and bred like rabbits (which represented the translation of my last name… *Conijn* is a hare). Although each of my parents and siblings in our immediate family of six were healthy, every medical issue imaginable was found somewhere among the twenty aunts and uncles and the countless cousins overseas. No one in white laughed.

After a night of no repeat performances, no further signs of a stroke, I was released with a diagnosis of TIAs, transient ischemic attacks, which were explained as "mini-strokes." A flurry of questions and a thick wad of discharge instructions: See a cardiologist within the next week. Contact your primary physician tomorrow. Can you be with someone at all times for a while, in case it happens again? Monitor your diet for reduced sodium. Explore stress relief possibilities. How are you getting home? Who do you live with? Who will you call on a regular basis to check in?" It was too much. I just wanted to turn off the noise and go to sleep.

My parents brought me back to my studio apartment in Wallingford, a quaint neighborhood in Seattle, and they left after I promised to call three times a day. I slept much of the following day, calling the high school in between naps to let them know the story and to set up another day off. The next day was filled making appointments for my doctor and the recommended cardiologist and then researching TIAs. As promised, I called my worried parents three times, and Kathy, to assure them that I was fine, despite the nagging questions of why these three TIA's happened...and *would they happen again?*

Yet, as with many twenty-something-year-olds, life went back to normal very quickly. It was easy to ignore this anomaly and return to teaching, time with friends, skiing, running, hiking, and sharing as much as possible with Tim in our blossoming relationship. A trip to Europe shortly after the 1987 fall of the Berlin Wall with my sister, kayaking the Stikine River in Alaska with a group of friends, and many other adventures closer to home. The courtship with Tim during that time was filled with shared outdoor challenges and a growing love for each other, eventually resulting in a fun wedding and, later, two children. I was strong, confident, and ready for what life had to offer. The TIAs were a distant memory.

Until eight years later.

Following a series of recurrent UTIs (urinary tract infections), my new primary physician referred me to a neurologist. Although an MRI exposed two demyelination spots, the neurologist said that he would need to wait and see for further symptoms and more progression of demyelination before he could give a firm diagnosis and treatment plan. Frustrated, I sought a second opinion.

The second neurologist asked me to bring a list of all medical oddities that had ever occurred in my lifetime. I painstakingly went through old records and called my parents to develop a timeline, which included the TIAs, the sudden and periodic vision drops, recurrent UTIs, difficulty swallowing, bouts of dysfunctional left leg and foot, heat sensitivity, and periodic intense waves of fatigue. Even shingles as an infant. Although the MRI results showed minimal plaques, he reported that these unexplained medical events were clearly "attacks," including what seemed like the TIAs back in 1987.

Devastating news. Frightening prospect for the future. However—*finally*, a firm diagnosis and a treatment plan. So began my journey with Relapsing Remitting Multiple Sclerosis.

The Queen Bee and Her Hive

M y body tensed, anticipating the brief, searing pain as the desperate bee thrust its venom into my skin. The poor bee. It was ultimately myself who knowingly sacrifices this innocent insect and its fellow hive mates for my personal benefit. As each stinger punctured my skin, the barbs caught into the initial epidermis layer. As the tweezers lifted each bee off of me, the barbs prevented the stinger's release and the bees' abdomens split open. An inevitable and gruesome death.

What number are we on? It was my daughter's turn. This was, in fact, a family affair. Like the complex job of each bee in the hive, everyone in my family had a role. Craig, only ten, was the self-proclaimed expert on handling the bees for this purpose. He took the job seriously as he eagerly gathered stories to later share with his cronies during recess. Terra, only six, was *sure* she was just as competent as her older brother and just wanted to be mommy's nurse.

Thankfully, Tim was there to navigate their enthusiasm and their hands as they took turns, gingerly holding the long-nose tweezer with a flailing and angry bee on the tip, guiding it out of the mesh-covered box through the tiny hole made for that purpose. The ice cube on my back was removed and the bee was then held onto my cold, reddened skin.

My role was to fight the tears and not twitch in pain for each of the twenty stings.

BST, or "Bee Sting Therapy," was the latest of my many attempts to combat the growing number of physical challenges multiple sclerosis had brought to my life. Bee sting therapy had helped my friend, Amy, with her arthritis. It was currently being studied by the MS Society and other organizations. There were so many promising claims on the internet for energy level and functionality. The manual I had ordered months ago touted success even dating back to ancient cultures, its diagrams clearly illustrating the method and acupuncture sites to use. There *must* be something to it. My doctor did not think so.

Yet, I was desperate. It was clear that my legs had progressed to yet another, less functional level and I was not sure that I would be able to walk much longer. It was winter and I had been regularly scanning our snow-covered yard from the living room couch. One day, it was uncharacteristically warm and a few bees had ventured out of their hive to investigate the possibility of an early spring. Tim joined me on the couch, watched the bees with me, reluctantly listening once again to my litany of accumulated physical and functional losses endured in the last several months. It had not been a good year. I had started needing to wall-walk, then progressed to a single walking pole, shortly afterward needing a pole for each hand, and then a walker. Now even that was difficult. I was exhausted. My hopes of it "all going away" was clearly not reality. We finally agreed that it was time to try another strategy.

We started that winter.

Tim collected the bees from the hive for a few months, knocking on the snow-covered structure to catch the guards who ventured out of the hive's small doorway to protect their queen. His jar was always ready. The brave souls had no chance. After several months, it was clear that the hive was not strong enough to sustain the multiple trips out of the hive into the cold winter air. The community weakened until it eventually disappeared. Now a small mesh-covered box of humming bees was regularly sent from a medical bee supply farm in California, the lady from our post office calling each month nervously to report, "Your bees are in…can you pick them up *today?*"

Bees are such gentle creatures. Not an adjective most people consider when stepping on one in the yard or accidentally interrupting a nest in the woods. Memories of tiny tongues licking the honey off my fingers when Tim showed me his two hives early in our courtship caused me now to smile. The bees had tickled my fingertips, making me giggle nervously. Watching the bees furiously buzz around Tim each time he tenderly worked the hive, it was clear that they trusted this white-clad man with the heavy gloves and large hat. They, in turn, pollinated his garden, helping produce robust crops of basil, tomatoes, garlic and peppers. The two hives produced a steady hum, adding to the sound of the rolling waves on nearby Alki Beach, to produce an ambiance unique to our tiny beach home. Even our neighbors loved Tim's bees. The bees were a source of joy on sunny days as we watched the insects venture out to find pollen to feed their queen and her young brood. And they brought sorrow after a hornet attack when many headless bees were strewn around the opening and base of the hive.

The arrival of baby Craig a year after Tim and I were married required the move from our tiny, single-room beach home to the large unfinished mountain house tucked between the bases of Mount Si and Mount Tenerife, an hour's drive away from the beachfront of Seattle to the mountains surrounding North Bend. Watching the bees now from the porch of our new home in the woods, I often think of the many mornings spent on the front porch of our beach cabin, enjoying the buzz of bees as they began their morning journeys from their sun-soaked hive to the garden. Here in the mountains they would have more room to roam, like our children would. There were foxglove, heather, and other meadow flowers. There were fruit trees nearby at the neighbors. Yet shortly after our move, those productive workers had been nearly decimated by the black bear that visited not one, but two nights in a row to gather honey. The winters were harsh, the drizzle of Seattle's winter rain replaced with higher elevation snow. Yet the queen survived and the hive seemed to thrive.

Now bees were the source of yet another treatment for my battle against MS. The bees would hopefully help stall the progression of the insidious spread of plaque on the myelin meant to protect my nerves from breaking down. They might stop the weakening of my runner's legs and allow me to climb and bike again. The energy these creatures unwillingly gave in their final powerful thrust would hopefully transfer to my fatigued body.

Returning to the living room couch, I noted that my lower back was aching. My stomach on the cushions caused an uncomfortable arch on my spine. Twelve pink spots on my back and six on my legs clearly marked the map of sting sites.

The "team" was nearly finishing. Yet, those final ankle sites would be the worst.

"Yes, I'm okay," I answered as Terra saw me flinch and wanted to make sure she had not hurt mommy.

"Really?" Her adorable, brown pixie face was level with mine as she crouched next to my face by the couch, chocolate orbs staring directly into my eyes.

"Yes, Terra…you are really helping mommy!"

Satisfied, Terra returned to my feet to wait for her next turn. It was now Craig removing the ice and holding the tweezers near my left ankle.

Brace.

First Craig, then Terra on the right ankle.

Done.

Tim retrieved the tweezers and deftly removed each stinger from my skin. He guided the two young assistants to the kitchen, knowing that I now needed time. It took a few minutes to let the pain subside as I visualized the poison surging through my body. Slowly, I stood up, gathered the litter of dead bees onto one of the discarded rags, picked up the tweezers and ice cube tray, and wiped the melting ice. After a few deep breaths, I joined my clan in the kitchen, knowing I had a forty-eight-hour reprieve before the next treatment.

My Bee Sting "Therapy" lasted a little over a year. We concurrently tried to monitor the research being conducted through the MS Society in the Netherlands and through other sources during that year. One study found no improvement, except reported improved energy. When another study was discontinued due to the thought that BST may actually *increase* the production of plaque internally (while seeming to temporarily help with external symptoms), we discontinued the "therapy." My energy did seem to improve, but it was not worth the postulation that the venom may accelerate an already overactive immune system.

Not an Option

The scene on the beach is bright and colorful. The purple, orange, and red Gore-Tex dry suits, worn by my family and our dear friends from Germany, contrast sharply with the light grey ocean, reflecting the slightly pink and dusty dawn sky. The aqua-blue and red kayaks are lined up on the beach. The diving sea birds are silhouetted against the ever-changing muted morning backdrop. Excited, but a little anxious, I sit on my log, just outside of my tent, watching the preparations. Everyone has a job. Mine is to conserve energy.

Well beyond insisting on helping in these situations, I accept my family's wishes to relax and let us all enjoy our family adventures…together. "Not an option, Mom," they told me when I suggested staying home. "We're not going if you're not going, Lucinda," said Tim when he finished the aggressive itinerary for our kayaking trip with our friends. My grown kids have always reminded me of the many times, decades ago in their young childhoods, when it was *never an option* for them to stay home when Tim and I wanted to explore. It had *never been an option* for them back then, and it was not now, for me. We just needed to adjust to my limitations.

Now I follow their lead and reluctantly allow them to help me. I remember needing to dress Terra into her tiny climbing harness at age five. Now, she now helps me into a dry suit, struggling to get the tight neck gasket over my thick skull. I remember teaching Craig to ski between my legs when he was three. Now, he firmly takes my arm and guides me down to the beach. I remember Tim's appreciation as I competently balanced child raising, working in Seattle, and assisting his elderly parents when he would be out of state on work trips. Now, he supports me into the water and carefully holds my upper arms as I submerge into the icy ocean and burp the air out of my air-filled dry suit. The Hauser and Emmelheinz families work as a team to stabilize the boat and help me awkwardly climb into the cockpit. It's not an option. It's never an option. I'm going, and I'm accepting their help.

This morning, our two families are leaving our remote camp on Island 44 in the Nuchaletz Provincial National Park on the outer north coast of Vancouver Island. We had only just arrived by kayak yesterday afternoon after a water taxi shuttled us on an eighteen-mile route from Zaballes to Rosa Island, where we unloaded five kayaks and a week's worth of gear, food, and water for the two families. After a languid paddle through the rest of the Nuchaletz Inlet, we approached the back side of Island 44. The protected cove where we hoped to camp, on the other side, required us to face the rolling ocean waves and strong head winds, with only a distant reef breaking the full force of the Pacific Ocean on us. We braced our legs against the boats, bent our bodies forward, and paddled like hell. We made it.

Last night had been magical. We had set up camp, looking to the water with its shallow rocky tidepools, birds swooping down to investigate the intruders and islands in the distance. My tent had been carefully prepared with the tools required for my special needs: the extra thick sleep pad, complete with bumper edges. My nighttime baclofen in the small bag near my sleeping bag for the inevitable night spasms. A bathroom area by large rocks, prepared to provide the balance and privacy I would need. A stump, strategically placed by the door of the tent to allow my arms to help push me up, since my legs weren't much help. I was ready for the week.

The Emmelheinz clan and my family returned from the tidepools, excited to show me what they had gathered. Their buckets were filled with intensely orange-red mini-mussels. We later gorged on the fresh steamed mollusks dipped in butter with no appetite left for our freeze-dried meals.

The sunset last night was intense, a palette melding the hues of orange, red, yellow, and magenta and showcasing the silhouettes of distant islands and sea stacks. Succumbing to the expected fatigue after the sustained effort of the day, I stayed at camp to enjoy the view from my log, hearing voices carry over the calm evening water as my family and dear friends went out in kayaks after dinner and discovered a large pod of sea otters sleeping in rafts among the kelp fields. It was lovely, but the nighttime rest we needed last night eluded us: I'd woken suddenly to Tim's instructions to get out and move our camp because the slapping water from the ocean was only a few feet from the tent. We had miscalculated the extent of the incoming tides when choosing out tent sites. Johannes had woken Tim earlier. They'd watched as the tide came in closer and closer to the sleeping campers.

Deprived of the full slumber our bodies needed to restore completely, we still woke early today, day number seven of our carefully planned two-week trip. Despite the usual detail provided on the itinerary for each day, today's entry simply read, "Explore, explore, explore." So, with tide charts, a plastic covered map of both Nuchaletz and Esperanza Inlets, and enough food for lunch, we are now finally launching from the beach. Soon, the camp behind us becomes smaller and smaller.

It is eerily quiet with only the subtle, rhythmic sounds of paddles dipping in the water, birds squawking in the distance, and a faint ten-year-old voice complaining that he is old enough to have his own kayak. We all smile. Timmy is the youngest in our group with the cocky self-assurance a typical ten-year-old has of his physical abilities. We knew it wouldn't be long before his father will be the primary force propelling their kayak forward. In the meantime, the sky is lovely, the water smooth, and the day is promising.

It will be important to pace myself during this physically demanding day. My energy is limited. I need to have it last. While kayaking, my legs will not need to carry me, but they are working while hidden under the spray skirt in the kayak. I feel the pressure of my abductors as they press to each side of the kayak, knees wedged firmly into the small space near the top outer edge of the cockpit. That pressure will be critical when turning the double kayak or if in rough water when bracing or just balancing against the waves. My weakened core needs to hold a sitting position all day. My arms need to help propel the double kayak forward. I lightly paddle, mimicking Tim's pattern to avoid the wasted energy of excessive splashing or paddles hitting each other.

Kayaking. Not what we imagined we would do until we grew older.

Yet, as my multiple sclerosis weakened my muscles progressively each year, Tim had discovered this sport to replace the mutual love of the mountains and the physical challenges of getting on, up, around, over and/or down them. To enjoy our mutual passion of the outdoors together, we needed to find alternatives to skiing, hiking, biking, and climbing. His solution is kayaking, and this is the result of that decision. He signed the family up for the Mountaineers Sea Kayaking class and told us afterwards. Not an option. We needed to be ready for our next family adventure.

So here we are. We have just approached the end of the cove with two choices ahead of us. To reach the first beach destination in the distance, we could opt for the smooth easy route around the bend or go a little further and ride the waves between the two sea stacks ahead. The German girls choose the first. The rest of us paddle ahead in four kayaks to the rocks ahead. Tim and I, then Johannes and Timmy, ride the swell and enter the cove in a thick floating bed of sea kelp. We hear a shriek and turn to see Terra's boat being tossed over by a rogue wave. Before I have time to panic, Terra has done a wet exit out of the flipped kayak and is in the process of a self-rescue, Craig already alongside her boat to keep it steady and hold her paddle. Beautiful, classic textbook rescue. Our course instructor would be proud.

After a short break on the beach, Terra is warm enough to get going again, although I would have welcomed more time to build up my reserves. We decide on Catala Island in the Esperanza Inlet for lunch. It requires a lengthy open ocean crossing, but the weather is good and the rolling waves seem innocuous.

Once on the water, it is clear the waves are much larger than they seemed from the shore. The exhilaration of rolling from the top of one to the bottom, looking up at a wall of water is only tempered by my need to see my kids. I exhale a breath of relief each time Craig or Terra appear as little dots on a distant roll. We paddle hard with no opportunities to sit back and give our arms a rest.

The island is finally in sight. Our anticipation helps to increase our pace and we get there in short order. The waves crash in small foamy rolls as we approach this picturesque island, the white sandy beach lined with driftwood walls, wind bent trees, and beach grass. The paddling has sapped more of my energy than expected and the boys need to help me to the sun-bleached logs up the beach. The warmth of the sun against the logs feels wonderful…to a point. However, soon the boys help me move to a shady spot after we have been basking for a half hour in the sun, the heat insidiously drain-ing my energy. My hands fumble to unzip my suit and open my water bottle.

After a few hours, we note that in the midst of relaxing, body surfing, and snacking, the water has slowly become more turbulent, roughly crashing its white caps on shore. Johannes and Tim encourage us to pack up and prepare to leave. Quickly. We pick up the pace. I look at Tim. He knows that stress increases my spasticity and instability.

"Just do your best," he says.

It is clear that we should have left earlier. Our suits are on, the kayaks are packed, and we are at the water's edge. The breaking waves have only increased in their intensity while we were preparing to leave. I see the men's concern as they instruct the others to move the kayaks to a part of the beach only nominally calmer. A plan is quickly devised. Tim's and my double kayak is the first into the water, with Johannes and Craig pushing us off. Then the mother-daughter double, followed by Johannes and Timmy, and then Terra pushed off by her brother. Finally, my first-born in his single. The unspoken question—how will he Craig able to push off, mount, secure his skirt, and then paddle like hell through the now crashing waves on his own? We all breathe a sigh of relief as he pulls it off. Fifteen minutes later, in what seems like a lifetime, all five boats are off the island and moving slowly against a headwind. The rolling open ocean waves obscure the land cropping ahead. Our destination.

Despite paddling efficiently and hard, the land remains stubbornly distant. It is difficult to know if we were making any progress. It sure doesn't seem so. Tim's urging to paddle harder pushes me to do so…harder…harder…with my repetitive mantra, *you can do it, you can do it, you can do it, yes, you can.* The winds prevent conversations. I catch the glances of the others as we try to stay close enough in range to see each other.

Finally, there is land. We think.

Another problem—the one we had read about when preparing for the trip. The predicted, ominous, thick fog has shrouded the water and islands, leaving visibility at barely ten feet. Plus, the tide must have gone out because the water is shallow with ridges in the sand clearly visible beneath our kayaks. Sandbars. We can barely put a paddle tip in the water. Unable to navigate visually and worried about grounding the kayaks, Tim is pulling out the plastic-covered map and his compass. Where is our island?

Honestly? I don't care. There are seven other able-bodied and smart outdoorsmen (and women) to get us home. I am toast. I just want to get out of this boat and into my tent. I miss my daily afternoon horizontal session on the couch. No more paddling, no more bracing, no more thinking. I lean back in the kayak, close my eyes, and lull myself into a half-sleep.

Terra shouts, "It's over there!" when she spies our tents in the distance two islands away. The fog had lifted for a few moments. I open my eyes and our group paddles in that direction, barely avoiding the sand bar that I had missed as the team's lookout.

Our boats finally hit land and I look at Tim, wearily letting him know that I am done, but I didn't need to. He knows my limits and today I have exceeded them. The fatigue has reached every inch of my body. Craig holds the boat, Terra the paddles, Tim and Johannes lift me by my arms. It takes both of them to lift me out of the boat. There is no *let me do it* this time. There is nothing more my body can do. With their help, I am returned to my log, barely moving my legs to help the men.

Exhausted, I watch the busy group clean up our gear. My family and friends work against this vibrant backdrop of ocean, sky, seabirds, a few sea otters, and a rainbow of colorful gear. I am incredibly thankful that multiple sclerosis did not stop my family from wanting to share the magic of this trip with me. Today was a wonderful adventure; each day of this trip has held new and exciting experiences as we enjoyed the beauty of coastal British Columbia.

Tim's itinerary shows that there is more planned with kayaking, whale watching, salmon fishing, and camping. More to experience, more to explore. No option except to embrace each new adventure with unquestionable support from my family and friends.

And I ask myself: what's next?

Acknowledgements

It is impossible to list everyone. However, I am indebted to my terrific children, Craig and Terra, my extended family, and our dear friends who have all filled my life with so many rich experiences to draw from.

"*Hartelijk dank*" to my mother, Maria DeGoede Conijn, who endured endless questions about her fascinating past growing up in a family of sixteen during WWII in rural Netherlands on a tulip farm, later emigrating to Canada with her new husband, my dearly missed father.

Thanks to our writing instructors, Richard and Evelyn, as well as my supportive writing partners: Katie, John, Carolyn, Laura, and Al. What a fun class! The shared humor, patience, and insight of this incredible group resulted in, not only improved writing skills but also a trusting community of writing friends. Kudos to the Swedish Medical Center Foundation and their donors for supporting this and other virtual classes for so many of us.

Finally, love and appreciation to my husband, Tim. He constantly finds new avenues for our shared outdoor adventures, supplies his wife with great almond lattes and scrumptious meals, cracks me up with his corny jokes, and now turns a blind eye to untouched projects and chores while I learn the art of creative writing.

Laura Nicol

About the Author

Laura Nicol is a Seattle native and has lived in the region most of her life. She attended the University of Washington and earned a degree in Aeronautical and Astronautical Engineering. Since Boeing was in a recession when she graduated, she moved to California for a couple of years and worked for NASA. The siren song of the Pacific Northwest called her back and she returned to Seattle as quickly as possible.

While working at Boeing, she met her husband-to-be, also an engineer, in the next bay over. Together they enjoyed many of the outdoor activities available in the Pacific Northwest, exploring from the murky depths of Puget Sound to the frozen mountain peaks of the Cascades. These experiences often create the backdrops for her stories. The arrival of their two children allowed Laura and her husband to experience the natural wonders from new viewpoints, including adding gummy worms to the ten essentials required for outdoor survival.

When her husband developed a neurological disease, her active outdoor life morphed into gardening and playing the piano. Learning to write stories rather than technical reports has become a new and challenging pastime.

Kayaking

A gentle push, sand scraping the hull, and we are floating free. Free. A few strokes and we are coordinated, pulling smoothly away from the shore. Our friends are waiting, their red, yellow, orange, and green kayaks like tropical flowers floating on the water. We begin our circumnavigation of the lake, staying together in a companionable flotilla.

The air is mountain fresh and the clouds are drifting apart. The ripples sparkle in the sunlight. We pause, staying quiet, as a family of common mergansers paddle by. The female always makes me smile because the rust-colored feathers on her head stick up; she looks like a very frazzled mother. We are drawn by the sound of water falling over rocks and slowly paddle into an inlet to investigate.

As we continue along the shore I twist around and ask Rob, "How're you doing?"

He has a lovely smile and gives me a nod. "This is great, honey. I feel good, really good," he replies. I feel my worries dissipate and I begin to relax and enjoy the day.

We used to be intrepid adventurers. We would save up

our vacation days at work and take fabulous trips. Sometimes we'd take leave without pay, never at risk of losing vacation days. We loved the outdoors and dabbled in lots of sports. Competent in many, masters of none.

Then one Friday Rob's feet were numb and by Monday he could hardly get out of bed. Doctors' appointments by the score. Finally, a diagnosis of an autoimmune disease. Cane, walker, manual chair, power chair, wheelchair van.

Our daughter said, "But you're my dad. You can't be sick." Well, there's sick that you get over in a week to ten days, and there is sick for the rest of your life. Most of our friends continued on with their outdoor lives, slowly drifting away. We were sad for a long, long time as we adapted to our new reality, missing our active outdoor life, missing friends. But we have new friends now, people who walk with a halting gait or not at all, who use aids for "activities of daily living," who deal with challenges every day, hour and minute of their lives. People who aren't defined by their illness.

My fingers trail in the cool water, leaving little V shapes on the surface as we slowly drift by the reeds. The current from the little stream flowing into the lake moves us gently along. The sun is dipping behind the ridge. We will have to be back soon, but we are dawdling, extending this magical day for as long as possible.

"Hey, Judy, look up and to your right. There's an eagle soaring," Rob says quietly. "Remember all the eagles in Glacier Bay?"

"Yes, I see it. And remember the Cry birds?" I ask. We both laugh at the well-worn joke. These imaginary birds sit on the icebergs and call, "Cry, Cry, Christ I'm cold." I pretend we are back in Alaska, a week in the wilderness with bears and whales and friends. But today's paddle is timed by a watch, not the sun and tides and available landings. Goldfinches flash in the trees as we paddle quickly back, not wanting to keep our friends from the MS Adventure Club waiting.

Four people from Outdoors for All are standing on the beach. As our bow plows into the sand, they pull our kayak out of the water. Two place a bench across the stern of the kayak and hold it steady. Two lift Rob onto the bench and help him slide across into his power chair.

"Cheated death once again!" he says with a joyful laugh.

The Strawberry Fields

Our parents are taking off for the summer to sail to Alaska. I really want to go, but *noooooo*. So, they had to decide what to do with me and my brother. I'm twelve, old enough to baby sit, so they could just pay me to stay home and look after myself. But *noooooo* again. Ron gets to go to science camp for the summer because he is just so darned smart. I get farmed out to our grandparents on, wait for it, The Farm. Does that sound fair? Don't get me wrong, I love my grandparents, but an entire summer on the farm? Please. Give me a break. What about my friends? Well, at least I know what I will write about for the obligatory back to school essay, "What I did this summer." Blech.

Mom gives me a list of rules about helping out, dishes, vacuuming, all that stuff I already know. Then she says, "And I don't want you riding on the tractor." What? She can't be serious. I love standing on the tow bar behind Gramps. He won't let me ride while he's plowing or harrowing or whatever, but I get to ride when he's bringing the tractor in from the field to put it in the barn for the night. Just because he rolled it last summer Mom thinks it is too dangerous. He wasn't even hurt. We'll see.

I have been packing for a week and the day after school's out, we leave town. First, they drop me off at The Farm, not even staying for lunch, and then take Ron over to Seabeck for the stupid science camp. They'll go back to Seattle and set sail for Alaska in a couple of days.

I help Grams fix lunch and Gramps comes in from the field, first washing up at the spigot outside. We sit down at the huge old antique dining table. It must have been intended for a much larger room because it takes up way too much space in the kitchen. I always bang my shins when I scoot my chair in. Stupid table. The kitchen smells like apples and cinnamon, so I know we will get pie for dessert, and nothing is better than Grams' apple pie. Lot of times Gramps has a big piece of pie for breakfast and he puts chicken gravy on it. Yuck.

It's June, so it's strawberry season. I love strawberry season. I am really good at picking. Gramps' rule is that you have to pick a row clean, starting at the top and going all the way to the bottom. You don't get to row hop, moving over to another row when you see a really nice clump of berries. Of course, the people who pay to pick get to do that, but I am paid to pick. So, I pick clean. I am really flexible, so bending over doesn't bother me. Sometimes I pick on one side and then the other and sometimes I straddle the row. I get paid by the pound, but that will be in a couple of weeks.

Right now, the berries are just beginning to show color. As soon as the flowers show, Gramps quits watering with the overhead sprinkler system. He runs water down between the rows so the leaves and flowers and fruit don't get wet and rot. I love helping him with this, so Grams lets me skip the washing up. He waits for me while I quickly change into my Farm Girl clothes.

We make a great team. He uses his small hoe to take out the weeds and his big hoe to make sure the water runs all the way down the slope, from the top of the field to the bottom. Every plant has to drink to make big fat red berries. I get to direct the water from the irrigation pipe into the ditches between the rows. We water several rows at a time and then I make little dams and divert the water into new rows. I have my own hoe to do this and it requires a lot of attention to detail. You can't have the water breaking through a dam and seeping into a row that has already been watered. That's just wasteful. Gramps helped build Grand Coulee Dam, so that's probably why I am so good at this.

The season is now at its peak and the warm air smells delightful. As my nose gets close to the plants, I can taste the juicy sweet berries even before I pop one in my mouth. Lots of people are coming to pick every day. Gramps assigns them rows, but, of course, they jump all over the place. They pay by the pound for the berries they pick and if they want more, they buy the ones I pick. Gramps also takes orders from people in town. Sometimes I ride into town with him to help make the deliveries. If there are extra cups of berries, I can always sell them on the steps of the Court House, which is fun because sometimes people give me tips. I save my money for when Grams and I go to town and visit the second-hand stores.

Well, strawberry season is over and we are plowing up one of the fields. To be accurate, I am sitting under the apple tree, which is covered with little green apples, reading my book, and Gramps is riding the tractor. The field is on a hill side, so when the dirt dries it's great for running down as fast as possible, and maybe falling and getting really dirty. It's the most fun when my brother and the cousins are here and we have races. There's a pipe at the bottom, which brings water from the spring. It's really cold and refreshing on a warm day. When I take a bath afterward, the dirt ring in the tub is epic. Oh yes, that is one of the things Mom reminded me to do. Always wash the bath tub and only use one towel to dry off.

Gramps disconnects the plow, so I know he's heading to the barn. I hop up, ready to stand behind him on the tow bar. But then he stops beside me and gets off. "Wanna drive it back?" he asks. And just like that I'm sitting in the big old tractor seat. It's metal, but contoured to fit, and the beat-up old blanket is soft and warm.

He shows me how to use the clutch and brake and gear stick, but I already know from riding behind him and watching so many times before. It takes a little practice to get going. Driving carefully along the dirt track, I pass the corn and bean fields. I concentrate really hard on the narrow path by the falling down shed, where Gramps rolled the tractor, and make it to the barn without mishap. I stop in front of the double doors and Gramps drives it on in. Giving him a big hug and thank you, I laugh all the way to the house. Super best day ever!

The Test

Lorraine was tired of waiting. Every time she asked when she would be assigned to a flight test she was brushed aside and told to be patient. Now she was really irritated and decided to take action. She quickly returned to her desk from the supervisor's office and sat down. Opening the big bottom drawer of her desk, she set her purse in her lap. Carefully stacking a few thick documents and two large books she lifted them up a good ten inches and let them drop onto her desk. A *metal* desk. A very satisfying boom sounded throughout the room. Perhaps that would get their attention since talking fell on deaf ears. Slinging her purse over her shoulder she walked toward the exit, grabbing her coat off the hook on her way past.

"Don't cry," she kept telling herself. The office contained thirty desks and she knew thirty pairs of eyes were following her. "Head up. Don't cry" she repeated over and over as she walked across the enormous room. She sat in her car for a few minutes, letting the tension and anger ease before heading home for the weekend.

That evening she was sitting on the couch with Mallow,

her big gray cat, contentedly purring beside her. With her feet propped up, she was eating chocolate fudge ice cream straight from the carton with a very large spoon when the phone rang. "Hello?"

"Hi Lorraine, it's Lizzie."

Well, this was odd. She and Lizzie were office friends, sometimes having lunch together, but they didn't see each other outside of work. Maybe she had some office gossip about her noisy exit this afternoon.

"Hey, Lizzie, what's up?"

"Uh, Lorraine, Steven asked me to call you and tell you that there is a flight test tomorrow morning. If you want to go be at the field at 7:00."

Steven was her lead at work. Lizzie was one of the engineering aides in the group.

"Lizzie, no hard feelings, I hope, but an aide doesn't call an engineer to give an assignment. That isn't the way it's done. Steven or one of the other engineers should have called me and not used you as a go-between. Tell them I am going to go visit my Grandma this weekend. Have a nice evening, see you Monday. Bye."

Looks like she finally got their attention.

Lorraine sat quietly, petting her cat and gritting her teeth. "Men!" she said exasperated. "Cowards." Mallow nudged her hand in total agreement.

On Monday, she arrived at work exactly on time. She didn't want anyone thinking she felt apologetic or give them an excuse to criticize her for being late. The room was unusually quiet. She could feel their eyes on her and hoped she didn't trip on the carpet. She hung up her coat, put her purse away, and got to work. Other than a few brief "Good Mornings," no one said anything to her about anything.

Mid-afternoon, Steven, her lead, came out of the supervisor's office. He took his seat next to her and said, "There is a flight test Wednesday. I want you to go."

She quelled a caustic response and simply said, "Good. Give me the details."

She had earned her Aeronautical and Astronautical Engineering degree at the University of Washington in 1971 and had thought she would be going to work at Boeing. However, the airplane industry was in a recession. Two years earlier, SPEEA, the union for aeronautical engineers, had actually sent reps to the school to encourage students to change their major. Reverse recruiting. Ninety students dropped to sixty by graduation and she was one of only two women in the class.

Job applications from Boeing were nonexistent. There were billboards around town that read, "Last person leaving turn out the lights." She accepted a job in the Bay Area and knew she was lucky.

Unfortunately, many of her classmates didn't get job offers. Someone, a friend no less, suggested she got the job because she was a woman. "Possibly helped," she responded calmly. "But it probably didn't hurt that I was in the top ten and I also worked in the wind tunnel for two years. Hard to tell, though."

After a few years of layoffs and a hiring freeze Boeing was hiring again. Now with a couple of years' experience, she'd returned to the Pacific Northwest and started working in Flight Controls in the Commercial Division. She was working on a derivative of the 747 Jumbo jet and looking forward to flight testing.

Just a few months ago, her supervisor had called her into his office. The company was doing employee reviews, asking the new hires what their five-year plans were. She had told him that her immediate goal was to be involved in the flight test program. She passed her flight physical and was looking forward to participating. But time after time, the other new hires, the male ones, of course, were sent. Never her. Every time she asked, she was told to be patient. She would be assigned soon.

The young men had master's degrees, but she had work experience. She had worked as a test engineer in the largest wind tunnel in the world while they stayed in school because jobs were scarce. Now she was the only woman engineer in the entire warehouse-sized building. But Boeing had hired her. She wasn't going to sit around as if her only reason for existing was to fulfill their affirmative action numbers. So she had staged a temper tantrum. Now she was finally going on a flight test.

Lots of different departments put in requests for flight test data. The Flight Test Department drew up the flight plans to acquire the data in the most efficient manner. She and her lead, Steven, looked over the portion of the flight plan that she would be responsible for. Fred, the lead who sat behind her, would be going along instead of Steven, since most of the data collected that day would be for his group.

Wednesday morning was bright and clear. She arrived early at Boeing Field, watched the fueling, and waited excitedly to board the plane. She wore her pink brushed cotton jeans, not that she was making a point or anything.

The air was cool and smelled of jet fuel as she walked across the tarmac and climbed the stairs. There were about thirty people on board and the senior test pilot, copilot, and engineer were settled in the cockpit. Catering had just delivered the box lunches, the stairs were being wheeled away, and a Flight Test crewman closed the door. Seat belts fastened, flaps down, engines spun up, and they accelerated down the runway. Rotate, lift off, landing gear up, flaps up, turning east to cross the Cascades. Flight testing would not be conducted over a populated area.

She sat by the window, so she could watch the spoilers and ailerons follow the pilot's commands to turn. That was her area of expertise. Fred, who was sitting next to her, would be collecting data from the elevators on the horizontal tail. They made the nose of the plane go up to climb and down to dive. Well, lose altitude anyway. He already had his briefcase open and was checking over the order of the tests.

"I am really not looking forward to this," Fred said to her.

"Why's that?"

He looked at her for a moment, a little frown on his forehead. "They didn't tell you?" he said slowly. "Today we're mainly testing the elevators. The stress and loads people are along to collect data, too. Mostly we will be flying roller coasters. I have Dramamine if you would like some now," he offered.

"Oh. Thanks, but I won't need it."

"Are you sure? I have plenty."

"No, I'm good, but that's very nice of you to offer. Thanks."

Oh boy, she thought. This is going to be a great day.

Watching out the window she tried to name some of the peaks passing below. No way to miss Mt. Rainier, its glaciers shining in the morning light. The terrain flattened out as they crossed the Cascades and the plateaus and wheat fields of Eastern Washington were passing below them.

The captain came on the intercom and announced they

would be starting the first run in five minutes. "Seat belts buckled? Is everyone ready?"

As Fred had said, there were a lot of roller coaster runs. Some of the runs involved fast elevator deflections, so the plane nosed up and down quickly without a lot of change in altitude. For some of the runs, the plane gained quite a lot of altitude and pitched forward quickly so Lorraine felt like she was weightless and only the seat belt kept her from floating away. Diving. The pull up at the bottom increased the gravity and pressed her into her seat. She imagined herself being an astronaut for these maneuvers. The elevator tests were interspersed with less dramatic tests to give everyone a break.

After a couple of hours, the captain announced that they would be flying level for thirty minutes for a lunch break. Lorraine grabbed her lunch. She had been so excited this morning that she had only had a bowl of cold cereal for breakfast, and she was starved. As soon as she started unwrapping the sandwich, Fred moved to a seat across the aisle. The chicken salad was on fresh bread and it didn't take long to consume. When she finished the mixed fruit and chewy ginger cookie, she noticed Fred hadn't opened his box lunch. So she asked, "If you aren't going to eat your cookie, can I have it?" Without even looking her way, he reached across the aisle and gave her his unopened box.

"Enjoy yourself," he mumbled.

When the captain announced that tests would resume in five minutes, she picked up her briefcase and went forward to sit with the Flight Test engineers. On her way, she noticed several unopened box lunches and smiled to herself. She sat down next to the test engineers and they looked up in surprise. One asked her, "Something we can do for you?"

"My tests are coming up soon and I want to be ready," she replied. "I might have some questions for you. By the way, I'm Lorraine, the Flight Controls engineer, along with Fred. I'm lateral controls and he's horizontal. He's in the back being sick," she said, trying to sound compassionate.

When her part of the tests were completed, she remained seated with the Flight Test group because they were a lot livelier than most of the engineers. It was interesting listening to them work and they seemed to enjoy sharing details with her. The next few hours went smoothly and she scored a few more cookies.

Test runs were finished in the late afternoon and they headed back to Boeing Field. The captain stuck his head out of the cockpit and invited her to join them. Lorraine tried really hard to look serious and keep the silly grin off her face when she took the Flight Engineer's seat. She expected to be asked to leave the cockpit for landing and was thrilled when she was allowed to stay.

Throttle back and flaps down. Landing gear down, touchdown. Speed brakes deployed. Her speed brakes. Thrust reversers, step on the brakes. As they slowed to a stop in front of the Flight Controls building, the captain honked the horn and waved with a thumbs up to the waiting crew. Now that was a surprise. She hadn't known that a 747 Jumbo jet had a horn and she couldn't help laughing.

Lorraine thanked the captain, copilot, and Flight Test engineers as she left the cockpit. While she was waiting in the Flight Test office, she heard the captain say to the chief of Flight Test, "Now that's what we need. More pink pants on board."

That was just too much. A smile of triumph flashed across her face.

The Conversation

I am going to tell you a story. You probably won't believe it, but I swear to you it is true. Cross my heart. I have changed names to protect myself. From what? You'll see.

Through no fault of my own, I am stuck at home. There is a worldwide pandemic raging outside and I am in the high-risk category, so I stay in as much as possible. I get my groceries delivered and do my shopping online. I go out for as few appointments as possible, always wear a mask with a hepa filter, and I wash my hands so often my skin is cracking. Household projects have all been put on hold. Traveling is just a dream. Quarantine is the new reality for as far as the eye can see.

I miss dressing up and going to the symphony. I miss dinner and drinks at the jazz clubs. And going to the movies and the library. I can't believe I am saying this, but I even miss going grocery shopping. Most of all, I miss my friends, meeting for coffee or lunch, going on a walk, sitting on a park bench. Conversation and companionable silence. Hugs.

I stay in touch with my friends and family by email, phone,

and Zoom. It certainly isn't as good as meeting in person, but it's better than nothing. But for long, chatty conversations, I still prefer the phone. I like to kick off my shoes, arrange the pillows, and lie down on the bed. I get comfortable, a cup of coffee, soda, or wine at hand. When I am really relaxed, I reach for the phone and call a friend.

I'm talking with my BFF Gwen. She and her husband Dan moved out of the city a few years ago and bought property in the islands. I like listening to her farming experiences and she likes talking about them. She's telling me about picking the first raspberries of the season and how delicious they taste. I can imagine her sitting on the couch with her feet on the coffee table. I hear her husband in the kitchen.

It's almost as if I see her sitting there. She is wearing her pink fleece jacket and Darn Tough socks. Dan is making lunch and the soup smells delicious. Suddenly I feel…dizzy. Disoriented. The way I feel when I totally lose track of time. When I really don't know what hour of what day of what month it is. As if I am just drifting free in time. But now I seem to have also lost track of my location. This has never happened before and it's frightening me.

I barely hear Gwen saying, "Lorraine, I have to go. Lunch is ready. Let's talk on Friday."

I manage to say, "OK, fine, give Dan a hug for me," and hang up. I just lay here feeling so strange and disoriented. I must be hallucinating. I am so lonesome from nine months in quarantine, and I miss my friends so much I am losing touch with reality.

It happens again the following week when I am talking with my cousin Kathy. She moved to Florida and I didn't make it down to visit before the pandemic hit. But I can see her sitting in her enclosed back porch with her gray cat Tolly in her lap and a glass of sparkling wine on the table. I ask her if she has bought any new orchids and she describes the cattlya I can see by the half empty wine glass. I feel the warm, humid air and smell the sweet scent of jasmine that is growing up the porch screen.

"Hey, Kathy, sorry, I gotta go. I'll call you back later," I tell her in a panic. This is too weird and I am really worried about myself.

These episodes begin happening more and more frequently when talking with close friends. I start keeping a record to see if this is for real or just my imagination filling in for reality. I am very leery of mentioning this to anyone for fear they will think I am crazy. Maybe I am.

For a couple of months, this strange phenomenon has only happens when I am talking with friends. At first it is with my closest friends, but pretty quickly it begins occurring with everyone I call. Today, much to my surprise, it happens when I accidentally answer a robocall. To investigate I start answering all the endless robocalls and push #1 to talk with the next available representative. The "dislocation" only occurs occasionally in the beginning, but with practice I can do it almost every time, complete strangers, knowing nothing about them, not even relaxed. Well, wow. Thinking about all the ways I can mess with these pesky callers really amuses me.

I try to "dislocate" to a favorite park bench where I used to sit and watch the birds. That doesn't work. I try visiting a friend's house when not on the phone. No, not then either. Then one day I adjust the radio antennae, and bam! I am in the radio studio. A little "eek" of surprise escapes me. The DJ hears me and looks around, but he can't see me. We are both really confused.

So what is going on? Why does it happen sometimes, but not other times? I seem to need some kind of connection to "dislocate". Obviously not a phone line because those are a thing of the past. So, no wires. Radios use electromagnetic waves of specific wave lengths. Wireless phone calls are transmitted using other wavelengths. I'm guessing that somehow I am traveling along the electromagnetic waves.

Slowly, as the pandemic drags on, "dislocating" happens more and more often. With practice I expand my abilities. I visit several of the local broadcast stations and refrain from squealing in surprise. I start traveling along the television frequencies as well as phone and radio.

I wonder, since we are engulfed in electromagnetic waves, can I just go anywhere? Am I limited to the path directly from me to the source, or can I travel along one wave and transfer to another? Do I have to stay with a certain frequency, or can I slide up and down the spectrum, changing from phone to radio to TV? I am pretty confident that I can, but before I try I need to make sure I can return home. My cat would be really sad if she didn't get fed on time.

I realize all of the electromagnetic waves carrying information must have identifiers, so I learn to parse out that data. Turning on both my radio and TV I spend time practicing. If I get a robocall, all the better because the caller really isn't going to know that I am not paying any attention to the conversation, but am involved in something else.

Fifteen months into the pandemic and I am fluent in surfing the electromagnetic waves. Radio, TV, phone, Wi-Fi, fiber optics, radar. You name it and I can hitch a ride.

I take the opportunity to travel. You can't beat the satellite phone for an exciting trip to a remote location, say the breath-taking Himalayas. It's hard to find these calls, so I am ready to grab one anytime I can. However, if it is an emergency call for help, I terminate as quickly as possible. I not only feel the caller's terror but I can also see it. It's actually visible in the ultraviolet frequency. The emotion is so intense it leaves me frightened and anxious and my heart is still skipping beats two weeks later.

I really missed the Blue Angels flying at Seafair last summer, so I hitch a ride in an F-18 every now and then. Please don't mention that to the NSA, FBI, CIA, NASA, or any of those alphabet organizations. Can you image how crazy they'd be if they learn I can visit the cockpit of a military airplane?

I transfer from an F-18 to a nuclear sub that is close to the surface and has its antennae deployed. As it makes a deep dive, the hull starts contracting and making lots of metallic creaks and groans as if it is going to be crushed by the pressure. The hydrophones pick up the sounds of marine animals, from the whales singing to the shrimp chirping. Fascinating. When the sub is pinged by radar from an aircraft carrier I take the opportunity to depart.

The aircraft carrier is even more exciting. Those jets catapulting off the bow and sinking out of sight before gaining enough speed to fly make me gasp every single time. Fortunately, the procedure is so noisy no one ever hears me cheering when they reappear above the deck instead of crashing into the sea.

Absolutely best of all is my trip to the International Space Station in the SpaceX Dragon. Five astronauts and me. The launch is thrilling and the docking is slow and nerve-wracking.

I love watching Kate's and Shannon's hair floating around in low gravity. And who knew the ISS smells like dirty socks?

But I can't stay until the Dragon returns to Earth. I have to take care of my corporeal self back home. After a couple of days, I catch a radio transmission and return to Earth, switch along a couple of frequencies, and make it home in a flash. Boy, am I hungry and thirsty.

As I rest between trips, I wonder if I can use this pandemic-induced talent to help others rather than just for my own entertainment. I give some thought to taking another person with me, say someone who can't travel due to health problems. But I have absolutely no idea how to get started and the thought of losing the person along the electromagnetic waves terrifies me. I am putting that idea aside for now.

Could I trace a kidnapper or track down a bomb threat? Could I prevent a cyber attack? My greatest worry is how I can be of assistance but maintain my anonymity. I don't want some fool to think I am a threat to national security and lock me up in a Faraday cage. So I am giving this some thought and will proceed with extreme caution.

We are coming up on eighteen months since the beginning of the pandemic. The vaccine is working and the number of people inoculated is finally approaching critical mass. I am so excited to escape quarantine and see my friends in person. I expect to have less time for dislocating and wonder if I will lose the ability. Maybe it is like riding a bike. You never really forget how.

Meanwhile, I think I will call a good friend who has fled the city to work remotely from a tropical island. No sunscreen needed.

If I'm Not Happy...

The alarm goes off. I am dreaming of our trip to Antarctica. We have seen whales, leopard seals, and so many wondrous birds. Today we are taking the Zodiacs to shore and walking over the glacier to the Emperor Penguin colony. I am so excited I reach over to poke my husband, Eric, making sure he's awake because he's such a heavy sleeper. But I guess he's as excited as I am because he's not there.

I open my eyes and confusion envelopes me. Where am I? This isn't our cabin on the cruise ship. This is my bedroom at home. Suddenly I realize it was all a dream. No trip to Antarctica. No safari in Africa. Scuba diving off the Great Barrier Reef? Trekking in New Zealand? Machu Picchu? Nope, dream on. Just never-ending trips to doctors' offices.

I want to put my pillow over my head and go back to sleep. I am so depressed I would like to sleep for the rest of my life. I'm taking antidepressants and I'm talking with a counselor, but sometimes it all just seems too much. Why us? Why can't we be that happy retired couple doing all the fun things our friends are doing? Sometimes I read a cheery Christmas newsletter and it's all I can do to keep from crying. Yes, I'm glad they are having fun; I don't begrudge them that. But I sure do envy them and wish we could join in. Why are we the couple stuck with an autoimmune disease?

The snooze alarm goes off and I resist hitting it again. I drag myself out of bed, get dressed, and go downstairs to help Eric. We no longer share a bed because he can't get up the stairs. He's in a hospital bed in what was my study. I'm not telling him this, but he sleeps so poorly that I am glad to have an excuse to sleep in another room. When he is in a lot of pain, he will ring me with the cordless door bell and I will stumble groggily down the stairs to help him. Really, there is nothing I can do to relieve his pain, but I keep him company, which maybe helps a little.

Okay, get it together. I can't show Eric how crappy I feel. Think of something pleasant. Think a happy thought. I got it. That was a great dinner Bonnie made for us last night. Once a week, she makes dinner for us and her husband drives her over to deliver it. How amazing is that? And since yesterday was Tuesday, today is Wednesday; piano lesson day. Yeah! We pay a person to stay with Eric for four hours every Wednesday, so I can go to my lesson and out to lunch. Let's see, I am meeting Joy today. That's gonna be fun. Okay, this will be a great day.

"Good morning, Eric. How was your night?" He's usually awake and waiting for me. I'd like to sleep in and he would like to get up earlier so we compromise somewhere in the middle.

"Not bad. How about you?"

"Oh, I'm good. I had a great dream about taking a cruise to see the Emperor Penguins. Our red down jackets kept us so nice and warm. It was amazing."

He gives me his lovely smile and says, "Next time for sure."

Eric has an autoimmune disease, not Multiple Sclerosis, but close enough. He's in a power chair and needs help with many of his "activities of daily living." You know, things like getting dressed, getting out of bed, going to the bathroom, and taking a shower. It takes two hours, more or less, to be ready for the day.

Friends don't understand and they don't want to modify their plans. "No, Gwen, I can't meet you for a hike at 8:00 a.m. How about we do a shorter one? No? Okay, well, have a good time." Skiing? "I know the snow reports are great, but I can't be gone an entire day." Going to the San Juans for the weekend? "Wow, it really would be fun, but, really, I can't go. I'd have to hire someone to stay with Eric, and it's $350 a night. No, he can't stay by himself for even one night." Our friends have their own lives to live and they drift away. I feel resentful.

Besides helping Eric, morning, evening, and all through the day, there are the chores around the house that he can't do any more. Taking out the garbage, for instance. That is *not* my job, but I have to do it.

Mowing the lawn. *Not* my job either. We have an electric mower, but the stupid grass bag keeps falling off. I go inside and ask Eric about it and he has the nerve to say, "Well, I never had that trouble."

"Come out and show me how it works," I snap back. Even after he gives me instructions, in great detail, it still falls off.

"Well, there are two solutions as I see it. You can buy a new lawn mower or get yard service."

I laugh and say, "That is only one solution." I really do love this guy.

It's all I can do to keep up with the place. I feel angry and unappreciated. And did I mention guilty? I feel so guilty for having these feelings. I know Eric would do it if he could. I'm not in a wheelchair. I don't have pain, I haven't had to give up my independence. But I'm not having any fun. I hate myself for feeling like this.

I am so stressed out and impatient I sometimes literally have to count to ten before responding to Eric. Not his fault. I know. Still, I am not having any fun. I haven't done any of the things we used to do together because I don't want him to feel bad that he can't participate anymore. Finally, I decide rather than exploding and being no use to anybody, I ask him if he would be all right if I went kayaking for a little while. "Sure," he says, "no point in us both being miserable." Oh my god, I love this man.

"How's Eric doing?" friends ask. Let's see, a brief summary or more detail, depending on whose asking. *And what about me?* I think. "Take care of yourself. It's really important," I'm told, kindly. *What does that even mean? And weren't you going to come and take Eric to the pub? Weren't you going to go for a walk with him, so I could have a little time to myself?"* I think. *Good intentions, no follow through. Doesn't do me much good.* Sometimes I hate myself. I'm such a bitch.

I am trying really hard to adapt to our new life, to be a loving wife and outstanding caregiver. I have chosen to stay with Eric and I want us to be happy. I go to the annual Care Givers Symposium, which covers both the practical day to day assistance and the "taking care of yourself" stuff. I have attended the six-week class, "Powerful Tools for Caregivers" where we made action plans to set reasonable goals to do something for ourselves each week. I have read several books by caregivers describing how they cope, but, of course, most of them have the money to hire lots of help. I recently participated in a couple of webinars for caregivers put on by the Can-Do MS organization. The only advice I hadn't heard before was directed to the people with MS. They need to make sure we, their partners, are getting the care and support we need so we don't burn out. Please, send us out to play. Then the time we take for ourselves would be even more rejuvenating because it would be guilt-free. If I'm not happy, no one is.

Patience; where do I get some? Resilience; please write me a prescription. Flexibility; an IV should do nicely. These really aren't my inborn personality traits and yet the MS Society keeps touting them. I like to plan ahead and have everything on the calendar. And yet, I am the one to convince Eric that it is OK to make a social engagement and then cancel it. An autoimmune disease is so unpredictable that rescheduling is the name of the game.

Mindfulness Meditation is the current fad for improving one's mental health. I took a ten-week class. I think it would helpful if I had the time for daily practice. It advises you to be kind to yourself. Treat yourself like you would a good friend. I really do try, but when I give myself a compliment, it always sounds sarcastic. I use the meditation when I go to bed and it helps get my cesspool mind to shut up and be still so I can fall asleep.

Best of all, I attend a monthly support group for the partners of people with MS. We call ourselves Carepartners because we include spouses, partners, parents, siblings, friends; anyone who loves and cares for a person with MS. Sometimes we have speakers, but most often we talk among ourselves. We can ask questions about anything, from the most detailed, intimate care giving issue, to which restaurants are wheelchair-friendly.

If I am in a bad mood and need to complain about my week, I get support from people who really understand. We share our troubles and offer suggestions. We laugh and cry together. And we become friends.

I find that having something to look forward to is always helpful. It helps to get my mind out of the tedium of the moment. Since Eric and I can't do all the fun outdoors stuff anymore, we have started going to concerts. It was hard at first to get him to leave the security of our home because so many things can go wrong. So I buy the tickets and then give him the choice. "Come with me or stay home. I hope you come with me; it will be more fun. The tickets are already paid for." Just a little pressure there. We go and have a great time, usually. Next week we are going to hear John Baptist. I keep that in my mind. I know that afterward he will say, "You were right, Honey. That was fun." Something to look forward to.

And the biggest cosmic joke of all? I have to be cheerful. Eric was always the one who could cheer me up with a quick-witted one-liner. Now it's up to me. Wow, talk about hard and unfair. Not that I am doing a very good job of being happy. On a scale of suicidal to Pollyanna, I definitely tip to the left. The inside of my head is negatively charged, swirling with anxiety, worry, criticism, and depression.

Eric and I have been married thirty years. We did everything together. It is as if we are two plants in one pot; our roots are entwined. It never crossed my mind to leave when he got sick. But sometimes it helps to remind myself that this is my choice. I choose to stay and help him. He is my one-and-only and I couldn't possibly live happily without him.

But sometimes I would really like a break. Wow, what a selfish thought. How about we both take a break? Maybe we can slip into a parallel universe where we are that happy, active couple living the lives we thought we would have. Just for a couple of days. A week maybe. A month.

But who am I kidding? If we could go there, we would never be coming back.

Born to Fly

When Lily was born, her parents were overjoyed and thought she was the most beautiful baby they had ever seen. It quickly became evident to Kay and Jack that she was also the cleverest little baby ever to live. They knew other parents probably felt this way too, but they believed Lily was extra special and they loved her entirely.

As a baby, Lily loved watching the birds and giggled with delight to see them fly. Her head always turned when she heard one sing and her beautiful blue eyes grew wide with wonder. She listened intently and began trying to imitate their calls even as she was learning to say *Mama* and *Papa*. Needless to say, the little mobile that hung over her crib was a flock of felt birds in primary colors.

When her parents put her in the baby backpack and went for walks, she would get so excited at the sight of a bird she would flap her pudgy little arms as if they were her wings. No one who saw her could help but smile. Not for her the picture books with cute little kitties or puppies or bunnies. It was books with birds that she wanted to see over and over.

As a toddler, Lily quickly learned that she could not run up to a flock of birds; they would fly away and leave her crying. No matter how hard she flapped her arms, she couldn't join them. She learned to sit quietly and watch. She could sit quietly for so long her parents would get restless and finally bribe her by promising to read a book about birds as soon as they got home.

Lily caused quite a stir when she entered kindergarten. At recess, she would extend her arms and swoop about the playground, emitting bird calls. At first the other children made fun of her, but she didn't care. Her joy was contagious and pretty soon other kids joined in. Within just a few weeks, there were so many children swooping about in unison that it became a murmuration. The teachers, in all of their years of teaching, had never seen anything like it.

With Parent Night approaching, the children all drew pictures of their families to hang on the wall. Lily's picture was a family of birds with papa bird sitting on the branch and mama bird feeding a baby bird in the nest. Ms. Clair, the teacher, said, "But Lily, this is a bird family and you are a person. Please draw a picture of yourself with Mom and Dad." She took away the drawing and gave Lily a new piece of paper. Lily sat frowning for a few minutes before drawing a picture of a different bird family.

When it was time for recess, Ms. Claire asked Lily to stay in.

"Am I in trouble?" she asked.

Oh, no," Ms. Claire told her. "I just want to have a little chat with you."

When the recess bell rang, Lily went to the restroom with the other girls and then returned to her desk. Ms. Claire sat down beside her and quietly asked, "Why did you draw pictures of birds when I asked you to draw your family?"

"But this is my family," Lily replied. "We are the bird family. We take turns picking a different bird and we learn all about that bird. We pretend we are that bird family. This week we are the grackles." She placed her little hand on top of Ms. Claire's hand and said slowly and carefully, "It's make-believe, Ms. Claire." She watched the little worry lines in Ms. Claire's forehead smooth out. She knew her parents were right; adults just couldn't understand.

Lily knew she couldn't fly like a bird, no matter how hard she flapped her arms. She had jumped off enough chairs, couches, tables, and windowsills to know that. But she enjoyed pretending and flying around the playground with her flock of friends.

Throughout elementary school, her interest in birds was a defining trait. She read as many books as she could about birds, both factual and fiction. Her science fair projects were always about birds, their habitat, food, behavior, song, coloring, and mating habits. Her most popular project was interactive and linked to bird cams around the world.

For a week in fourth grade, she and her friends spent the afternoon recess laying on the grass and looking up at the sky. Their teacher, Ms. Carla, asked, "Why were you children laying on the grass all week?" Everyone turned to look at Lily. "Because," she said, "we want to know how airplanes fly. They don't flap their wings, so how do they fly?"

Ms. Carla was young and enthusiastic. She knew a teaching moment when it presented itself. She said, "Raise your hand if you want to learn how airplanes fly." She counted the hands and declared a majority. She wrote their ideas on the blackboard as the class brainstormed what they already knew or thought they knew.

Throughout the year, Ms. Carla incorporated flight into the required teaching units. She arranged speakers from the Museum of Flight, Audubon, and the local Aviation High School. The class studied bird anatomy and feathers and how humans used that knowledge to learn to fly. They made paper airplanes and balsa wood gliders and learned about lift and thrust and directional control.

When they took a field trip to the Museum of Flight, Lily was amazed by how many different types of airplanes there were. That evening, she waved her hands with excitement as she told Mama and Papa what she had seen. "Not as many as birds, of course, but so many more than I ever imagined," she exclaimed. "And they have summer camp. Please, please, please can I go?"

Of course, she went to summer camp and as many classes as she could. She came home one day and announced, "I want to fly."

Kay smiled and said, "Of course, you do. You know, I plan on coming back as a seagull. I love the way they soar on the wind, how beautiful they are against the dark storm clouds. And they aren't endangered, so no worries. What kind of bird do you want to be?"

"No, Mama, I want to learn to fly an airplane."

Kay and Jack had known this day would come. "Tell you what, my little wren, we'll sit down with Papa tonight and discuss this. I think we have some planning to do."

It took a few weeks of phone calls and research and discussions to come up with a long-range plan. The local flight school recommended waiting until Lily was sixteen before starting lessons. She couldn't solo until sixteen and couldn't get her license until seventeen. Starting sooner would just cost more money.

Lily was very disappointed, but understood the reasoning. They discussed activities that would give her the sense of freedom she craved. She agreed that joining the local sailing club sounded like fun, especially since she knew that a sail operated on the same principle as an airplane wing, which was just an imitation of a bird wing. She didn't want to ice skate because she thought the skaters looked like they were trapped in a cage. Lily asked about skiing and her parents agreed that she could give it a try. She already swam on the Parks Department summer swim team and asked about scuba diving. They decided to take a vacation where they could snorkel. She would have to wait until she was older to scuba dive.

Lily studied hard in middle school because her goal was to be accepted into the Aviation High School. From competitive swimming, she switched to the diving team. She and several friends left the sailing club and began kite boarding. She loved skiing, flying down the steep moguls with the speed of a peregrine falcon, or floating weightless through the powder with the grace of a swallow. She knew ninth grade would be her last year to ski because in high school she would be studying harder and working as many hours as possible to save money for flying lessons.

The night before her sixteenth birthday, Lily's sleep was filled with dreams of flying, even crazier and more fantastical than usual. She planned to study her ground school lessons, review the instrumentation in the Cessna 172, and take a couple of runs on her flight simulator when she got up in the morning. But she was just too excited to settle down. She felt like a bird trapped in a cage, so she slipped quietly out of the house and went for a run.

She talked her parents into taking her to the airport early, so she could have the paperwork done before lesson time. Stepping outside the flight school office, she sniffed the air. Instead of the clean scent of grass and trees she had smelled on her morning run, she now smelled aviation fuel. It was both repellent and heady at the same time. She tried to identify the various airplanes sitting on the apron and speculated as to which one she would soon be flying.

When she heard the office door opening behind her, Lily twirled around, bouncing on her toes. Kim, her instructor, walked over, smiling. "Happy Birthday, Lily. What a beautiful day for your first flight. Now, I know you have been studying ground school and flying your simulator, but I want you to put that out of your mind for now. I want you to watch me and listen to me as if this is all new to you. Real life, actually seeing and feeling, is a different way of learning."

Lily nodded her head enthusiastically and said, "Yes, Ms. Kim, I can do that." She carefully listened and precisely followed Ms. Kim's directions as they walked around a beautiful canary yellow plane. They inspected each item on the preflight check list, looking for physical damage, oil leaks, flat tires. Moving the ailerons, flaps, elevators, and rudder; making sure the control surfaces were free.

Awkwardly climbing into the right-hand seat, she placed her hands on the yoke. She adjusted her seat, so she could reach the rudder pedals, turned the yoke to watch the ailerons deflect, and worked her way carefully through the remainder of the checklist. They taxied out to the runway and waited for clearance from the tower. Ms. Kim applied thrust and they accelerated down the runway. Lily shivered with delight as the tires lifted clear of the ground. She was flying, not quite as free as a bird, but earth was receding below her.

Flying was now the highlight of her life. She had a feather-light touch and was quick and accurate during simulated emergencies. Her instructor told her she was a natural, the best she had ever taught. On the day that she soloed, Lily was calm and self-assured. In the air, she felt as if she were integrated with the airplane. She wished this feeling could go on forever; that she would never have to return to the ground. When the time was up, she made a perfectly coordinated turn to head back to the airport. She landed as if she had been flying all her life.

Kay and Jack were waiting for her outside the flight school office and she ran to them, her face radiant. "Thank you, Mom and Dad. Thank you. This has been the most wonderful day of my life. I know you made it possible for me. I can never thank you enough." She threw her arms wide and exclaimed to the world, "I was born to fly!"

At Aviation High, Lily attended ground school in the evenings and passed the written test with a perfect score. On her seventeenth birthday she was certified for her Private Pilot's License.

Lily was thrilled when she graduated high school and entered the university, majoring in Aeronautical and Astronautical Engineering. The huge introductory classes held in overly warm auditoriums and the obligatory electives felt like she was being held at the starting gate. On the other hand, she was able to spend her weekends with the local glider club, which she had joined as soon as she moved onto campus.

The club was a co-op, so she was able to pay for most

of her membership and air time by working. A local farmer rented them a field. Her first job was helping maintain the runway; mowing, filling potholes, attending to the windsock, and other unskilled tasks. At the same time, she was learning how to help maintain the gliders, watching over shoulders and then talking her way into helping. Skills learned at Aviation High let her quickly advance to being on the repair team and she was able to pick up extra credits for flight time.

Lily flew as often as possible. She smiled every time she pulled the tow rope release and was slowly enveloped in quiet as the red Super Cub banked away, returning to the field. After soloing in the Blanik training glider, the high performance single-seater became her first love. She always used her allotted time, never landing early. The more experienced members said she seemed to have an innate ability to sense the invisible air currents and catch the thermals to stay aloft.

The second year at university, the students separated into their specialties and Lily was quickly immersed in topics that fascinated her. Instead of being with two hundred students, class size was around thirty. She stood out since she was one of only two women. Lily was friendly and quite a few guys asked her out, but she always replied, "Thank you so much. I would really enjoy going out with you, but between working and studying I just don't have the time." After a while, to salve their egos, they decided she must be gay and quit asking. Lily was amused when she heard the rumor and was relieved she didn't have to keep turning the boys down. It made it easier to be just friends.

It quickly became obvious to Lily which students were serious and which weren't. In the study hall, the serious students sat together and talked about the assignments rather than sports and girls. Lily sat with them and they soon realized she had a lot to contribute. She was delighted when Brian, the student she was secretly competing with for top grades, asked her, "Hey, some of us meet at Jack's apartment Wednesday evenings to study. Would you like to join us?" Brian was holding his breath, hoping she would say yes. He didn't believe the rumor that she was gay. At least, he hoped it wasn't true. He had been drawn to her ever since he had seen her in the giant lecture hall and had never been able to get close until now. She was as elusive as a will-o'-the-wisp.

"Who else will be there?" she asked.

Not very encouraging, but when he told her, she seemed very pleased to join the group. His quiet little smile appeared. He hoped this would be a first step toward getting to know her better.

Three weeks later, as the study group was breaking up, he asked her if she would like to go the football game on Saturday. "No, thanks," she told him. "With studying and work, I just don't have the time. But thanks for asking. Have fun." Maybe he hadn't heard the rumors, she thought.

As she walked out the door, Jack called to him, "Hold up a minute, Brian. You know, if you are interested in her, you need to find out what she is interested in. She is obsessed, and spending time with her will be on her terms only."

"Well, what the heck does she do besides work and study?"

"Why don't you ask her about her work?"

A couple of weeks later, Brian accompanied Lily to the glider field. He took a demo ride in the silver Blanik and was afraid and exhilarated, both at the same time. Later, as he watched Lily circling far above in the club's orange single-seater, he decided to sign up for lessons.

Not a bad trade, he thought. *I'll happily give up tailgate parties and football games with the guys to spend more time with her.*

Lily was delighted by his newfound enthusiasm and invited him to a lecture and exhibit at The Museum of Air and Space. Pretty soon, he was joining her wherever she went and she realized how much she loved having him share her interests. It wasn't long before he came to the conclusion that he was willing to follow her anywhere, forever.

Lily and Brian entered grad school with the idea of gathering a group of students and designing and building a high-performance glider. They joined a cross-country soaring club and began working on their Soaring Association badges. Brian knew before they even started earning badges that Lily, with her intense commitment and almost supernatural, innate abilities would quickly outpace him. He wasn't concerned.

One cool day in March they were soaring with some friends, practicing along a ridge, trying for lift in less-than-optimal conditions. They were all logging shorter flights than normal, but it was good practice for when conditions were difficult on a cross country flight. Lily was working her way along the ridge, barely maintaining altitude. Without warning, a cloud materialized around her. She had an inborn compass, always knowing the direction, and smoothly turned away from the ridge. Checking her instruments, she was surprised at how quickly she was losing altitude in a down draft. Completely focused, no time to worry, she fought with all her skill to slow the descent. Hoping to clear the bottom of the cloud with enough elevation to return to the landing field, she was mentally preparing to make an emergency offsite landing. When her instruments told her she was going to be landing with zero visibility, she deployed the flaps and speed brakes to slow her speed and pulled back on the stick to raise the nose. It would have been a good landing, but the tail hit a fence post.

Her friends were watching for her, each facing a different direction. Brian, terrified, saw the glider appear in the fog and yelled to the others. He watched, relieved, as she flared to make a spot landing. He was already running as the tail of the glider hit the post, flipped, and crashed upside down. His heart felt as if it had stopped as he threw himself on the ground beside the shattered canopy, screaming her name over and over.

At the memorial service, Brian was talking with Lily's parents, telling them how he had admired her focus and determination, how he loved her effervescence and joy of life. How much she had changed his life. He paused, trying not to cry, then continued. "I haven't told anyone this. It just sounds crazy, but when I got to the glider, I saw a bird sitting on the wing. It was a bright yellow bird; I don't know what kind. It took off and flew a few circles around the glider, warbling as it flew. It was so out of place on that cold foggy day, I think about it and wonder if I just imagined it, but I wanted to tell you. I know it sounds fanciful, but that little yellow bird seems to always be superimposed on my memories of Lily."

Kay and Jack looked at each other, and the lines of grief in their faces smoothed a little. Kay gave Brian a long, tight hug and said, "Thank you for telling us. That makes all the difference in the world."

Go Buy a Lift, You Cheapskates

I was so mad I thought my head was going to explode.

"Mary, what's the matter?" Nick asked when I walked into the living room.

"The Clinic. The Clinic is ignoring me. What's-his-name has put me on ignore and isn't returning my calls. I am so mad I could spit."

"Uh oh. He's doesn't know what a mistake he's making. And please go outside to spit."

My husband, Nick, the nicest man in the world, was a quadriplegic. It had all started innocently enough on a Saturday afternoon. His toes were a bit tingly after we walked around Seward Park. By Monday he could hardly get out of bed. We were fortunate to get an appointment with his primary care physician (PCP) the same day. Examination, CAT scan, spinal tap. We were told it wasn't MS, but the doctor didn't have a diagnosis. Worried and scared, we left the clinic with Nick in a borrowed wheelchair.

He began a treatment of steroid infusions, which was frequently the starting point for Multiple Sclerosis and similar diseases. Several referrals later he was diagnosed with an autoimmune disease with characteristics similar to MS. It was Devic's disease, which is now called Neuromyelitis Optica. The neurologist said, "I suppose you are going to go home and look this up on the internet. Let me warn you not to read anything older than ten years. Everyone with this disease died back then. We can do better now."

Oh my god. Not like that was scary or anything.

Fortunately, there were only two steps up to our front porch. We quickly bought an aluminum ramp, so Nick could stay in the wheelchair rather than try to use a walker to climb the stairs. When he could no longer manage the stairs to our bedroom, we converted my study on the main floor into a bedroom. As he got weaker, we bought a hospital bed that we could raise and lower, so he could scoot downhill going either direction.

There was no manual on learning to live while disabled. The PT and OT who started coming to our house were invaluable in teaching us how to adapt. To get the wheelchair up over a curb, tip it back. To get pants on, roll side to side. When you tip your husband over backwards when over enthusiastically lifting his feet onto the couch, call 911. And why didn't the chair come with anti-tip bars?

Adjusting was really hard. In addition to the constantly changing physical needs, we were struggling emotionally. We had to give up the outdoor activities we had enjoyed and our life was taken over by medical appointments. We were feeling resentful, cheated out of the retirement we had planned. We were envious of friends who continued enjoying our previous lifestyle. Disappointment, uncertainty, and fear engulfed us and our emotional reserves were drained away. Smiles were endangered and laughs were extinct.

I don't know how he managed, but Nick was amazing. Even with all the pain from demyelinated nerves, he refrained from taking it out on me. I wasn't so even tempered. Sometimes, frequently, I had to actually stop myself before speaking and count to ten to avoid snapping at him. We were tired, frustrated, angry. It was exhausting just getting through the day.

His disease was rare and there were no FDA-approved drugs. A treatment for MS would help for a while, briefly giving us hope, and then quit working. The doctor would prescribe a different treatment and we would give that a try. But Nick continued to get weaker and we had to keep adjusting to his deteriorating condition. Rather than scooting in and out of bed on his own, he started using a slider board. When he continued to lose upper body strength, we bought a patient lift. This required putting a sling around him, manually pumping up the lift, swinging him into position and letting him down gently. He was too weak to use the manual wheelchair. The fancy new power chair relieved me of having to push him around the house. The recline feature also helped reduce the chances of another deep vein thrombosis and more pressure sores. Despair was closing in.

Nick's primary care physician was at the Clinic, a large, independent medical practice. It was a good-looking building with the name emblazoned on the side; originally an office building but now converted to a medical clinic, nine stories tall, 205,000 square feet.

A major flaw in the renovations was that the planners forgot to include a patient lift. They couldn't transfer Nick from his wheelchair onto an examining table. He couldn't get a proper physical. I was asked to bring in digital pictures of his skin issues, including what turned out to be a pressure sore, a very painful and serious situation. If he needed a CAT scan or any tests that required him to be out of his chair, he was sent to the hospital.

We were outraged. It was hard enough getting to one appointment. It took three exhausting hours just getting ready to leave the house. It was irritating having to make arrangements for transportation to a second appointment. This wasn't equality. It was beyond unreasonable and he *still* wasn't getting proper medical care.

When we asked his PCP about getting a patient lift, he said that he had tried but couldn't make any headway solving the problem. Nick's cardiologist also practiced at the Clinic and said he wasn't happy about having to receive reports from the hospital doctors. He preferred to read the tests himself, as he did with all his other patients.

I couldn't find any information on the Clinic website to file a complaint or a phone number to call and try to resolve this issue. I called the executive director and CEO and explained the situation that Nick was not receiving appropriate medical care because he couldn't transfer to an examining table. The man was amazed to hear this and sounded very concerned. "Surely you husband can't be the only one. I'll look into it and call you back." He even gave me his direct line.

Okay, we were overwhelmed just trying to get through the day and up to our eyeballs in medical appointments. A couple of weeks went by before I realized I hadn't heard from him. I called his direct line and left a message. A week later I called again. I called his secretary and left another message. I was beginning to get the feeling the executive director was ignoring me. Despair turned to rage. This is why I was so angry my head was going to explode.

Previously, we had solved a similar problem with the Hospital Infusion Center. Nick was required to be in bed for the new treatment he was starting there. When we arrived for the first time, they didn't have a lift to transfer him. The staff quickly borrowed one from the emergency room, transferred him, and began the process. It was a long day. We had arrived at 10:30 in the morning and were ready to leave at 4:00 p.m. It then took two hours to borrow the lift back from the emergency room. Nick, a very gentle and patient person, was miserable and uncharacteristically cranky. I was so irritated by the time the lift arrived I could hardly talk. The charge nurse wasn't happy either. She gave me a phone number to call and file a complaint.

I woke up the next morning still fuming and called the number, detailing the problem at great length. The ombudsman was very understanding and explained the lengthy, cumbersome procedure for buying new equipment. He said he would look into it. Several phone calls and a couple of months later, the Infusion Center had their very own shiny new lift.

Inexplicably, I was so naive as to think it would be easy to solve the same problem again at the Clinic. Unfounded optimism. Wishful thinking. Delusional. The Clinic website boasted that they put the patient first. So why did they fight us instead of just going out and buying a lift? No idea. Now we were faced with dealing with an uncooperative adversary.

Did we have the emotional energy to take on the Clinic? We discussed filing a complaint with the U.S. Department of Justice (DOJ), which would take an entirely different level of commitment than talking with a sympathetic ombudsman. Fortunately, our daughter was as incensed as we were. She wrote our letter to the DOJ and emphasized this wasn't just about us; many more people would benefit. This was undoubtedly a key consideration when involving the DOJ.

Thanks goodness we had her support because it took a year to resolve the complaint.

The U.S. Department of Justice accepted our claim that under the Americans with Disabilities Act, the Clinic was discriminating against us. We were not receiving health care equal to that of a person without disabilities.

The DOJ suggested mediation and we agreed, but it never happened. There were many phone calls between us and the DOJ. They continued to ask for more details in response to the Clinic's claims. It dragged on for so long the agent assigned to our case was transferred and we had to bring a new person up to speed. Whenever they called, I had a jolt of anxiety that they were going to say they were dropping the case. However, they assured us that our case was important; they were moving forward.

Each time I had a chance, I asked the DOJ agent, "Please talk very slowly when you are discussing the case with the Clinic lawyers."

"Why?" he would ask.

"I want this to cost the Clinic as much as possible," was my spiteful response.

It would have been so much cheaper for them, so much

easier on our frayed nerves, if they had just bought the stupid lift to begin with.

When the case was finally concluded, the Clinic signed an agreement to have a dedicated lift room and a trained lift team. When a person called to make an appointment, the receptionist was required to ask if the patient needed help transferring. In addition, the Clinic had to establish a means to resolve patient grievances. I hope, in the end, they really regretted making that decision to ignore us. Ha, take that, you cheap bastards!

The best part of all was the first time we went in and met the lift team. We told them how pleased we were and jokingly said we thought there should be a plaque on the lift dedicating it to Nick. We gave them a quick explanation why. The lady who had been hired to head the team and who was responsible for training gave us a warm smile. "We're delighted to meet you and glad to be here. We have already helped eighteen people since we started just a few months ago."

Hearing that felt so good.

Nick gave me a smile and asked, "Mary, are you happy now?"

It didn't wipe out all the aggravation of the past year, but yes, it certainly made me happy. Yeah for us and yeah for the Department of Justice!

Sailing

My love affair with sailing began when I was twelve. We had a summer cabin on the north end of Lake Washington and my parents tore it down and built our permanent home. We moved over the summer and when we started school in the fall my brother, Ron, and I were in junior high. He quickly made friends with a boy named Reid who, at fourteen, was already a sailing maniac. Reid's family didn't live on the water, so arrangements were made and he kept his Sea Scouter, a ten foot sailing dingy, at our place.

My Mom was a very serious person, a hard worker who didn't really have any hobbies. She took care of us four kids (five, including my Father), the large house, and the garden. I guess gardening was her hobby because she enjoyed it. Much to my surprise, she wanted to learn to sail, so Reid gave us lessons. She enjoyed it so much we quickly had a Sea Scouter of our own.

Just let me say that the person who designed the Sea Scouter was brilliant. Besides being a sailboat it was also a rowboat, and we carried the oars at first, just in case. They came in handy when we couldn't figure out how to get home, or when we ran into the neighbors' docks. We'd quickly put the sail down and row home, engulfed in a cloud of shame. It took some practice before we really got the hang of it.

And then there was over-confidence. I talked my father into going out with me. He wasn't interested in learning to sail, but he did like to encourage us. It was December, cold and windy, so maybe not the best decision either of us had ever made. Fortunately, we weren't too far from shore when a hard gust slammed us sideways and swamped our little boat. Oh my god, it was breathtakingly cold. I forgot the bailing bucket. It was really hard to row a boat full of water. It felt like an eternity, but we finally made it back to the dock. We were shivering so hard we had trouble tying the dock lines. Fortunately, Mom sent my brother down to help take care of the sodden sail. Dad was a good sport about it, but I could tell it would be a long time before he would go out with me again.

By our second summer, Mom and I were masters of our destination. We could get wherever we wanted to go and back home again. The little boat would pass lightly over the sparkling ripples or bounce on the choppy waves, sending cool spay splashing in our faces. The warm sun on our backs, the wind in our faces, we skimmed across the lake, as free as the gulls. Who knew ten feet of blue and white molded fiberglass and a triangle of Dacron could be so much fun?

Next came the Lightening. Cool name. It was designed on the east coast and very popular for racing. Nineteen feet long with a beam (width) of six-and-a-half feet, this boat was as sleek as a greyhound. Because of the one hundred and thirty-pound center board, she behaved like a sailboat with a heavy keel. This meant it could sail in much heavier winds than the little Sea Scouter with its dinky dagger board. Also, it had two sails, a main sail, and a jib. Boy, did we have fun in that boat.

It took us a while to learn its capabilities and trust ourselves. At first, we were leery of going out when there were white caps on the lake. As we gained confidence, we went out in stronger and stronger winds, with white froth blowing off the waves as they raced down the lake before the wind.

In a strong wind a sailboat lists, tipping sideways. There is an optimal angle of tilt for the fastest sailing, so we would lean backward over the side, into the wind, to prevent the boat from leaning too far. We would hook our toes through hiking straps to keep from doing backward somersaults over the side and into the water. We practiced "man overboard" maneuvers just in case.

If the wind was really strong and we didn't have enough weight leaning over the side, the water would run along the gunwale and sometimes into the cockpit. This always scared the daylights out of my sister and made my brother laugh. Mom would just say, "Stop that," which certainly left room for interpretation, but seemed to cover her responsibilities.

When the waves broke over the bow, the spray was blown into our faces. Whoever was seated closest to the bow would try to duck, so the next person would get hit with the spray. It was such a laugh.

When sailing downwind, that is, the wind is coming for behind, there's a thing you can do with the sails on opposite sides of the boat, one on the starboard and one on the port. It's a little tricky, but it looks really nice. It's called wing and wing because it looks like a bird in flight. My mom loved sailing that maneuver. If the wind was shifty and the waves choppy, it was even harder. We didn't have a whisker pole to hold the jib in place, so Mom would stand on the bow and hold the sail in position. My Mom, the human whisker pole.

When I was away at college Mom traded in the Lightening for an Aquarius. It was twenty-three feet long, eight feet wide, and had a cabin. It was designed for cruising and could sleep five, very snugly. Dad now enjoyed going sailing for a few hours because he could go below and take a nap. The Aquarius was certainly not a racer like the Lightning, but we had fun. Having a cabin with seating and a head was a luxury. If it rained, not everyone had to get wet. If the wind died, we had a motor, so we didn't have to wait to be rescued. This was an advantage because we could sail farther from home port and explore new areas of the lake.

We grew up and moved away. When I was living south of San Francisco, my boyfriend, Jeff, and I would rent little boats and sail on a lake so small it wasn't much more than a pond. When my brother came for a visit, the three of us rented a boat in Sausalito. It was one of those perfect days with warm sun, puffy white clouds in a brilliant blue sky, and a strong wind. The white caps were blowing in under the Golden Gate Bridge as we left the dock and headed toward Angel Island.

Sailing the Bay was so different from Lake Washington in Seattle. Added to the fresh smell of the outdoors was the tang of salt water, algae, and sea wrack on the beaches. There were so many more birds, including my favorite, the goofy pelican. As we passed close to a red marker buoy, it was rocking in the waves and clanging mournfully. Sea lions were pulled out resting and barking as we slipped past. The salty spray on my face left a gritty residue on my glasses.

The surface of the water was a kaleidoscope of motion.

Besides the white-capped waves pushed by the wind, great ocean swells came in under the Golden Gate and rolled the boat. We kept a sharp eye out for freighters, both to stay clear and to be prepared when the wake slammed into us. With all this added motion, my boyfriend was feeling queasy. When I started making roast beef sandwiches with lots of mayo, he turned green, so we headed back to the dock.

As we approached the dock, we dumped the wind from the sails, back winded the jib, and came to a perfect stop. Reid, our instructor so many years ago, would have been proud of us. As Jeff stepped ashore, we filled the sails and headed back out. The rental agent walking down the dock started running and waving his arms. I assumed he thought we were coming in because it was so windy and rough out for us. We pretended we didn't see him. When we returned the boat, not one minute early, the grins on our faces said it all.

My brother and sister and I got married. With our new spouses, we chartered a boat in the British Virgin Islands for a week. It was "bare boat," which meant we were good enough sailors to not need to hire a captain. The boat, a Morgan Forty Two, was designed for comfortable cruising: six berths, water tank, shower, a retractable sun shade over the cockpit, and lots of other delightful amenities.

The water was so clear we didn't need to use the depth sounder; the many shades of blue told us all we needed to know. In the shallows we could see the sparkling ripples in the waves reflected off the white sand bottom. We snorkeled in the warm water with tropical fish in shades of reds, blues, greens, purples; all the colors so vivid they dazzled the eye.

Some evenings we ate ashore at picturesque little restaurants. Most of the time we ate aboard, preparing meals with the provisions we had ordered. Drop anchor in a quiet bay, maybe swim to shore and tie the stern to a tree. Grill the steaks, serve with juicy fresh tropical fruit and local beer. Listen to the native birds in the trees, watch the blue sky gently turn to cream and mauve, silhouetted palm trees fading to black. Sleep like a baby rocked in a cradle, kissed goodnight by a tropical breeze. Truly paradise.

My husband, Dave, learned to sail and loved it, too, although maybe not quite as much as I did. We sailed my mother's Aquarius and my brother's Hobie Cat with the rainbow sails. We bought a Cal 29 and cruised Puget Sound, anchoring in various cozy ports. We enjoyed looking for orcas and the occasional school of dolphins, and watching the seals play. We tried to identify all of the various marine birds we passed; red beak, silly head feathers, golden eyes, green ring around the neck?

One time we saw a disturbance is the water a couple of hundred feet behind us and thought an orca or grey whale was about to surface in our wake. Instead, the battleship gray of a submarine conning tower broke the surface, a rush of water streaming down its sides. The displaced water created a wave that tossed our boat about and made the sails and rigging snap angrily. I yelled and shook my fist as it went by.

One of Dave's coworkers raced a Thunderbird and invited us to crew for the Tri Island races. Like the Sea Scouter, the Thunderbird was designed in Seattle. It was twenty-six feet long and both a cruising and racing boat. We had never raced before, but John was a wonderful captain. He gave very precise direction in a quiet voice, never impatient or angry.

Racing added many exciting new experiences to our repertoire of sailing stories. Before the race began, all the boats would be tightly packed, jockeying for position, trying to be first to cross the start line when the horn sounded. If you crossed the line early, you had to circle back around and re-cross it, which put you well behind rather than out ahead. It was hectic, with quick direction changes in tight quarters. It was nerve-wracking, as collisions were avoided by mere inches. The captains had to know the rules of right of way so thoroughly they didn't need to think about them.

There were interesting moments in each race, such as running aground on a sand bar just minutes after starting the first of the three races. The third race was by far the most memorable. From Seattle to a buoy off Port Townsend, it required a canny knowledge of sailing Puget Sound. Due to the tides, the water generally flowed north for an ebbing tide and south when flooding. But the bays and promontories created currents that modified the general flow. The land masses also interfered with the wind direction. John made a bad decision early in the race, staying close to shore, hoping to catch the current. Most of the boats stayed farther out, catching more wind, and quickly pulled ahead. We were the last in our class to round the buoy at Port Townsend.

Later, I went below to sleep. Dave stood watch, occasionally relieving John at the helm. When I went on deck to take my turn, I was met with one of the most stunningly beautiful sights of my life. We were surrounded by the fleet flying their spinnakers under the full moon. The wind filled the gossamer sails, all colors of the rainbow, lifting them up toward the sky. I was spellbound by what looked like hot air balloons ready to launch from the dark surface of the water. Not that it mattered, but the gun sounded when we crossed the finish line. We had come from behind to win the race.

As other interests absorbed our time, we sold the Cal 29. Many years later, as we approached retirement, we bought a Ranger 23 and moored it in a little marina on the lake about a mile from our house. Tragically, after only a few years, Dave developed a neurological disorder and could no longer go sailing.

Ten years later, I still had the boat. Trying to coordinate free time with the weather was difficult and I only got out a few times each season. The cost of moorage was too high to justify my occasional outing, but I clung to that boat as if it were a life raft. It represented a more carefree time in my life. A chance to go out on the water gave me something to look forward to. When I was sailing I was free. My mind cleared of daily problems and worries and I existed only in the moment. Every time I managed to sail wing and wing, I dedicated the moment to Mom. Sailing brought me joy. Just me and my Ranger, we were off on a great adventure. The feeling of rejuvenation stayed with me for days after I docked the boat and returned to earth.

Acknowledgments

Of course, I will start by thanking my parents for passing on their joy of reading. Who could possibly hope to become a writer without first loving to read?

Thanks to my amazing husband, Dave, who has shared his life with me.

I thank my good friend Evelyn Arvey. I never felt that I had the next great American novel in me demanding to be written and shared with the world. Since graduating college, technical writing was part of my job. Without Evelyn twisting my arm and convincing me to give this class a try, I would not have signed up. I would never have dipped my pen into the genre of fiction and would have totally missed this enlightening experience.

My classmates have been amazing. Their critiques, suggestions, support, and humor have made this class so much more than I ever expected.

Our brilliant teachers, Evelyn and Richard Arvey, have guided the way from the first attempt to construct a proper paragraph. Their kind guidance and critical editing have helped me write stories I am willing to share.

Last but not least, I would like to thank the people of the Swedish MS Center and their benefactors, the Swedish Medical Center Foundation, for sponsoring the class. It would not have come into existence without their support.